D0349724

DORMIA

WRITTEN BY

JAKE HALPERN & PETER KUJAWINSKI

HOUGHTON MIFFLIN

HOUGHTON MIFFLIN HARCOURT

BOSTON NEW YORK 2009

Interior illustrations by Stephanie Cooper.

Houghton Mifflin is an imprint of Houghton Mifflin Harcourt Publishing Company.

www.hmhbooks.com

The text of this book is set in Aldus.

Library of Congress Cataloging-in-Publication Data

Halpern, Jake.
Dormia / written by Jake Halpern & Peter Kujawinski.
p. cm.
Summary: After learning that he is a descendant of Dormia, a hidden kindgom in the Ural Mountains whose inhabitants possess the ancient power of "wakeful sleeping," twelve-year-old Alfonso sets out on a mission to save the kingdom from destruction, discovering secrets that lurk in his own sleep.

ISBN 978-0-547-07665-2

[1. Sleep disorders—Fiction. 2. Sleep—Fiction. 3. Fantasy.] I. Kujawinski, Peter. II. Title.
PZ7.H16656Do 2009
[Fic]—dc22
2008036108

Manufactured in the United States of America
QUM 10 9 8 7 6 5 4 3 2 1

To my wife, Kasia Lipska-Bardzo
Ciękocham. —J.H.

To my parents, Frank and Jo Kujawinski, who taught me
to read, to love, and to live. —P.K.

DORMIA

CHAPTER 1

A DANGEROUS PLACE TO WAKE UP

DID YOU EVER go on vacation, wake up in a strange bed, and struggle to remember where *exactly* you were? Well, twelve-year-old Alfonso Perplexon had never gone on a vacation, but he often felt this very sensation. For him, waking up was always an odd experience, and today was no exception.

As he woke up from a late afternoon nap, Alfonso blinked open his eyes and discovered that he was perched at the top of a gigantic pine tree—some two hundred feet above the ground. The view was spectacular. Alfonso could see for miles in every direction, and he could even make out his house in the distant hamlet of World's End, Minnesota. Unfortunately, there was no time to enjoy the view. The small branch that Alfonso stood on was covered with gleaming snow and creaked dangerously under the pressure of his weight. Icy gusts of wind shook the entire treetop. Alfonso looked down grimly at the ground far below. If he fell, he would most certainly die.

"Oh brother," muttered Alfonso. "Not again."

This wasn't the first time Alfonso had woken up in a tough spot. He was always doing crazy things in his sleep. Of course, there were times when he enjoyed a good night's sleep in bed, just like other people. But often enough, within a few seconds of drifting off, Alfonso's eyes would flutter back open and he would enter a peculiar trance. Although technically asleep, it was the strangest type of sleep anyone had ever seen. While in this trance, he ran, cross-country skied, climbed trees, cooked fantastically delicious pancakes, walked tightropes, read Shakespeare, and shot deadly accurate arrows. These trances had begun a few years back, and lately they were happening more often.

In recent weeks, Alfonso had been waking up from his trances in this particular tree, which was in the middle of an old-growth pine forest known locally as the Forest of the Obitteroos. Very few people had the skill to climb a tree in the Forest of the Obitteroos and no one ever attempted to do so in the depths of winter. No one except Alfonso, and even he wasn't sure how his sleeping-self did it. He simply woke up and there he was at the top of a tree.

Of course, his immediate concern was his own safety. Although his sleeping-self was an expert at climbing the most dangerous of trees, Alfonso's waking-self had no aptitude for it whatsoever. He was quite short and skinny for his age, and when awake, he didn't feel particularly athletic. His large green eyes and thick, dark eyebrows were the only outsized parts of his body. In every other regard, he was very small.

Alfonso stared down at the ground below and felt so dizzy that he almost threw up. A small clump of snow fell off the branch on which he was standing and he watched it plummet down for several long seconds before it finally hit the ground. Cold gusts of air continued to blast fiercely from the north, and the icy branches of the tree swayed and crackled in the wind. Then, rather suddenly, he heard a high-pitched scream. Alfonso glanced to his left and saw a two-foot-wide mass of sticks and mud sitting on a nearby branch. It was a bird's nest, and the current occupant—a brown falcon with white-tipped wings—was staring at him and moving restlessly around her nest. Underneath the falcon Alfonso could see three trembling balls of downy fur. They were baby falcons, no more than two weeks old.

Strangely enough, Alfonso wasn't surprised by this turn of events. His sleeping-self seemed attached to falcons and eagles and, consequently, he often woke up near these fierce predator birds. Very slowly, Alfonso reached into his coat pocket and took out a handful of raisins, leftover from his lunch. He sank into a crouch and whispered, *"Kee-aw, kee-aw, sqrook!"* He was imitating the sound that baby falcons make. It had taken him weeks of practice to do this properly. Basically, whenever he spent time near a falcon's nest, he listened carefully to the noises that the baby falcons made, and then later practiced imitating their cries. He had gotten very good at this. In fact, this was one of the few things that he did very well when he was wide awake.

Alfonso made his cry once again: *"Kee-aw, kee-aw, sqrook!"*

The mother falcon circled nervously around her chicks but soon moved to a branch on the far end of the nest. Alfonso leaned in closer. Below him, the three baby falcons looked up and opened their tiny beaks. Alfonso tore the raisins in half and carefully dropped them into the three open mouths. Meanwhile, the mother falcon stared unblinkingly at him. As soon as Alfonso had finished feeding the chicks, his thoughts inevitably returned to his own predicament. For Alfonso, the task now at hand was getting down from this tree, and the key was to fall asleep. Unfortunately, it was far too cold and windy for Alfonso to feel the slightest bit tired. He was left with nothing to do but sit and think.

As usual, Alfonso wondered what was wrong with him. It was a question he had pondered a great deal lately. Doctors at the big hospital in St. Paul, Minnesota, claimed that Alfonso suffered from a very rare sleeping disorder known as Morvan's syndrome, which made it impossible to sleep in a normal fashion. Morvan's syndrome was once common during the Middle Ages, but nowadays the disorder was exceedingly rare. Indeed, the doctors in St. Paul claimed that only a handful of people in the entire world had it. One well-known case involved a man from Mongolia named Ulugh Begongh. Apparently, Mr. Begongh had been awake for thirty-eight years, or 13,870 consecutive nights. Yet every evening, between nine P.M. and eleven P.M., Mr. Begongh's eyes closed halfway, his breathing softened, and he appeared to sleep—only during this time Mr. Begongh actually experienced increased amounts of speed and strength. His wife claimed that on one occasion her husband lifted a one-thousand-pound ox cart above his head.

Doctors in Mongolia, and elsewhere, believed that Morvan's syndrome originated from a rare form of cholera, known as the sleeper's cholera, which supposedly swept through Central

Asia sometime during the seventh century. At that time, it was called *quiesco coruscus,* which is Latin for "sleep shaking." But by the time Alfonso had developed the syndrome, doctors felt Morvan's syndrome was a genetic disorder. Alfonso's father had also been prone to sleepwalking.

Of course, the kids at school loved it whenever Alfonso fell asleep. They had taken to calling him the "sleeping ninja" and had been clamoring for him to join the fencing team, the cheerleading squad, the spelunking club, and the society for amateur tightrope walkers, as long as he agreed to participate while asleep.

For a while, Alfonso was immensely flattered. What twelve-year-old wouldn't be? There were just two problems. The first was that Alfonso never remembered anything he did in his sleep and, as far as he knew, he had absolutely no control over what his sleeping-self did. As a result, he never felt any pride in his sleeping accomplishments. The second problem was that his sleeping-self appeared to be quite a show-off. Inevitably, every time that he fell asleep, his sleeping-self would do whatever it could to grab the spotlight and impress everyone around him. There was, for instance, the time when he climbed out of the third-story window of his social studies class and tightrope-walked along a set of power lines to the top of a telephone pole where some baby falcons were nesting. This had nearly gotten him expelled from school, but his classmates were still begging him to do it again.

The branch below Alfonso trembled in the wind as his thoughts continued to wander. He began to feel a bit drowsy, especially when he thought about the roaring fire waiting for him back home in World's End. Alfonso focused on his breathing and with each exhalation he allowed his eyes to close a little more. His head grew heavy and his mind became cloudy. Then, in what felt like a second later, Alfonso woke up at the foot of the massive pine tree. He was back on the ground! As usual, he had no memory of what he had just done.

Alfonso glanced at his watch. It was almost five P.M. and the forest was filled with the murky glow of winter twilight. Alfonso did not like being caught in the Forest of the Obitteroos at night. Truth be told, no one did. The forest, though peaceful and very beautiful, had a spooky and slightly unnerving quality. The trees themselves had a presence about them. Many were older than the United States and some were alive even before Christopher Columbus sailed to America. And they still stood there, watching and waiting.

Suddenly, Alfonso flinched. A half-second later, he heard a rustling noise behind him. He whirled around but saw nothing.

"Who's there?" he yelled.

Silence.

"Who's there?" he yelled louder. "What do you want?"

Silence again.

Alfonso shrugged, reached down to the ground, and began to pick up his cross-country skis, which he had used to get here. Just then, he heard another rustling noise. This time when he looked up, a tall, gaunt man stood in front of him, about four feet away. He was smiling awkwardly, and dressed in sheepskin boots, a wide-brimmed hat, and a heavy fur cloak, the sort of clothing that Canadian fur trappers wore centuries ago. The man's skin was sickly in color—a pale green—and it looked like it was stretched a bit too tightly around his bony face. His eyes were hidden by the brim of his hat, but his long, angular chin was visible. A ghastly scar coiled and squiggled along the entire length of his jaw. The skin along the scar was irritated by the cold and had turned a raw pinkish color.

"Well done! That was quite a climb for a young boy," the man with the scar said. His voice sounded ancient and raspy, as if he had not exercised his vocal cords in a very long time.

"Uh, thanks," Alfonso said nervously. He swallowed hard and his heart began to pound.

"Perhaps my eyes deceive me, but you appeared to be sleeping as you climbed," observed the man. "Is this true?"

Alfonso nodded.

"Very impressive," the man said slowly. He coughed. It sounded like the growl of a truck. "*Very* impressive."

Alfonso wanted to run, but something kept him rooted in place. "All I did was fall asleep," he said.

"Nonsense," replied the man in a friendly manner. "All a runner does is run, yet does he doubt the value of his talents—or hand over his gold medal at the end of a race—because all he did was place one foot in front of the other?"

"Sleeping is different," began Alfonso.

"Yes it is," interrupted the man. He smiled again. As he did, the coiling scar along his jaw twisted awkwardly, like a wounded snake. "Sleeping, or rather the *manner in which you sleep,* is the rarest of gifts and should not be taken lightly. I've seen a few exceptional sleepers in my day, but to climb this massive tree in the dead of winter at the age of . . . How old are you?"

"Tw-twelve," said Alfonso.

"Yes, at the age of twelve, well, that is something most unusual."

"Oh," said Alfonso rather softly, almost to himself.

"I suppose you have other sleeping skills?" asked the man. He took a step closer. Alfonso shivered and took a step back.

"Don't be alarmed," said the man softly. "My name is Kiril. I am a stranger to this area, but rest assured, I mean you no harm. I have nothing but admiration for your sleeping skills. What else can you do?"

"I don't know," stammered Alfonso. "But I really must be going."

"Indeed," replied the man. Neither he nor Alfonso moved. "Just out of curiosity," the man asked, "are you a green thumb? Isn't that the phrase in your country? A skilled gardener?"

"Sir, I'm not sure what you mean," replied Alfonso. "And I really must —"

"Please," interrupted the man again, "let us converse as friends. What I mean to say is this: are you interested in plants? Unusual ones? And have you grown any plants in your sleep? That would be *most* interesting."

Alfonso said nothing.

"Hmm," said Kiril. "You should know that I am a *passionate* collector of unusual plants. Such specimens interest me—and they interest my father as well."

"Your father?" inquired Alfonso. "Who's that?"

"Let's save that discussion for a later time," said Kiril. He smiled. "For now, let us talk—as friends—about the plant that you may have grown in your sleep. Such specimens are of considerable interest to me and I am willing to pay handsomely, though, I should warn you, I will be forced to pay you in gold bars. My resources are vast. You and your family—your mother is Judy, yes?—will never need to work again."

Alfonso stared at Kiril, who was now standing so close that Alfonso could feel the heat of Kiril's foggy breath.

Kiril smiled again. "You have such a plant, don't you?"

"No," said Alfonso. "I never bother with plants or flowers when I'm asleep."

The wind howled through the Forest of the Obitteroos. Snow fell from the tree branches and pattered thickly onto the ground. Kiril nodded. "Well," he said, "I did my best to help you and to give you a fair deal. Be careful. Someone far less trustworthy than I may soon come knocking on your door."

Kiril looked as if he were about to say something else, but at that very moment, the wind gusted violently and lifted Kiril's wide-brimmed hat from his head. Alfonso gasped and an icy tingle of fear crept up his spine. The wind had revealed Kiril's eyes: they were large, vacant, and *entirely* white.

Alfonso stumbled backwards, snatched up his cross-country skis, and ran off in a terrified sprint. In his haste and fear, he never once turned around to see if he was being followed.

CHAPTER 2

A MOST CURIOUS PLANT

IT WAS PITCH-BLACK and bitterly cold when Alfonso arrived at the cluster of small, snow-covered houses that made up World's End, Minnesota. He was wide awake now and therefore his skiing was labored and awkward. Gradually, Alfonso made his way along the shore of a small body of water, known as Lake Witekkon, and then continued up a curving, snow-covered driveway to the ramshackle cottage where his family lived. The windows were coated with frost, but he could still see a roaring fire in the cottage's large stone fireplace. The air was ripe with the scent of burning wood. By the time he made his way into the kitchen, dinner was already on the table and his mother, Judy Perplexon, appeared both worried and annoyed.

Judy was a plain woman with thinning blond hair. She always wore sensible shoes and ankle-length skirts. The only jewelry she owned—besides a plain gold wedding band—was the small, wooden medallion that hung by a copper chain around her neck. Leif, her husband and Alfonso's father, had whittled the medallion for her just before he died. Judy never took it off.

Judy hadn't been the same since Leif passed away. Leif, like Alfonso, had been a very active sleeper and was famous for swimming the local lakes in his sleep. Three years ago, as he was in the middle of the lake taking one of his sleep-swims, a freak lightning storm passed overhead. The storm lit up the lake with blast after blast of lightning and Leif Perplexon was never seen again.

After her husband's death, Judy had given up her job as a librarian at the local public library and stayed close to home. Most days she helped her father, Pappy Eubanks, tend to the flowers and vegetables he grew in the enormous greenhouse nursery next to their cottage. Pappy grew most anything, but he specialized in rare flowers that he then sold all over the world. These flowers were the family's main source of income. Ever since he was a boy, Pappy had a knack for raising flowers that no one else could seem to grow. Over the years he had grown Tanzanian Violets, Weeping Carpathian Clovers, Giant Birds of Paradise, King Leopold Roses, and Manchurian Moonglow Tumblinas. These plants didn't make the family rich, but they paid the bills and gave Pappy and Judy something to do.

"Where have you been?" asked Judy as Alfonso walked into the kitchen.

"I fell asleep on the way home from school," Alfonso replied with a shrug of his shoulders. "I ended up climbing that tree and feeding the falcons."

"Again?"

"That's right," said Alfonso. "And then I couldn't get back to sleep, so it took me forever to get home."

For a moment, Alfonso considered telling them about his encounter with Kiril, but he quickly decided against it. His mother was already in a depressed state and Alfonso didn't want to get her all upset about some spooky guy who was lurking in the woods.

"Never mind how slow you went," said Pappy Eubanks, who was already sitting down at the kitchen table, a fork and knife sticking out of each fist. "I'm glad to see you awake on your skis. That is a long journey, a hard journey, and you should be proud of yourself that you made it with your eyes open." For his part, Pappy had absolutely no interest in what Alfonso did in his sleep. Alfonso was quite glad about this, and he always smiled when Pappy griped, "All that sleep craziness is nothing more than tomfoolery." *Tomfoolery.* That's what Pappy called everything that Alfonso did in his sleep.

Pappy smiled approvingly at Alfonso and revealed a set of crooked, jack-o-lantern teeth. Pappy was a small man with a large potbelly framed by a pair of old leather suspenders. His face was dominated by an enormous pair of reading glasses that magnified his pupils to the size of golf balls. Traces of potting soil sat in small clumps on his bald, gleaming head. "Sit down my boy," beckoned Pappy. "Let's have a nice meal, shall we? How were the baby falcons today? Hungry, I bet! It's the dead of winter!"

Alfonso nodded. The three turned to the food on the table and ate dinner in silence. Afterward, Alfonso went to the greenhouse to do his evening chores. He wasn't particularly fond of them. It took him almost an hour to sprinkle teaspoons of Pappy's special, homemade, fluorescent red plant food into each of the two hundred or so potted flowers in the greenhouse. The one bright spot was that he could spend time with the strange plant that he had recently grown. Neither Alfonso, nor Judy, nor Pappy Eubanks, nor the botanist from the University of Minnesota who had once paid them a visit, had the slightest idea what type of plant it was.

The plant was about a foot tall and very skinny. It had seven dark green leaves that looked too big for the long turquoise stem. And just recently, it had grown the most amazing flower. The flower's petals changed colors every few minutes so that, over the course of an hour, they went from green to blue, to violet, to red, to pink, to yellow, to orange, to maroon, to purple, and then back to green.

A long-time client of Pappy's from Greenwich, Connecticut, offered Alfonso ten thousand dollars on the spot for the plant. Alfonso refused. Without a moment's hesitation, the man upped his offer to twenty thousand dollars. This was an awful lot of money. It was about half of what Pappy's flower and vegetable business made in an entire year. Both Judy and Pappy begged Alfonso to accept the deal, but Alfonso still refused. He was obstinate because, through a most unusual turn of events, Alfonso was convinced that the plant was his father's.

As it turns out, Alfonso had always loved a particular family heirloom—an old wooden maraca, or rattle. The rattle had belonged to Leif, who had carried it with him from the Ural

Mountains, in northern Russia, where he had been born. Very little was known about Leif's journey from the Urals to North America; in fact, all that Judy knew for certain was that Leif arrived at an orphanage in Vancouver, Canada, at the age of eight. The records also noted that Leif had an older brother named Hill, who was sent to a different Canadian orphanage in Winnipeg. Hill didn't stay there long. Shortly after his arrival in Winnipeg, he ran away and was never heard from again. Judy said Leif had tried to find his brother, but had never succeeded.

After Leif's drowning, Alfonso treasured the small rattle, with its hand-carved foreign writing, as the strongest connection he had to his father. And then, one night a few months ago, something terrible happened. While Alfonso was sleepwalking around his room, he accidentally stepped on the rattle and cracked it open. The next morning, Alfonso discovered the broken toy. He was beside himself with anger. It was bad enough that his sleeping-self was constantly upstaging him at school, but now it had gone and broken his most treasured possession.

As he examined the broken rattle, seven large yellow seeds fell onto the floor. Alfonso picked up the seeds in his hand, but when he opened his fingers, he noticed that the seeds had turned orange. A few moments later they turned maroon, then purple, then green. Alfonso placed the seeds in an old pickle jar beneath his bed for safekeeping. The following night, however, his sleeping-self took the seeds, brought them down to the greenhouse, and planted them in a large clay pot. The night after that, Alfonso sleepwalked to a nearby creek, retrieved three small, crescent-shaped stones, and placed them in the pot.

The next night, Alfonso sleepwalked to a nearby hilltop, collected two pinecones and a small bag of wolf droppings, and then placed all of this into the pot as well. All told, these nightly missions went on for almost three weeks. It was almost as if Alfonso's sleeping-self were following the directions to some strange recipe, and for once, Alfonso didn't resent these sleeping escapades. Somehow they left him feeling closer to his father. Of course, he had no idea what would come of all of this until, on the fourth week, the seeds he planted sprouted into the remarkable plant that now proudly sat in Pappy's greenhouse.

After Alfonso finished his chores, he walked over to his plant to admire it for a moment. The petals were turning from violet to red. The change came in a ripple, as if someone had spilled a jar of ink across the face of the flower. Moments later, a loud sound interrupted his observation of the plant.

Thwack! Thwack! Thwack!

It sounded as if someone were smashing a plank of wood with a hammer. He grabbed a flashlight that was resting on a nearby bench and walked cautiously toward the noise. The greenhouse was quite large—more than three times larger than the cottage in which the Perplexons lived—and as Alfonso walked along the concrete floor, his footsteps echoed across its cavernous ceilings.

Thwack! Thwack! Thwack!

The noise grew louder. Alfonso flicked on his flashlight and let the beam roam over the greenhouse's plant-filled tables until it fell upon a large wooden crate sitting in a dusty corner.

Thwack! Thwack! Thwack!

The entire crate was rattling and shaking as if it contained a wild animal. Slowly, Alfonso took a step closer. To his surprise, he realized that the top of the crate was broken and almost completely yanked off. His flashlight shone on the black writing stenciled into the wood:

FROM: BLAGOVESHCHENSK SHIPPING & HANDLING
34 NORIL'SK
CITY OF BARSH-YIN-BINDER
URAL MOUNTAINS, RUSSIA

TO: MASTER ALFONSO PERPLEXON
WORLD'S END
STATE OF MINNESOTA IN
THE UNITED STATES OF AMERICA

Alfonso was confused. When did this package arrive? Where was Barsh-yin-Binder? And what was making such a racket? Before Alfonso could begin to answer these questions, he heard another strange noise—a loud engine sputtering its way up the Perplexon's driveway. Alfonso glanced at his watch. It was almost nine. No one ever visited the Perplexon home at this time of night. Alfonso rushed back to the door of the greenhouse. In the distance, he saw a man with a flowing mane of white hair riding a motorcycle. The man was taking the icy turns of the Perplexon driveway at such great speeds that Alfonso felt certain he would wipe out. But he didn't. He rode expertly to the front door of the cottage and dismounted. Then, without a moment's hesitation, he turned toward Alfonso and waved.

"Hello?" yelled Alfonso. "Can I help you?"

The man simply gestured with his hand for Alfonso to come over.

"You need some help?" asked Alfonso again.

The man nodded.

Alfonso glanced back at the crate and then walked reluctantly toward the man. The motorcyclist was very tall, almost six and a half feet. He had a great deal of white hair, a finely maintained handlebar mustache, and a long crooked nose. He wore an old bomber jacket, a tightly fitted leather aviator's cap, and an ancient-looking pair of racing goggles.

"Hello, my name is Hill Persplexy, though you should feel free to call me 'Uncle Hill,'" mumbled the man as he took off his racing goggles. "And you must be Alfonso. Yes, you look like your father."

"Uncle Hill?" said Alfonso incredulously. "You mean you're my father's . . ."

"Older brother," muttered the man. "Yes, that's me."

"Wow!" said Alfonso excitedly. "I never thought you'd —"

"Show up?"

Alfonso nodded and then beamed at his uncle. In the years after his father died, Alfonso often hoped that his uncle Hill might magically appear. And, suddenly, here he was. Yet, as Alfonso took a closer look at his long-lost relative, he noticed something peculiar. His uncle's eyes were half closed. Moments later he let out a very audible snore.

"You're asleep!" said Alfonso.

"Why of course I'm asleep," Hill mumbled. "Do you think I could have ridden that old motorcycle in these conditions if I were awake? I just sleepdrove here all the way from Chicago, where I live. Nonstop. There's not a moment to lose."

"Why?"

"I'll tell you more as soon as I wake up," Hill said briskly. "Let's go inside and get some coffee, shall we?"

"But in the greenhouse there's —"

"Never mind that now," said Hill. He drew nearer to Alfonso. "We have urgent matters to discuss — lives are at stake."

CHAPTER 3

McBRIDGE'S BOOK OF MYTHICAL PLANTS

INSIDE THE HOUSE, Judy Perplexon overcame her initial shock at seeing her husband's long-lost brother and quickly put on a pot of coffee. They all sat down with him in the small living room, next to the fireplace. For at least five minutes, Hill said nothing but snored loudly. It was enough to make Pappy and Alfonso very tired. At last, Judy served him a mug of piping hot Colombian coffee. Hill downed it in several large gulps. He then blinked furiously, rubbed his eyes, looked around the room, and gasped: "Where on earth am I?"

"You're in World's End, Minnesota," Judy Perplexon calmly explained. "I am Judy, this is my son, Alfonso, and this is my father, Pappy Eubanks."

"Pleased to meet you. I am Hill Persplexy," he said with a

polite nod. "I believe you were acquainted with my brother, Leif Persplexy."

"Of course I was acquainted with him," Judy softly replied. "H-he was my husband."

"I see," said Hill. He looked at Judy. "It appears I've missed both his wedding and his funeral. I'm very sorry for your loss. My failure to see Leif before he died will haunt me forever." They sat silently for a few minutes until the silence seemed unbearable. "When did he pass away?" Hill asked.

"Three years ago," replied Judy.

"What a horrible pity," said Hill with a sad shake of his head. He reached across the table and grasped Judy's hand tenderly. "You must forgive me for not calling sooner. I only just found out about the whole sad affair myself. When I was driving through town on my motorcycle, I asked for directions to the Persplexy place and this big fellow at the general store told me that Leif had died. Drowned in the lake, he said. This was news to me. As I'm sure you know, the two of us were separated as kids. I've had the darndest time tracking him down. I even hired a private detective at one point. No signs of Leif Persplexy anywhere in the Western Hemisphere. That's what the detective told me. Paid him near seven thousand dollars for that tidbit. Anyway, I'm so glad to have found you. So very, very glad indeed."

"Uncle Hill?" said Alfonso.

"Yes," replied Hill kindly.

"Why are you calling my father Leif *Persplexy?* His name—our name—is *Perplexon.*"

"Afraid not," replied Hill with a large, rather apologetic smile. "That was a mistake made by the orphanage in Vancouver. The name is 'Persplexy'— always has been—it's an old Dormian name. Quite a respected one actually. If I remember correctly, there were a number of distinguished Dormian sword makers by that name. Of course, they were asleep while they made the swords, but they still made fine weaponry . . ."

Judy and Pappy Eubanks exchanged uneasy looks.

"I'm sure Leif told you all about Dormia so I won't bore you with the details."

"He didn't mention anything like that," said a suspicious-looking Pappy.

"Oh dear," said Hill with a sudden look of concern. "Not a word, eh? Leif always was a bit of a secretive fellow. Didn't like to talk about himself. Yes, well, er . . . I have some explaining to do. You see, Alfonso, even though I know very little about you, I am willing to wager that you are a most unusual sleeper."

"Tell me about it," said Alfonso with a sigh. "The doctors say I've got Morvan's syndrome."

"Those doctors are fools," said Hill. "They insist on coming up with fancy, complicated names for any so-called disorders that baffle them. When I was in an orphanage in Winnipeg, they told me I had the same thing, and claimed it was because I had contracted a rare form of cholera. Nonsense! Let me tell you, dear nephew, what you have is not a disorder, or a syndrome, but a gift! It's the gift of *wakeful sleeping*. Your father had it because he was Dormian, and obviously he passed it on to you."

"Is that right?" inquired Pappy Eubanks skeptically.

"Yes," replied Hill in a matter-of-fact tone. "Dormia is a place where everyone goes about their business—wielding swords, writing books, building palaces, cooking dinner—while asleep.

And this is no coincidence. Ever since the beginning of Dormian history, which I confess to know precious little about, the Dormians have been at war with a nasty lot of roaming barbarians known as Dragoonya. Unfortunately, these Dragoonya fellows outnumber us and they're unusually skilled in battle. Don't ask me why they hate us—I forgot. Anyway, at some point along the way, we Dormians took to defending ourselves in our sleep. We simply couldn't afford to waste our sleeping hours in bed. It was necessary to muster every man, woman, and child—sleeping and awake—to be on guard against our eternal foe. We hid ourselves in a series of great mountain fortresses deep within the Ural Mountains. They eventually became the eleven great cities of Dormia."

"There are eleven cities of Dormia?" inquired Alfonso.

"There *were* eleven cities of Dormia," corrected Hill. "The Dragoonya destroyed most of them, although at least one city—Somnos—still exists in the Ural Mountains. That's where Leif and I were born."

Pappy's eyes looked massive behind his reading glasses. He furrowed his eyebrows and uttered a theatrical sigh.

"Hmm," grunted Pappy. "You claim these *Dormians* can defend themselves while asleep? How's that possible? When you're asleep your eyes are closed!" He spoke the last sentence slowly and with great exasperation, as if talking to a very slow person.

"Not in this case," Hill briskly replied. "Even in the world outside Dormia, it's possible. When normal people sleepwalk, their eyes are often open even if they're in a deep sleep, snoring away. It's the same for Dormians. They may shut their eyes for a few seconds at the beginning of sleep, but then their eyes pop back open. Think of it as a trance."

Judy glanced at Alfonso. The doctors in St. Paul had described Alfonso's sleeping disorder exactly the same way. Pappy fell silent but soon his eyes lit up again. "Dormia is in the Urals, you say? That should be easy enough to verify. We'll just look it up in my trusty old atlas over here —"

"Oh, don't bother," interrupted Hill. "You won't find it in an atlas or any other reference book."

"Is that so?" asked Pappy. "And you expect us to believe this claptrap nonsense with no proof?"

"To the contrary, my good man," replied Hill. He stood up and took off his old leather bomber jacket. Beneath this he wore a heavy wool turtleneck and a shoulder-strap holster that contained a well-polished Colt .45 revolver. Both Pappy and Judy stiffened at the sight of the gun.

"Don't worry about the revolver," said Hill. "I'm a well-trained marksman. I got her during my days in the air force. The two of us have been through a lot together. Anyway, what I want to show you is this . . ." Hill reached into his jacket and pulled out a crinkled December issue of the magazine *American Botanist.* Alfonso recognized the issue immediately because his plant was featured in its pages. The botanist from the University of Minnesota had snapped a few pictures of the plant during his visit and submitted them to the editors at *American Botanist.* The article said nothing about Alfonso or Pappy. In fact, it wasn't really an article. It was just a series of photos with a small caption that read, "This remarkable, color-changing plant was grown organically in a greenhouse in World's End, Minnesota."

"What kind of proof is that?" Pappy demanded. "You can buy that magazine anywhere."

"Let me explain," said Hill. "Every night during the last month, when I fell asleep I promptly sleepwalked to the nearest newsstand and purchased a copy of *American Botanist.* This happened every night without fail. Of course, I couldn't understand why I was doing this, but I figured there had to be a reason. At times I may be a fool, but my sleeping-self is a very clever man. I looked through the magazine and there, on page thirty-eight, was a remarkable yet strangely familiar image. Long ago—in another time and place—I knew I had seen this flower with petals that changed color. And then it hit me: this was a Dormian bloom —"

"This is all very interesting," Pappy Eubanks said impatiently. "But, kind sir, we are still waiting for a shred of proof!"

"Yes, of course," replied Hill. He reached into his jacket again and this time pulled out a small leather-bound book that wasn't much bigger than a deck of cards. On its cover, in ornate gold writing, were the words *McBridge's Book of Mythical Plants.* Hill handed it over to Pappy, who stared at it in his hands.

"What's this?" he asked. "Mythical plants? What kind of made-up nonsense are you peddling!"

"Oh, it's real," replied Hill. "A palm reader and occult store owner I knew in Chicago was going out of business and selling all his books. He sold the whole lot to me for two dollars, and this one was at the bottom." Hill pointed to the leather-bound book. "Yes, it's been my source of knowledge for quite a few things. You'll see. Turn to section *D.*"

Alfonso and Judy quickly gathered around Pappy as he opened the well-worn cover of the book. It was ordered alphabetically. The first entry was the Achaemenian Rose, whose petals supposedly turned to gold dust when rubbed together.

According to the book, it was last seen in ancient Persia during the reign of Cyrus the Great (559 B.C.). Next there was the Afrinagan orchid of Atlantis, whose roots apparently burst into flames whenever they were exposed to direct moonlight. "Yeah right," muttered Pappy as he flipped through the pages until he came upon section *D* and found an entry for Dormian bloom. Next to it was a drawing of a plant that looked similar to the one sitting in the greenhouse. The book noted:

Dormian bloom:

This rarest of plants is distinguished by its remarkable petals, which change color every few minutes in a cyclical fashion. It supposedly possesses a number of magical powers including the ability to turn frozen earth into ripe, fertile soil. The plant is indigenous to the mythical kingdom of Dormia, where it has always been closely guarded by the Order of Dormian Knights, who are renowned for their ability to fight in their sleep. Little is known for certain about Dormia, but it is believed that this ancient symbol is the nation's insignia:

When a Dormian bloom is fully grown, it becomes a Founding Tree of Dormia. At this point, its trunk stands over one thousand

feet in height and its roots, which stretch out for hundreds of miles in all directions, pump nourishment into the soil. These trees are the lifeblood of Dormia and are exceptionally prized.

The legend of the Dormian bloom is widespread throughout much of Central Asia. Even the Venetian traveler Marco Polo mentions hearing of it during his travels to the Far East in the late thirteenth century. It is speculated that the plant is native to the Ural Mountains. Yet even here, there is a saying in Russian, which hints at its rarity. The saying is used by locals to describe highly improbable occurrences. It goes:

Это столь же вероятно как видеть реку,
которая течет в верх или найти цвет
Дорми.

Roughly translated this means:
"That is as unlikely as seeing a river
that flows uphill or stumbling upon a
flower of Dormia."

According to legend, the plant can only be hatched by a Dormian outside the realm of Dormia. This event almost always coincides with the death of a Founding Tree in one of the eleven mythical cities of Dormia. During this precarious transition period, known as Dormian Autumn, the bloom must quickly be delivered to the city whose Founding Tree is dying. If this task is not accomplished in time, both the Dormian bloom and the Dormian city in question will wither and die. Or so the legend goes.

Pappy looked up at Hill. "You haven't convinced me!" he declared irritably. "Some palm reader sells you this book and you believe it? Hah! This is all very curious, isn't it? You've been out of the picture for the last twenty years and then, as soon as Alfonso grows a valuable plant and it shows up in the pages of a magazine, you come to Minnesota with this far-fetched tale and a book of made-up plants. It's like those folks who win the lottery and suddenly dozens of distant cousins start coming out of the woodwork. And the kicker is: we don't even know who you really are! I don't mean to be rude, sir, but I have a grandson to protect."

Hill let out a heavy sigh, but said nothing.

"Maybe his story is true," said Alfonso nervously. "I mean . . . Uncle Hill, if that's who he really is, does seem kind of familiar in a weird way. And, if you think about it, Dad said he was born in the Ural Mountains and the only thing he brought with him was his maraca. That means the seeds inside the maraca—the ones that I used to grow the plant—also come from the Urals. It all does kind of fit together. But —"

"But what?" interjected Hill.

"Well," said Alfonso sheepishly, "Pappy has a good point. It's tempting to believe your story, Uncle Hill. I mean, it might be true. But how can we be certain that you are who you say you are?"

"The truth is," added Judy, "you really don't resemble Leif. I mean, judging just by appearances, it doesn't look like you two were brothers."

Alfonso studied Hill closely. He looked old—more like a grandfather than an uncle. If he were truly Leif's brother, that would make him roughly fifty years old. Of course, some people aged more rapidly than others, but even if that were the case, Hill's story had some holes in it.

Hill smiled awkwardly, shifted his weight in his seat, and then said, "I realize it doesn't look good—me showing up after all these years with this crazy tale—but I'm afraid you'll just have to trust me. I want to help you protect the plant."

At that moment, Alfonso thought back to his encounter with Kiril in the Forest of the Obitteroos. He recalled Kiril's warning that in the near future someone with uncertain motives would come knocking on his door asking for the plant. And now here was Hill. It all gave Alfonso an uneasy feeling.

"Well," Judy said to Pappy, "you have to admit, the drawing of the Dormian bloom in Hill's book looks exactly like the plant that's sitting in our greenhouse right now."

"The greenhouse!" gasped Alfonso. He had forgotten completely about the greenhouse and the large wooden box that was making the strange thumping noise.

"What about the greenhouse?" Pappy asked irritably.

"There's a box in the greenhouse addressed to me with something strange in it."

"Oh yes," replied Pappy. "It had plants from some foreign shipping company. You know, you should ask your mother and me before ordering such foolish-looking plants from overseas."

"But I didn't order it," said Alfonso. "And whatever is in that box isn't a plant—it was thrashing about like a wild animal."

"No, it was a plant," said Pappy. "Saw it with my own eyes."

Hill sat up straight. "Where was the box from?" he asked.

"Can't remember exactly—some foreign port," said Pappy. "In any case, it was a heck of an odd-looking plant—kind of looked like a turtle."

Hill stared hard at Pappy. "Was it about four feet in height, with a sturdy stem, and a large bud with a hard covering that looks like a shell?" asked Hill.

"Why that's exactly right," replied Pappy. "How'd you guess? Did you send it?"

"Absolutely not," said Hill as he grabbed *McBridge's Book of Mythical Plants* and began flipping pages frantically. He stopped at an entry titled "Dragoonya plant of war." The entry included a drawing of a plant that looked like a cross between a Venus flytrap and a giant snapping turtle. Alfonso read the following entry aloud:

Dragoonya plant of war:

A fierce snapping plant with actual teeth teeth and a nimble root system that helps it move with surprising speed. Supposedly it was used in battle by the nomadic Dragoonya of Central Asia. Handle with extreme care. In fact, best if avoided altogether.

Renowned for their seeming ability to predict the future, the Dragoonya are a fierce and cruel . . .

"Holy smokes," interrupted Pappy Eubanks as he pointed to the drawing. "That's the plant. I'm certain of it."

"And it's in the same greenhouse as your Dormian bloom?" asked Hill.

"Yes," said Pappy. "In fact, there were at least three in the box. Maybe more."

"By Jove!" exclaimed Hill as he snatched up his bomber jacket and goggles. "Quickly—to the greenhouse. Those Dragoonya plants will destroy the bloom!"

CHAPTER 4

RUN FOR YOUR LIVES!

THEY RAN TOWARD the greenhouse, with Pappy and Alfonso in the lead. They scrambled through the snow and then stopped abruptly at the greenhouse door. The building was dark and completely silent. "Not a word," whispered Hill as he reached into his leather bomber jacket and pulled out his Colt .45 revolver. "We have to get the Dormian bloom."

"I can show you where it is," said Alfonso.

"Good," said Hill. "Lead the way."

Inside the greenhouse, the many plants and rows of tables were illuminated in a milky glow from the light of the moon, which was now shining brightly overhead. Cautiously, the foursome made their way down the center aisle of the greenhouse until they came to the large table where Pappy kept most of his orchids. The Dormian bloom was sitting right where Alfonso had left it. Alfonso quickly scooped it up and nodded to Hill. Just then, however, they heard the sound of feet scampering. Or at least it sounded like feet. Something low to the ground was moving very quickly and headed directly for them. Dark shapes surrounded them. Pappy let out a scream and in the moonlight Alfonso saw a gnarled, slimy green bud—bigger than the head of a horse—with a set of massive jaws and sharp yellowish teeth clamped tightly around Pappy's leg. Moments later, they heard a crunch.

Pappy screamed again. "M-MY LEG!"

"Stand back!" shouted Hill. "Give me some room!"

Alfonso and Judy stumbled backwards. Hill set his gun down on the table, picked up a nearby shovel, raised it over his head, and brought it down fiercely on the head of the plant. Pappy let out another scream. The plant released its grip. In one swift, powerful movement Hill scooped up Pappy Eubanks like a child and flung him over his shoulder. Pappy had turned white. Just above his ankle, his leg was obviously broken. The ankle and foot dangled loosely, as if only the skin was holding it to the rest of his leg.

"Hill! Behind you!" screamed Judy.

"My revolver," barked Hill. "Grab my revolver!"

Alfonso grabbed the heavy gun and tossed it to his uncle. Hill turned, raised his pistol, and aimed it at two more charging Dragoonya plants of war.

Pow! Pow! Pow!

Hill fired three shots. The noise was deafening. They all heard the bullets ricochet off the concrete floor and break through glass. The plants were momentarily stunned, but recovered quickly and resumed their charge. Hill fired two more shots and looked at Judy and Alfonso.

"Run for your lives!" he yelled.

All three of them scrambled across the greenhouse and made for the door.

"Grab my Gobi desert orchid!" moaned Pappy. "I-it's worth a fortune."

Judy nodded, snagged a large purple and green orchid off a nearby shelf, and then continued running with the others. Judy carried the orchid, Alfonso carried the bloom, and Hill carried Pappy. They pushed through the door of the greenhouse, slammed it shut behind them, and rushed into the snowy yard.

"There are five of them," groaned Pappy, who was the only one facing backwards. He moaned again and then slumped loosely against Hill. He had passed out from the pain.

They could hear the plants pounding against the inside of the greenhouse door. Clearly, the door was about to break. Hill surveyed the snow-covered landscape.

"Is that a plane over there?" he asked, pointing down toward the edge of Lake Witekkon. Alfonso nodded. Several hundred feet away, near the ice-covered surface of the lake, sat a rusting seaplane. The long-range plane, which had been used in the South Pacific during World War II, belonged to the Perplexons' neighbor, Martin Edlund.

"It belongs to Old Man Edlund—he bought it at some auction," said Judy. "He claims it can fly, but I've never seen it off the ground."

"We'll have to take that chance," Hill shouted. He started running across the field toward the plane. The others followed him. Seconds later, the greenhouse door burst open. Alfonso glanced backwards and saw the Dragoonya plants of war moving effortlessly over the snow.

Hill made it to the seaplane first. He cranked open the main cargo door and pushed Pappy in. He then settled into the cockpit and, to his great relief, saw the fuel indicator pointing toward the word *full.* Hill hit the starter button and after a few seconds of grinding, the plane's dual-propeller engines roared to life. Alfonso and Judy arrived and climbed inside.

"Close the door!" yelled Hill.

"Already done," yelled Judy.

"Good!" said Hill. "Judy, grab that large wrench over there and hit me over the head with it."

"What?"

"Hit me over the head with that wrench—you need to knock me out. I really shouldn't take off in this plane in these conditions, if I'm awake, and I'm not feeling sleepy after that coffee."

"I can't do that!" said Judy.

"I'll do it," said Alfonso sheepishly.

"Good lad," said Hill. "Give me a good whack, but not too hard, just enough to make me see stars. I need to be fast asleep to pull off a stunt like this!"

Alfonso picked up the wrench that was sitting on the floor of the plane, raised it as high as he could in the cramped cabin, and brought it down on his uncle's head. It hit his skull with a dull thud. Hill immediately went slack and his head slumped off to the side. He lay motionless in the pilot's seat.

"Oh my goodness," said Judy. "I think you may have done your uncle in."

Alfonso glanced out the window. The Dragoonya plants of war were just a few feet away. The nearest one opened its massive jaws and leapt for the door handle. It was locked. The plant snarled. All five gathered on the ground below the window and lunged at it together, crashing into the glass. The window held, but spidery cracks appeared.

Suddenly Hill's eyes twitched open. His nose wiggled. His lips puckered. An instant later he was sitting erect in his seat, squinting sleepily through the windshield. "Not exactly sure where I am," muttered Hill. "But I think it might be best to depart promptly." With that, he gunned the engine and the plane began to slide across the frozen lake. The plants of war lunged again but missed the window and hit the metal fuselage with such force that the plane rocked as it built up speed. "Up, up, and away," muttered Hill. He pulled back on the plane's steering wheel. Moments later, they were airborne and Hill navigated the plane expertly through a tight space between two large trees.

As the seaplane gained altitude, Alfonso looked out the window and saw the frozen landscape of Minnesota expand beneath him, all those ice-covered lakes and snowy fields. From this height everything looked so peaceful, like a soft white carpet lit up by the moon. Inside the cockpit, however, things were far less calm. It sounded as if someone was banging together two frying pans directly in Alfonso's ear, and the noise seemed to be coming from the plane's rickety propellers. Plus, everything rattled—the floor, the seats, even the steering wheel. The vibrations worked their way through Alfonso's feet, up his legs, along his spine, and into his jaw.

Hill piloted the plane and snored peacefully for about an hour until, rather abruptly, he woke up and gingerly rubbed his head.

He looked at Alfonso. "You really gave me a good whack with that wrench."

"Hill, what are you doing awake?" asked Judy nervously. "I thought you could fly the plane only when you were asleep."

"Actually," said Hill, "I can fly well enough when I'm awake, but I'm really much better at piloting when I'm asleep, especially when it comes to tricky operations—like taking off in a rickety old seaplane in the depths of winter." He paused. "How's Pappy? I haven't heard anything from him since the greenhouse."

"I don't know," Judy gravely replied. "His foot is completely broken at the shin. He's been passed out now for a long time. He's still breathing, and I want to wake him up, but he should rest while he can. He needs medical attention quickly."

"He'll be fine," replied Hill. "I suspect he's as healthy as a horse. I'm not a doctor, but being in the military, I saw my fair share of injuries, and I can tell that it was a clean break."

"I hope so," replied Judy. She glanced at Pappy. "You say you were in the air force?"

"Indeed," Hill said, nodding vigorously. He eased back into the pilot's seat and began to explain. Back in his air force days he'd actually set a world record for flying a transport plane—56.8 hours straight—on a trip from Los Angeles to Miami. There was just one problem: he had gone the wrong way. He had, of course, intended to take the direct route of flying across the United States from Los Angeles to Miami, but he had fallen asleep at the wheel and gone the other way around the world instead. He flew over the Pacific Ocean, Asia, Europe, and then over the Atlantic Ocean to Miami. The following day the *Miami Herald* ran the following banner: MAN TRAVELS AROUND THE

GLOBE BACKWARDS IN HIS SLEEP: AIR FORCE IS ANNOYED BUT PROUD.

The highlight of his flying career, said Hill, came when he and a Soviet pilot named Yuri Napinoff, who was also famous for flying in his sleep, were asked to do a joint mission in the early 1970s, to show that the United States and the Soviet Union could get along. When the two pilots finally met in Moscow, Hill discovered that Yuri was actually a quarter Dormian on his mother's side. Hill wasn't entirely surprised. According to him, the globe was sprinkled with men and women like Hill and Yuri who had some kind of connection to Dormia and who yearned to go back, but could never find the way. During their mission, Hill and Yuri were supposed to practice dropping bombs into the Caspian Sea, but instead they flew over the Ural Mountains—for eighty-two hours straight—to try to catch a glimpse of Dormia. They saw nothing; it was too cloudy. Ever since, Hill had rather sadly given up hope that he would ever go home again. In time, he quit the air force and repeatedly turned down opportunities to become the spokesman for countless sleep-related products such as nightcaps, pajamas, earplugs, and of course, sleeping pills. Instead, he became a watch repairman in Chicago. His would be a quiet and uneventful life. Or so he thought. And then came the day when Hill saw the photo of the Dormian bloom in the pages of *American Botanist* and everything changed. He turned around and smiled at Alfonso.

From the look on her face, Judy was still unconvinced. "That's very interesting," she told Hill, "but I'd really like to know where we're going."

"We're going to Dormia," replied Hill matter-of-factly.

"We're flying directly to Dormia?" asked Alfonso in total disbelief.

"Oh goodness no," replied Hill. "I wish we could, but we'd never make it there in this plane. Besides there's a bigger problem, as I just explained: I have no idea where *exactly* Dormia is. We're flying to a little island off the western coast of Canada called Fort Krasnik. I'm friends with a highly placed longshoreman there by the name of Dusty Magrewski. Hopefully, he can help us book passage on a boat to Russia."

"You've got to be kidding," said Judy. "We are *not* going to Russia. I'm sure I don't need to tell you that I have a house to look after, we have a plant business to run, and Alfonso has school to attend."

"And all those things will be waiting for you when you return," replied Hill. "In the meantime, at least come as far as Fort Krasnik. They've got a great doctor who will fix Pappy right up. Then, if you still want to go home, I'll fly you back. Besides, I think you'll really enjoy meeting Dusty Magrewski."

"Why's that?" asked Alfonso.

"Well," said Hill, "for starters, Dusty knew both your father and me when we were kids. You see, we came through Fort Krasnik on our way from the Urals to Canada. So Dusty can vouch that I am who I say I am. Hopefully, that'll put your minds at ease."

"So then Dusty knows about Dormia?" asked Alfonso.

"No, no, no," replied Hill with a chortle. "Hardly anyone knows about Dormia except the sort of crackpots who believe in old wives' tales and a handful of actual Dormians like myself."

At that moment, Pappy stirred awake. Even in the gloom of the cabin, his face looked pale and sweaty. No one wanted to look at his leg, which had begun to swell. "Dormia," he wheezed. "A-are you still tryin' to sell us your magic stories?"

"Perhaps this would interest you," said Hill. He reached deep into the inside of his leather jacket and fished out a small, well-worn pocket watch. "This timepiece is Dormian," he said as he handed it to Alfonso. "It's the only thing I brought with me. Take a look—open it."

Alfonso pressed down on a thick knob at the top and the cover of the smooth metal watch swung open, revealing an intricately painted tree on the inside of the cover. The tree bore little resemblance to the Dormian bloom, but it did have a number of flowers on it, and these flowers changed color every few seconds in the exact same manner as the bloom. Alfonso thought that this was very odd because the timepiece appeared to be a windup device with no batteries. How exactly were these leaves changing color? Directly beneath the image of the tree was a small numeric panel, much like the date wheel on an ordinary watch, but instead of providing a date, it simply read: 55.

"What does the fifty-five mean?" asked Alfonso.

"Not sure," said Hill. "Ever since I got it, decades ago, that date wheel was stuck on the number one hundred and forty three. Then, about three months ago, it just started counting backwards—going down one number each day. I'll be darned if I know what exactly it means, but I have a hunch."

"What an odd watch," said Alfonso softly, almost to himself.

"Yeah," agreed Hill. "That timepiece has been with me since I left Dormia and it keeps perfect time, too, although it makes a strange ticking noise."

"What do you mean?" Alfonso asked. He brought the watch to his ear. Hill was right—it did make a strange sound that went like this: *tick-tick-tick-tick-tick-tick-TOCK tick-tick-tick-tick-TOCK TOCK-TOCK* (pause) *tick-tick-tick-tick-tick-tick-TOCK tick-tick-TOCK TOCK-TOCK.*

Alfonso looked at Hill. "It sounds like it's broken," he said.

"True enough," replied Hill. "And yet, as I said, it keeps perfect time."

"You still haven't convinced me," Pappy bitterly muttered. "You've got nothing but a bunch of cheap trinkets in the way of evidence as far as I am concerned."

Hill let out a deep, exasperated sigh.

"I don't know what else I can tell you," said Hill. "I've shown you everything." He glanced back at Pappy and Judy. His eyes wandered to the floor, where he saw the Gobi desert orchid. It appeared to be in very bad shape. The temperature was quite cold in the cabin of the plane and the orchid's stem was covered with a layer of frost and its flowers had withered.

Hill smiled. "I've got an idea," he said. "Judy, would you mind handing that orchid to Alfonso? Alfonso, I want you to take the orchid out of its pot and place it next to the bloom. Then I want you to take the bloom out of its pot as well."

"What?" Pappy shouted. "You can't re-pot a rare Gobi desert orchid on a plane. It'll die!"

"I'm afraid the orchid is already dead," replied Hill. He looked at Judy.

"All right," Judy said. "I'll play along." She handed the orchid to Alfonso.

Alfonso carefully removed the orchid from its container and placed it next to the bloom. Then he removed the bloom from its container. For a moment, nothing happened.

"I told you!" Pappy said. "Tomfoolery!"

"Wait!" exclaimed Judy. The frost on the orchid's stem was glistening. Over the next minute, they all watched with rapt attention as the frost melted into beads of water, the orchid's stem straightened, and the delicate purple and green petals unfurled and blossomed outward. Upon closer examination, Alfonso noticed that several small roots from the bloom had extended outward and connected with those of the orchid.

"Oh my word," mumbled Pappy. "I don't believe it."

"So I've finally gotten your attention," said Hill with a smile. "Good! Now, Alfonso, I want you to pull those two plants apart—but be careful—I don't want you to tear their roots."

Alfonso did as he was told. Very gently he pulled the Dormian bloom away from the Gobi desert orchid. The orchid immediately began to wither. Its stem wilted, its flower lost its petals, and the soil took on the color of dust.

"What happened?" asked Pappy.

"I think it's quite obvious," replied Hill. "The Dormian bloom revived your orchid."

"Little good that did," winced Pappy. "As soon as the plants were separated my orchid withered again."

"That's my point exactly!" he said. His eyes shone with a fierce determination. "Without the Dormian bloom the orchid returned to its natural state, which was close to death. It's exactly how *McBridge's* explains it."

Hill fixed his gaze on Alfonso. "The same exact thing is about to happen in Somnos—only on a much grander scale. Don't you see? When the Founding Tree of Somnos dies, the snow will reclaim its ground, winter will descend, and everything around the city will die: the trees, the bushes, the grass, the crops, then all the farm animals, and eventually—when all the food is gone—the people will perish too. They'll freeze to death—freeze in walls of ice . . ."

Hill paused for a moment and fell into an eerie silence.

"I remember a story as a boy," he continued slowly, "about a Dormian city that froze over. An expedition force from Somnos went to this place—its name was Quartzor or Quartin or something like that. They found hundreds of Dormians frozen in walls of ice. Apparently, you could see entire families huddled together in frozen blocks. Their faces, which held these terrifying expressions, were perfectly preserved. My goodness, what an awful way to go."

"So, if we fail to deliver the Dormian bloom, that's what is going to happen in Somnos?" asked Alfonso.

Hill nodded solemnly.

"And the date wheel on your watch, which has been ticking down, you think that's how many days we have to deliver the plant before Somnos freezes?"

Hill nodded again.

"Fifty-five days," said Alfonso. "That seems like plenty of time, doesn't it?"

"Oh, my dear boy," said Hill with a rather sad laugh, "I am afraid you haven't the faintest idea just how long and hard the journey will be. It could take us years to find Somnos."

CHAPTER 5

A DEN OF SMUGGLERS

SEVERAL HOURS LATER, the first light of dawn began to make its way over the horizon, and the plane's cabin warmed up. Everyone soon fell asleep as they flew across the Rocky Mountains and on toward the west coast of Canada.

Alfonso was the first to wake up. Immediately, he noticed that his left ear hurt, as if it had been punched. He straightened up in his seat. Something fell onto his lap. It was Hill's pocket watch—the one that kept time but ticked as if broken. Alfonso picked up the watch and stared at it. Its exterior had a curious pattern etched on it. It looked like this:

Alfonso pressed the watch to his left ear. It fit exactly where his ear hurt. For some reason, his sleeping-self had pressed the watch to his ear the entire time he had been asleep. Why?

He listened to the strange ticking for a while: *tick-tick-tick-tick-tick-tick-TOCK tick-tick-tick-tick-TOCK TOCK-TOCK* (pause) *tick-tick-tick-tick-tick-tick-TOCK tick-tick-TOCK TOCK-TOCK*. All of a sudden, he wondered if the ticking was a riddle.

Alfonso had always loved solving riddles. He had a giant book of them back home in World's End. Alfonso would often mull over a given riddle for hours at a time until his brain throbbed with pain. In his opinion, the key to solving the toughest riddles usually involved looking at them from another perspective. In other words, he had to forget about the watch all together and simply focus on the ticking itself. The first thing that came to mind was Morse code, which Alfonso had just learned about in his history class. The code, which was used during World War II, involved a series of short and long beeps, each of which stood for a different letter in the alphabet.

The ticking on Hill's watch also appeared to be a code, though it wasn't Morse code—it was something else. Alfonso furrowed his brow as he tried to figure it out. What did the *ticks* and *tocks* stand for? He knew he could solve this.

After several minutes of intense concentration, one possibility occurred to Alfonso: the ticks were numbers and the tocks were spaces. He grabbed a pen from his pocket and began scribbling on an old scrap of paper that he found on the floor. He wrote out the code: 6-4---6-2---. The ticking revealed two numbers: sixty-four and sixty-two. Excitedly, he woke everybody up and announced what he had discovered.

"There's no rhyme or reason to that broken old watch!" Pappy complained. "What you came up with doesn't even make sense! Sixty-four and sixty-two? What's that supposed to mean anyway?"

"I don't know," said Alfonso. "But it's got to mean something."

"I doubt it," said Pappy.

"Sixty-four and sixty-two," said Hill to himself. He appeared to be deep in thought. "Those numbers are very curious. You know, back in my air force days, I used to fly to Reykjavík, Iceland. You know what we pilots used to call that place? We called it 'sixty-four by twenty-one.' You know why? Because those were the city's coordinates: sixty-four degrees north latitude by twenty-one degrees west longitude."

"What's your point?" asked Pappy.

"My point is that I think that sixty-four and sixty-two are coordinates!" exclaimed Hill. His eyes quickly strayed toward an old atlas on the dashboard of the plane. "I think Alfonso has just come up with two coordinates—latitude and longitude.

I'm guessing that it's sixty-four degrees north latitude by sixty-two degrees east longitude." He laughed. "What's the matter with me? All these years I thought that crazy ticking was just some mechanical defect."

Hill grabbed the atlas and matched up the numbers with the markings for latitude and longitude. They pointed to an area in the middle of the Ural Mountains. Hill grabbed Alfonso's pen and marked the spot.

"You did it!" yelled Hill. He leaned over and gave Alfonso a giant bear hug. "That's where we've got to go! And to think that over all these years, the first clue to finding Dormia was ticking away in my pocket."

"What do you think we'll find there?" asked Alfonso.

"I'm not sure," said Hill. "I wish I could say that we'll find Somnos, but I doubt it will be that easy. After all, this place has remained hidden for thousands of years. But by Jove, this is a very good start!"

Alfonso turned and looked at Judy and Pappy. His eyes shined with excitement.

"Hmph," muttered Pappy, but he said nothing further.

Several hours later, Hill and Alfonso were walking along an old wooden boardwalk in the seaside town of Fort Krasnik, looking for any sign of Dusty Magrewski and the doctor's office. They had left Pappy in the seaplane—he was in no shape to walk—and Judy had insisted on staying with her father.

At first glance, Fort Krasnik looked like a massive boulder

jutting out of the sea. There were no trees, grass, or vegetation of any kind. All the structures on the island—even the distant rooftops and lampposts—were made of the same dreary-looking gray stone. The only trace of color came from the boardwalk, which was painted a dull blue. The boardwalk was lined with a number of dilapidated shops. One shop advertised "peg legs and wooden teeth," another boasted "the best glass eyes in the North Pacific," and yet another had a display window filled with hundreds of razor-sharp daggers. The boardwalk itself was packed with pedestrians—mainly fishermen with dirty beards and leathery skin. There were also at least a dozen men rolling dice in the gutter and yelling. One of them, who appeared to have just won a sizable jackpot, was brandishing a knife and yelling,"Keep yer distance boys, keep yer distance. 'Dis jackpot is mine and I intend to keep 'er."

"Don't be nervous," Hill shouted to Alfonso above the din of the crowd. "This has always been a rough place, but they usually don't harm kids." He lifted his arm just in time to deflect a bottle that had been thrown out the window of a nearby bar. "Just don't get anyone mad," he added. "And, of course, always watch for flying bottles."

As they continued onward, Hill assumed the role of a tour guide and began spouting bits of history, as if they were a family on vacation. According to Hill, Fort Krasnik was founded by a group of surly Russian sailors who rebelled against their captain during the infamous Long Voyage of 1703. After eating all of the biscuits aboard their ship and throwing their captain into the icy waters of the North Pacific, the sailors landed on a small rocky island that they named Fort Krasnik, after the Krasnik Bakery in St. Petersburg, which made a particularly tough, jaw-breaking biscuit. These sailors vowed never to return to the high seas. Instead, they built docks and shops along the shore and dubbed themselves "along-the-shore-men" or simply "longshoremen."

The longshoremen of Fort Krasnik, who never had much regard for rules or regulations, soon developed a reputation as masters of the black market. They bought, sold, and traded stolen goods of all kinds. As a result, smuggling boats from all over the world came to do business on this island, which operated as its own little nation-state. Hill knew about the place because he and Leif had passed through on their way to North America.

"So how *exactly* did you and my dad get here from the Urals anyway?" asked Alfonso.

"Now that's a good question," replied Hill calmly as they walked past two old sailors fighting over a scrap of stale bread. "As I've told you, I was just eight years old when I left Dormia, so my memory is rather fuzzy, but I do remember some things. I know that Leif and I got lost outside the city of Somnos. Terrible day that was. We wandered through the city's gates and strayed into the surrounding mountains. Somehow we ended up in this very deep and dark forest. For several days we just huddled there—cold, starving, and alone. And then, well, er . . ."

"What?" asked Alfonso. "What happened next?"

"That's the thing," confessed Hill sheepishly. "It's kind of a blank. The next thing I can remember is being on this old ship bound for North America. The finer points of how exactly we got onto the ship are still a complete mystery to me."

"The ship's captain was a woman smuggler en route to Fort

Krasnik. When the ship finally laid anchor, the old sea captain—who never had any interest in children—handed Leif and me over to a longshoreman friend of hers named Dusty Magrewski. It all worked out rather well because Dusty had always wanted children of his own, but over the years, he had been too busy with his work. Dusty took us in and he became almost like a father to us—that is, until we ran away."

"Why did you run away?" Alfonso asked.

"Never mind that," said Hill awkwardly. "Oh, would you look at that! We're here!"

Hill came to an abrupt halt in front of a large stone warehouse with two enormous sliding doors in front. Directly above the doors hung a sign that read:

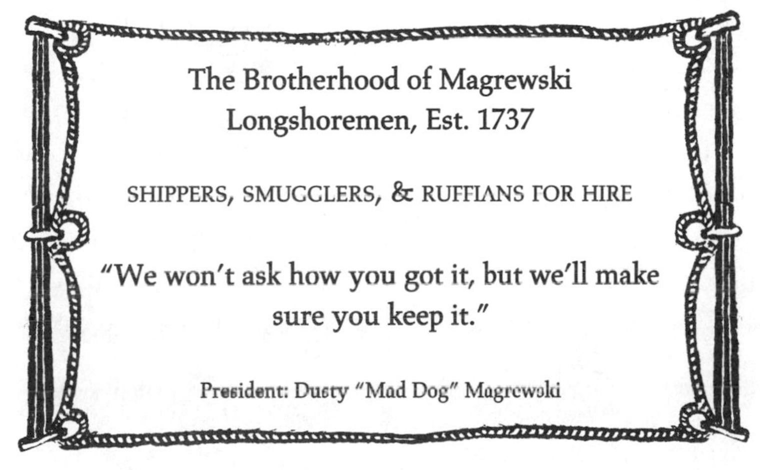

In the distance a whistle blew and longshoremen began streaming out of the front doors. Apparently, this was their lunch break. Hill and Alfonso stood to the side to avoid the mad rush. The longshoremen were of all shapes and sizes but most had the same thick upper body that comes from the daily lifting and moving of heavy objects. They all wore strudy jeans and hooded canvas jackets but there was something else about them that made them all look alike: they all had muttonchops, long sideburns that ended just below their mouths.

"That was the fashion a long ways back," Hill explained. "And once Fort Krasnik longshoremen have hit upon a way of doing things, they don't like to change. You'll see—they're a stubborn bunch and quick to suspicion. But it's for survival purposes. If they were nice to everyone, they'd probably get more visitors, and that's exactly what they don't want."

"And these guys are all longshoremen?" asked Alfonso.

"They're Magrewskis," replied Hill. "They're all members of the Magrewski Brotherhood, which is one of the two ancient brotherhoods of longshoremen in this city." Hill went on to explain that the Magrewskis were established in 1737 by a sailor named Ivan Magrewski. Ivan had a half-brother named Boris Popov and the two men couldn't stand each other. According to legend, both men had taken turns burning down each other's houses for over thirty years. Eventually, Boris founded his own brotherhood—known as the Popov Longshoremen—and the two groups had been competing, fighting, and cursing one another ever since.

"So is your friend Dusty Magrewski related to Ivan Magrewski?" asked Alfonso.

"Yup," said Hill. "I believe he is Ivan's great-great-great-great-great-grandson. Or something like that."

When all the longshoremen had filed out, Hill and Alfonso stepped toward the entrance and came face to face with an ancient-looking longshoreman with a bald head and a sawed-off shotgun. His scraggly muttonchops gleamed with grease.

"Hey snoopers, whur do ya think yer a-goin'?" he shouted, exposing a mouth empty except for two lonely teeth, both of which were crooked.

"We're old friends of Dusty's," replied Hill. "Dusty Magrewski that is."

"Ya know Dusty?" he asked suspiciously, pointing the gun at them. "Doesn't seem right. Ya look like yer from some-place else."

"That's true," said Hill. "I am from somewhere else, but I lived here for a while. They called me Little Hilly back then."

The old man peered at Hill closely. "Yer a lot taller than the Little Hilly I remember. And what's more, I remember him bein' a nice lad, at least at first . . ." He straightened up. "If ya are Little Hilly, ya've got a lot of 'splainin' to do. And if Dusty don't like it, I'll take care of ya myself." He motioned the two inside with his shotgun. "Don't think about runnin'. I may be ninety-four years old but I'm a good shot. Eyes haven't clouded up yet. Oh I'll shoot ya all right. Shoot ya right in the buttocks. How'd ya like that, boys? Heh, heh, heh. I'd like it just fine."

Hill and Alfonso avoided eye contact with the old longshore-man and walked into the massive warehouse. It was hard to tell what was being stored there because nearly everything was piled in boxes and wooden crates. The sound of their footsteps on the stone floor echoed sharply throughout the building.

When they arrived at a wooden spiral staircase and looked up, they saw someone glaring suspiciously at them. "Is that Dusty up there?" Hill shouted.

"An' who's askin'?" came the response.

"It's me!" shouted Hill. "Uh, Little Hilly. I've come for a visit with my nephew here, Alfonso. He's Leif's son."

A flashlight shone uncomfortably in their faces. "Little Hilly?" came the response. "Ya look more like a tall scarecrow than Lil' Hilly!"

The longshoreman behind them cocked his shotgun. "Ya want me to throw 'em out?" he asked. "Or should I shoot 'em in the buttocks first?"

"Wait just a minute," said Dusty. He was scowling fiercely. Dusty turned to shine his flashlight on Alfonso's face. "Who are ya, small fry?"

"My name is Alfonso," replied Alfonso timidly.

"Sakes alive!" said Dusty. "Yer the spittin' image of yer father—are ya as talented a sleeper as Leif was?"

"Probably more so," said Hill quickly. "You should hear about the things this boy can do in his sleep."

"Mr. Magrewski, you knew my father?" Alfonso called up.

"'Course I did," replied Dusty. "I knew both yer father and yer uncle! And I loved both of 'em like sons until they stole from me."

"Yes, I'm very glad you brought that up," said Hill nervously. "As it turns out, I have a very good explanation for that whole unfortunate episode."

"I'm listenin'," said Dusty gruffly.

"Well, er, you see, we were tricked," explained Hill. "Leif and I were young, homesick, and stupid. Very stupid. We met this swindler who said he could take us back to the Urals. So we stole that money from you and paid the swindler who then ran off on us. Afterward, we were too ashamed to return. So we snuck onto a boat headed for the mainland and eventually we ended up in these Canadian orphanages. I still feel rotten about the whole thing. Darn rotten. And it hardly feels right to return after all these years to ask for a favor —"

"Ya don't say!" boomed Dusty. "Yer barely done apologizin' and yer already askin' for a favor. Ya got nerve, Lil' Hilly!"

"All right, that's it!" yelled the ninety-four-year-old longshoreman. "Yer both gettin' a buttocks full a lead!" He prodded Hill in the shoulder blades with the loaded shotgun.

"C'mon Dusty," pleaded Hill. "I'm sorry. Leif and I only stole the money because we were homesick!"

Dusty shone his flashlight on Alfonso again. "If this is Leif's boy, where's Leif?" he asked.

After a moment's pause, Hill explained that Leif had died in an accident while Alfonso was still very young. Alfonso felt his cheeks go red. Moments later, Dusty's flashlight clicked off.

"Well, that's sad news," said Dusty. "Mighty sad news indeed." He stood silently for a moment and his angry scowl softened into a rather sad frown. "Well, yer here now . . . Come on up here and lemme have a decent look at the both of ya."

Hill and Alfonso walked up the spiral staircase and emerged into a small nook with a desk, a chair, and dozens of stacks of yellowing papers. Apparently, this was Dusty's office. Dusty himself was built like a bulldog. Though Hill later said Dusty was at least seventy years old, he still looked tough, with meaty fists, iron biceps, and shoulders rippling with muscles. In contrast, his face was filled with oversize pudgy cheeks, a slightly askew nose, and ears that stuck out like a rabbit's.

"I can't believe Lil' Hilly has come back to visit," said Dusty with a shake of his head. "Now tell me, while ya got me in a tolerably good mood, what's this favor ya need?"

"Two things," said Hill. "First off, Alfonso's grandfather is with us and he's got a busted leg. He needs to see the doctor."

"Easy enough," said Dusty. "An' the second favor?"

"Well, um, you see, we need to book passage on a ship to the northern Urals," said Hill.

"Oh boy!" said Dusty with a dry chortle. "That'll be much, much, much trickier. The only one who makes that run is Vice Admiral Purcheezie."

"Vice Admiral who?" inquired Alfonso.

"That's the sea captain I was telling you about," explained Hill excitedly. "She's the one who brought us here from the Urals all those years ago."

"The thing is," continued Dusty, "there's absolutely no chance that she'll take ya with 'er. None at all! She never takes passengers—not anymore. But she does owe me a favor—a very big favor. And I might be willin' to call that favor in for ya, and get ya onboard that ship, but ya got to do somethin' for me. Understand?"

"I'll do whatever you need me to do," said Hill eagerly.

"Not interested," said Dusty. "It's gotta be young Alfonso."

CHAPTER 6

THE GAME OF BALLAST

LATE THAT evening, Alfonso, Hill, Judy, and Pappy found themselves in a cramped windowless bunkroom in the Magrewski warehouse. The Dormian bloom lay hidden under an old-fashioned top hat that someone had left behind and long since forgotten. A small potbelly stove burned in the corner, giving off heat and casting a warm, cozy glow across the room. For the time being, everyone seemed content—even Pappy. The doctor's office had been quick and efficient, and the on-duty nurse had set Pappy's leg, wrapped it in a sturdy cast, and tested him to make sure there was no infection. Pappy would be on strict bed rest for a few days, but then he'd be able to move around with crutches.

All evening long, various older longshoremen had been stopping by the room to say hello to Hill and to pay their respects to Leif's wife and son. These were welcome visits, especially since they seemed to confirm that Hill and Leif were brothers. The longshoremen were happy to see Hill, but they were even happier to see Alfonso. One at a time, at least a dozen big, gruff longshoremen came into the bunkroom, smiled shyly, and then asked to shake Alfonso's hand. One longshoreman even asked for Alfonso's autograph. At first, Alfonso found this very perplexing, but eventually Hill explained what was going on. "Your father was an extremely talented mole rat," said Hill. "He was really a superstar around here."

"My dad was a mole rat?" Alfonso asked. "What does that mean?"

"It's a sporting term," explained Hill. "It involves a game called ballast. On any given ballast team, the mole rat is the most important position. He's a little bit like the quarterback in a football game."

"Still, I don't get it," said Alfonso. "Even if my father was a good mole rat, why are the Magrewskis so excited about *me* being here?"

"Because your father always played ballast in his sleep," explained Hill. "And the word is out that you are an even more talented sleeper than he was."

"How did that happen?" asked Judy suspiciously.

"I don't know," said Hill awkwardly. "I guess I might have said something of the sort to Dusty."

"Now listen here, Hill," said Judy. "In the future, you really shouldn't tell folks —" At that very moment, the door swung open and in walked Dusty with a big smile on his face.

"Hope I'm not disturbin' ya," said Dusty. "I won't be but a minute. I just have some quick business to discuss with ya."

"Business?" asked Judy.

"Well," said Dusty, "as ya may or may not know, tomorrow is our annual ballast match against the Popov Longshoremen, and so ya might say that yer timin' is auspicious—mighty auspicious. Ya see, once a year the Magrewskis face off against those miserable Popovs in a match that the whole island gathers to see. Unfortunately, for the last decade or so, we've been havin' a very bad losin' streak. Then, to make matters worse, our mole rat has just gone missin'. Chances are, he probably ran away out of fear of losin' again. The fink! Anyway, we could use some help from young Alfonso here. If he's half as good as his old man was, he might just lead us to victory. And, ya see, a victory is just what we need right now. People are startin' to lose faith in the Magrewskis. There's talk that we ain't as tough or clever as we once was. That's bad for business—mighty bad. And so I've got a little proposition for ya: Alfonso, if ya lead us to victory, I swear I'll get ya a spot on the vice admiral's boat to the Urals. What do ya say?"

"But I don't know the first thing about the game of ballast," began Alfonso. "So I really doubt I can do your team much good."

"That don't matter a lick," said Dusty. "Your father didn't know the first thing about ballast either, but the minute he fell asleep, he performed like a champ."

"This is a sorry business," declared Pappy, who up until now had been silent. "Hill is a grown man and he led us to this strange den of thieves. Let *him* be your blind mouse, or mole rat, or whatever you call it."

"I would if I could," said Hill dejectedly, "but I was never any good at it."

"It doesn't matter anyway," added Pappy. "Because neither Judy, nor Alfonso, nor I, nor any plant life that might be in our possession—*if you know what I mean*—is going to the Urals. For goodness sake, Hill doesn't even know where he is going."

"I do too!" said Hill. "We know the exact coordinates."

"I'd like to help," interjected Alfonso. "I mean, I guess I could give it a try . . ."

No one replied to Alfonso's half-hearted offer and instead a tense silence descended on the room.

"Tell me this," said Judy finally, "is this a dangerous game? I mean, could Alfonso get hurt playing it?"

Dusty didn't reply immediately. Instead, he looked at Hill for some indication of how to answer this question.

"Ballast just takes a little skill, that's all," said Hill confidently. "Alfonso will be perfectly safe."

The next morning, just before breakfast, Hill led Alfonso to a cleared area of the beach. In front of them sat the remains of a massive old Russian cargo ship known as the *Nyetbezkov.* The ship had run aground during a bad storm in the 1920s and had been sitting there ever since. The *Nyetbezkov* was enormous—at least three football fields long—and completely covered with rust. Entire pieces of the ship had fallen off, including the rotting skeleton of a lifeboat. Bits of torn-away metal lay scattered everywhere across the sand. The whole ship leaned heavily to one side. The only evidence of recent attention were two new rope ladders dangling off the side. These ladders, apparently, were the means by which brave souls climbed onto the ship. But why would anyone want to do that? Well, as Hill explained, this bizarre vessel was the actual playing field for the annual game of ballast between the Magrewskis and the Popovs.

The goal of the game was to remove ballast from the depths of the *Nyetbezkov.* Technically, *ballast* was the name for any heavy material placed in the hull of a ship in order to make it more balanced. Often ballast was just crushed gravel. But, in this case, the *Nyetbezkov*'s hull was filled with hundred-pound cannon balls. On the day of Fort Krasnik's annual ballast match, the two teams of longshoremen gathered on the beach in front of the *Nyetbezkov.* Each team climbed up onto the ship via the ropes dangling from either end, crept through the utter darkness inside, located the cannon balls on the lowermost level, and then brought five of them back to the beach. The team to do this first was the winner. Each team was led by someone who was light, flexible, and comfortable navigating in complete darkness. This person was known as the mole rat. Five brawny longshoremen followed closely behind and were linked to the mole rat by rope. The game had many pitfalls. Perhaps the most serious of these was that the floors inside the ship were all rotting away and, if you took a wrong step, you could easily fall to your death.

"I thought you said this game wasn't dangerous," Alfonso said.

"It's not dangerous if you're a good mole rat," replied Hill. "And I feel certain—deep in my bones—that you're going to be the best mole rat there ever was."

Alfonso gave his uncle a very unconvinced look.

"Listen," whispered Hill urgently, "if you don't want to do this, just say the word, but I believe you can do it. Remember: you're no ordinary sleeper. *For heaven's sake, you grew a Dormian bloom!* All you have to do is trust yourself."

"But that's the problem," said Alfonso. "I can't trust myself. I might go to sleep intending to play ballast, and then end up building a sandcastle instead."

"No," said Hill sternly. "You have to focus. Before you fall asleep, you must picture yourself climbing the rope ladder onto the ship—again, and again, and again, and again—until your brain gets the idea. That's what I do whenever I need to do something in my sleep. Then, when you doze off, you'll be on your way."

"I don't know," said Alfonso. "You flew the wrong way around the world—maybe I'll get it backwards too!"

"You won't!" said Hill.

"You really think I can do this?" asked Alfonso.

Hill clapped Alfonso on the shoulders. "I've only just met you," said Hill, "but I believe in you with all my heart."

A few hours later, every single able-bodied person on the entire island of Fort Krasnik had gathered in front of the *Nyetbezkov* to watch the annual ballast game. Most of the spectators were longshoremen, sailors, or the kind of sketchy-looking characters who had to be thieves or outlaws of one kind or another. There were also a great many gamblers. Most of the fans seemed to be brandishing fists full of dollars (American and Canadian) and calling out various odds on the match.

"I'll bet two hundred smackeroos on the Magrewskis if ya give me ten-to-one odds," yelled one short, pudgy sailor.

"I'll bet five hundred on the Magrewskis if ya give me fifteen-to-one odds," yelled another sailor.

"I'll take both yer bets," announced a tall longshoreman. "There's not a chance in the world that the Magrewskis will win. Yer money is as good as mine."

"I heard the Magrewskis got a new mole rat," added an old woman with a patch over her eye. "They say he's Leif's son. Still, I'm bettin' my money on the Popovs. You'd have to be nuts to bet on the Magrewskis."

As the spectators continued to bet and speculate on the outcome of the match, Judy and Pappy—laying in a movable bed—watched on nervously. Neither of them was happy about Alfonso participating in this event, but it was too late to object now.

Meanwhile, Hill and Alfonso were walking to the place where the Magrewski team had gathered. Along the way, however, they were stopped by a small, impish man with white hair, reddish eyes, and tiny hands.

"The name is Timmons, mole rat for the Popovs," said the man. "I heard yer the new mole rat."

Alfonso nodded.

"Yer a bit young, ain't ya?" asked Timmons.

"He's old enough," replied Hill.

"They say yer Leif's son," said Timmons. "I knew yer old man. They say he was the most gifted mole rat there ever was. But I say he was a cheater and a thief too—stealin' money from his own brothers!"

Alfonso blushed fiercely and his hands curled into fists.

"That's enough Timmons," warned Hill.

"Be careful," added Timmons. "The *Nyetbezkov* can be a dangerous place—I'm lucky it ain't claimed my life yet. If I was ya, boy, I'd think twice about playin' this game or ya might end up disappearin' like yer old man. I think —"

But Timmons never finished his sentence because he was interrupted by the most powerfully built man that Alfonso had ever seen. He must have weighed upwards of three hundred fifty pounds—all of which appeared to be rock-solid muscle. His arms looked stronger than the legs of an elephant. His hair was jet-black, rather oily-looking, and pulled back into a short ponytail. He wore a dirty pair of longshoreman overalls, had a bushy set of muttonchops, and sported a massive tattoo of a sea dragon on his arm.

"I think it's time ya shut yer trap," the man said to Timmons in a very deep voice. "If ya don't leave now, yer liable to end up with a few broken bones." The man smiled in an unfriendly manner.

Timmons gave a peevish look and scampered away.

The man turned to Alfonso and stuck out a beefy hand. "The name is Paks Bilblox," said the man with a kindly smile. "But everyone just calls me Bilblox. I'm your muscle."

"That means he's the guy on your team who walks directly behind you," explained Hill. "You'll rely on him the most."

"You're gonna do just fine, Alfonso," said Bilblox. "Don't pay any mind to Timmons. He's just tryin' to mess with ya. Yer old man was no thief or cheater. He was the best there ever was at this game."

Alfonso nodded in what he hoped was a confident way. Bilblox put his massive arm around Alfonso's shoulder and led him over to where their other teammates were standing. There were four of them—all tough, muscular men with mutton-chops and hard brown eyes. Bilblox introduced Alfonso, then they all walked to the starting line directly in the middle of the clearing, alongside Timmons and his teammates. At the starting gun, the two teams would run to their respective ladders and begin climbing up onto the ship.

"Okay, everybody," Bilblox announced. "It's time to buckle in."

Everyone on the Magrewski team lined up behind Alfonso. Each person wore a body harness with straps that went around the waist and chest. One at a time, the members of the team ran a rope through their harnesses so that they were all connected. When this was done, Bilblox instructed Alfonso to announce that they were ready.

"We're all ready!" yelled Alfonso as confidently as he could.

"We're all ready too!" yelled Timmons.

Everyone waited for the referee to shoot off the starting gun, as Alfonso stared out at the crashing waves. He could hear his heart pounding in his ears. How would he ever fall asleep? The rope. He had to focus on the rope—just as Hill had told him to do. He closed his eyes and pictured himself climbing it. He pictured the scene perfectly and slowly it happened: he began to feel drowsy. Soon Alfonso was asleep. In fact, he was so deeply asleep that, when the starting gun went off, he didn't even budge. Meanwhile, Timmons and his team ran to their rope and began climbing up it with great speed.

"What's goin' on?" shouted one of the members of the Magrewski team. "We're losin' already!"

"Be quiet!" whispered Bilblox. "Give him a minute. Then he'll be racin' outta here like a missile—just like his old man."

Timmons had nearly reached the upper deck of the *Nyetbezkov* when Alfonso finally entered his sleeping trance. His body snapped to attention, his eyes opened, and he let out a loud snore. He turned to face the rusted ship. A moment later, he was running for the rope ladder. A great cheer rose from the crowd, but Alfonso didn't wake up—he didn't even hesitate—he just shimmied up the rope ladder like a monkey gone wild. His teammates followed closely behind, making as little noise as possible.

"That-a-boy," muttered Bilblox as he climbed. "That-a-boy."

When the Magrewski team arrived on the upper deck, all five longshoremen winced from the pain in their burning red hands and aching shoulders. Alfonso, however, just stood there, as if waiting for a bus. Seconds later, he started again. The entire team crab-walked up the steeply slanting deck to a darkened doorway. The doorway opened into a narrow stairway filled with trash, dead seagulls, and thick strips of rusted-off paint.

"No one goes down this way," gasped one of the Magrewski longshoremen. "This stairway is too dangerous. We'll fall to our deaths!"

"Zip it!" hissed Bilblox. "The kid knows what he's doin'."

Alfonso avoided stepping on the actual stairs and instead pressed his legs against the narrow walls of the stairwell and slowly moved down. His teammates followed. Soon they were in absolute darkness. According to the rules of the game, the mole rat carried a flashlight that contained a half-hour's worth of battery life. Alfonso switched his flashlight on and continued on.

Suddenly everyone heard a crunch, as if rusting metal had just given way. Alfonso's light disappeared and Bilblox felt a jerk on his rope. "Steady, boys!" yelled Bilblox. All five longshoremen slid forward and braced themselves in time. Bilblox peered at Alfonso, who was dangling through a portion of the floor that had just collapsed. Alfonso looked up blankly. They could hear him snoring. In one swift movement, Bilblox grabbed the rope and hoisted Alfonso up.

"Are ya all right?" asked Bilblox.

Alfonso nodded sleepily.

They continued their slow descent down the stairwell until they entered what appeared to be crew quarters. In the gloom illuminated by Alfonso's flashlight, thick piles of rust sat in every corner, like dark sawdust. They slid through the crew's quarters, pushed open a heavy steel door, and looked down another long corridor, although this one was even narrower than the stairwell they had just descended. Alfonso's flashlight panned along a whitewashed wall, revealing a number of dark areas that looked like ink blots. "Lots of rust," he said sleepily. "Follow my feet. Think like a squirrel."

Alfonso walked along the wall—which was tilting at a crazy angle—and kept his hands outstretched for balance. The longshoremen tried to imitate his steps as closely as possible. A few times, Alfonso tested an area with the tip of his foot only to see it crumble through the wall as easily as through paper. Still, he had learned from his initial fall and they made it through the hallway unharmed.

Passing through the next door, they entered a hallway with

a metal ladder that led down through a hole in the floor and into the blackness below.

"What's wrong?" Bilblox whispered. "That's our way down."

"Not this time," Alfonso replied with a yawn. "Rusted through." Alfonso continued down the hallway until they came to a large pipe that descended directly down in the same direction as the metal ladder. They peered into the pipe and saw the cannonballs roughly fifty feet below them.

"All right, men," said Bilblox. "Lower me and Alfonso into this hole. Then I'll bring back the cannonballs and we'll be out of here." The men nodded eagerly and adjusted their rope so that there was plenty of slack to lower Bilblox and Alfonso. Alfonso went first and landed directly on top of a cannonball. Seconds later, Bilblox landed alongside him.

"Holy smokes!" said Bilblox excitedly. "I can't believe ya found them so quickly. If we can just get back alive, we'll make history!"

௸

Back outside the ship, the crowd was growing restless. With all the gamblers in attendance, large sums of money were riding on the outcome of this match. On top of this, for all the Magrewski longshoremen, a great deal of pride was at stake. The Magrewskis had not won in over ten years, and, if their luck didn't change, the brotherhood's reputation would only sink deeper. Last but not least, for all the family members of the contestants, there was the added worry that something might go horribly wrong inside the belly of the ship.

Judy and Pappy watched the deck of the ship nervously, but said nothing.

"There's no way the Magrewskis can win," an old sailor standing nearby loudly declared. "I only hope that Leif's boy don't take a nasty fall and bust open his noggin like that mole rat from two years ago. What a pity that was. I think he's just learned how to eat with a fork again."

Judy winced. *How could Hill have possibly assured her that this was a safe sport?* If anything happened to Alfonso —

Just then, however, a massive roar came from the crowd. There, standing on the upper deck of the *Nyetbezkov* was Alfonso. Behind him were five triumphant Magrewskis. One at a time, the longshoremen threw their cannonballs over the side of the deck. The crowd grew louder. Soon the Magrewskis were all shimmying down the rope ladder toward the beach. When they arrived at the bottom, they ran with the cannonballs back to the starting line. Alfonso followed behind. His feet dragged but he managed to jog. It was only then that they saw Timmons's team appear on the upper deck.

Alfonso and his team had won.

A whooping, hollering horde of at least one hundred Magrewski longshoremen rushed toward Alfonso. Dusty and Hill led the charge. "Ya did it!" yelled Dusty. "By Jove, ya did it!"

Alfonso awoke to the sound of this cheering. As he blinked sleepily, he became aware that he was sitting on someone's shoulders. They belonged to Bilblox. All around him people were cheering. Longshoremen were pushing and shoving to get close and shake Alfonso's hand. Bilblox, however, kept them all safely at bay.

"We did it in record time," yelled Bilblox. "Yer old man woulda been proud—mighty proud!"

"How did ya do it so quickly?" asked Dusty.

"I don't know," Alfonso yelled over the din of the crowd. "It's all a blur."

"I told you!" Hill yelled. "I knew you could do it. Now we'll be on our way—on our way to the Urals!"

"Yes indeed," said Dusty. "I'll make all the arrangements."

Alfonso climbed down from Bilblox's shoulders and drew close to his uncle. "Uncle Hill, I can't go with you to the Urals," he said. "Mom will never agree."

"I'll convince her!" promised Hill. "I'll beg her."

Alfonso shook his head. He simply knew it would never work.

Hill frowned.

"We have no choice," Alfonso said. He leaned in close and whispered into his uncle's ear, "Can I trust you to take the Dormian bloom?"

CHAPTER 7

ALFONSO'S DECISION

THAT NIGHT, as he lay in his bed, Alfonso stared at the ceiling and watched the flames from the potbelly stove cast a flickering light on the ceiling of the bunkroom. Judy, Hill, and Pappy were fast asleep. The only sounds in the room were the crackling of the fire, the rumble of Pappy's snoring, and the ticking of Hill's old-fashioned windup alarm clock. Hill's alarm was set for four o'clock in the morning. As soon as it rang, Hill would set off to meet Vice Admiral Purcheezie. By midday, Hill would be sailing westward toward Russia and the Ural Mountains. And, in keeping with Alfonso's wishes, Hill would be taking the Dormian bloom with him.

At first, both Judy and Pappy were stunned by Alfonso's decision to hand over the Dormian bloom to his uncle. "That's crazy!" said Pappy. "That plant is worth a fortune!" This was true, admitted Alfonso, but he quickly reminded Pappy that the plant was *his* and he could do with it as he pleased. In truth, Alfonso was not particularly eager to give up the Dormian bloom, but what else could he do? He was just twelve years old. He couldn't set off halfway around the world to go roaming around the Ural Mountains in search of some hidden city, even if he had discovered its location. He had school, chores, and life back in World's End, Minnesota. Besides, his mother would never, ever agree. So Alfonso had done the only thing he could do. He entrusted the plant to his uncle.

"Don't worry," Hill had told his nephew. "I'll keep the Dormian bloom on me at all times." Then, to show Alfonso just how serious he was about this promise, he produced the old top hat that they'd been using to cover and hide the plant. Hill had done some handy work on the top hat. He had removed the circular top of the hat and replaced it with a glass panel. "It's like a skylight," explained Hill. "This way I can put the plant inside the hat and the plant will still get plenty of light. I'll just keep the hat—and the plant—on my head at all times!"

Alfonso had been impressed with Hill's cleverness, but it did little to lift his spirits. It was now almost midnight. In four more hours, Hill and his plant would be gone—perhaps forever. It was a very depressing thought. The only thing to do now was to go to sleep. Yet, as hard as he tried, Alfonso simply couldn't fall asleep. His mind was still racing with images from the day: the crowds at the beach, the rusting hulk of the *Nyetbezkov,* the view from Bilblox's shoulders of the overjoyed

Magrewski longshoremen, and the embarrassingly long hug that his mother had given him.

At some point, Alfonso's thoughts were interrupted by a loud noise: *Bang! Bang! Bang!* It sounded as if someone were rapping their knuckles on a large slab of wood, perhaps the front door of the warehouse. Alfonso glanced at Hill, Judy, and Pappy, but they were all still fast asleep. The knocking stopped and then a few seconds later began again. Alfonso lay in bed wide awake, staring at the ceiling and trying to ignore what he heard. What was going on? Maybe one of the longshoremen had gotten locked out? He was tempted to answer the door, but Dusty had warned him not to go snooping around the warehouse at night because the guards had orders to shoot all intruders on sight. But the knocking persisted. In fact, it grew louder. *Bang! Bang! Bang!*

Finally, Alfonso climbed out of bed, walked out of the bunkroom, and tiptoed over to the massive oak doors that sealed the entrance to the warehouse. The doors were at least fifteen feet high. There was no way Alfonso could open them. There was, however, a small peephole that he could open to get a glimpse of who was standing outside. He was tempted to open the peephole, but instead he simply said, in a very meek voice, "Who's there?"

"Alms for the poor, please . . . alms for the poor," came the reply.

"I'm sorry," Alfonso replied. "I don't have anything."

The person on the other side emitted a wheezy, gasping laugh. "Surely there are things to help the poor somewhere in this impressive warehouse."

"They're not mine and I don't live here," said Alfonso.

"Where are you from?"

Alfonso hesitated before answering that he was from Minnesota.

Another laugh. "I know it well," said the voice. "The trees there grow very tall. Come my young friend, a fellow traveler like you must have something of value, be it coins, food, or perhaps something else . . ."

There was something familiar about this person's voice. Who was he? Alfonso looked at the door's peephole, took a deep breath, reached up, and slid it open. Two wide-open eyes, totally white, stared back at him. Alfonso gasped, not only because of their hideous appearance but because he recognized them immediately. He was staring face to face at Kiril. His face was no longer hidden by a hat, and his long, snakelike scar gleamed a pale blue in the moonlight.

"You followed me here," stammered Alfonso. He felt frozen in place, just as he had in the forest back in World's End.

"No, my friend," said Kiril. "I was here long before you arrived. It was you who followed me."

"I don't understand," Alfonso replied.

"Of course you don't," said Kiril. His voice was kindly, but somehow it gave Alfonso a creepy feeling, as if a bead of ice-cold water were running down his spine. "You are too young to understand," continued Kiril. "When are you going to come to your senses and let me help you? Besides, what makes you trust the man who claims to be your uncle? Do you really know him? Why wasn't he around when you were growing up? And why does he know so little about his own past? Strange, isn't it? And soon he will lead you into a trap . . ."

"What do you mean?" demanded Alfonso.

"This man who professes to be your uncle will deliver you directly into the hands of the enemy," explained Kiril. "And then he'll blame all of his missteps on his faulty memory. I have foreseen the entire thing. Trust me."

"Why should I trust you?" asked Alfonso. "I don't know who you are."

"I've been nothing but honest with you," replied Kiril. "If anyone has been underhanded it has been *you*. Tell me: why did you lie to me about the Dormian bloom? I know you have it—and so does my father."

"Your father?" inquired Alfonso. "Who are you talking about?"

"He's your only true friend," replied Kiril. "It would be a mistake to trust anyone else."

"Well, I'm sorry," said Alfonso, "but I don't trust him either."

Alfonso started to back away, but before he could, a long, pale, bony hand shot through the narrow peephole and clasped Alfonso tightly around the throat.

"Blasphemy!" hissed Kiril. "My father is the only one who can help you—how dare you question him!"

"Let go," gasped Alfonso. He used all of his strength to grab Kiril's middle finger and bend it backwards. Kiril howled with pain and released Alfonso's throat. Alfonso slammed the peephole shut and stumbled backwards, grabbing his throat. Outside the door, Kiril was still talking. "Don't go," he begged. "Let me help you! I've acted in a fit of anger! I am sorry! *Come back!*"

Alfonso said nothing in response and instead ran back to the safety of the bunkroom. Only then did he realize he was holding something in his hand.

It was a ring.

In the struggle with Kiril, Alfonso had somehow managed to pull a ring off the man's middle finger. It was made of a dull gold, and carved on top was an intricate coat of arms. The coat of arms showed a picture of a Dormian bloom in front of a setting sun. Alfonso shuddered at the thought of the ring's owner. He shoved the ring deep into his pocket and forced his eyes closed. Although he was covered in sweat from the encounter, he fell asleep almost immediately.

Alfonso awoke a few hours later, just before four in the morning. It was one of those strange waking moments when, as soon as he opened his eyes, Alfonso found that his mind was as crystal clear and as wide awake as it had ever been. He was overcome with a single, unquestionable, overpowering feeling. *He had to go to the Urals. He himself had to deliver the Dormian bloom to Somnos.* This feeling came from deep within Alfonso's gut. It was obvious to him now that he had to be very careful about whom he trusted. He certainly didn't trust Kiril, but suddenly, he didn't fully trust *anyone* except himself. Although he believed that Hill probably was his uncle, he still wasn't sure about Hill's motives.

The simple truth was that he, Alfonso Perplexon, had grown this Dormian bloom. There had to be a reason for it. True, he was just twelve years old, but somehow Alfonso knew that he alone could deliver this plant to its rightful home. He had never felt so certain of anything in his entire life. This was *his* journey to make; oddly enough, as soon as he came to this realization, he was overcome by a great sense of calm.

Alfonso got out of bed and crept over to the bunk where Judy was sleeping. He shook his mother gently. She opened her eyes groggily. "What's the matter, Alfonso?" she asked. "What are you doing awake?"

"Mom, I have to go," said Alfonso in the most determined voice that he could muster. "I have to go with Uncle Hill to the Urals."

Judy sat up quickly. "What do you mean you *have* to go?" she asked. "What kind of talk is that?"

"It's hard to explain," said Alfonso. "But I woke up with this clear idea. I-It's just something I have to do. I *feel* it."

"Did something happen during the night?" Judy asked.

"No," Alfonso lied. He didn't want to tell her about the encounter with Kiril and the ring that sat in his pocket. "I have to do this," he repeated.

Judy stared into Alfonso's face for a full minute. She sighed. "Oh boy," she said. "Your father said that this would happen someday. I just didn't think it would happen so soon."

"What do you mean?" asked Alfonso in disbelief. "I don't understand."

Judy threw her arms around Alfonso and hugged him tightly.

"Your father always wanted to return to his homeland," she explained. "Of course, he never did. But he told me . . . he said, 'One day Alfonso will want to return as well and I'm afraid you'll have to let him.'"

Alfonso swallowed hard, but said nothing.

"Is this what you really want?" she asked.

Alfonso nodded.

"You know that I can't go with you," said Judy. "I have to look after Pappy. We'll have to stay here in Fort Krasnik until his leg heals."

"I'll meet you back here," said Alfonso. "I promise."

Judy nodded and then offered a rather sad smile.

"It shouldn't take too long," said Alfonso.

They sat there for a few minutes, just looking at each other.

"Well, if you're going to go, you should probably have this," said Judy. She reached around her neck and took off the chain with the wooden medallion that Leif had whittled for her. It was a strange piece of jewelry. Carved into the wood was a hand with five fingers extended and a + symbol etched into the palm. The words *YOU ARE* were written across the top. And, at the bottom, was a series of numbers. It looked a little like this:

Judy never knew what any of these carvings meant, but she treasured the medallion. She said it was her good luck charm. "Your father wanted me to give this to you when you grew up," she whispered. "I figure now is as good a time as any. He said he whittled it while asleep."

Alfonso hugged his mother as tears rolled down their cheeks. At that moment, Hill's alarm clock went off.

About a half-hour later, Alfonso, Hill, and Bilblox were standing on a darkened Fort Krasnik street, outside a sorry-looking pub known as the Missing Limb. The pub was just a giant, windowless box made of stone. Outside the entrance, the muddy ground was littered with empty beer bottles, cigar butts, and piles of discarded chicken bones.

"This place is the roughest pub on the island," explained Bilblox. "Stick close to me." This was, in fact, precisely why Bilblox was here. Dusty had asked him to tag along to offer his protection. "Don't worry," added Bilblox. "I won't let nothin' bad happen to ya."

"Thanks for coming along," said Hill. "We appreciate it."

"Well, before yer done thankin' me, I have somethin' else to tell ya," said Bilblox. "Somethin' *important.*"

"What is it?" inquired Hill.

"I'm comin' with ya," declared Bilblox.

"You mean, into the pub?"

"Nope," said Bilblox. "I mean I'm comin' with ya to the Urals. I guess, after a lifetime of workin' on the docks, I've always wanted to see a bit of the world. Besides, in a place like the Urals, you'll need a bit of muscle."

"That's a mighty generous offer, but —" began Hill.

"It's not an offer," interrupted Bilblox. "It's my decision."

"Does Dusty know about this?" asked Hill.

"Yup," said Bilblox. "It was his idea, especially after Alfonso said he was goin' along with ya. Dusty doesn't want anythin' bad happenin' to Alfonso. Neither do I. In fact, neither do any of the Magrewskis. We feel like Alfonso is one of us now. And we always look out for our own."

Alfonso grinned and looked embarrassed.

"Well, we probably could use a bit of muscle," admitted Hill. "All right then — let's go inside and meet the vice admiral."

"I'll lead the way," said Bilblox. He headed for the pub's door and soon came upon a bouncer who was almost his size. Bilblox gave the bouncer a careful smile and walked past him toward the entrance. The bouncer immediately grabbed him by his shirt. "Ya know the rules, Bilblox," he growled. "No missin' limb, no entrance."

"We don't intend to become regulars," explained Bilblox. "We just have a meetin', that's all."

"No missin' limb, no entrance," repeated the bouncer.

With a wink at Alfonso, Hill walked up to the bouncer, took off his shoe, and showed him his right foot, which was missing its pinky toe. The bouncer laughed and shook his head.

"A missing limb is a missing limb," proclaimed Hill.

"All right," said the bouncer. "That's a mighty sorry excuse for a missin' limb, but I'll let it slide. As for the rest of ya, however, I ain't lettin' ya in."

Suddenly, around the corner a tall woman appeared and in a hoarse voice said, "This here limb's for me, this here limb's for the lad, and this here limb's for the four-hundred-pound guy next to him." The woman then displayed three missing limbs:

a hook for her left arm, a wooden stump for her left leg, and a bump where the index finger of her right hand used to be.

The bouncer's fierce expression melted and he smiled officiously. "Of course, Vice Admiral," he said. "The Missin' Limb is mighty pleased to be yer home away from home."

They entered the bar and glanced around. In the corner, two ancient-looking men, each with a missing right leg, played a sad ballad with a violin and banjo. The bar was filled with a vast mix of people, and all of them appeared as dirty and shabby as the bar itself.

They sat at a wooden booth adorned with initials and crossed-out declarations of love. Theirs was the only empty booth in the place, perhaps because it was the one nearest the horrible-smelling bathroom. Hill grimaced and pinched his nose. They all stared blankly at Vice Admiral Purcheezie. She looked every bit of her eighty-some years, with a thin, sunburned face filled with wrinkles. Her ears and nose bore the scars of numerous bites. But all this faded away before the brilliance of her blue eyes and the expression they wore, like an ever-watchful hawk.

"I never take passengers," the vice admiral announced. "Not on my ship. But I owe Dusty big and I reckon he owes you, which means I got no choice in the matter. Mind you, though, I'd just as soon throw the lot of you overboard, so when you come aboard, step lightly—especially you Lil' Hilly—I still remember the headaches you caused me all those years ago."

Four mugs of steaming hot milk were set down in front of them. "Don't drink the grog here," said the vice admiral. "It's not right. But the milk's fine and on a ship like my *Success Story,* we get to missin' it after a couple weeks." She drained the mug in one gulp. "Right," she said. "I don't know if Dusty told ya, and I don't particularly care either, but we're leavin' at noon today. Polar ice ain't broken yet but we'll have to take our chances. I can't be waitin' for the authorities . . ." She stood up. "*Success Story.* Be on it at noon or we're leavin' without you jokers. If all goes well, we'll be in Barsh-yin-Binder in three weeks' time!"

"Barsh-yin-Binder," Alfonso repeated. He remembered the name stenciled on the wooden crate in their greenhouse. The word felt strange on his tongue.

"That's right!" said the vice admiral with a loud cackle. "It's the only port town in all the Urals and, let me tell ya, it's an absolutely God-awful place. Tell ya the truth, I can't imagine why on earth ya want to go there, but I suppose ya have yer reasons."

Alfonso glanced at Hill.

"Don't worry," said Hill as reassuringly as he could. "It can't be that bad."

"Oh yes it is!" said the vice admiral with another cackle. "Barsh-yin-Binder makes Fort Krasnik look like Beverly Hills."

The vice admiral turned to leave but then took a step back and looked at the three of them once more. "And remember this," she said, "don't be thinkin' that my bein' a woman will make me any more kindly. I'm tougher and meaner than any man and a whole lot smarter too."

"What kind of trouble could we cause?" asked Hill innocently.

"Smugglin' trouble," she snapped. "Let me make this perfectly clear: there's room for only one smuggler on this ship and yer lookin' at 'er. Ya better tell me right away if yer carryin' any contraband."

"Contraband?" asked Alfonso.

"She means illegal cargo," explained Bilblox.

Alfonso was silent for a moment. "No, ma'am," he said. "We don't have anything like that."

"Hmm," grunted the vice admiral. "Two things are for certain: the first is that yer a lousy liar! The second is that there'll be serious trouble on this trip—I can feel it—and I ain't gonna be too concerned with protectin' ya. Ya hear me? When the trouble comes, yer on yer own!"

CHAPTER 8

THE *SUCCESS STORY*

As HE CLIMBED aboard the *Success Story,* an ancient-looking icebreaker with two slanted smokestacks and streaks of orange rust running everywhere, Hill vaguely recalled his first voyage on the ship many years before. He remembered climbing on giant coils of rope and playing hide-and-go-seek with Leif in the ship's vast cargo bays. He also remembered the vice admiral's fierce blue eyes and the sound of her wooden peg leg as she walked around the ship. Most of all, he recollected what awful shape the ship was in.

In the years since then, the ship's condition had gone from bad to worse. The *Success Story*'s few windows were so caked with sea salt that they had long since ceased to be transparent. The anchor was nothing but a giant boulder attached to a heavy chain. The ship would be very lucky to make it across the Pacific without sinking, thought Hill, but of course he kept this worry to himself.

"Hurry up, gents, hurry up!" barked the vice admiral, who was standing at the top of the gangplank. She wore a Russian-style fur hat and a heavy dark blue sailor's jacket. She was smoking a corncob pipe with a lump of tobacco inside that smelled distinctly like burning seaweed.

"Aye, aye, Captain," replied Hill, trying to sound as cheerful as possible.

"It's Vice Admiral," she growled. "The title is hereditary but it still means something ya know?"

"Hereditary?" inquired Alfonso.

"She comes from a long line of vice admirals," explained Hill. "They go back a few hundred years I believe."

"Did they all sail on this ship?" Bilblox asked in a half-whisper, half-taunt. "Gee willikers, this thing looks older than Columbus."

"She's seaworthy, I assure ya that," the vice admiral declared with an intense glint in her eyes and a puff of her pipe. "The men and women in my family have been sailin' 'er for ages. If ya know anything about yer history of the sea—and, from the looks of ya, I suspect the answer is no—ya may recall that a Norwegian by the name of Nils A. E. Nordenskjöld was the first sea captain to complete the legendary Northeast Passage from Europe to Asia by breakin' through thousands of miles of ice and crossing the Arctic Ocean. Afterward, the king of Norway gave him the honorary—and hereditary—title of vice admiral. Well, that brave sailor was me great-great-grandpappy on me mother's side. And this here ship, the one that yer looking so aghast about boardin', was the very one to make that famous journey. So mind yer manners! She's not a fancy ship. And we won't be setting any records by sailing 'er. But me pappy sailed 'er, me grandpappy sailed her, me great-grandpappy sailed her, me great-great-grandpappy sailed her, and I don't mean to quit. No sir! Ya won't find me in my old age loungin' about some home for old sailors, readin' nautical books and pullin' saltwater taffy."

Vice Admiral Purcheezie reached into her jacket and pulled out a small brass bugle. She placed the mouthpiece of the bugle between her lips, puffed out her cheeks, and then played a short melody that was—without a doubt—the most shrill and awful-sounding tune that Alfonso, Bilblox, or Hill had ever heard. The tune was apparently a signal of some kind because moments later someone else on the ship called out: "Right away, Vice Admiral!" In the next instant, the deck beneath them shook with the mighty roar of churning engines, and a cloud of heavy black smoke began pouring from the ship's smokestacks. In no time at all, visibility dropped to zero. Alfonso lost sight of his uncle, who was standing only three feet away. Everything went black with smoke and soon it was difficult even to breathe.

"I think ya've got an exhaust problem," Bilblox gasped.

"Oh, ya'll get used to it," said the vice admiral, who was apparently still standing nearby. "The smoke toughens up the lungs. And besides, once the ship gets goin', it'll clear away."

A few minutes later, the boat began to move and soon everyone could see and breathe properly. The first thing Alfonso noticed was that all four of them were covered from head to toe in heavy black soot, as if they were a gang of chimney sweeps. He was glad Hill was wearing the top hat, which protected the bloom from the soot. The vice admiral, however, didn't seem the least bit fazed. Instead, she gazed back toward shore, nodded her head, and puffed on her pipe contentedly. They all watched the skyline of Fort Krasnik recede into the distance as the boat shuddered its way out to sea.

As he took in the view, Alfonso said a silent goodbye to his mother and Pappy. He would miss them, to be sure, but at least they were in good hands. Dusty had invited them to stay in the warehouse, in the little bunkroom, until Alfonso and Hill returned. The only problem was, of course, that no one could say exactly when they would be returning.

"So," said Hill, "where should we bunk up?"

"Oh right," said the vice admiral absentmindedly. "Me first mate, Shamus, will show ya to yer quarters."

Seconds later, a very small man with a shock of bright red hair appeared. He wore overalls, rubber boots, and a plaid wool hat. He seemed to be muttering quietly to himself, but he spoke so softly that it was impossible to hear what he was saying.

"What's that ya say?" asked the vice admiral.

Shamus cleared his throat and said loudly in a thick Irish brogue, "Nothing madam, just reciting the Lord's prayers."

"Take our guests to their quarters," she ordered.

"Aye, madam, and where would that be?"

"In the windmill, Shamus," she replied. "They should be plenty comfortable there."

"Aye, aye, madam," said Shamus loudly. He then muttered very softly—so Alfonso, Bilblox, and Hill could barely hear him—a bit of additional commentary: "Anything you say, madam, you blasted, senile blowhard, calling yourself a vice admiral and ordering me about like we was the Royal Navy."

"What's that ya say?" demanded the vice admiral. "Blast it all, speak up! Ya know I can't hear ya when ya mumble."

"Nothing, madam," said Shamus. "I'll just be showing our esteemed guests to their quarters."

"On the double!" ordered the vice admiral.

Shamus promptly led Alfonso, Bilblox, and Hill down the length of the upper deck toward the bow of the ship, where they would be staying. The upper deck was stacked with open cargo, most of which looked to be at least a hundred years old. Lashed to the deck with thick ropes were horse-drawn buggies (without the horses), old potbelly stoves, massive iceboxes, several large cannons, fifty or so foot-powered sewing machines, a case of old swords, a small, steam-powered tugboat up on cinder blocks, and, at the very end, an ornately carved, twenty-foot-high mini-windmill with a bright red door. The freshly painted door looked to be the only thing on the ship that had received any recent attention.

As he walked past all the cargo, Alfonso stepped along carefully, since the entire ship was rocking back and forth with the sea. At one point, he almost lost his balance altogether.

"You'll get used to this," said Hill assuredly. "It's just the natural rocking of the sea."

"Yeah right," muttered Shamus with a dark chuckle. "Wait till the sea gets rough. Truth is this ship shouldn't be rockin' like this already. We're barely out of port. The problem is that the *Success Story* is overloaded. Dangerously overloaded! The vice admiral shouldn't be putting all this cargo on the deck. The boat is so top-heavy it rocks like a drunk old man carrying a case of whiskey on his back. One good storm, or a rogue wave, and all this stuff is going overboard including this here windmill. Of course, I told the vice admiral that. Told her more than once, I did! After all her great-great-grandpappy was Nils A. E. Nordenskjöld. Bloody idiots, all of them! I only hope —"

"Why are ya fellas draggin' all this junk across the ocean?" Bilblox interrupted impatiently.

"A good question," replied Shamus. "The truth is that the vice admiral — in her infinite wisdom — is determined to honor her illustrious past by continuing to navigate the waters of the Arctic Ocean in the same ship and along the same route as her forebears. Mainly we do the route from North America to Barsh-yin-Binder."

"And they actually want this junk in Barsh-yin-Binder?" asked Bilblox.

"Absolutely," replied Shamus. "There is a great demand for antiquated technologies in the Barsh-yin-Binder area."

"Antiquated technologies?" asked Alfonso.

"Yes, all of this junk — antique merchandise — is valuable in Barsh-yin-Binder," explained Shamus. "As I'm sure you know, Barsh-yin-Binder is a lawless, backwards place at least a century behind the times. So this old stuff, which you couldn't give away in North America, is worth quite a bit over there. Of course, we can't rely on the local Barsh-yin-Binders to keep us in business. Though the city is a dump, it's a haven for a number of 'business associates' of the vice admiral. We ply this route, do some tradin' . . ." He leaned in closer. "'Course it's the high-value smugglin' that pays the bills, but you won't hear me talkin' about it. No sir, I won't say a word about all those *borrowed* goods."

"Borrowed?" asked Alfonso.

"Stolen!" said Shamus with a roll of his eyes. "Yee gads, do I have to spell everything out for you lugs?"

"Is this windmill where we'll be staying?" asked Bilblox.

They were all now standing in front of the thirty-foot-high windmill, which was, rather sloppily, tied down to the deck of the ship with several lines of rope.

"That's right," declared Shamus. He nodded reassuringly and then muttered to himself, "And I hope to goodness the whole thing doesn't go overboard 'cause I certainly warned the vice admiral that only a fool stacks a windmill atop the windiest part of a ship. 'Course even bigger fools decide to stay in such a windmill."

Shamus smiled brightly and opened the red door to the windmill. Inside, there was just one large room with old hardwood floors, a small stone fireplace, a few bearskin rugs, some old French leather club chairs, two bunk beds, a bookshelf packed with old leather-bound books, and a high ceiling with a lone light bulb. It was a very cozy space and suddenly the journey across the Pacific looked like it actually might be bearable—so long as the windmill stayed firmly planted on the deck of the ship.

"So here are your quarters," said Shamus. "Make yourselves at home." Shamus then cleared his throat and extended his hand. It was clear that he expected a tip. Alfonso looked about awkwardly. Bilblox rolled his eyes. Hill finally dug into his pockets and placed a one-dollar bill in Shamus's outstretched hand. Shamus cleared his throat again. Hill reached back into his pocket, pulled out a five-dollar bill, and placed it in Shamus's hand as well. "Much obliged!" said Shamus. "See you at dinner tonight, which will be around ten o'clock."

Once Shamus was gone, Hill sat on a bunk bed and took off the top hat.

"What's the deal with that big ol' hat yer wearin'?" asked Bilblox. "It ain't too practical for this voyage. Why don't ya throw it away?"

Alfonso and Hill looked at each other.

"What's goin' on?" Bilblox asked.

"It's all right," said Hill. "I think we have to tell Bilblox. I mean, after all, he is making this journey with us. He's going to find out sooner or later."

"Okay," said Alfonso. He opened the glass panel on the top hat and pulled out the Dormian bloom. The plant's flower was currently changing color from bright pink to a deep custard-yellow.

"What in the name of Ivan Magrewski is that?" asked Bilblox.

"It's our contraband," explained Alfonso.

"I suspected that ya were smugglin' somethin'," said Bilblox. "I mean, I knew ya were deliverin' contraband to Barshyin-Binder, but this is it? Some kind of gimmicky trick plant that changes colors? Ya gotta be kiddin' me!"

"This is no gimmicky trick plant," said Hill sternly. "This is a Dormian bloom — perhaps the rarest and most powerful form of organic life on the planet. Now sit down and pay attention."

Hill went on to explain the entire story of how they'd rescued the plant from World's End, fended off the Dragoonya plants of war, fled to Fort Krasnik, and committed themselves to finding the ancient city of Somnos. Bilblox listened patiently, occasionally nodding in amazement.

"So you see," concluded Hill, "there's just one of these little plants on the whole planet! It *must* arrive at its proper destination in Dormia."

"So," said Bilblox with a mischievous smile, "we're not going to tell the vice admiral about any of this?"

"There's no point in doing that," said Hill. "Besides, we're not going to cause her any trouble. It's not like we're being followed. There's not another person in the whole world besides Judy and Pappy who knows what we're up to."

Alfonso cleared his throat and looked about rather uncomfortably.

"What is it?" asked Hill.

"Well, um, that's not exactly true," Alfonso reluctantly said. "There's someone else." Alfonso told them about his two encounters with Kiril. He described what Kiril looked like and what he had said. "The guy really gives me the creeps," said Alfonso. "And I'm pretty sure he's following us."

"Hmm," said Hill with a heavy sigh. "Are you absolutely sure that this happened? I mean, perhaps these were just nightmares. Both times you met this Kiril right after waking up."

"This was no dream," protested Alfonso. "And I have the ring to prove it."

"The ring?" inquired Hill.

"I pulled it off his finger by accident," explained Alfonso. He reached into his coat pocket and pulled out the gold ring. Hill grabbed it and inspected it carefully. "Hmm," he said. "This is just as I've feared. Well, there's no doubt about it now."

"What?" asked Bilblox.

"Here, have a look," said Hill. He walked across the windmill and picked up a tattered canvas duffle bag that he'd been carrying with him. He pulled out his copy of *McBridge's Book of Mythical Plants* and quickly flipped through the pages until he came to the entry for the Dragoonya plant of war. The entry included a highly detailed picture revealing the plant's muscular jaws, its yellow fangs, its tortoiselike outer shell, and its dangling roots, which served as its feet.

Alfonso stared at the picture, remembering Pappy's screams as the plant broke his leg in two. He glanced down at the writing below the picture, which he had skipped in the rush to their greenhouse:

> *Renowned for their seeming ability to predict the future, the Dragoonya are a fierce and cruel people. At different points in history, they dominated the Asian steppes behind the leadership of their knights who, according to legend, had eyes that shone like the fog. They enslaved or killed everyone they encountered. The origins of the Dragoonya are unknown, but many speak of their capital, named Dargora, hidden in the far north deep within a petrified forest. According to legend, it is visible only from a distance at twilight. Those who ventured into the growing darkness to catch a glimpse of it never lived to tell.*

Alfonso felt a shiver travel up his spine. He looked at Hill, who had been reading along with him. "Don't worry about all that," said Hill. "I've got no intention of taking us to Dargora. Come on now, let's focus on the picture of this plant. If you look closely, you'll see something like a dog collar around the plant's neck. There's a metal tag on that collar."

Alfonso and Bilblox both studied the picture carefully.

"Yeah, I see the tag yer talkin' about," said Bilblox. "So what's the big deal, huh?"

Hill reached back into his duffle bag, rummaged around some more, and finally pulled out a leather case containing a small magnifying glass. He handed it to Alfonso. "Go ahead," said Hill. "Take another look."

Alfonso did so and gasped. When he looked through the magnifying glass, he could see—as clear as day—that the metal tag was emblazoned with a picture of a Dormian bloom in front of a setting sun. It was the exact same image as the one on Kiril's ring.

"Whoa!" said Bilblox. "That's pretty spooky! It's the same picture as on the ring. What does it mean?"

"It means that we're in serious trouble," said Hill. "That image is the emblem of the Dragoonya and I'd wager this Kiril fellow is a Dragoonya henchman."

"Who in the heck are the Dragoonya anyway?" asked Bilblox.

"They're the eternal enemies of Dormia," said Hill gravely. "And they're a very powerful and nasty lot."

"So," said Bilblox, "if the Dragoonya are so powerful, why ain't they captured ya yet?"

Hill shrugged. "I don't know," he said. "I've been wondering that myself."

As Bilblox and Hill continued to chat away, Alfonso took hold of Kiril's ring and began to study it with the magnifying glass. He stared at it intently without blinking. The plant carved into the ring's coat of arms was clearly a Dormian bloom. The stem, the leaves, and the flower itself were a perfect match to his own plant. This was no surprise. He'd noticed this even without the magnifying glass. What was surprising, however, was the image behind the plant. Initially, it seemed that this image was a setting sun whose fiery rays were casting light onto the plant. But, as Alfonso examined the image closely, he realized that the sun was in fact not a sun at all, but a bonfire whose leaping flames were actually *burning* the plant. Odd as it seemed, the image on this coat of arms was clearly of a Dormian bloom on fire.

Alfonso sat up and then called over Bilblox and his uncle. "Look what I've found!" he whispered urgently. "It's not a setting sun—it's a bonfire!" Both Hill and Bilblox looked through the magnifying glass. Alfonso was right: the Dormian bloom was being consumed by fire.

"Strange, isn't it?" asked Alfonso. "Why would it be on fire?"

"I think it means we ought to torch this plant and see what happens," said Bilblox eagerly. "It may unlock some kind of secret."

"You brawny, cargo-lugging imbecile!" retorted Hill. "That's the stupidest, most dangerous, and irresponsible idea I've ever heard. You all listen to me and listen good: we are delivering this plant to Dormia—unharmed—and that means you should forget this business about flames right now, before I knock both of your heads together!"

"What about burning off a single leaf?" asked Alfonso. "We could just do it as an experiment."

"Absolutely not," replied Hill.

The matter was settled. Or so it seemed. Yet throughout the remainder of the day the possibility of burning a single leaf continued to linger in Hill's thoughts, for he was a curious man—not well suited to playing the role of the disciplinarian—and he had lived much of his life by doing things on a whim. Now, thanks to Alfonso, a clue had fallen into his lap. Could he really afford to ignore it? Besides, what harm could come from such a small experiment? All trees occasionally lost a leaf or two—this was a natural occurrence—so what would it matter if they burned a single leaf?

CHAPTER 9

VICE ADMIRAL PURCHEEZIE HOLDS COURT

JUST BEFORE ten o'clock that night, Hill, Alfonso, and Bilblox left the windmill and headed out along the upper deck of the *Success Story* toward the ship's bridge. The night was dark and the sky shimmered with thousands of stars shining brilliantly. The ship itself was heading almost due north and the wind was already frosty with gusts of polar air. When the three arrived at the bridge, they encountered Shamus, who was standing at the wheel of the ship. The room was a mess of scattered maps, old sailing books, heavy rubber boots, ashtrays overloaded with used lumps of tobacco, and an old phonograph that was playing marching-band tunes from the 1920s. "Good evening," said Shamus wearily. "Sorry for the mess, but I pretty much live in this room. We're a wee bit short on help these days. Don't get much sleep, but who's complaining? Not me. Oh, not me. Just head down that set of stairs and dinner will be served shortly."

"Thanks," said Alfonso.

"Don't thank me yet," he muttered. "If you can eat the slop that Hellen cooks then you've got a hardier stomach than I do."

"Who's Hellen?" asked Alfonso.

"You'll see," Shamus replied.

They parted ways with Shamus and headed down a narrow flight of stairs that led into a dining room of sorts. Actually, it was a small room with a billiards table in the middle that had been converted into a dining room table. Above the billiard table hung a crystal chandelier that looked as if it had belonged in an opera house. It was enormous—far too big for the small space—and the lowermost crystals actually touched the surface of the billiards table. Dust lay everywhere. The place smelled of rotting fish, stale books, mildewed wood, and burned cooking oil. As Alfonso took a seat at the billiards table, a small mouse scurried into the corner pocket.

"Hello, boys!" said a large, matronly woman who emerged from a door at the far end of the room. She wore an apron that nearly covered her entire body, a filthy-looking chef's hat, and a pair of large rubber gloves. "The name is Hellen. I am the cook, though I occasionally do the navigating as well. I expect you met Shamus already, and of course you've met the vice admiral, so now you've met the entire crew."

"The entire crew?" asked Bilblox with a dumbfounded look. "Ya mean there are just three of ya runnin' this whole ship?"

"That's right, honey," said Hellen. "The vice admiral doesn't take a liking to folks too quick. She prefers to operate with a bit of a skeleton crew. Keeps costs down. Of course, there have been other members of the crew over the years, but they never seem to last."

Bilblox raised his eyebrows. "I see," he said.

"Anyway," said Hellen, "what can I get you fellows to eat?"

"What's on the menu?" asked Hill.

"Fried seal—that's all we ever serve."

"We'll take three of those," said Hill.

"Three fried seals coming up!" said Hellen cheerfully. "Do you want any hot sauce with that? It helps kill the taste and the germs as well."

Alfonso, Bilblox, and Hill all nodded.

While they were waiting for their fried seal, they heard the vice admiral's peg leg poking its way down the stairs. "At ease, gentlemen," she said as she entered the room. "How are my passengers doing?"

"We're doing just fine, Vice Admiral," said Hill.

"Good," she said. "Now tell me, Hill, do ya remember yer way around the ship at all? Last time ya were on board, when ya were just a little feller, ya and yer brother played around all day in every nook and cranny of this ship."

"I don't remember much," explained Hill. "But there are some things, like playing hide-and-seek with Leif in the *Success Story*'s cargo hold or climbing ropes on the deck. But other than that, my memory gets pretty hazy. It's like I've got amnesia or something."

"Pity," said the vice admiral as she sat at the billiards table and lit her pipe. "Then ya've got no memory from before I found ya in the Urals?"

"Hardly any," said Hill. "In fact, I have no memory of leaving my parents at all. I've tried everything to remember what they look like, but nothing works . . ." He let out a painful, drawn-out sigh.

"Well," said the vice admiral as she puffed on her pipe and sipped her beer, "it was really the oddest thing. I'd hired a fellow I knew in Barsh-yin-Binder to take me on a huntin' trip into the Ural Mountains. They have great big bears in those parts, a good bit bigger than the grizzlies in North America, and I was aimin' to shoot one. We must have traveled almost a week, passin' through some wild mountain passes, until we came to the edge of a fearsome forest known as Straszydlo. I'd have to say that it's just about the spookiest place I've ever visited. Anyway, we were aimin' to venture into them woods, when we found ya in an old horse-drawn sled. Not sure where the horse was. Ran off, I guess. Anyway, ya and yer brother were all by yer lonesome and fast asleep to boot. I couldn't believe it. Of course, I'm not much interested in kids—never have been—but I couldn't leave ya there to freeze and die. So we cut the huntin' trip short, hooked yer sled up to our horses, and took ya back to Barsh-yin-Binder."

"I don't remember —" began Hill.

"Figures," interrupted the vice admiral, who seemed slightly annoyed. "I go to the trouble of savin' yer life and ya don't remember a moment of it. And now here I am doin' ya a favor again. I must be the most generous vice admiral on the seven seas —"

Rather suddenly, a loud coughing echoed down the stairway from the bridge above. Then came the sound of Shamus's muttering.

"What's that ya say?" yelled the vice admiral.

"Nothing, madam," yelled Shamus. "Just something stuck in my throat."

Vice Admiral Purcheezie shook her head and took a puff on her pipe.

"What happened in Barsh-yin-Binder?" asked Alfonso. "What did you do with my dad and Uncle Hill once you arrived there?"

"Well, as ya can imagine, there are no proper orphanages in Barsh-yin-Binder so I took 'em back to Fort Krasnik where I entrusted 'em to Dusty Magrewski. And from there, well ya know the rest." She turned to look at Hill. "So ya still haven't told us why yer so eager to go back. Homesick, are ya? Tryin' to find yer family?"

"Something like that," replied Hill. "Plus, I want to show my nephew the Ural Mountains."

"It sounds to me as if yer lookin' for Dormia," replied the vice admiral as she took a long drag on her pipe. "Ya and Leif kept mutterin' about that imaginary place."

"You've heard of Dormia?" blurted out Alfonso.

"Of course!" said the vice admiral. "Every visitor to those parts has. It's the greatest wives' tale in all of northern Asia. People lookin' for adventure or people with no past, like yer uncle here, get caught up in it. They buy some cheap, dime-store book on fantastical places, like Atlantis or Dormia, and believe every last made-up word of it. Well, lemme tell ya— it's just as foolhardy as lookin' for the Fountain of Youth, and *much* more dangerous. The mountains and woods over there are filled with nasty beasts and dangerous sorts of men an' women."

"That's enough now," said Hill sternly. "I don't want you scaring Alfonso."

"He should be scared!" growled the vice admiral. She slapped the table with her meaty fist, stood up, and stared fiercely at Hill. "A boy of Alfonso's age has no business in those parts. And I ain't sure what kind of uncle would take him there either. Alfonso may trust ya—he's just a gullible young feller—but not me. Not for a minute! What are ya really up to anyway, Hill? How about ya come clean?"

Hill stared back at the vice admiral defiantly, but said nothing.

"Suit yerself," she grumbled. "But don't expect me to come to yer rescue if ya get into trouble in the dark woods of the Urals. I already done that once and ya can bet yer life I ain't gonna do it again."

"We'll be just fine," said Hill with a rather forced smile.

CHAPTER 10

A PILE OF PURPLE POWDER

BACK IN THE windmill, Alfonso, Bilblox, and Hill prepared for sleep. Bilblox lit a fire in the small stone fireplace, Hill found an extra stash of wool blankets in one of the closets, and Alfonso discovered an old music box that played a soothing Irish lullaby. When it finally came time to go to sleep, Alfonso noticed that his uncle had taken a clock off the wall and placed it on the nightstand by his bed. He was staring at it with fierce intensity.

"What are you doing with that?" Alfonso asked.

"It's broken," replied Hill sleepily. "I am going to repair it."

Bilblox looked confused. "Repair it when?" he asked.

"When I'm sleeping," said Hill with a yawn. "That's when I repair things."

Bilblox simply rolled his eyes. He had heard so many crazy things today that he no longer had the energy to ask questions.

"So you're focusing?" inquired Alfonso. "You're doing the same thing that I did before the ballast match?"

"More or less," replied Hill. "Only I'm using a slightly more advanced technique. It involves meditation. I'll stare at this clock and, all the while, I'll block out all other thoughts. I do this by repeating a sacred phrase—what the Hindus call a *mantra japa*. The mantra that I use sounds like this: *Aum namah Shivaya*. Basically, I just keep repeating this mantra—for exactly one hundred and eight times—and, afterward, I fall asleep almost right away. The next thing you know—presto!—my sleeping-self is doing exactly what it is supposed to be doing. Well, most of the time anyway."

"Why do ya do it one hundred and eight times?" asked Bilblox skeptically.

"Oh that's easy," said Hill. "It turns out that one hundred and eight is a magical number. Didn't you know that? I've read quite a few books on this subject matter and let me tell you the facts: the Hindu gods have one hundred and eight names. There are exactly one hundred and eight sins in Tibetan Buddhism. Chinese astrologists believe that there are one hundred and eight sacred stars. The number of stitches on a baseball is, yes, one hundred and eight. The number of episodes of my favorite TV show—*Dr. Who*—that were accidentally destroyed in the nineteen-seventies, once again, one hundred and eight."

"Wow," said Alfonso. "So all this helps you control what you do in your sleep?"

"My dear, dear nephew," said Hill with a laugh. "The power of sleep is a very mysterious thing. There is no guaranteed or certain way to control it. Goodness knows, some nights I've gone to sleep meditating on the image of a broken watch, but as soon as I drift off, my sleeping-self overrules this and heads across town to get a burrito. That's the way it was with those copies of *American Botanist* that I kept buying. I didn't intend to do that. My sleeping-self just did it. But the things that we do in our sleep almost always have a reason behind them. After all, those copies of *American Botanist* led me to you."

"It's just like me growing the Dormian bloom," added Alfonso. "I didn't understand what I was doing at the time, but I guess there was a reason for it."

"Exactly," said Hill. "Whatever you did in your sleep was done for a reason. Or at least, I think so."

"That makes me feel a bit better," said Alfonso with a smile. "Hey, would it be all right if I tried your meditation technique?"

"Sure," said Hill. He handed Alfonso the broken clock. "Why don't you try to fix this tonight?"

Alfonso nodded. He said goodnight to Hill and Bilblox and immediately began concentrating on the clock. As he did this, Alfonso repeated the ancient Hindu words—*Aum namah Shivaya*—exactly 108 times. As soon as he was done, Alfonso drifted off into a very deep sleep. He slept very soundly and, the next thing he knew, it was morning. At first, he was disappointed. Nothing had happened. Then, rather hazily, he became aware of a noise in the room—*tick, tick, tick*—it was the clock. It was on the wall, ticking away perfectly.

It didn't take long before Alfonso, Hill, and Bilblox settled into the routine of life on the *Success Story*. Each night, just before they all went to bed, Hill usually gave Alfonso a new task to do in his sleep—cleaning the windmill, mending some socks, organizing a box of cargo, or even reading a book on how to sail a ship. Alfonso then meditated, went to sleep, and promptly got to work. "I've never seen a boy work harder in his sleep," marveled Hill. "And I can't believe how quickly he picked up this technique." Alfonso was thrilled with his progress, although he still had no memories of what he did while sleeping.

On most mornings, the three of them woke up around eight and proceeded directly to the mess for breakfast. Hellen always served the exact same meal: twenty-year-old hardtack, coffee, and fried seal. It was a disgusting combination, but they all got used to it, mainly by drenching every meal with generous amounts of hot sauce. Sometimes the vice admiral came down and joined them. She often shared stories about her distinguished family, especially Nils A. E. Nordenskjöld. Of course, the stories were extremely long and often quite boring—filled with details of highly complicated nautical maneuvers—but it helped pass the time. Gradually, the days began to blend together. The only thing that marked the passage of time was the date wheel on Hill's watch, which was steadily working its way down to zero. According to the vice admiral, it would take them almost a month to complete the journey to Barsh-yin-Binder.

This wouldn't leave them much time to find Somnos. Not much time at all.

Generally, in the early afternoons, Alfonso scraped ice off the deck of the ship and gave what he collected to his Dormian bloom. He had discovered that the plant thrived on a diet of ice and winter sunshine. Later, after dinner, he would read in the windmill. On one such evening, just as he was drifting off to sleep with a book in his lap, Alfonso was startled by a shout from his uncle Hill.

"Dash it all!" yelled Hill. "We probably shouldn't do it, but it might answer some questions."

"What are ya talkin' about?" an annoyed Bilblox asked.

"I'm talking about taking a leaf from the bloom and, uh, burning it," Hill replied. He looked at Alfonso. "What do you think?"

"I thought you said we weren't going to do that," said Alfonso.

"I know, I know," said Hill. "But I just keep thinking about what clues it might yield. I can't get the blasted thought out of my head!"

"Well," said Alfonso, "it is just one leaf."

"Yes," said Hill excitedly. "That's exactly right! Exactly right! So it's agreed. We burn just one leaf and that's it. Never again. Understood?"

Alfonso and Bilblox nodded. Hill took the Dormian bloom out from his top hat and placed it on the floor. Hill identified the smallest of the seven leaves and held his breath as he broke it off cleanly at the stem. Nothing happened, although the tearing away of the leaf left a milky-white scar on the bloom.

Hill then placed the leaf on the floor, lit a match, and stuck it next to the leaf. In one single, brilliant flash, the entire leaf burst into a ball of flames that leapt up, hovered for a moment in midair, darted left and then right, gave off a few greenish sparks, and promptly disappeared. On the floor, directly beneath the spot where the leaf once lay, were roughly a dozen barely visible granules of purple powder.

"Most remarkable," said Hill, with a touch of fear in his voice.

"Wow!" said Alfonso giddily. "That was cool."

"I told ya this was the thing to do," boasted Bilblox. "Now the question is, what do we do with these little specks of purple ash?"

"I have no idea," said Hill. "But I suppose one of us will have to touch them."

"I volunteer," said Bilblox eagerly.

"Hmm," mumbled Hill. "All right, go ahead."

Very cautiously, Bilblox moved his right index finger toward the small granules of ash. He paused for a moment, glanced at both Hill and Alfonso with a hopeful smile, and then touched the bright purple granules.

Nothing happened.

"Well, I guess it's safe to touch," said Bilblox with a shrug. "Don't seem poisonous or anything like that."

For the next hour or so the three of them experimented with the granules in every possible manner. They touched them, smelled them, tried to set them on fire, and even tasted one of them. Nothing happened. They had reached a dead end. It was now very late, well after midnight, and all three of them were quite sleepy.

"I think it's time for me to go to bed," yawned Bilblox as he rubbed his eyes. "I'm so tired . . . I'm . . . whoa . . . what's happening? What's going on?" Bilblox was blinking furiously and glancing about in a wild disoriented fashion like a startled animal. "I can't see!" he yelled.

"It's the purple granules!" said Alfonso. "I think he accidentally rubbed them into his eyes."

Both Alfonso and Hill took a closer look and, sure enough, several granules of the purple ash were rapidly dissolving into the moist film of Bilblox's eyes.

"Holy cow!" yelled Bilblox. "Ya wouldn't believe what I'm seeing!"

"What is it!" asked Alfonso.

Bilblox rose clumsily to his feet and stumbled toward the door. He fumbled for the handle. In frustration, he pounded on the door. It flew open as if made of tissue paper. Wind gushed into the room and the remaining purple powder blew away. Bilblox staggered onto the deck and clutched one of the thick wooden rails. It snapped in his hands. Alfonso was astonished. Bilblox was a strong guy, but not *that* strong.

"I can't believe this!" yelled Bilblox. "This is *amazing!*"

Alfonso and Hill ran toward him.

"It's like my eyes are two giant telescopes," Bilblox exclaimed. "I'm still tryin' to get the hang of it—ya can kind of zoom in and out—but I can see a long ways off! In fact, I can see the shore!"

"That's impossible," said Hill. "The nearest shore is the Alaskan coastline and that must be a good three hundred miles away."

"I can see it perfectly," said Bilblox. "There are giant rocks, quite a bit of blue ice, some evergreens, and wait . . . yes, that's a seal . . . wait . . . yes, there are three big seals and a baby one too!"

"What's behind us?" asked Alfonso. "Can you see that way?"

"H-hold on," said Bilblox, who seemed out of breath. "I'm lookin'. I don't see anythin' yet. Just miles and miles of open sea . . . wait . . . yes, I see a ship. It's a big black ship. It has some cannons on the front and it's really movin'. Now, my eyes are goin' blurry. Wait . . . Oh no! I-I've gone blind." Bilblox fell to his knees and rubbed his fists into his eyes.

"What do you mean blind?" yelled Hill. "What have you done!"

"Wait, I see somethin'," gasped Bilblox. His eyes were closed. He was taking short, hard breaths of air—as if he had just run a race. "I see flyin' fish jumpin' across the bow of the ship . . . Now mist is closin' in . . . Someone just spilled a cup of coffee . . . And there's an iceberg . . . There's a low-lyin' iceberg, barely visible, just off the starboard bow . . . Purcheezie! She's got to turn the ship or we'll smack inta it!"

Alfonso and Hill exchanged puzzled glances. It was a clear night with no mist or flying fish or anything remotely out of the ordinary. Bilblox fell silent.

"Bilblox? Are you okay? Can you see?" Hill was obviously very concerned.

After a long pause, Bilblox slowly stood up. His eyes began to creep open. "T-t-tired," he muttered. Alfonso and Hill each took one of his arms and helped him back to the windmill. Groggily, Bilblox climbed into his bed. All of his movements seemed slow and lazy—except for his eyelids. Indeed, Bilblox was now blinking furiously as if he had something in his eyes.

"Holy mackerel!" gasped Hill. "Look at his eyes!"

Alfonso was noticing the exact same thing. Bilblox's eyes had turned a milky white, and his pupils were only barely visible.

"Oh no," gasped Alfonso. He couldn't believe it. Bilblox's eyes looked like Kiril's.

The next morning, just after breakfast, Hill and Alfonso went around to see Vice Admiral Purcheezie, who was manning the wheel on the bridge of the *Success Story*.

"Where's the big longshoreman?" asked the vice admiral as she took a puff on her pipe. "Feelin' lazy?"

"Not really," replied Alfonso. "He's just a little under the weather."

The vice admiral raised her eyebrows skeptically, but said nothing.

"Looks like we got some low visibility ahead," said Hill, pointing to a bank of fog in the distance. "Are we headed that way?"

The vice admiral nodded. "We're headed right into that fog. All the better; a black ship has been on our tail for the last few hours and it's startin' to make me nervous."

"A ship is following us?" inquired Hill.

"Indeed," said the vice admiral. "I've been keepin' a sharp eye on 'er. Looks to be an old warship, judgin' from the cannons on 'er bow."

The vice admiral stood up and looked due south with her telescope. "Well, she's not there now, but I'm pretty sure she's gainin' on us. I've seen these ships before. They're old relics from the Russian navy favored by hijackers, pirates, and mercenaries of one kind or another. I've had my run-ins with them in earlier years. They target ships leavin' Fort Krasnik. After all, we're not gonna call the police, are we? Still, I don't know why they'd be after me right now, especially this far north. They couldn't have figured out what I got onboard—only me and the crew know." She looked at Hill and Alfonso. "As I said, it's mighty strange they're still followin' me. Ya wouldn't know anythin' about this, would ya?"

"No," Hill quickly replied.

"No matter," continued the vice admiral. "We're almost into that fog, and luckily we're near an ice field as well."

"Why is that lucky?" asked Alfonso.

"It's lucky because there's no way that black ship is followin' us into a foggy ice field. Too dangerous. Only a fool or a savvy veteran of the polar seas—like meself—would do somethin' like that."

The fog was now only a few hundred yards away. It looked to Alfonso as if an enormous dark cloud had fallen from the sky and was resting on the water. Just as they were about to enter the fog, several small dark gray objects leapt out of the sea and shot over the bow of the ship. They looked like bats.

"Flyin' fish!" roared Vice Admiral Purcheezie with a burst of girlish laughter. "I haven't seen them in years."

Just then another of these fish smacked into the windshield in front of them. This startled Hill and he stumbled backwards into Vice Admiral Purcheezie, causing her to drop the mug of coffee she was holding.

"Watch yourself!" she growled.

Alfonso's eyes grew wide with alarm. It was exactly what Bilblox had foreseen.

"Vice Admiral, watch out!" yelled Alfonso at the top of his lungs. "There's gonna be a low-lying iceberg just off the starboard bow! You've got to turn now!"

"What in tarnation are you talkin' about?" asked the vice admiral. She peered ahead and saw an ominous shape loom into view. "Holy smokes, yer right! Hold on, we're goin' full-tilt to port!" The vice admiral grabbed the steering wheel and spun it quickly to the left. The boat lurched violently to port. Books fell off shelves and bottles clattered to the floor. Below deck, Hellen—who was still cleaning up from breakfast—screamed as her pans and dishes fell from their shelves and crashed to the floor.

The *Success Story* veered sharply out of the path of the iceberg and missed it only by several feet. The vice admiral let out a sigh of relief. "I can't believe I didn't see it," she said. "A few seconds more, and this ship woulda been sunk."

She turned to Alfonso with a fierce look in her eyes. "Young man," she said, "how in blazes did ya see that comin'?"

CHAPTER 11

THE ICEBERG FORTRESS

ALFONSO stared back at the vice admiral. What could he say? He was a truthful boy, but how could he explain that Bilblox had taken the burnt ash from a magical plant, rubbed it into his eyes, and by doing so, foreseen an iceberg that could sink their ship? It was absurd. Even though Alfonso knew that this is *exactly* what happened, he could hardly believe it himself.

So instead of telling the truth, he told the vice admiral that Bilblox had a dream the night before that they would hit an iceberg. "It got me pretty worried," Alfonso explained, "so I guess I was on the lookout."

Fortunately, Vice Admiral Purcheezie believed this yarn. Tears welled up in her eyes and she embraced Alfonso with the tenderness of a proud grandmother. "Ya saved m' ship, lad," she said. Her voice choked with emotion. "Sure, the *Success Story* is an icebreaker, but it's pretty old and that iceberg would've snapped it in two. Ya saved my ship and the whole Nordenskjöld family is in yer debt."

"Don't be too grateful," replied Alfonso.

"An' why not?" she asked.

"Because it's our fault that the black ship is following us," said Alfonso. "I think they want something we have."

"Tell me somethin' I don't know," she replied with a chortle. "I knew ya were smugglin' somethin' from the moment I laid eyes upon ya."

"You did?" inquired Alfonso.

Alfonso looked nervously at Hill, who was just getting up. He had fallen during the near miss with the iceberg and was bleeding from a large gash on the forehead.

"I'm feeling a bit shaky," he murmured.

"Go see Hellen," said the vice admiral. "She'll fix you up."

Hill nodded groggily and headed down the tight staircase to the deck below in search of Hellen. Alfonso attempted to escort him, but Hill waved him off. Reluctantly, Alfonso returned to the bridge.

"How'd you know about us smuggling something?" Alfonso asked the vice admiral.

"I've been in this business for more than half a century," she replied. "I can spot a smuggler a hundred yards away and the three of ya had it written all over yer faces."

"I suppose we should tell you what we're smuggling —"

"Don't ya dare!" barked the vice admiral. "I don't want to know a blasted thing. Ya don't ask about my cargo and I don't ask about yers. That's how it goes with smugglers. That way, if we ever got boarded, I can say I honestly had no idea that this young lad was smugglin' her majesty's royal jewels —"

"But we're not smuggling jewels," interjected Alfonso.

"I don't want to know!" bellowed the vice admiral. "Now come here and help me keep watch over the sea. I need those eyes of yers. This fog is thicker than clam chowder 'n there are icebergs all around us." Alfonso nodded and stood next to the vice admiral as they peered out the front windshield of the ship.

After two intense hours, the fog lifted and revealed a dozen or so massive icebergs floating nearby. Most were at least a hundred feet tall and colored a very bright blue, especially in contrast with the dark waters. It was exciting stuff, being so close, but Alfonso also felt small and powerless. One wrong move, and the *Success Story*—and everything in it—might end up on the bottom of the North Pacific.

"Where are we?" asked Alfonso.

"Still in the thick of an ice field," said the vice admiral. "But we're very close."

"To what?"

"We'll be makin' a pit stop at one of these bergs and now I'm just tryin' to find it," she explained. "It's a great big berg with two giant horns of ice and it belongs to a nasty character by the name of Lars."

Alfonso stared at the desolate iceberg-filled water. How could anyone live around here?

"I don't blame ya fer bein' surprised," said the vice admiral. "Only smugglers and thieves know 'bout him. This Lars fella took over an iceberg and hollowed it out with rooms and meetin' areas and those kinds a things. It doesn't get a lot of unwanted attention, so it's been a regular stop on my route fer many years now. Ya can spend the night, get some decent fried whale, pick up some provisions, and—most importantly—sell a bit of *merchandise,* no questions asked." She squinted into the distance and nodded enthusiastically. "Ah, there it is," she said. "Dead ahead of us." Roughly a mile or so in front of them was a tall, very narrow iceberg with two slender horns of ice protruding up. It looked as if a Viking was underwater with only his helmet sticking up out of the ocean.

"So," said the vice admiral, "ya want to come along with Shamus and me and check the place out?"

Alfonso nodded excitedly.

"Fine then," said the vice admiral. "Just stick close to us—real close."

An hour or so later, the vice admiral, Shamus, and Alfonso readied themselves to leave the ship. Hellen would stay behind to watch over things. Hill and Bilblox were both fast asleep in the windmill. Bilblox was sleeping off the aftereffects of the powder and Hill was recovering from the nasty blow that he'd taken to the head. Alfonso had tried to wake them, but neither of them batted an eye.

As usual, Shamus was complaining under his breath, but this time, he had good reason. On his back was a large wooden trunk that the vice admiral had instructed him to carry. It appeared to be about as big as he was, and it probably weighed more than he did. Alfonso knew better than to ask what was in the trunk. In fact, it was best to pretend that the trunk and the contraband it contained were not even there.

With the *Success Story* snugly lashed to two ice boulders, the vice admiral lowered the ship's gangplank onto a narrow shelf of ice jutting out from the iceberg. The three of them made their way across the gangplank to the slippery ice shelf. A bitter wind whistled across the ice and chilled them almost immediately, despite their thick winter coats.

"I hate this part," muttered Shamus. "It's always me carrying this trunk on the slippery ice and, of course, I'm never moving fast enough —"

"Quit yer complainin'," said the vice admiral. "We're lucky to get a break from Hellen's cooking."

Taking quick, deliberate steps, the vice admiral led the way along the narrow shelf until she came to a crevice where someone had carved a perfectly formed set of stairs into the ice. The stairs led down several hundred feet into the mouth of a large cave, which was marked by two burning torches.

The three of them descended the icy stairs, into the cave, and continued down a narrow tunnel that burrowed deep into the iceberg. The tunnel was lined with torches, so it was possible to see, but just barely. They walked in silence for several minutes. Then, rather faintly, Alfonso heard what sounded like a fiddle. Its soft, haunting melody echoed dully along the ice. He soon heard another sound: a constant, low-level roar of water. These two sounds grew louder and louder until the three of them emerged into a giant underground cavern in which several dozen people were sitting at tables made of ice. They all appeared to be drinking out of frosty glass mugs and having a good time. The center of the room featured a giant waterfall that rushed down from a hole in the ceiling. The water filled a large pool and then snaked through the room via a quickly moving stream. In the stream at least a dozen penguins and a few baby walruses splashed about. Several ice bridges crossed the stream at various points.

The cavern was decorated with a number of massive, twenty-foot ice sculptures of fierce-looking men toting swords. Near the base of the waterfall was a bar, where waiters dressed in black-fur jackets poured drinks and scurried to and fro with overflowing trays filled with slimy, stinky-smelling fish dishes. Next to the kitchen was a large elevated stage, also made of ice, where a band of fiddlers was finishing a slow, doleful tune that sounded like a lullaby. When the band finished, the lead fiddler struck up a new, faster-paced tune and his fellow fiddlers joined in. The entire cavern was soon echoing with the sound of clapping as everyone rose to their feet and began to dance on the icy tabletops. A good number of these dancers fell immediately, crashing down onto the floor in wild tumbles, but a handful of the more talented dancers kicked their legs up toward the ceiling and spun around with perfect precision. One of the dancers was a plump redheaded woman dressed in a one-piece snowsuit made of fine white fur.

The vice admiral, Shamus, and Alfonso just stood there, overwhelmed by the spectacle. Shamus was wearing a most uncommon smile on his face, and his cheeks were flushed a deep red. "Oh my goodness, I haven't heard this tune in years," he mumbled. "I should like to join in the merriment and dance a jig with that fetching redhead."

"Go ahead," said the vice admiral with a smile. "I'll take the chest from here. We'll meet back at the ship by midnight. That black ship is on our tail, and there's a full moon out tonight."

"Aye, aye, Vice Admiral," replied Shamus. He dropped the chest and walked quickly toward the redhead in the one-piece snowsuit. Soon he was dancing on the tabletop next to her. He was very skilled: he kicked his legs way up in the air and on every sixth kick he did a perfect backflip. A crowd soon gathered around his table.

"Wow," said Alfonso. "Shamus is really good!"

"Yes he is," said the vice admiral with a smile. "He'll be dancin' from now till midnight."

Together the vice admiral and Alfonso picked up the heavy trunk. They hauled it through a maze of tables, crossed the nearest ice bridge, and proceeded around the back of the waterfall. The sound of the roaring water drowned out the festivities. Here there were two windows carved into the ice. Above one of them, the word *supplies* was etched into the ice. Above the other were the words *We pay gold—no questions asked.* Alfonso and the vice admiral set down the trunk and walked up to the window marked *supplies.* Almost immediately, an attendant dressed in black fur appeared.

"Greetings. What can I get for you, Vice Admiral?" asked the attendant.

"Twen'y pounds of flour, ten pounds of sugar, four pounds of chocolate, six gallons of rum, thirty yards of heavy wool, two large plastic tarps, and, uh —" The vice admiral leaned closer and dropped her voice. "If ya have it, a good book with adventure, friendship, bloodshed, and, uh, a—a bit of romance."

"Not a problem," the attendant crisply replied. "Would you like these taken out to your ship?"

"'Course," said the vice admiral in a louder voice. "We don't plan to stay."

"And will you be doing business at the other window as well?"

"Indeed," she replied. The vice admiral then walked over to the *We pay gold—no questions asked* window and heaved her chest up onto the window's ledge. A moment later the same attendant appeared behind that window. He looked excited.

"What do you have?" asked the attendant. "Is it jewels? Oh, is it more of those rubies you brought just —"

"Hold your horses," interrupted the vice admiral. She turned to Alfonso. "All right, my friend," she said. "Why don't ya mosey on outta here. Ya remember the rules: I mind my business and ya mind yers. Now this may take a while. Sometimes I'm here hagglin' with these fools for hours. Go back into the main room and get somethin' to eat. Tell them to put it on the vice admiral's tab. Make sure not to leave the main room. I can't afford to have ya gettin' lost. We need to be outta here at midnight sharp. Got it?"

Alfonso nodded. "I'll be there."

"Good," she replied. "Now be gone with ya."

Alfonso headed back into the main room, found an empty table by the edge of the waterfall, and waited for someone to take his order. A few minutes later, a heavyset, middle-aged woman in a white-fur coat and a matching white-fur hat waddled over to Alfonso's table.

"Da name is Gertrude," said the woman. "What'll it be tonight, young sir?"

"What do you recommend?"

"Fried whale is always good," said Gertrude. "Most of the fellas always seem to order that, often with a side of baked walrus, and some reindeer sausages for dessert."

"Great," said Alfonso with a forced smile.

While waiting for his food to arrive, Alfonso returned to a puzzle he had recently become obsessed with: the necklace that his mother had given him back in Fort Krasnik. He reached into his shirt, unfastened the necklace, and held the wood medallion in his hand. Alfonso studied it carefully.

The numbers at the bottom were clearly a code. Leif, like his son, loved riddles and always had books on codes lying around the house. Initially, Alfonso suspected that his dad had constructed a very simple code where each of the numbers stood for a letter such as 1 = *A*, 2 = *B*, 3 = *C*, 4 = *D*, and so on. But this didn't work, because it spelled

FQKTSXT

JJU JJU PJJ

Obviously, it meant nothing, or at least nothing Alfonso could understand. Clearly, the hand with the + on the palm had something to do with the code. But what was the connection?

Alfonso glanced up to see if his food was coming, but the waitress was nowhere in sight. He returned his attention to the medallion. What did the hand mean? Or maybe it was the fingers? What did the fingers mean? It was just an ordinary hand with five fingers, except that the palm had a plus sign.

Wait a minute, thought Alfonso. What if the hand and plus sign went together and they meant "plus five"? Alfonso then returned to his original idea in which each of the numbers at the bottom of the medallion stood for a letter. But this time, he added five to each number in the sequence so that the starting point was actually 6 and not 1. What if the code went as follows: 6 = *A*, 7 = *B*, 8 = *C*, 9 = *D*, and so on? Alfonso took a pencil and a scrap of paper from his pocket and wrote out a whole chart. It looked like this:

A - 6	H - 13	O - 20	V - 27
B - 7	I - 14	P - 21	W - 28
C - 8	J - 15	Q - 22	X - 29
D - 9	K - 16	R - 23	Y - 30
E - 10	L - 17	S - 24	Z - 31
F - 11	M - 18	T - 25	
G - 12	N - 19	U - 26	

When he applied this code to the medallion, Alfonso leapt up in excitement. The entire message, including the *you are* at the top read:

YOU ARE

ALFONSO

EEP EEP KEE

This had to be right. After all, his father had written his name in code! The only remaining question was: what on earth did *eep eep kee* mean?

CHAPTER 12

LARS

ALFONSO CONTINUED staring at the wooden medallion until the waitress, Gertrude, arrived at his table with a large silver platter of seafood. There was enough food on the platter to feed the entire crew of the *Success Story* for a week. The whale and walrus dishes were thoroughly disgusting—the very smell was enough to make Alfonso want to vomit—but the reindeer sausages weren't bad and he did his best to eat them. When nobody was looking, he threw the rest of the food to a few nearby penguins, who feasted on it happily. This turned out to be a bad idea, because soon Alfonso found himself surrounded by a dozen or so hungry penguins. When it became clear that he had nothing left to give them in the way of food, the penguins began to close in on him and peck at his legs. Gertrude waddled over and tried to shoo the penguins away.

"Didn't you see the sign?" asked an annoyed Gertrude. She pointed to a small wooden sign by the edge of the stream that read:

DO NOT FEED THE PENGUINS!

"Sorry," said Alfonso sheepishly. In that instant, one of the penguins closed its beak around the chain of the medallion, which was still dangling from his hand. In the next instant, the penguin was scurrying away at top speed, with the medallion in its mouth.

"Hey!" yelled Alfonso.

Gertrude tried to intercept the little bird, but it simply made a quick turn and headed over to one of the nearby ice bridges instead. Alfonso jumped to his feet and raced after the penguin.

"Hey!" yelled Alfonso. "He's got my medallion!"

"Forget it," called Gertrude. "You'll never get it back." Alfonso ignored her. He chased the penguin down the length of the main room and into a large ice tunnel that was lit with a series of torches. The penguin was surprisingly fast and Alfonso had to sprint hard to keep up with it. The penguin, sensing that it was being hunted, turned off the main tunnel and proceeded down a smaller side tunnel. Alfonso followed. The penguin made several more turns. After the sixth or seventh such turn, the bird disappeared. Alfonso stopped and looked around. The light had become dim, but something on the floor stood out against the ice. It was the medallion! The penguin must have dropped it. Alfonso felt elated as he picked up the medallion and hung it around his neck. He sighed with contentment and started back, but suddenly he realized that nothing looked familiar.

After a few minutes of walking, he came upon a large octagonal room he had never seen before. He walked to the center of the room and looked around. There were eight ice tunnels to choose from, and they all looked the same. Panic began to pulse through Alfonso's veins. He realized he was completely lost.

For the next hour, Alfonso walked into each of the eight tunnels to try to find a way back, but his efforts were fruitless. He returned to the octagonal room and sank down next to an icy wall. He felt like crying. How would he get back to the *Success Story*? He wouldn't. It was as simple as that. He was lost. Miserably lost. And no one would ever find him. *Why had he fed the penguins? Why had he left the main room?* These were very stupid things he had done. Alfonso slumped down even further and burrowed his head into his jacket. Just then, however, he heard something in the distance: footsteps. It was clear they were coming toward him from one of the tunnels.

"Hello?" Alfonso called timidly.

There was no reply—just the sound of footsteps getting closer.

An enormous man in a long fur jacket emerged from the gloom. In the dim light, he almost resembled a bear. One of the few signs that he was human was his beard—it came down almost to his waist and it was thoroughly encrusted in ice. The man was breathing heavily, as if he had been walking for some time, and steam rose off him as it does from horses on cold mornings. His coat bulged curiously on the right side. In his left hand, he carried a long, sharp sword.

"What is this?" demanded the enormous man. His bushy eyebrows turned up and his hooded, glittering eyes narrowed in anger.

"I-I-I'm here with Vice Admiral Purcheezie," stammered Alfonso. "I was chasing a penguin and I got lost. Wh-who are you?"

"WHO AM I?" boomed the man. "What kind of question is that? In fact, anyone who asks such a question has no business being on this iceberg at all. Especially a boy like you! Who am I?" The man laughed darkly. "I am Lars—that's who. The real question is: *who are you?*" Lars took a giant stride toward Alfonso, who was still slumped up against the icy wall of the tunnel. It was impossible for him to back away. Lars placed the sharp point of his sword on Alfonso's throat. "Tell me," boomed Lars, "before I slit your throat: *who are you?*"

"A-Alfonso," he replied.

"Alfonso?" Lars repeated. "Never heard of anyone like that."

The tip of the sword pierced Alfonso's skin. He felt a trickle of blood running down his throat. Lars dragged the sword tip down, across Alfonso's medallion, and rested it just above his heart. One thrust and it was over.

Alfonso felt the medallion resting on his heaving chest. It was worth a try.

"I am Alfonso. *Eep, eep, kee.*"

A look of surprise and shock crept across Lars's face. He took a step backwards and withdrew his sword.

"Do you have any idea what you just said?" asked Lars.

"No," said Alfonso weakly.

"Incredible," said Lars. "If you are being truthful, then I have been expecting you for a very, very, very long time."

Lars turned and strode down the corridor from which he came. Alfonso jumped to his feet and raced after him. They made numerous turns along the way and eventually came to a spiral staircase carved into the ice. "I hope you like climbing stairs," said Lars gruffly. "It's twenty flights to the top." With that, Lars turned and began gliding up the stairs, taking two and three steps at a time. Alfonso hesitated for a moment, unsure of whether it was wise to follow this giant man into a remote corner of the iceberg, but he could think of no alternative. He was soon scurrying up the stairs of ice as quickly as he could. After several minutes of climbing, they came upon a large opening that offered a stunning view of the surrounding icebergs—many of which were illuminated in the light of the moon. Alfonso could see the *Success Story* below them, moored to the side of the iceberg. Lars was leading him to the top of one of the iceberg's two giant horns.

"Tell me," said Lars as they climbed, "how is it that a boy like you becomes a Great Sleeper?"

"What do you mean?"

"That's what you said in the Dormian tongue—*'Eep eep kee'—I am the Great Sleeper.* Though I'm not sure if I believe you."

"I have no idea what you're talking about," gasped Alfonso as he struggled to keep up with Lars.

But Lars didn't explain. He didn't even turn around. He simply continued climbing.

"Among other things, I'm talking about what you're smuggling," said Lars. His harsh voice echoed throughout the dim staircase.

"You must be mistaken," Alfonso replied. "I'm not smuggling anything."

"You're a poor liar," said Lars. "I know exactly what you are smuggling and you're a fool to have hidden it where you did. Did you really think I wouldn't find it simply because you placed it inside a hat? I found the Dormian bloom within fifteen minutes of boarding the *Success Story.* And your two friends were so deeply asleep in their beds that I could've been singing aloud as I robbed them and they still wouldn't have noticed."

"What have you done with my plant?" asked Alfonso in alarm.

"The plant is not *yours,*" replied Lars. "You're merely the delivery boy—and a poor one at that. Given how careless you seem to be, I can't believe that someone didn't steal it sooner." He turned to glare at Alfonso. "In any case, this Dormian bloom is much safer with me than it is with you." Lars patted his massive fur coat, and the bulge Alfonso had noticed on the right side of the coat made sense: it was the top hat, with the plant inside.

"You can't do that!" yelled Alfonso.

"I can do whatever I like!" growled Lars. The staircase they had been ascending ended abruptly in a cavernous room with open windows that looked out on all sides. The space was barren except for a few bearskin rugs, a copper urn that contained a roaring fire, and a rack containing six or seven gleaming swords as well as a wooden walking stick. Moonlight and a biting wind poured into the room. Lars took off his coat and, sure enough, there was the top hat snuggled inside. Lars placed the top hat gently on the floor. Then he walked across the room and took a short sword from the rack. He placed it on the ground and slid it across the ice toward Alfonso.

"Pick it up!" ordered Lars.

"Why?" asked Alfonso.

"You'll see," replied Lars.

Alfonso reached down to the ice and picked up the sword. It felt cold, heavy, and quite clumsy in his hands. He struggled to raise it up so that the tip pointed toward the ceiling.

"Eep eep kee," Lars muttered to himself darkly. "We'll see about that." Lars's eyes closed and then seconds later opened again. His eyes stared blankly at Alfonso. Air poured from his nostrils in a drowsy sigh. Suddenly, he charged. In a wild frenzy of movement, the enormous bearlike man thrust out his sword and sprinted across the room toward Alfonso with the unmistakable intent of killing him. Alfonso saw him coming, but he was too paralyzed with fear to move. He simply stood his ground as if death were inevitable. At the last possible moment, however, something very unexpected happened. Despite the fact that his heart was pounding rapidly, Alfonso felt a ripple of extreme fatigue pulse through his body and his eyelids began to shut. An instant later, he was asleep.

His sleeping-self quickly sprang into a defensive position, crouching down low, so that his head was no higher than Lars's kneecap. In response, Lars hesitated for a brief moment, and in that instant of indecision, Alfonso dropped his sword, dove toward the ground, and somersaulted deftly in between Lars's massive legs. Lars spun around, blinked rapidly, and charged again. This time Alfonso darted over to the rack of swords, grabbed the wooden walking stick, and charged directly at Lars. Just before the two collided, Alfonso planted the walking stick into the ice—exactly as an Olympic pole-vaulter would do—and vaulted clear over Lars's head. Alfonso soared through the air, hit the far wall with his feet and then sprang off into a backflip, after which he gracefully landed on his feet.

The battle went on for several more minutes. The various skirmishes soon formed a pattern. Each time Lars charged it seemed certain he would kill Alfonso, but at the last minute the boy would always escape. After ten minutes or so of the most ferocious fighting, Lars set down his sword, breathing heavily, and yelled, "Enough!" This shout roused Alfonso from his sleeping trance.

"Do you have any memory of what just happened?" gasped Lars.

"No," said Alfonso. His voice was trembling with fear. "What happened?"

"You were in mortal danger and so, as a Dormian, your greatest defense mechanism kicked in: you fell asleep," Lars explained. "You performed remarkably well. How long have you been practicing those moves?"

"I don't know," replied Alfonso timidly. "I've never been in a fight in my life, but I can't vouch for my sleeping-self."

"You're too young to move so expertly in your sleep," muttered Lars. "Few can move so quickly, let alone a boy. Once, in my youth, I remember a Dormian knight who moved with as much speed, but he was a master sleeper at the height of his powers. And now you are already his equal. How do you explain this?"

"I can't," said Alfonso.

"And the plant that you carry," continued Lars, "did you grow it yourself?"

Alfonso nodded.

"I cannot believe it, but I must," said Lars. "You are indeed the Great Sleeper. What a frightful twist of fate. The last city of Dormia is in the hands of a mere boy."

Lars gave a weary, half-defeated sigh.

"Come along now," he said finally. "I have much to tell you and the hour is late."

CHAPTER 13

THE GREAT SLEEPER

LARS PICKED up the two swords that were lying on the ground and returned them to the rack. He strode across the room and peered out a large open window onto the sea below. Moonlight illuminated his face. He stood there for almost ten seconds, silent as a ghost, until he finally turned to face Alfonso.

"You're a Dormian, aren't you?" asked Alfonso.

"Of course I am," replied Lars. "I am a Dormian knight from the Order of the Wanderers. For many years, we have been waiting for the arrival of you and your plant. And to think it is being carried by a *child* —"

"I'm not a child!" said Alfonso defiantly. Normally, Alfonso would have been far too afraid to speak up like this, but he had just been attacked—and apparently he had put up a rather good fight—so he spoke his mind.

"Hmm," said Lars, though he said nothing further. He simply stroked his beard, rubbing out the small icicles and clumps of snow that had formed within the tangles of his hair. "It is our duty, as Wanderers, to spread out across all corners of the earth and wait," explained Lars. "We wait, and wait, and wait until a Dormian bloom is hatched. Of course, hardly any Wanderers ever live to see a Great Sleeper or a Dormian bloom. After all, a new bloom comes along only once every few centuries. In any case, when this happens, it is the duty of the Wanderer to help the bloom find its way back to Dormia. We're not nearly as strong as we once were, but we do our best. As I'm sure you know, the bloom has great powers, but in order for them to be fully realized, it must be planted in Dormia, in one of the eleven ancient cities. There, the plant will grow from a sapling—a Dormian bloom—into a Founding Tree of Dormia."

For a brief moment, Lars allowed himself to smile, as if he were involuntarily being whisked away into the memory of a far better time and place. "As a boy, I used to play with my friends around the base of it," he continued softly. "The trunk was so thick it took almost two minutes to run around. The leaves of this tree were like the sails of the greatest sailing ships. And the roots! They worked magic on the ground: they turned frozen earth into ripe, fertile soil. They are the lifeblood of Dormia. Without them, the entire place will wither and die . . ." His voice trailed away.

"You see," Lars continued, "a typical tree will live for many hundreds of years. When it starts to die, somewhere in the world—*outside Dormia*—a person will grow another bloom. This person may have only a tiny amount of Dormian blood in his or her veins. We really don't know much about *how* or *why* a given person becomes a Great Sleeper, but when this happens, that person must bring his or her bloom directly to Dormia, where it is promptly planted in the ground. Usually, within a year's time, that bloom grows with astounding speed and matures into a thousand-foot-tall Founding Tree. In effect, it replaces the Founding Tree that has just died.

"Of course, timing is crucial with all of this. If the Dormian bloom is not delivered in time . . . well, a great many Dormians will starve in the cold. This has happened more than once. Four of the eleven cities of Dormia—Prenjuk, Majlom, Zuydhoek, and Quartin—all perished because a Great Sleeper didn't show up in time. My mother's family hailed from the city of Quartin and all of them, every last one of them, perished. People who freeze in this manner tend to get colder and colder and then, just before death comes, they actually feel a burning, searing heat. It becomes so agonizing that they actually rip away their clothing for relief. *What a miserable way to die!* Trust me, Alfonso, that's not the sort of thing anyone wants on their conscience. No matter the cost, no matter the hardship, the bloom must be delivered."

"So you won't be keeping the bloom?" asked Alfonso.

"No, but I had to test you," snapped Lars. "You are the Great Sleeper—a Dormian with extraordinary powers, especially in combat. It's hard to believe—I've never heard of a Great Sleeper being so young. It's far too much responsibility for someone your age. After all, the Great Sleeper automatically becomes the leader of the Dormian knights. Strange as it sounds, by ancient law, you are now the head of my order."

Lars stepped away from the window. He walked to the far end of the room, took a seat on one of the bearskin rugs, and began to warm his hands over the fire crackling in the copper urn. He tossed a few pieces of charcoal onto the flames and then grabbed an old brass teakettle and hung it from a hook that dangled above the urn. "Come have some tea," said Lars. Suddenly his tone was much friendlier. "Your ship leaves in just over an hour and you must return before then. I know Vice Admiral Purcheezie well—she will leave even if you are not onboard."

"Will you give me my plant back?" asked Alfonso cautiously.

"I will," said Lars. "But first we must talk. I have much more to tell you."

Alfonso walked across the room and sat down facing Lars. The warmth of the fire felt good and for the first time in hours he relaxed a little.

"Tell me," Lars began, "have you received any training in the art of sleep trances?"

"Well, my uncle Hill—he's Dormian—he taught me this trick where I can fix a clock or clean my room by meditating before I go to sleep," explained Alfonso. "It works most of the time."

"Child's play," said Lars dismissively. "Any Dormian can do it. We all have enhanced agility, concentration, and strength in a sleep trance. That's one of the main reasons that we as a people have survived against such great odds over the centuries. Most Dormians, however, have little control over their powers. They may go to sleep hoping to sharpen their sword, but they end up mending their socks instead. They simply go wherever their sleep trance takes them."

"And most people in Dormia are like that?" asked Alfonso.

"All but the Dormian knights," replied Lars. "We Dormian knights are trained to shift at will between sleep trances and our waking state. In the span of twenty-one seconds, for example, I can complete three separate naps or sleep trances. In between these sleep trances, I wake up for two seconds at a time."

"Why would you want to do that?" asked Alfonso.

"So I can control what I am doing," replied Lars. "How do you think that I remembered the fight that we just had? I woke up dozens of times during that fight and contemplated what I wanted to do next. Like most Dormians, I do my best fighting and physical work when I'm in a sleep trance, but I do my best thinking when I'm awake. Dormian knights have the best of both worlds. I am constantly jumping in and out of sleep trances—fighting, thinking, fighting, thinking, fighting, thinking."

"I wish I could do that," Alfonso said.

"But you don't have to," replied Lars. "You can do something better." Lars removed the teakettle from its hook, and poured the piping hot water into two large clay mugs. He then reached into his jacket and pulled out a small sack of crushed mint leaves, which he sprinkled into the mugs. The warm, moist scent of mint soon wafted into their nostrils. "Drink up," said Lars. "This mint comes from my own small garden here on the iceberg."

"What can I do that's better?" asked Alfonso.

Lars leaned back and took a sip of hot tea. "Well," said Lars, "to begin with, your sleeping powers of agility, concentration, and strength are above average. That's why you performed so well in the skirmish we just had—even though you, like your uncle Hill, have no real training. However, because you are a Great Sleeper, even your basic skills are amazingly good. Those skills alone, however, aren't enough for you to succeed. Your real gift lies elsewhere. As a Great Sleeper, you can enter something called the hypnogogic state."

Lars stared at Alfonso, took another sip of tea, and continued.

"It's the state that exists between waking and sleeping," explained Lars. "Normal people and Dormians enter it for only the briefest of moments. Sometimes we enter it late at night or early in the morning. Normal people just feel groggy during these moments, but for the Great Sleeper, this is a time when incredible powers can be summoned. When you are in it, you will enjoy all the powers of sleep—and all the alertness of being awake—and all at once! There will be no need to vacillate between waking and sleeping as we knights do. You will be both asleep and awake at the same time. What's more, your eyes will remain firmly shut, and yet you will be able to see directly through your eyelids."

"Cool," said Alfonso. "How do I—"

"I'm not finished," snapped Lars. "There's more. The real magic of hypnogogia—the true value of being in that state—involves a special power of perception known as the delicate ear. Essentially, it heightens all of your senses, but especially your hearing. This power allows you to sense everything that happens in a room: the quiver of a finger on a trigger, the slightest rattle of a sword, the softest whisper, even the faintest smell of poison. You must learn to use the delicate ear to your advantage. This is crucial."

"Well, how do I do it?" asked Alfonso excitedly. "You have to teach me."

"I am afraid I will be of no use to you," said Lars. "I've entered hypnogogia for only a second at a time and I had no stomach for it. The main problem is that you are immediately overwhelmed with feedback. When I was still living in Dormia, I heard stories about a few errant knights who attempted to stay in hypnogogia for more than a few seconds. They lost their minds."

"Why?"

"Just think about it," replied Lars. "Imagine being in a world where every detail, however small, is as clear to you as a thunderclap—the beat of a mouse's heart a mile away or even the movement of each particle of dust as it swirls around a room—all the billions of movements that occur every second are plainly obvious to someone in hypnogogia. Only the Great Sleeper can filter all of this information. Without such a filter, hypnogogia is just a recipe for quickly and painfully losing your mind."

Lars paused. "You must learn quickly," he said finally. "Danger is bearing down upon you. You realize that you are being followed?"

"Yes," said Alfonso. "There's a black ship behind us. And there's this man with white eyes who's also been following us."

Lars nodded, as if he weren't in the least bit surprised.

"What do you know about the man with the white eyes?" asked Lars.

"Not much."

"Is he blind or can he see?"

"I assumed he was blind, but I'm not certain," replied Alfonso.

"You should find out—it is very important," said Lars. "Did he give you his name?"

"He calls himself Kiril," explained Alfonso.

"I have no idea who he is," said Lars. "But I suspect that he is in league with the Dragoonya, and that means that he is answerable to Nartam."

"Nartam?"

"Yes, he is the king of the Dragoonya," explained Lars. "Little is known of him for certain, but we know that Nartam was born a Dormian."

"A Dormian?"

"Nartam is a fallen Dormian," said Lars. "According to historians, he was a cruel child, but brilliant, and as a young man he committed the greatest crime that anyone can commit: he burned a leaf from the Founding Tree in the Dormian city of Dragoo."

Alfonso swallowed hard. He instantly thought back to the small leaf that they had burned the day before.

"Nartam didn't stop after one leaf—he eventually burned the entire tree for the ash that it creates," explained Lars. "You see, when a tree burns, it actually yields very little ash. A tree that weighs fifty tons and is as tall as this iceberg, for example, may produce only a few pounds of ash when burned. Perhaps Nartam intended to burn only part of the tree, but this didn't give him enough of what he wanted and so he burned the whole thing. Of course, without its tree, the city of Dragoo died soon thereafter. From that moment on, Nartam has continuously menaced all Dormian cities. He *needs* the ash. Those who possess it gain several temporary but extraordinary abilities: glimpses of the future, long-range vision, overwhelming strength, and a blooming of physical health. And for Dormians who use the ash there is an added benefit powerful enough to drive men mad: immortality. In fact, if taken in sufficiently large quantities, it can turn back the clock of time, making an old man young once more. The city of Dragoo was destroyed in the Dormian year 2386. Now, according to the Dormian calendar, it is the year 4920. That means Nartam is more than two thousand years old."

Lars's face clouded over in sadness. "His is a greedy way of life. He burns the trees so that he can live forever, but to do so he destroys the lives of all the Dormians who depend on the Founding Trees for that nourishment that it provides. There were once eleven cities of Dormia. Each of them was carefully hidden deep in the Ural Mountains. Yet one by one they perished either at the hands of Nartam and his Dragoonya or because for unknown reasons the Great Sleeper failed to appear. Only the capital city—Somnos—remains."

Lars stared intently at Alfonso. "It is to Somnos that you must deliver your plant, as fast as you possibly can," he said with quiet intensity. "The hatching of a bloom is triggered by Dormian autumn—the period during which a Founding Tree dies. The fact that you grew the Dormian bloom means that the Founding Tree of Somnos is dying. As I told you before, only your successful delivery of the bloom to Somnos will save that city."

Alfonso thought back to *McBridge's Book of Mythical Plants.* The book's definition of the bloom was correct. Somewhere in the middle of the desolate Ural Mountains, the last Dormian city was dying and only Alfonso's little plant could save it.

"Here's the thing," said Alfonso. "I have some coordinates where I think Somnos might be near, but I don't know how we'll get there. Is there a road or a trail that we can take?"

Lars shook his head. "If I knew the exact route back to Somnos, I probably would have tried to return home long ago." He stared at the fire. "I still remember the day I left with the other Wanderers. It was the month before my fourteenth birthday. A door opened in the mountain and I stepped into a howling wind filled with snow. I took three steps forward into the blizzard and then glanced over my shoulder, but the door had shut and no trace of it remained on the mountain rock. Though I had departed only seconds before, it was as if I had been gone forever."

A cold blast of wind poured in through one of the windows and Alfonso took a sip of the mint tea. He glanced at Lars and noticed a familiar look on Lars's face. It was a sad, wistful look—the look of a man who longs for his old, half-forgotten home. Alfonso had seen the same look many times on his father and on Uncle Hill.

The spell of the moment was suddenly broken by the sound of the *Success Story*'s foghorn.

Lars stood and looked out the window. "That's the vice admiral's final call," he said. "You and the bloom must board that ship."

Lars rushed down the stairs with Alfonso running just behind. Soon they were in front of the *Success Story*. Lars stopped, turned to Alfonso, and carefully removed the bloom from his cloak. "There is much more to say, but I'm afraid our time is gone," Lars said. "Good luck."

"Just one last question," blurted out Alfonso. He wondered briefly about the wisdom of what he was about to say, but he continued anyway: "The ash from the bloom. What happens if a non-Dormian uses it?"

Lars hesitated. He looked at Alfonso carefully. It was clear that Lars understood perfectly well why Alfonso was asking this question. Alfonso expected Lars to get angry, but he did not. Instead, he sighed heavily and shook his head.

"Your friend will go blind," said Lars.

"Blind?" said Alfonso incredulously. "You mean he won't be able to see anything?"

"Yes," said Lars. He leaned toward Alfonso and when he spoke, his voice was low and urgent. "When a Dormian uses the ash, his eyes go white—and his vision may be a bit blurry at times—but he can still see. When a non-Dormian uses the ash, however, his blindness is complete. That's why I asked you if Kiril was blind. I wanted to know if he was a Dormian traitor. But that's another matter altogether and we've run out of time to discuss such things. Your friend's blindness is regrettable, but the real problem is this: once his vision begins to disappear, the only way he will regain it is by burning the plant again and using more of the ash. And I assure you he will try to do just this. I don't care who this person is, he can no longer be trusted."

Alfonso felt his throat tighten. His heart began to beat rapidly. *How could he stop trusting Bilblox?* Bilblox and Hill were the only people whom he *could* trust. Besides, if Bilblox wanted that plant, there would be no stopping him. He shivered as if suddenly he remembered he was cold.

"Do you understand?" insisted Lars.

Alfonso nodded.

"Why don't you come with us?" pleaded Alfonso.

"I can't," said Lars. "I would only draw suspicion to you and you *must* not be followed. Besides, if you can master hypnogogia, your powers will far exceed mine. Now run—and don't stop until you reach Somnos!"

Alfonso stared back into Lars's steel gray eyes, and nodded. He took the bloom from the Dormian knight's outstretched hands and ran aboard the icebreaker.

CHAPTER 14

RACE TO THE POLAR ICE PACK

ON THE BRIDGE of the *Success Story,* Alfonso found Vice Admiral Purcheezie in a worried mood. "Things ain't lookin' good!" she muttered while steering the ship away from Lars's iceberg. "I saw a light on the water a couple miles away—I think it's that miserable black ship closin' in on us. I'm not sure what yer smugglin'—and I don't aim to know—but whatever it is, that ship is mighty desperate for it."

"What can I do?" Alfonso asked.

The vice admiral shook her head angrily. "We got other problems too," she said. "A bad winter storm is comin' our way, so I'm steerin' us into open water. Go tell yer friends. We've got nasty seas ahead."

By dawn, the wind was howling across the deck and rattling

the ship's old windows. Twenty-foot waves slammed against the side of the *Success Story*. Sleet began to fall from the sky and storm clouds closed in. The only good news was that they could no longer see the black ship pursuing them. To be certain of this, however, the vice admiral asked Alfonso to climb up the ship's skinny emergency mast to a small platform known as the eagle's nest. From this perch, which sat about thirty feet above the deck, it was usually possible to see quite some distance.

Alfonso climbed up the mast and into the eagle's nest. The sea looked incredibly rough. Waves rollicked in all directions and churned up eddies of foam that swirled around the ship. Below him, Alfonso could see Shamus rushing around the deck, tidying this and that and cinching down loose objects. Menacing black clouds covered the entire sky and it seemed as if the morning was turning back to night.

Suddenly, a far-away pinprick of light on the southern horizon drew Alfonso's attention. He squinted and concentrated, but saw nothing. Taking out an old monoscope from its holster on the eagle's nest, he looked again and focused on remaining still. After a minute of looking, he saw it: a dull but distinct bobbing light that revealed the unmistakable shape of the black warship.

Alfonso shouted down to Shamus and pointed at the warship with his monoscope. Shamus dropped his chores and ran to the heaving stern of the ship. The vice admiral joined him. Moments later, she bellowed for Alfonso to come down. Shamus sprinted off toward the engine room. Thick black smoke poured out of the *Success Story*'s two smokestacks. The deck rattled from the increased speed. By the time Alfonso climbed down from his perch, the *Success Story* had sped up to the point where walking or even standing on deck required firm handholds.

Alfonso clawed his way to the bridge, where the vice admiral—her eyes bloodshot from lack of sleep—was at the wheel. "Can we outrun that warship?" Alfonso asked.

The vice admiral shook her head. "That beast has twin screws, and we got only one. Can't go dodgin' them forever."

In a few hours, the entire crew except for Shamus, who was at the helm, gathered in the ship's dining area for an early dinner. No one ate much of the fried seal that Hellen prepared. Midway through dinner, the vice admiral lit up her pipe, took several long puffs, and announced matter-of-factly, "Well, the situation don't look good. That warship is drawin' closer and, if we both keep our present speeds, she'll be upon us in less than eight hours' time."

"Who's sailin' that black warship?" asked Bilblox.

"What's the matter with your eyes?" asked Hellen. "How come they've gone white?"

"Oh, my eyes . . ." stammered Bilblox. "Well, uhh . . ."

"It's just a case of temporary snow blindness from all the sun," interjected Hill.

"Hmm," said Hellen. "Can you see?"

"Not too well," replied Bilblox.

"Anyway," said the vice admiral, "as I was tellin' ya, those mercenaries or pirates that someone has hired to do their dirty work, oh, they're after us. Ya can be sure of that. And once they get us, they'll take what they want and sink the ship, probably with us on it." She let out a big sigh. "Somehow or another we need to get away. We got two options. The first is to keep goin' across the East Siberian Sea, through the Laptev Sea, and on to Barsh-yin-Binder. But if we do that, the black warship will catch us like a cat pouncin' on a mouse."

"What's our other option?" asked Bilblox.

A rather mischievous smile crept across the vice admiral's face. There was a long pause and everyone listened to the wind howling and the rain splattering heavily onto the wooden deck above.

"The other option," she said, "is that we pull out of the water and go over the ice."

"What? Are ya kiddin'?" inquired Bilblox.

"Is that possible?" asked Hill.

"'Course it is," snapped the vice admiral. "Hellen, have ya oiled the retractable skating blades recently?"

"What—those things?" replied Hellen with a laugh. "Not in decades!"

"Well, better get to it," said the vice admiral. "Shamus!" she shouted. "Due north, full steam ahead. We need to get to the pack ice in eight hours or less!"

After a few hours of fitful sleep, Alfonso woke up when it was still dark. Hill and Bilblox were already gone. Alfonso dressed quickly and exited the windmill. As soon as he stepped foot on the deck, he stopped in his tracks. His mouth hung open as he stared at the incredible scene. Massive icebergs surrounded them. Wind screamed across the deck. Icicles hung from every corner of the ship. Snow was falling so heavily that, at times, he could barely see anything at all. It was a blizzard like none he had ever encountered. Alfonso quickly covered his mouth and nose to keep out the falling snow and made his way to the mess hall below. Here he found everyone finishing their breakfasts and in the middle of a heated discussion.

"With all due respect, Vice Admiral," said Hill testily, "we've got a warship just behind us, we're in the Arctic Ocean in wintertime, and you're proposing that we pull a nautical maneuver that has never been done before? This seems foolhardy!"

Instead of being furious at such direct language, the vice admiral simply smiled. "Now, now, Lil' Hilly," she said, "don't ya get upset. It can be done, that's for sure. Right, Hellen?"

"Theoretically," said Hellen with a curt nod. "It's possible."

"Ya see, boys," said the vice admiral with a hearty laugh, "all ya need is some womanly courage! Lemme explain."

The vice admiral relit her pipe and in a dry, professorial tone gave her crew a little history lesson. She explained that back in the 1890s, when the *Success Story* was first built, it was considered a prototype—or the first ship of its kind—which meant that it came with a number of experimental gizmos. The most curious of these were two retractable steel blades that spanned the length of the ship. When resting on top of an ice field, these blades transformed the ship into a giant, double-bladed ice skate of sorts. Unfortunately, said the vice admiral, the device had been tried only once and ended in complete failure. The *Success Story* fell on its side and had to be towed to a dry dock for months of repairs. Since that time, the retractable skating blades had never been used. "So there ya have it," concluded the vice admiral with a cheery smile. "My great-grandpappy tried it once and failed. But I've been workin' on some calculations and I'm sure it'll work!"

It sounded ridiculous, but the vice admiral's wild confidence was infectious. Besides, what other choice did they have?

"How will it glide?" asked Alfonso. "I mean, what will power us along?"

"Sails!" replied the vice admiral merrily. "At this time of year, we regularly get winds of eighty knots or more 'round here. Even a small sail will move us like a jet engine, specially when we're on double ice-blades!"

"This I gotta see," said Bilblox with a roll of his white eyes.

"Oh, ya'll do more than see it," said the vice admiral. "If this is gonna work we'll need every ounce of yer strength, Bilblox." She tapped out her pipe onto the table. "All right, then, let's get goin'. We've got work to do before the *Success Story* starts skatin'."

On deck, everyone could see that the black warship had narrowed the distance to only about a half-mile. The ship was so close that Alfonso could clearly see its bow. It was a strange-looking ship, almost ghostlike in appearance and obviously larger than the *Success Story*. The only sign of people was two bundled-up figures dressed in fur coats and manning a large artillery gun that was pointed at them. One direct hit from this gun and the *Success Story* would be badly wounded. Using a monoscope, Alfonso repeatedly looked for any signs of Kiril, but it was impossible to tell if he was onboard.

Alfonso felt a bit too exposed on the deck and soon joined the vice admiral on the bridge. She was artfully weaving the *Success Story* around the icebergs. With each turn that she made, the vice admiral brought the ship as close to the floating hunks of ice as she dared. The warship failed to mimic these maneuvers and did not draw closer.

"Where is that blasted pack ice when we need it?" asked the vice admiral irritably. "Wait a minute . . . There it is—dead ahead!" She pointed out the window excitedly with her metal hook. Several miles in front of them was a solid crust of ice sitting on the horizon. It looked like a thick coat of vanilla frosting resting on the sea.

"You found it!" shouted Alfonso.

"Ya bet yer land-lovin' legs I did!" yelled the vice admiral. "Now get down below deck and help Bilblox and yer uncle get those skatin' blades ready!"

Alfonso dashed down the stairs leading to the mess hall and then continued all the way to the lowest level, where Hill and Bilblox were waiting. They stood in a small dingy hallway next to a wall panel with two sets of iron cranks. One crank was marked LEFT SKATING BLADE. The other was marked RIGHT SKATING BLADE. Above both cranks dangled a large sign that read OUT OF ORDER!

"I got a bad feelin' about this," whispered Bilblox.

"Don't worry," said Hill with a forced smile. "This ship is old but reliable."

Moments later the entire ship shuddered as if it too were having second thoughts about what the vice admiral was attempting to do. Outside, the seas were getting rougher.

"How are your eyes?" asked Hill.

"Blurry," replied Bilblox. "But I'm sure my vision will come back."

Alfonso shifted awkwardly, but said nothing.

"So what's the plan?" asked Bilblox.

"The vice admiral said to lower the skating blades," said Alfonso.

"Let's do it then," said Bilblox. "I'd just as soon get this over with."

Bilblox, Hill, and Alfonso all placed their hands on the LEFT SKATING BLADE crank and began pushing on it with all of their might. Slowly, the old, rusted mechanism began to turn. Beneath them they heard a loud creaking noise. "Good grief," grunted Hill. "This crank could use some oil." The three of them continued pushing on the crank for the next five minutes until they heard a giant thud. "I think that means the skate is locked into place," said Hill. "Either that or it's busted."

"Well," gasped Bilblox, "what do you say we get to work on the other one?"

Hill nodded.

It took ten minutes of backbreaking labor before they managed to lower the right skating blade. When this was done, they were thoroughly exhausted. Wearily, all three limped back up the stairs to the bridge, where they found the vice admiral yelling at the top of her lungs.

"For cryin' out loud we need more speed, Shamus!" she shrieked. "We ain't gonna make it if ya don't get this ship movin' faster. Shovel more coal into the furnace, for goodness sake, shovel *more* coal, ya good for nothin' Irishman!"

Shamus, who was downstairs in the ship's engine room, was now muttering so loudly that it really wasn't a mutter at all: "I'm trying, you senile blowhard—I'm trying!"

The vice admiral turned and saw Alfonso, Bilblox, and Hill staring out the front windshield of the ship. Directly in front of them, about a quarter of a mile away, was a wide slab of ice that marked the beginning of the polar ice pack.

"Finally, you're back," she said. "All right, lads, go find Hellen on the main deck and help her hoist up the sails. Quickly! This has to happen before we hit the ice or we'll get stuck."

The three of them hustled onto the main deck and helped Hellen hoist up two giant blue sails. The first sail hung from the ship's emergency mast; the other hung from one of the ship's smokestacks. The sails weren't especially tall, but they were exceedingly wide, and when they filled with wind they eclipsed the entire horizon.

Just as they had finished unfurling the sails, a hair-raising SCREEEEEEEEEECH reverberated throughout the ship. Alfonso plugged his fingers into his ears. Bilblox and Hill both winced. The only person who seemed completely unruffled was the vice admiral. "Don't worry!" she shouted to them from the bridge. "Those're the blades goin' on the ice!"

Howling wind poured into the round bellies of the sails. Thick black smoke poured out of the ship's smokestacks. The *Success Story* creaked awkwardly out of the water, like an old horse trying to stand. Water poured off the hull and splashed onto the ice below. The blades underneath the ship slid forward and the ship slid onto the ice. Improbably, the vice admiral's plan seemed to be working. Everyone cheered in celebration until they realized that the ship had stopped moving.

"What's goin' on?" called out the vice admiral from the bridge. "Why are we stopped?"

"We're stuck on a bump on the ice!" yelled Hellen as she peered over the side. "It's right about midship and it's holding us up like we're in the middle of a seesaw. Any minute now, we're gonna start rocking back and forth!"

Hellen was exactly right. Just seconds later, the entire ship started wobbling back and forth.

"Bilblox!" yelled the vice admiral. "Ya big lug! Get down there with some rope and help us out."

"Ya crazy? I can't pull this entire ship by myself," yelled Bilblox.

"Just give it a good yank," yelled the vice admiral. "That should be enough! Now get goin'!"

"I can barely see," protested Bilblox.

"Ya don't need to see," snapped the vice admiral. "Ya just need to pull!"

Bilblox nodded seriously, grabbed a large coil of rope tied to the front of the ship, and climbed down a rickety old ladder that clung to the side of the ship. Suddenly, everyone's attention was diverted back toward the water, where—not more than a hundred yards away—the black warship had suddenly reappeared out of the blizzard.

"Oh boy," muttered the vice admiral. "This is gonna be close."

CHAPTER 15

HYPNOGOGIA

BILBLOX groped his way down the ladder that was affixed to the side of the ship, and as he climbed, the black warship rotated slightly to get a clear shot at the *Success Story. Ba-boom!* The warship let loose with a thunderous volley from its onboard gun. Seconds later, the rounds splashed in the water a hundred feet behind the *Success Story.*

"Hurry up, Bilblox!" yelled the vice admiral. "They're not gonna miss us next time!"

Down on the ice, Bilblox quickly assessed the situation. Blurry though his vision was, he still saw what needed to be done: he had to pull the entire ship forward just a few inches. Of course, under normal circumstances, there was no way that a single man could pull a ship that weighed hundreds of tons.

Yet, as it now rested, the ship was balanced in such a way that one good tug on the rope might effectively tip the scales and move the vessel down off the bump. In situations like this, sometimes the smallest of things can make the biggest difference. It was like the old story of the straw that broke the camel's back, and Bilblox was the straw that would move the *Success Story.*

Bilblox ran away from the ship until the rope was taut. He then began pulling on it with all of his might. "Arrrrrrrgh!" he yelled as he put every last ounce of strength into the effort. "Arrrrrrrgh!"

The ship slid forward an inch. The black warship fired again at the *Success Story.* This time, the gunshot whistled only feet above the upper deck of the ship and peppered both the sail and mast with iron pellets. Bilblox gave the rope another massive pull. "Arrrrrrrgh!" he yelled. His legs trembled and he felt his face go red. The entire ship moved forward a solid four inches. The bow tipped down, and the *Success Story* began to move.

They were over the bump!

Clumps of ice and snow shot out from under the *Success Story*'s skates and, within what seemed like only seconds, the ship had picked up considerable speed. Bilblox sprinted for the ladder on the side of the ship and took hold. The boat continued to accelerate as the wind filled the sails and the skates slid cleanly along the ice. The vice admiral let out a wild, whooping cry of joy. Hill, Alfonso, and Hellen embraced one another. Shamus wept. Bilblox held onto the side of the ship for dear life and carefully climbed up the rickety wooden rungs of the ladder. The *Success Story* whizzed north, leaving the mysterious black warship far behind.

For the first few days on the ice, everyone spent a lot of time just staring around, amazed that they were on a ship that was skating steadily across the polar icecap. The ice wasn't the dull-looking stuff that floats on the surface of cold drinks. The vice admiral had done her homework well. The ice fields that they were skating across were made of thick old sea ice, the type that takes on a wondrous blue-green color. It wasn't smooth like new ice, but the bumps weren't large enough to be uncomfortable. The air had become much colder and soon the deck and every other exposed piece of the ship grew a thick layer of frost. Shamus brought up Russian polar jackets and thick Eskimo mukluks for everyone to wear. It was so cold that they began wearing them even at breakfast and dinner.

Thanks to all the ice, the bloom was in great health. It was still about the same size as when they had left World's End, but the leaves were green and vibrant, and the colors of the flower became more intense. Still, every time Alfonso checked on the bloom, which was at least once a day, he couldn't help glancing at the little scar on the stem of the plant where they had snipped off a leaf and burned it. He felt uneasy every time he looked at it. Lars had made it quite clear that burning the leaf of a Founding Tree or a Dormian bloom was "the greatest crime that anyone could commit." After all, this was what Nartam had done! The very thought of this made Alfonso's gut tighten into a knot.

Alfonso's real concern, however, was Bilblox. Just as Lars had predicted, Bilblox was beginning to go blind. The longshoreman couldn't see anything for several hours each day. Bilblox stuck to the story that this was simply a result of snow blindness—a temporary form of blindness caused by the sun reflecting off the ice and snow. Of course, Alfonso knew that this wasn't true. Again and again, he recalled exactly what Lars had told him: "Once his vision begins to disappear, the only way he will regain it is by burning the plant again and using more of the ash . . . I don't care who this person is, he can no longer be trusted." Alfonso wanted to share this information—whether it was true or not—with both Hill and Bilblox. It seemed like the right thing to do. After all, they were all in this together. The problem was this: Alfonso didn't want to make Bilblox angry or give him any ideas about burning the plant. In truth, Alfonso wasn't sure that Bilblox could be trusted; and so he decided to remain silent on the subject of Bilblox's blindness.

In the end, Alfonso resolved that he should at least tell Hill the gist of what Lars had said. So, one afternoon when the two of them were alone in the windmill, Alfonso explained what had happened on the iceberg. Hill listened with rapt attention as Alfonso retold the story of Nartam and how he was a fallen Dormian. Hill became even more excited upon learning that Alfonso—*his very own nephew*—was a legendary Great Sleeper of Dormia. "I knew there was something special about you!" said Hill gleefully. "I guess your father did too—or at least his sleeping-self did. That's why he carved that medallion in his sleep. I only wish Leif were here to see all of this. It's fantastic! You'll be famous in Dormia. You'll be the sort of person that kids learn about in their sleeping classes."

"Sleeping classes?" inquired Alfonso. "What are you talking about?"

"I'm talking about school," said Hill somewhat defensively. "I don't recall much from my school days in Somnos, but I do remember focusing on the basics at an early age: reading, mathematics, and sleeping."

Alfonso sat up in his chair. "You had a class in sleeping?"

"Of course," Hill replied. "We're a land of sleepers, after all. We took it quite seriously."

"What do you remember from sleeping class?" Alfonso asked. "Maybe something can help me."

"I don't remember much," replied Hill with a dejected sigh. "I remember the lovely redhead who sat in front of me in level one sleeping. I recall our teacher, Dr. Soskis, who was an awful snorer. And I remember something called the ten-second counting game . . . no, wait . . . the ten-second drill . . . yes, that's what it was. The ten-second drill. If my memory rings true, the idea was that you counted to ten, and that with each number you got a bit drowsier, so that by ten, you were totally asleep. I prefer my one hundred and eight chants, but then again I was never interested in sleep classes anyway."

"Why ten seconds?" Alfonso persisted.

"That was the starting point," replied Hill. "With practice, you could stuff the ten-second period of falling asleep into eight seconds, or six or even less. I was never much good at it, but that shouldn't stop you."

"I'll try it!" declared Alfonso.

He leaned back in his chair, closed his eyes, and began counting to ten. He said each number slowly, as if he didn't want to let it go. It didn't work. He succeeded in getting drowsy, but not in falling asleep. So he tried it again, only this time he continued counting all the way to twenty, and by the time he said *seventeen* he managed to fall asleep. He spent the next few hours working on this drill and, eventually, he was able to fall asleep exactly as he muttered the word *ten.*

"You really seem to have mastered this," said Hill proudly at the end of the day. "Here, let me have a try. I bet you I can still do it." He sat down, closed his eyes halfway, and began to count out loud. Alfonso watched silently. By the seventh second, Hill's head drooped and Alfonso was sure he would make it to ten right on time. At eight, Hill's jaw opened. At nine, however, something unexpected happened. Bilblox, who had spent the day in the mess hall, burst in through the front door of the windmill. Hill had just finished saying *nine* when the door clattered open. Hill's reaction to the noise was completely bizarre: he leapt to his feet and crouched low to the ground like a panther about to pounce. Hill's eyes fluttered heavily—not quite awake and not yet asleep.

"Uncle Hill?" said Alfonso.

Hill twirled to face Alfonso in a blindingly fast movement. His entire face quivered with excitement, as if every muscle was poised for action. A second later, his body relaxed into a normal position and his eyes opened fully.

"Wh-wh-what happened?" muttered Hill. He looked around the room and saw Bilblox standing in the doorway.

"You!" he said. "I heard you kick open the door and then everything was happening at once, like my mind was drowning." He shook his head to clear it and turned to Alfonso. "What happened? Did I fall asleep?"

"I'm not sure," replied Alfonso. In truth, it wasn't clear whether Hill had been awake or asleep. Rather suddenly, Alfonso recalled his conversation with Lars, who spoke of Great

Sleepers and their ability to balance between waking and sleeping. Could Hill have stumbled into hypnogogia?

"Bilblox, could you do that again?" Alfonso asked. "I'm going to count to ten and when I say 'nine,' I want you to slam the front door."

"This is ridiculous," said Hill.

"Let me just try it," replied Alfonso. He looked at Bilblox, who nodded that he was ready.

Alfonso sat back down and made sure the area around him was clear. He began the count, focusing not only on the numbers, but also on the spaces between them. At six, his eyes grew heavy and his muscles began to relax. His legs and arms jerked in preparation for sleep. At seven, his eyes closed halfway and his head drooped toward his chest. At eight, his mind began to shut down all conscious thought and his lips could only barely mouth the word *nine.* Then, *wham!* Bilblox slammed the front door. Alfonso's legs spasmed and he fell from his chair.

As he lay there, Alfonso discovered he had entered another world. It was a world where the slightest action was as clear as a hammer blow to his head. He heard Hill approaching, his footsteps loud on the wooden floor, his voice concerned, but then he also heard Hill's shoelaces rubbing against each other, the scratching of Hill's big toe against the inner wall of his sneakers, the rumbling of hunger in Bilblox's stomach, the vice admiral's pen scratching along a blank sheet of paper twenty feet below them, a peeler in Hellen's hand slicing off potato skin, the awful scratch of the skating blades cutting into the ice, the creak of the snow as it shifted under the *Success Story,* the slow heartbeat of thousands of semihibernating fish, and even the distant, low calls of two humpback whales. These noises and billions of others washed over Alfonso like a tidal wave and he felt as if his brain itself were crumbling like a sandcastle in the surf.

Slowly, Alfonso opened his eyes. He could see everything: the dust that swirled around him in a frenzy, the tiny wads of dirt underneath Hill's fingernails, each woven thread on Bilblox's red plaid shirt, and the beady eyes of an ant hiding in a dark corner of the windmill.

Confronted with all this intense stimulation, Alfonso felt disoriented and dizzy. He couldn't shut down his ears or eyes, so instead he tried to focus. He knew he was in danger of throwing up his breakfast. He staggered toward the stove and looked above it at the mantel, where he saw an hourglass slowly dropping grains of sand from the upper chamber to the lower. Bilblox had found this hourglass under one of the beds and they had been using it to help keep time. Alfonso now brought all of his concentration to bear on this device. In his highly alert state, it was easy to look at the hourglass and see each individual grain of sand as it passed through the narrow opening in the middle and fell into the lower chamber. Gradually, the nausea in Alfonso's stomach began to dissipate. He forced himself to concentrate as hard as he could. He imagined that the world was made up of only him and the hourglass. It was hard to do, but eventually the other noises and sights began to diminish until they were only a murmur in the background. Still, it took massive concentration. He was holding back an ocean with only the power of his mind and any letup would cause him to drown. The effort proved unbearably difficult. Alfonso quickly became exhausted. The world spun around him, and he fell onto the floor, unconscious.

CHAPTER 16

SKATING ON THIN ICE

ALFONSO woke up sometime later, sputtering, as freezing water poured over him. He opened his eyes. Hill and Bilblox crowded above him, their faces etched with concern.

"Alfonso?" Hill said slowly. "Are you all right?"

Alfonso nodded weakly.

"Ya've been passed out for hours. We've been tryin' to wake ya up, but nothin' was workin'," said Bilblox.

Alfonso took a deep breath of air and then exhaled. Slowly, he came to his senses. The first thing he noticed was how incredibly still the ship seemed. Maybe it was just an aftereffect of the trance he had been in.

"Wh-what's going on?" he asked.

"There's a problem on the ice," replied Bilblox. "We had to stop."

As soon as Alfonso could stand on his own two feet, he joined the rest of the crew in the ship's mess hall. Alfonso still felt shaky from his jaunt into hypnogogia, but he was desperately curious to see why the *Success Story* had come to a stop. It was clear that they were nowhere near Barsh-yin-Binder. When he glanced out the front door of the windmill, all Alfonso could see was miles and miles of pack ice.

"Ah, there y'are!" said the vice admiral. "Fine time to wake up! Just look at the mess we've run into." She used her good hand to unfurl a large map on the billiards table. It was of the entire North Pole region. Using one of her old, gnarled fingers, the vice admiral pointed to a section of sea that said "Presumed to be solid ice in winter."

"What does 'presumed to be solid ice' mean?" asked Alfonso.

"It means we're in trouble because we don't know what's ahead of us," snapped the vice admiral. She explained that, a few hours ago, they had come upon an expanse of open water, which appeared to be at least fifty miles across. They couldn't float across because they didn't want to risk doing another water-to-ice transition. From the eagle's nest Shamus had seen a number of ice-filled pathways that spider-webbed across the open water ahead of them. The problem was this: they had no idea which one of these icy pathways would lead them all the way across the water to the solid ice on the other side. "So ya see, it's kind of like a maze," said the vice admiral. "And we need to find which pathway is the right one to take."

"How will we do that?" asked Alfonso.

"That's where ya come in," said the vice admiral. "We need a higher perspective on things. Hellen remembered that we have an old hot-air balloon in the cargo hold. Arctic explorers have been usin' balloons like these since the days of Amundsen and Scott. Hellen is down there now getting it ready for you."

"For me? I just woke up and I still don't feel good."

"Too bad," the vice admiral curtly replied. "Yer the only one light enough. As I mentioned, it's a very old hot-air balloon. We'll need ya to go up in it and sketch a map of the best route to take. Think ya can do it?"

"I don't think so," said Alfonso.

"Oh, I'm certain ya can," said the vice admiral. "Besides, ya don't have a choice—either ya do it or we all freeze to death out here."

Everyone soon gathered on the deck around the steadily inflating hot-air balloon. A makeshift stove dangled above the tiny wicker basket that would hold Alfonso. Shamus shoveled coal into the stove as they watched puffs of smoke emerge from a long, skinny funnel that went into the actual balloon. The funnel was filling the patchwork balloon with the warm air that would, in theory, make the whole contraption rise.

Hellen commanded Alfonso to climb into the wicker basket. A rope tied to the basket would allow them to guide the balloon up and then pull it back down after Alfonso finished with his observations. The vice admiral handed Alfonso a pad and pencil.

"Just tug on the rope when you're finished," said Hellen with a smile. "And we'll pull you down 'fore you know it."

"Okay," said Alfonso as he climbed into the wicker basket. He tried to sound confident. "That sounds easy enough."

Once seated inside the basket, Alfonso raised his hand and

gave a thumbs-up sign. Shamus released the rope. The balloon shot up. Alfonso sat in the bottom of the basket and held on tight as the wind whistled through the wicker. The balloon seemed even more unsteady and fragile than it looked when tethered to the ship. It bounced wildly as the wind gusted. Several embers from the stove landed on the wicker and burned for a few seconds before dying out. One landed on Alfonso's head and burned away a small patch of his hair before he managed to get it out.

Eventually, the balloon jerked to a stop and quivered there, held in place only by the long, old rope that was connected to the ship. Alfonso prayed that the rope wouldn't snap. He stood up carefully and shivered as the fierce wind tore at his clothes. Dark gray clouds hovered just above the balloon. He took out his monoscope and looked over the vast field of ice and water below him. Instantly he knew that his task was next to impossible. Strips of ice zig-zagged everywhere across the open water, but there was no telling whether they were stable enough to support the weight of the ship.

At that moment, a terrifying gust of wind struck the balloon. Alfonso screamed as the wicker basket went sideways. He grabbed hold of a rope and felt his stomach drop. After swaying crazily for a few seconds, the basket steadied and Alfonso let out a sigh of relief. He sank to the floor of the basket and looked around in confusion. Everything was gone: his extra pair of gloves, a sandwich, the pencil, the pad of paper, and worst of all, the monoscope. Miserable and freezing cold, Alfonso buried his head in his hands.

He had failed.

Alfonso stared blankly at the wall of the basket. It had begun to snow again, and through the holes in the wicker, Alfonso could see light flakes swirling around with the wind. In one area of the basket's wall, there was an opening just large enough for one flake at a time to squeeze inside. It reminded him of the narrowest part of the hourglass, which allowed only one particle of sand at a time to fall. Alfonso lifted his head. Maybe if he entered hypnogogia, he'd have a better chance of finding a route through the ice. But how could he enter that state? Of course, he could do the ten-second drill, but Bilblox wasn't around to interrupt him at the count of nine. He needed to improvise a new solution. Then it came to him.

Alfonso made himself as comfortable as possible in the bottom of the basket and began the count. At five, he raised his arms above his head; at six, he felt drowsy; at seven, his mind went blank; at eight, his entire body relaxed; and at nine, his arms flopped down to his side and smacked against his legs, giving him a good jolt. The jolt worked perfectly and Alfonso immediately entered hypnogogia.

Sensations flooded Alfonso's mind and, for a second, he felt both disoriented and nauseous. He was bombarded with stimuli of all kind—the whistling of the wind, the creaking of the wicker basket, the smell of each burning chunk of coal, and the incredible, beautiful complexity of every snowflake as it fluttered past. He had to focus. He had to concentrate on the individual snowflakes as they shimmied through the minute hole in the wicker basket. With fierce determination, he did the same exact thing that he'd done with the hourglass: he focused on each particle as it squeezed through the narrow opening. He focused on snowflake after snowflake after snowflake—until his concentration was so tight that he felt as if all of his powers of perception were being channeled into a single laser beam that he could point anywhere he wanted to. He was now ready to study the ice below.

When he finally peered over the side of the basket, Alfonso noticed the hundreds of paths that could be taken and, in the blink of an eye, he identified the three paths that spanned all the way across the water. Then he listened. He listened to the sound of the ice as it bent, creaked, and cracked. These soft, almost nonexistent sounds, which would mean nothing to a normal person, told the half-awake, half-asleep Alfonso exactly how thick each of the three paths were. He knew immediately that, of the three paths, the southernmost one was the best. No sooner had he made this realization than exhaustion passed over him like a wave. He grabbed the rope to tug on it, but it was too late. He slumped unconscious to the floor.

Below, on the ship's deck, everyone waited for the tug that never came. Finally, the vice admiral gave the order to pull in the balloon. Hill and Bilblox could barely breathe. What had happened?

The instant that the balloon touched down, both of them ran to the basket and carried Alfonso out. They checked his pulse. It was slow but steady. Alfonso was alive, although his skin was pale and cold to the touch. They rushed him inside.

That night, in the ship's mess, the mood at dinner was grim. Hill, Bilblox, Shamus, Hellen, and the vice admiral merely picked at their food. Alfonso lay asleep in a corner, on a cot, wrapped in a cocoon of heavy wool blankets. He was now running a high fever and shivering uncontrollably. To make matters worse, Alfonso had returned without a map.

Bilblox eventually gave up on dinner. He wiped his mouth, stood up, and stumbled across the room to check on Alfonso. His eyes had become worse, and he had to grope with his hands to find his way. Very gently, Bilblox ran his hands over Alfonso to see if the boy was still shivering. "You better have a look at Alfonso," said Bilblox nervously. "There's something definitely wrong with him."

The entire party rushed over. Alfonso appeared to be fast asleep. His entire body was resting except for his right arm, which was extended up and fluttering wildly, like a bird caught on a string.

"Why's he doin' that?" asked Bilblox nervously. "What's wrong?"

"I have no idea," said Hellen. "It looks like his hand is having some kind of spasm."

"Darn it!" said the vice admiral. "I never should have sent him up there."

"No, wait, he's okay!" exclaimed Hill. "Get a pencil and paper!"

Hellen shot Hill a puzzled look, but indulged his request and found a stubby pencil and a piece of tissue paper lying in a drawer. Hellen handed both items to Hill.

"You got real paper?" he asked.

"I'll have to look for it," she said.

Hill shook his head. "No time—this will have to do." He tiptoed toward Alfonso and maneuvered the pencil into his grip. Hill then grabbed a serving tray, placed the tissue paper on it, and moved it within range of Alfonso's outstretched arm. Immediately, Alfonso began to write. His movements were quick, but incredibly precise and so delicate that the tissue never tore. In less than a minute, he was done. The pencil fell from his grasp and his arm returned to his side. He began to snore softly.

Hill turned and presented the tissue to everyone else. It was clearly a route across a narrow pathway of ice—complete with latitude, longitude, and a small direction finder indicating north, south, east, and west.

"Holy smokestacks!" said Shamus.

"No jostlin'!" commanded the vice admiral. "One good breeze and that tissue is torn through." She took the tissue map from Hill and placed it safely within the pages of a nearby book, the massive *Advanced Encyclopedia of Surgical Practice,* 1860 edition.

"Unbelievable," muttered the vice admiral. She then ordered Hellen and Shamus to prepare the ship. "We've got our route," she announced happily. "And we're leavin' tomorrow mornin' at first light."

The following day, Vice Admiral Purcheezie navigated the *Success Story* according to Alfonso's hand-drawn map. They crept through an intricate series of turns and twists, usually with water on both sides. By the time they successfully arrived back on the solid ice pack, everyone was exhausted and in no mood to celebrate, even though Alfonso had woken up and was feeling much better. With time, though, they began to relax. It was the start of a seven-day period of blissful monotony.

Although the temperature was still ferociously cold, the sun shone during the day, and at night the sky glowed with billions of stars. They marveled at the northern lights, which shimmered in the evening and put on shows that lasted for hours. Everybody went on the deck and stayed there despite the cold. Rays of light blue, green, purple, and orange twisted in front of them, appearing and reappearing like ghosts. It was magical. Alfonso had seen the northern lights before, but never like this, when they took over the entire night sky.

The only problem that cropped up during this time involved Bilblox's eyesight or lack thereof. He was steadily going blind. There were occasional moments when his vision returned, but those moments were becoming less frequent. Meanwhile, the vice admiral had exhausted every known remedy for snow blindness and none had worked. It was becoming increasingly apparent that Bilblox's condition was *not* related to the snow. It was undoubtedly the ash.

One evening, Alfonso returned to the windmill and discovered Bilblox crawling on the floor with Hill's magnifying glass in his hand.

"What are you doing?" asked Alfonso.

"Oh, uh, well, er, nothin'," stammered Bilblox. "My eyesight's come back for a few minutes, so I decided to look for somethin'."

"What were you looking for?" asked Alfonso.

Bilblox shrugged awkwardly.

"What is it?"

Bilblox sighed. "I'm lookin' to see if any of that purple ash might still be around here, maybe stuck in the cracks or somethin'," said Bilblox. "I dunno, I figured it was worth a shot. Ya know, it might help my eyesight."

"I don't think that's such a good idea," said Alfonso cautiously. "I mean, you shouldn't use that powder anymore."

"Easy for ya to say," said Bilblox with a sigh. "Ya ain't the one who's goin' blind!"

At breakfast on their seventh day of steady sailing, the vice admiral announced they'd soon be leaving the pack ice. They were only two days steaming from Barsh-yin-Binder. The news jolted them. Reluctantly, their thoughts turned to Barsh-yin-Binder, the city that Shamus described as "evil to the core."

"Vice Admiral," said Bilblox, "is the city really as bad as they say it is?"

"Well," she replied, "it's a strange place, that's for sure. It's a former British colony so most of the folks speak English. Truth is, though, the British gave up on the place pretty quickly. There's nothin' to speak of in the city itself—nothing but trouble, backwards people, and a whole lot of thieves. Ya'll see soon enough. It's a place where time stopped 'round 1850. Ya won't find a radio, or a light bulb, or a single motor car in the whole city. The only good part is that the city's reputation scares away enough respectable types, so it's a good place for smugglers to meet and do a bit of business. That's the only reason I'm here."

The *Success Story* easily transitioned from the ice to the water, and two days later, in the early afternoon, they arrived just up the coast from Barsh-yin-Binder. For the first time in weeks, they saw land, although it wasn't much different from the ice because it was also covered with snow. The vice admiral announced that she had some business to do with a smuggler in Barsh-yin-Binder. She also planned a hunting trip. Once this business was done, she would return to Fort Krasnik.

"If yer back from yer wanderin' by then, yer welcome to come with me," said the vice admiral. "Otherwise, I'm afraid yer on your own. I can't imagine ya'll want to stay around here any longer than a few weeks."

Alfonso shot his uncle a worried look. The date wheel on Hill's watch was down to 19. They had less than three weeks to find Somnos.

"Trust me," said Hill. "We are going to be as quick as we can."

When the *Success Story* finally pulled into harbor just outside Barsh-yin-Binder, a dark mood hung over the ship. Everyone gathered on deck. Hill was wearing the top hat that contained the Dormian bloom. The vice admiral eyed the hat suspiciously but said nothing. Hellen nodded curtly and left to help Bilblox prepare the lifeboat that they would row to shore. A few minutes later, all was ready. Everybody shook hands and tried to smile, but it wasn't an easy goodbye. The vice admiral gave them a sack of gold coins for Barsh-yin-Binder. "Take it," she said gruffly but with emotion. "It should more than cover yer expenses."

As the three adventurers clambered into the lifeboat, the vice admiral reminded them to hurry back. The *Success Story* wouldn't stay near Barsh-yin-Binder any longer than was absolutely necessary.

They nodded, reluctantly waved goodbye, and pushed away from the ship. Under Bilblox's steady pulling, the lifeboat made good progress and soon the *Success Story* was no longer visible. Evening fell quickly, as it always does in the northern regions in the winter. The moon began its slow ascent across the sky, lighting up the gray hairs in Hill's mustache and illuminating Bilblox's ghostly white eyes.

CHAPTER 17

BARSH-YIN-BINDER

ALFONSO strained to see through the inky darkness of Barsh-yin-Binder's harbor. He soon noticed a few docks, but they looked abandoned. The only ship visible in the entire harbor was a barely floating steamship that looked about as old and torn apart as the *Nyetbezkov* in Fort Krasnik. On its deck a battle was taking place—a gang of at least twenty sailors was fighting with fists and daggers. At one point, a man fell overboard and hit the water only a few feet away from their rowboat. The man was laughing violently. In one of his clenched fists he held a razor-sharp dagger. He continued to cackle and snort until the water lapped above his head and he sank beneath. No one aboard the ship even seemed to notice the man's drowning and the small rowboat carrying Alfonso, Hill, and Bilblox slipped past undetected.

Bilblox rowed them toward a remote corner of the harbor, where several rundown docks jutted out into the water. Alfonso surveyed the view in all directions. The city's only visible landmark was a darkened castle that loomed in the distance.

"Bilblox, pull us into that dock at the very end!" commanded Hill in a hard whisper.

Bilblox turned around to get a better look. He blinked furiously into the darkness. It was obvious that he could see nothing at all.

"Don't worry about it, my friend," said Hill apologetically. "I'll row us in the rest of the way." The two men switched places and within minutes they bumped lightly against a dilapidated dock. It was nothing more than a few pieces of rotten wood sticking up from the water.

They secured the rowboat to the sturdiest piece of wood they could find and entered the knee-high water just a foot or two from the shore. It felt like liquid ice. All three hurried to get out of the water and stumbled onto solid land for the first time since leaving Fort Krasnik.

Little did they realize that they had landed in the old Slave District of Barsh-yin-Binder, which was without question the poorest and most dangerous part of that ill-fated city. Rats were everywhere, scampering beneath their feet and nibbling at their boots. Whimpering old men and women dressed in rags limped past. Several small fires burned in partially destroyed buildings. The smell of rotting food wafted through the air.

And far down the street, several wild dogs were fighting over the carcass of a dead horse.

"Where on earth are we?" asked Bilblox. "It smells awful."

Before anyone could reply, they heard the approaching sound of hundreds of hooves clattering against the cobblestone street. There was another sound too. It was an eerie *swooshing,* as if thousands of feathers were fluttering madly in the wind. In the next instant, the hordes of rats were gone. So too were the old beggars dressed in rags. The streets were now completely empty. Hill and Alfonso looked at each other, their eyes wide with worry. A high-pitched voice called to them through the darkness: "Hide over here with me if you value your lives, good sirs!"

"Let's go!" said Alfonso.

They ran across the street to an alleyway where they found the person who had called to them—a girl, perhaps thirteen years old, standing in the shadows. She stepped into the middle of the alley and a narrow beam of moonlight illuminated her face. It was filthy, covered in dirt and grime, but her eyes glittered darkly and her hair was a fine, golden blond. She wore a heavy fur robe so caked in mud it looked like it might have been formerly used as a doormat. In her hand, she held a dagger with a shriveled, smoking tomato skewered on the tip. Behind her the remnants of a fire crackled.

"Keep your lips sealed when the horsemen pass," whispered the girl. "They will gladly kill us just for the pleasure of it."

The sound of the horses grew louder and instinctively all of them stepped backwards, deeper into the darkness of the alley. Bilblox tripped on a rock, bumped into Hill, and fell heavily. In the commotion, the top hat fell off Hill's head, hit the ground with a dull thud, and began to roll into the street.

"The bloom!" yelled Alfonso.

The girl darted out, snatched up the hat, and promptly disappeared into the shadows of a dock on the other side of the street. Then the horsemen came. They were fierce-looking men, dressed in a leather armor that was covered with feathers. The feathers made a strange flapping noise that sounded as if thousands of birds of prey were swooping in for the kill. The horsemen were all armed with either swords or lances, and some had both. All of them wore helmets with sharp pointy beaks. There were at least fifty of them and they passed together as a single group so massive that it created its own swirling wind.

As far as Alfonso was concerned, the only thing louder than the pounding of the horses' hooves was the sound of his heart, which was throbbing in his ears. Even Bilblox, who never seemed to be scared of anything, clutched Alfonso's shoulder tightly as the horsemen passed. Finally, when the last horseman had disappeared, Hill dashed out into the street to get the top hat.

"Get back in the alley, good sir! And pray stay there until I say otherwise," hissed the girl from the far side of the street. Hill hesitated, then nodded and retreated back into the alley. For a minute no one moved or said anything. Eventually, the girl called to them. "Sirs! We're safe now!" She walked casually into the middle of the street, holding the top hat in her arms.

Hill grabbed the hat from her, checked quickly to make sure the bloom was still inside, and placed the hat back on his head.

"Who were those horsemen?" he asked.

"They were Dragoonya," replied the girl, as if this was the stupidest question that anybody had ever asked her. "Didn't you see their armor with all those feathers? Who else dresses like that?"

"That's what I was afraid of," said Hill. "What are they doing here in Barsh-yin-Binder?"

The girl gave Hill a puzzled look.

"My good sirs, do you know *anything* about this place?" she asked. "The Dragoonya control this city!"

Hill's face turned a sickly white. "Wh-what do you mean?" he asked.

The girl shook her head in amazement. "The Dragoonya are *in charge here,*" said the girl, who spoke with a precise British accent. "Of course, we have a Guild of Merchants, but the Dragoonya sit in the castle, and are the real authority."

"The Dragoonya control Barsh-yin-Binder?" muttered Hill. "But, how . . . I don't believe it . . . How is it that I have no memory of this place? I must have passed through here as a boy but I don't remember any Dragoonya . . ." He stared in anguish at Alfonso. "Have I led us into a trap?"

Alfonso said nothing. All he could think of was Kiril's warning back in Fort Krasnik: *This man who professes to be your uncle will deliver you directly into the hands of the enemy. And then he'll blame all of his missteps on his faulty memory. I have foreseen the entire thing.*

"Well what do ya wanna do?" asked Bilblox. "Maybe we oughta head back to the ship. If this is a trap, we need to regroup and put in someplace else. We can bypass the city, right?"

"I don't think so," said Alfonso. "We need supplies. Where else are we going to get them? No, we've just got to get in and out of this city as quickly as possible."

"That's right," concluded Hill. "We need only a few things, like a map and winter supplies . . ." He looked around the desolate area. "But first we need to get off these streets."

He turned to the girl. "Is there a place to sleep nearby?" he asked. "We'll pay you for your help."

The girl smiled. "I know this city as well as anyone," she said. "My fee is four gold coins a day. It is a bit steep, but you will have my undivided attention and loyalty." She looked at Hill, who nodded.

"Excellent choice, gentlemen! Come with me." She started up the street in the same direction as the Dragoonya had gone minutes before.

"Why are we trustin' her?" Bilblox muttered. "It ain't right. She'll cut our throats just like anyone else."

"Do you have other suggestions?" Hill asked. "We have to find shelter, and I don't see anyone else here. We either follow her, go back to the ship, or strike off on our own."

"What do you think, Alfonso?" Bilblox asked.

Alfonso said nothing. He looked at the girl, who was standing about ten feet away and waiting for them to follow her. She wore a tired but eager expression on her face.

Alfonso sighed. "I agree with Uncle Hill," he said. "Let's go along with her for a little while. If she had wanted to rob us, she could've done it already." He walked toward her.

"What's your name?" he asked.

She stood up straight and stuck out her hand. "The name is Resuza," she said. "And I am indeed pleased to meet you. Your uncle looks familiar. Is he a frequent visitor to these parts?"

"No," said Alfonso grimly. "I don't think so."

They started walking down the empty streets.

"Where exactly are ya takin' us?" asked Bilblox.

"The Prince Binder," replied Resuza in a confident tone. "If you can afford it, it's the only decent hotel in town—a fine resting place and eminently comfortable."

Alfonso stopped. "We probably shouldn't go to a hotel," he said. "We don't want to raise any . . . suspicions."

Resuza laughed. "Come, Master Alfonso! A group of three strangers sleeping someplace *other* than the Prince Binder would raise great suspicions. Indeed, the hotel is the only safe place for strangers in this city. You will see."

For the next half-hour or so, the four of them trudged through snowy streets hemmed in on both sides by high stone walls. Behind the walls were houses that were either abandoned or in serious disrepair. They could see caved-in roofs, collapsed doorways, and darkened windows. Barsh-yin-Binder looked like a city that had fallen upon very hard times.

As they walked, Resuza explained to the group that the Prince Binder Hotel was located in the Trawpoy, the city's best neighborhood. The name came from an ancient tongue and meant "deep caverns," which is exactly what the Trawpoy was—a series of deep caverns nestled beneath the city. In ancient times, when the city was under siege, everyone in Barsh-yin-Binder flocked to the caverns for safety. Within these caverns there were streets, homes, shops, and the city's only hotel. The caverns were also perfectly protected from the wind, sun, and rain. This made them warm in winter and cool in summer. The caverns had many natural hot springs, where warm mineral-rich water bubbled up from the earth's depths and created bathing pools that could be used even in the depths of winter.

"Doesn't sound that bad," remarked Hill.

Resuza nodded in agreement. "And because it is run by the

Guild of Merchants, the Dragoonya are on their best behavior. The common soldiers are forbidden from entering the place."

"Is that where you live?" Alfonso asked.

Resuza laughed bitterly. "If only I could," she replied. "But fate has handed me a different road." She looked at Alfonso. "I live in an abandoned building near where we first met. There are a few of us there—those unlucky enough to have no family—"

Resuza stopped mid-sentence as they turned a corner and came upon an awful sight. In the middle of the street, a stone's throw ahead of them, stood twelve Dragoonya soldiers dressed in full battle gear. Instinctively, Resuza ducked behind a nearby stone wall. The others followed her lead. Fortunately, the soldiers were facing the other direction and didn't notice them.

The soldiers stood next to a rusted dog cage. Inside the cage were three people lying huddled together. Their bodies were entwined, and they had no room to move. There was a man, a woman, and a child. Perhaps the prisoners were a family. They wore only rags for clothes and looked near death. Although the child's feet were wrapped in a blanket, the man's and woman's feet were bare. It was far below freezing, with snow piled everywhere, and the parents' bare feet—blackened and bleeding—were exposed to the elements. Being from Minnesota, Alfonso was no stranger to the cold. He knew it was only a matter of time, perhaps less than an hour, before their feet would be lifeless from frostbite. He had to do something. He couldn't go back to his mom and Pappy knowing that he had ignored the situation. Alfonso stood up and began walking toward the cage.

Resuza pulled hard on Alfonso's coat. "Do nothing!" she hissed. "Unless you want to end up dead!"

Reluctantly, Alfonso returned to his hiding position.

Hill recoiled in horror. "What's going on?" he asked. "We have to help —"

"We can do nothing to help them!" whispered Resuza harshly. "They are Dragoonya slaves who tried to escape and are now being punished. The Dragoonya put them in the dog cages for a few hours to teach them a lesson. They will probably live, and if they do, they'll never again try to escape."

"What kind of people are these Dragoonya?" asked Bilblox angrily.

"Not the sort of people that you want to cross," said Resuza. "There is no fate in life worse than being a Dragoonya slave, but we can't help them."

"She's right," said Hill. "It'd be suicide to pick a fight with them."

"You just want to leave that family to die?" asked Alfonso angrily. He couldn't believe what his uncle was saying.

"I understand how you feel," said Hill. "But we have something of our own to protect—something very important."

"But it's just —" began Alfonso.

"Have you forgotten everything I told you?" snarled Hill. It was the first time Alfonso had ever seen his uncle angry and it gave him pause. "The lives of tens of thousands of people are at stake. People are going to starve and freeze in droves if we don't make our little delivery. So keep your head about you, nephew! We have a responsibility to them—to all of them!"

Alfonso bit his lip and said nothing.

"Now look," said Hill tenderly to his nephew, "we'll be face to face with Dragoonya soon enough, but let's wait at least until we have a fighting chance."

Bilblox nodded.

"I don't know what either of you are talking about," whispered Resuza, "but let's get out of here."

"Okay," said Alfonso quietly. "Let's go."

Resuza led the way down several deserted side streets and the others followed in a gloomy silence. Eventually, after roughly fifteen minutes of walking, they came upon a set of enormous wooden doors built into the side of a hill. In front of the doors stood three men dressed in heavy fur coats and carrying ancient-looking muskets. Curved swords hung from their waists.

"Say nothing!" Resuza whispered. "We have come to the Trawpoy gates. I will speak to the guards. Don't worry, they're not Dragoonya. They're hired men who work for the Guild of Merchants."

She stepped forward and approached the guards.

"What is your business here?" demanded one of the guards. "The gates are closed!"

"These three wealthy travelers will be guests at the Prince Binder," Resuza announced.

"It will be ten gold pieces to pass," replied the guard.

Resuza looked expectantly at Hill. He nodded, reached deep into his coat pocket, and pulled out ten gold pieces.

Once paid, the guards opened the massive wooden doors, and the four of them entered a wide tunnel that led deeper into the cavern. The air in the tunnel was moist and warm and smelled rotten. The walls were lined with hundreds of small torches that shed a great deal of flickering light on the sweaty rock walls. Eventually, the tunnel opened into an expansive cavern, and here they noticed steam rising from small holes in the ground. Alfonso also noticed a few openings in the cavern's ceiling, which allowed the night sky to pour in. Several of the openings were covered with dangling vines and white flowers that glowed in the moonlight.

The walls of the cavern were carved on both sides into rows of fashionable homes, complete with columns, porticos, steps, windows, and balconies. These homes were still in use and, unlike those in the rest of the city, their windows were lit with candles and revealed people going about their business. Many of these homes had large bathing pools in front of them. Even at this late hour, many of the pools were occupied by men who sat idly stroking their beards and enjoying the comfort of the piping-hot waters on their old bones.

At the far end of the cavern they saw an impressive-looking mansion carved completely out of the rock wall. Two guards dressed in ornamental tunics stood on either side of the entrance. The front door was open and they saw a roaring fire inside. Above the door was a scarlet-colored banner that read:

Inside, the Prince Binder Hotel looked like something from Paris or perhaps Istanbul in the early 1800s. It was fancy, but completely out of date. There were wooden floors, very low ceilings, kerosene lights, ancient-looking Persian carpets, and several overstuffed pillows occupied by old men who were playing backgammon and smoking water pipes. In the corner sat an old player piano, playing a sad and sleepy melody all by itself.

They followed Resuza to a registration window at the rear of the room. It was empty, save for an ornate bell that sat on a wooden ledge at the bottom of the window. Resuza rang the bell loudly. Half a minute passed and no one appeared. Resuza rang it again. Immediately they heard muffled shouts and the sounds of furniture tipping over. A tall man wearing a three-piece suit, a fluffy neck cravate, and a monocle appeared at the window. A nearby hanging lamp made his bald head gleam. He smiled broadly and bowed.

"Greetings and salutations, most honored guests," he began. "And welcome to the Prince Binder, the Arctic's most exclusive luxury inn. I am Count Zippricz, owner and manager of this establishment. How may I assist you?"

Hill cleared his throat. "Just a room," he said. "We are tired and won't trouble you with anything else."

Count Zippricz bowed so low that his head almost touched the wooden ledge. "With the greatest pleasure," he said. "You'll find the Prince Binder has everything you could possibly desire. And of course, the Trawpoy itself is a splendid area for any sporting or cultural pursuits you might have. Yes, the Trawpoy is an oasis for weary travelers. And nowhere is that more clear than in the Prince Binder!"

"So we're perfectly safe?" asked Hill.

Count Zippricz's smile faded. "Within reason," he replied. "This is Barsh-yin-Binder, after all. Indeed it has an illustrious name, but I won't lie to you, these are difficult times." He leaned in close and whispered urgently, "Go upstairs to your room immediately. It's on the third floor. Lock the door and let no one in. *No one.* Say nothing while you are here, and if you can help it, do not leave the hotel. Do you understand? The

Dragoonya have a stranglehold on our fair city. And even they, wretched creatures that they are, can't keep the thieves at bay. I've been robbed three times this month."

He straightened up, handed them a rusted key attached to an oversize wooden knob, and proclaimed, "Welcome again, kind sirs! And enjoy your stay!" With that, he reached up to the top of the registration window and abruptly pulled down a metal grate that securely closed off all access to the window. He then turned and ran away.

They all looked at Resuza. She nodded in a determined way, took the key, and led them up three flights of stairs, down a musty hallway, and into a large room with four beds and a small balcony that looked out onto the street.

"This room suits me fine," said Hill with a nod. "Thank you, Resuza." He paused and looked at Alfonso and Bilblox. "That was a nasty business with that family in the dog cages," he said. "Do the Dragoonya have many slaves?"

Resuza's eyes darkened. She nodded, but said nothing.

"You've lived in Barsh-yin-Binder all your life?" Hill asked.

"No," Resuza replied softly. "I grew up in a little village in the foothills of the Urals. I came to this miserable city only a few years ago."

"We're going to the foothills very soon," said Alfonso. "Can you help us buy supplies and get out of the city as soon as possible?"

Resuza beamed. "Of course, of course. I am the only dependable guide in Barsh-yin-Binder with extensive experience in the surrounding regions. You won't be disappointed!"

Bilblox looked uneasy with this arrangement, but Alfonso's

mind was made up. They needed to trust someone, and after all, Resuza had already helped them once.

That decided, they swiftly prepared for bed. If all went well, they would spend only one night in the Prince Binder, and they all knew it might be the last real bed they would see for many weeks.

Alfonso fell asleep with one arm around the top hat containing the Dormian bloom. He slept soundly until three in the morning, when he woke to the sound of a muffled cry. He sat up in bed with his heart pounding and glanced at his companions. They were all fast asleep.

Alfonso looked around the room and immediately noticed that the door leading out to the balcony was open. It swayed back and forth thanks to a gentle breeze entering the room. *Who opened that door?* Alfonso crept out of bed and made his way across the room. He paused to see if he could hear anything. Utter silence.

He continued forward and poked his head out onto the balcony. The street below was quiet. He was about to duck back into his room when he sensed another presence on the balcony. He turned quickly to his right. There, standing flush against the outer wall, stood Kiril. Kiril's face was drenched in sweat and he was breathing heavily. In his right hand he held a sword. A second sword was sheathed and tucked into his belt. Alfonso's entire body convulsed in a spasm of fright. He tried to speak, but no words came to his mouth. Finally he managed to stammer, "Wha-wha-what are you doing here?"

"You fool!" hissed Kiril. "I'm protecting you and the bloom!"

"What do you mean?"

"This cursed city is filthy with thieves," hissed Kiril. "You're being stalked. You'll need to protect yourself. Here, take this!" Kiril quickly reached into his jacket and pulled out a dagger whose blade was covered with blood. With trembling fingers, Alfonso grasped the weapon's handle. Instinctively, Alfonso glanced once more at Kiril's sword and—this time—he noticed that it too was streaked with blood.

"Now go back inside!" snapped Kiril.

Alfonso shrank backwards and stumbled into the room. Seconds later, someone began pounding furiously on the door that led to the main hallway.

Hill sprang up from bed, holding his Colt .45 pistol. "Who's there?" he yelled.

"I-I-It's Count Zippricz!" came the stammering reply. "Is everyone all right?"

Hill walked over to the door and opened it. Count Zippricz emerged from the shadows. His face looked ashen white and his hands were shaking. "A band—of—four thieves—broke—into the hotel," he explained between terrified gasps. "They killed the—two guards—out front and they would've—killed us all until—*someone beheaded all—of them.*" Count Zippricz stared at Bilblox and Resuza, who had jumped out of bed at the commotion and were standing behind Hill.

"I pray that all of you are safe," he said.

Hill nodded and lowered his pistol. "Come," he said to Alfonso. "Let's search the room and make sure everything is fine." Alfonso put on a heavy sweater and, very stealthily, he took the dagger that Kiril had given him and slipped it under his sweater. He could feel the blood on the dagger's blade dampening his undershirt. Alfonso said nothing—it was best to keep the weapon a secret for now.

Hill and Alfonso searched every nook and cranny of the room—including the bathroom and the balcony—but there were no signs of anything unusual.

"I wonder where he went?" muttered Alfonso.

"You wonder where *who* went?" asked Hill.

"Kiril," replied Alfonso. "I saw him on the balcony just before Count Zippricz arrived."

Hill stopped short. "Are you certain it was Kiril?" he asked.

Alfonso nodded.

"Then somehow he found us," said Hill. "But I don't understand. If he's Dragoonya, why haven't we been captured?"

Alfonso shook his head. "I don't know," he said. "It doesn't make sense."

Later that night, once everyone had returned to their beds and fallen back asleep, Alfonso reached into his sweater and pulled out the dagger that Kiril had given him. A small candle was burning on a nightstand near Alfonso's bed and in its dim, flickering light he could make out the intricate carving on the dagger's handle. Most prominently, there was an insignia that looked quite familiar: [symbol]. It took Alfonso a moment to identify the symbol and then, quite suddenly, he recalled seeing it in *McBridge's Book of Mythical Plants.* This was the symbol of Dormia.

CHAPTER 18

DR. VAN BAMBLEWEEP

THE MORNING light didn't make Alfonso feel any better. He couldn't stop thinking about what had happened. Kiril's actions made no sense. After all, from the very beginning—back in World's End—Kiril had focused on acquiring the plant. If Kiril was skilled enough to single-handedly behead four thieves, he could've stolen the plant while they were sleeping, even if Alfonso had his arm around it. What kind of devious plans did Kiril—and his "father"— have for Alfonso? Or was it possible, as improbable as it seemed, that Kiril was actually trying to help?

These questions spun through Alfonso's mind that morning as he and Bilblox prepared to leave the Prince Binder Hotel in search of a shop that belonged to one Dr. Van Bambleweep. According to Resuza, Dr. Van Bambleweep was the closest thing to a real doctor in the entire city of Barsh-yin-Binder. Alfonso hoped that Dr. Van Bambleweep could examine Bilblox's eyes to see if anything could be done to help him regain his sight. Meanwhile, Hill and Resuza would spend the morning buying supplies for their trip into the Ural Mountains. They would need food, tents, maps, sleds, dogs, and plenty of warm clothing. If all went well, they would leave Barsh-yin-Binder by evening.

Alfonso and Bilblox exited the Prince Binder Hotel and walked out into the massive Trawpoy cavern. They passed the large hot spring where they had seen several old men bathing the night before. It was hard to shake a feeling of deep uneasiness as they walked around and remembered Count Zippricz's warnings, as well as the incident from the previous night.

The hot springs were all empty except for a few small turtles swimming about in them. The entire cavern was still quite dark. The only indication that it was morning came from the holes in the ceiling of the cavern that allowed in a few beams of dim sunlight. Alfonso and Bilblox walked several hundred yards across the cavern until they found a small storefront carved into the rock. It had a window, which was far too fogged with steam to see through, and a round green door with a sign that read VAN BAMBLEWEEP & SONS: BOOKS, MAPS, ANTIQUES, & SAGE MEDICAL ADVICE SINCE 1369 OR THEREABOUTS. Alfonso and Bilblox stared at the sign for a moment.

"What the heck kind of doctor's office is this?" asked Bilblox.

"I'm not sure," said Alfonso. "But we might as well find out."

Alfonso stepped up to the door and knocked on it heavily. A minute or so later, the door creaked open. An elderly man, with only his white hair and chin visible, peered out at them.

"Come in *quickly.* No one must know that I am here!" the man furiously whispered.

Alfonso and Bilblox were confused, but followed the man's instruction and stepped through the door. After they entered, the door slammed shut and they stood in near darkness. The old man peeked out his front window to see if Alfonso and Bilblox had been followed. He was very tall and he wore a white doctor's coat and a pair of glasses whose lenses were tinted dark green. He had a scraggly white beard and raw pink-colored skin that looked as if it had been scrubbed vigorously with a rough brush. His hands, which were trembling, had spindly fingers with enormously long yellowish fingernails that curled into curlicues. He smelled of sour pickles.

"I don't mean to be rude, old chaps, but I don't want the Dragoonya to know that I'm home," explained the man in a quavering and very creaky voice. He had the same sort of old-fashioned English accent as Resuza. "Those thugs are a wretched lot—not one of them is fit to hold a wax candle—so I usually keep a low profile. But obviously, you're not Dragoonya. What can I do for you?"

"We need to talk to you about a medical problem," explained Alfonso.

"Really? Well, that's too bad. I'm quite busy at the moment," replied the doctor.

"Please," said Alfonso. "You have to help us—my friend is going blind."

"Blind?" inquired the doctor. This seemed to resonate with him and he nodded approvingly. "Well, I will never turn away a blind man," he said. "Why don't you come into my examining room? My name, by the way, is Dr. Van Bambleweep. Sorry to be so rude at the door, but these are bad times in Barsh-yin-Binder. Very bad times indeed."

The doctor led them through a room filled with rows of dusty bookshelves filled with books, maps, and hundreds of small glass jars containing various powders and elixirs. Alfonso was able to read the labels on some of the jars: Root of Mountain Lilac—found by Tatars; Ground Tusk of Black Rhino; Bile of Kazakh Green-Cheeked Parrot; Teeth of Blunt-Nosed Leopard (molars); and Skin of Male Copperbelly Snake. On the other end of the room was a small but clean office with a desk, a threadbare carpet, and a few rickety chairs.

"Please have a seat," said the doctor cordially. "So, your friend is going blind?"

Bilblox and Alfonso sat down, but neither of them spoke.

"You'll have to speak up," said the doctor. "I am very old and I don't hear well anymore."

Bilblox cleared his throat and declared, "I'm really not blind all of the time—just sometimes."

"Just sometimes?" inquired the doctor.

"Well it comes and goes," explained Bilblox awkwardly. "Fer instance, right now, I can see all right—even though it's pretty dark in here—but most of the time I can't see a lousy thing."

"How long has this been going on?" asked the doctor.

"About a week or two," replied Bilblox.

"I see," said Van Bambleweep. "And can you describe what your eyes look like? Under other circumstances I would give you an eye exam, but my own eyes are in rather poor shape, so I think it would do little good."

Alfonso glanced again at the doctor's strange green-tinted glasses. They were as dark as sunglasses and, in the dim light of the room, it seemed doubtful that he could see anything at all.

"I don't know what to tell ya," said Bilblox testily. "I haven't looked into a mirror in weeks."

"I can describe his eyes for you," interjected Alfonso.

"Good lad," said the doctor. "What do they look like?"

"Well it depends," said Alfonso. "If you look really closely, you can almost see the outline of where his pupils used to be—but, other than that, his eyes are entirely white."

"Entirely white?" asked the doctor. There was a sudden eagerness in his voice.

"Yes," said Alfonso. "Entirely white. Well, almost."

"Most intriguing indeed," said the doctor with a cluck of his tongue. "And before all this happened, how was your long-range vision? In other words, were you able to see things off in the distance just before you went blind?"

Bilblox said nothing.

"I can't hear you," said the doctor. "If you want help, you'll have to speak up!"

"Okay," said Bilblox. "I did have very good long-distance vision just before I went blind. I saw lots of things, but I don't see how that matters."

Van Bambleweep looked excited. "And then, just after that, did you get a quick moment of prescience?"

"Prescience?" inquired Bilblox.

"Yes," said the doctor. "Were you able to see into the future?"

"What kind of question is that?" growled Bilblox. "I thought ya were supposed to be a doctor. What kind of crazy hokum are ya peddlin'?"

"Just answer the question," Van Bambleweep said.

"No," said Bilblox. "That's the most preposterous thing I ever heard."

"Suit yourself," said the doctor. "But, based on what you are telling me, I'd say you're suffering from an acute case of Dragoonya dim-sightedness. It's very rare these days. It means your blindness is irreversible and it's only going to get worse." He crossed his arms and leaned back in his chair.

"Oh really, *doctor!*" said Bilblox with a forced laugh. "That's a heck of a diagnosis considerin' ya didn't even examine me. Dragoonya dim-sightedness! Who ever heard of such a thing? Alfonso, let's get outta here."

Bilblox stood up, but Alfonso remained seated in his chair.

"How can you be sure that his blindness is irreversible?" Alfonso asked.

"Oh ya can't be serious!" interjected Bilblox irritably.

"I want to hear what he has to say," said Alfonso. "You did kind of glimpse into the future when you saw those flying fish and the iceberg."

"Just as I suspected," said Van Bambleweep. "Let me ask you another question: did you rub anything into your eyes just before you had that long-range vision?"

Bilblox said nothing.

"A certain type of powder, perhaps?" pressed the doctor.

"Maybe," mumbled Bilblox.

Alfonso felt his stomach tighten into a knot.

"I knew it!" the doctor exclaimed. "How in the name of Prince Binder did you get your hands on the purple ash? There hasn't been any of that stuff around this city for at least two hundred years."

"I-I don't know what yer talking about," stammered Bilblox.

"Oh come now, my friend," replied the doctor. "I've been a sage of medicine in this town for a good many years—as have my grandfathers and great-grandfathers before me—and there is only one thing that causes the pupils to disappear entirely: purple ash. One major side effect is whiteness of the eyes and blindness. Other, more desired effects are telescopic vision and a moment of clairvoyance in which you see into the future. Does any of this ring a bell? Yes, I suspect it does. The curious thing is how two travelers like you got your hands on purple ash. The only people who *ever* have purple ash are the Dragoonya. They use it and their eyesight suffers. Almost all who use it go entirely blind. Of course, there are reports of a very few who have managed to keep their eyesight, but I don't put much stock in those claims. In any case, it's almost always the Dragoonya who suffer from this. That's why we call the ailment Dragoonya dim-sightedness. Don't you see?"

"I guess so," said Alfonso. He paused. "And there's no cure?"

"No," replied the doctor matter-of-factly. "There's no cure. At least, I've never seen one. But I've never really treated anyone with this particular ailment. As I said, that purple ash disappeared over two hundred years ago."

"Why did it disappear?" asked Alfonso.

"Hard to say," said the doctor. "I'm not sure where the Dragoonya find the ash—there are all kinds of fantastical tales about where it comes from—but the source seems to have dried up. And, let me tell you, things have been going downhill for the Dragoonya ever since. Look around this city. It's a catastrophe! But two hundred years ago . . . that was a different story. Back then, the Dragoonya used the ash shrewdly to their advantage. For centuries, they attacked commercial ships and made small fortunes as pirates, thanks to the powers the ash gave them. You can understand why I'm curious how you two gentlemen managed to get some."

"Curiosity kills cats," said Bilblox menacingly.

"Suit yourself," grumbled the doctor. "But I wouldn't go walking around Barsh-yin-Binder with those white eyes of yours or you're bound to attract a lot of attention."

"We have another question for you," said Alfonso, who was only too eager to change the subject. "Your sign says you sell maps, and we need one."

"What kind of map?" asked the doctor.

"We need a map of the Ural Mountains," said Alfonso. "We're trying to get to a location near —" Alfonso stopped himself. Was it really wise to share the coordinates of their destination with this stranger?

"Where in the Urals?" asked the doctor. "You'll need to be more specific. It's a huge mountain range. I can't help you unless you tell me where, exactly, you're headed. I have hundreds of maps. I'm just trying to find out which one you need."

"We want to get to sixty-four degrees north latitude by sixty-two degrees east longitude," said Alfonso with a sigh. "Can you help us?"

"Hmm," said the doctor. "If I am not mistaken, those coordinates place you right in the high peaks of the Urals and, unfortunately, most of that area is terra incognita."

"What's that mean?" asked Bilblox.

"It's a Latin phrase," explained the doctor. "It means 'unknown land.' In other words, no one has taken the time to explore it. It's just too dangerous and too remote. Why are you interested in that area?"

Alfonso ignored Van Bambleweep's question. "Don't you have *any* maps of the high peaks?" he insisted. "Anything at all?"

"Well, I do have one," said the doctor. "It was made by a smuggler from Estonia. The map is incomplete, but it might help."

The doctor disappeared into the shadows of his shop and soon reemerged with a timeworn piece of rolled parchment, held together by a small chain and a silver clasp engraved with the following words: *õnne proovile panama.*

"As you can see," explained the doctor, "the smuggler who made this map was named Õnne Proovile Panama."

The doctor then unfurled a map titled "Uralid." In the center of the map was a large blank section marked with these strange words: *End teiste asjusse mitte segama.*

"This appears to be the map of a route leading directly through the high peaks of the Urals," explained the doctor. "You can see the word *Uralid* at the top. I think that must be referring to the Urals. There is also a marking for Straszydlo. This must refer to the legendary Straszydlo Forest, which sits on the northwestern edge of these mountains."

Alfonso looked at Bilblox. "Straszydlo Forest!" he exclaimed. "That's where the vice admiral found my father and Uncle Hill."

Bilblox nodded, but the doctor ignored them.

"You see," he continued, "the intersection of the two coordinates you gave me is in the center of that white space. I'm afraid this map is of no use to you."

Bilblox squinted at the map. Apparently, his short window of being able to see was not yet over.

"It's Estonian," Bilblox said. "I know 'cuz my family is Estonian. We immigrated to Fort Krasnik when times got hard for longshoremen back in the old country. My first name, Paks, actually means 'thick' in Estonian. That's why I go by Bilblox—sounds tougher."

"You speak Estonian?" asked Alfonso.

"Jah, absoluutselt," replied Bilblox in a very proud manner. "That means, 'yes, absolutely,' in Estonian."

"So what does the map say?" asked Alfonso.

"Well the text written over the blank space says: 'Mind your own business!'"

"You don't say!" cackled the doctor. "I guess this Panama chap didn't want anyone using his smuggling route."

"That's another thing," said Bilblox. *"Õnne proovile panama* ain't the guy's name. It's a sayin' in Estonian that means: 'Press your luck.'"

"How curious," said the doctor. "What on earth do you suppose that means?"

"Maybe it means that if you enter the blank area you're pressing your luck," guessed Alfonso.

"Maybe," said Bilblox. "Or maybe I oughta just press my thumb down on the spot where it says press your luck. Here, gimme that thing." The doctor handed the clasp to Bilblox and he used his large, calloused thumb to press down gently on the silver clasp. Nothing happened. He pressed down again with considerable effort. This time there was a soft clicking, barely audible, and the clasp yawned open. It revealed a small space with enough room for a carefully folded piece of tissue paper. Bilblox took out the paper and smoothed it out. It was the exact shape of the missing space on the map.

Dr. Van Bambleweep gasped.

Bilblox took the tissue paper and placed it over the blank spot, thereby completing the map. Sure enough, it showed a clear route through the mountains. The doctor, who was now brimming with excitement, rushed over to a nearby bookcase and began consulting a number of atlases.

"What are you doing?" asked Alfonso.

"Some calculations," replied the doctor distractedly. "I'm trying to determine the exact location of sixty-four degrees north latitude by sixty-two degrees east longitude on that map."

Several minutes later, he returned to the Estonian smuggler's map and marked a large *X* on the exact spot where he believed those coordinates to be. It lay directly on the path of the Estonian smuggler's route.

Alfonso and Bilblox looked at each other. Alfonso didn't say anything, but his smile said it all. They had found it. Somnos, the capital of Dormia.

"How much do you want for this map?" Alfonso asked Van Bambleweep.

"This is a very old map," said the doctor, who suddenly seemed quite attached to it. "I would have to charge at least twenty gold pieces."

"We'll take it," replied Alfonso.

CHAPTER 19

LOAFER'S CORNER

MEANWHILE, IN THE commercial district of the Trawpoy, Hill and Resuza were busy buying supplies for their journey. Resuza did all the legwork. She took Hill to the shops, advised him on what to buy, and then haggled furiously over the prices with the shopkeepers. Once a purchase was made, they loaded it onto the back of a donkey cart they had rented and drove on to the next shop. Their list was as follows:

40 pounds of salted meat
30 pounds of coal
2 heavyweight sleds (insist on well-sharpened runners)
Bullets for a Colt .45 pistol—if they can be found
2 short swords

¼ keg of gunpowder
½ gallon whiskey
10 huskies (8 followers, 2 leaders)
4 hats (look for newly shorn wool, and make sure they have earflaps)
8 gloves (thin, so that two pairs can be worn at the same time)
2 pots (1 medium and 1 large)
2 sturdy tents
6 lanterns
Cooking utensils
Sharpening steel
Medium-size roll of raw cotton
8 full-length blankets
Large bottle of iodine
Whistle (as piercing as possible—for wolves)
8 waterproof sealskin bags
4 snow goggles
Dried medicinal herbs
2 pounds of Turkish coffee
Tea

That morning, they purchased all of the goods and, by early afternoon, they were done. All the goods were loaded onto the donkey cart, including the dogs, who sat perched on every conceivable nook of open space.

As Resuza navigated them back toward the Prince Binder Hotel, they passed through a remote and especially dark section of the Trawpoy, where they came upon a hot spring that smelled of rotten eggs. Next to the spring was a large flat rock on which nearly a dozen men in tattered clothing were lounging about. All of them were lying on their backs and staring up at the ceiling. They didn't appear to be sleeping. In fact, a few of them were chatting quietly. The others simply seemed to be resting.

"This place smells awful," gasped Hill.

"The smell comes from the water," explained Resuza. "This is an especially sulfurous place—Loafer's Corner they call it."

"Why are these men here?"

"They are loafers," replied Resuza disgustedly. "They simply lie around all the day and *loaf.* They are the laziest men in all of Barsh-yin-Binder. No one bothers with them because they keep to this terrible-smelling corner of the cavern."

"Don't be too harsh on us," said one of the men in a quavering, tired-sounding voice. "I assure you: lying around all day and doing nothing can actually be quite difficult."

Suddenly Hill noticed a large coffin sitting on a pedestal in the middle of the group of loafers. He pointed and asked about it.

"That coffin belongs to the so-called Queen of the Loafers—a woman named Spack who sleeps in it all day long," explained Resuza. "They say she's awake for less than ten minutes each day. She does everything in her sleep—eats, walks, talks, even swims—"

"Stop the cart!" yelled Hill. He hopped off the cart and bounded through the steamy sulfur fumes toward the coffin. It was very large and made of well-polished wood. The following words were carved prominently onto the lid of the coffin: I WAKE FOR NO ONE!

"Don't . . . bother," muttered a nearby loafer. He was so filthy with dirt and grime that Hill winced. "'Tis true—I am a pitiful sight," said the man. A thick band of drool hung from his lower lip. "But I washed my clothes last year."

Hill attempted a half-smile. "What can you tell me about the woman in this coffin?" he asked.

"Our . . . queen! The . . . Lady Spack . . . is the greatest loafer there . . . ever . . . was," said the man sluggishly. "Always telling the rest of us to work . . . less, especially if you . . . lift a finger . . . to help someone . . . else."

Hill inspected the coffin further and saw that it had two ivory handles, one at each end, so that it could be carried if need be. He leaned forward and heard a faint whimpering coming from inside the coffin. It was Spack.

"She's singing," Hill remarked.

"In . . . deed," said the loafer. "That Spack is . . . a great . . . singer in her . . . sleep."

Hill placed his ear directly against the coffin, just above three tiny breathing holes drilled into the wooden lid. He heard a voice singing a squeaky-sounding lullaby: The language was incomprehensible. The words, if you could even call them that, sounded like high-pitched yelps. Hill scrunched his chin thoughtfully. "That tune sounds familiar," he said. "Reminds me of a lullaby from long ago."

"All lullabies sound familiar," Resuza said.

"Maybe," replied Hill. He tried to open the coffin, but the lid wouldn't budge.

"You . . . won't get in," said the nearby loafer. "Spack locks that coffin . . . from the . . . inside. She decides when . . . to wake up."

Hill looked at Resuza. "This Spack character could be of use to us. Bring the donkey cart over here. We're taking the coffin.

It looks like it has a small set of wheels on the bottom here. We should be able to move it pretty easily."

"Why would you want to do that?" asked Resuza.

For a brief moment, Hill considered telling Resuza about Dormia—and why exactly he was interested in unusual sleepers like Spack—but he quickly decided against it.

"I have my reasons," said Hill. "Now help me with this coffin."

"What? Our . . . queen," said the loafer. In a massive effort, he rose up on one elbow. "You . . . can't . . ." The loafer's eyes fluttered, his elbow began to quiver, and he lay back down in mid-sentence, fast asleep.

CHAPTER 20

CLASH WITH THE DRAGOONYA

As THEY RETURNED from their day of shopping, Hill and Resuza bumped into Alfonso and Bilblox, who were also on their way back to the Prince Binder. They greeted each other happily. Hill showed off all the goods Resuza had helped him purchase, and afterward, Alfonso explained their discovery of the Estonian smuggler's map. Hill's eyes shone with excitement and he grabbed Alfonso in a playful bear hug.

"You've done it, my boy!" he exclaimed. "You found what we needed most—a route to the watch's coordinates!"

"Why are you gents so keen on going to that exact place?" asked Resuza.

"We're going back to the little mountain town where I was born," explained Hill in a kindly manner. "That's all."

"Strange," replied Resuza. "I didn't know there were any towns in the high peaks of the Urals."

Alfonso tried to change the subject. "What are we doing with that coffin?" he asked.

"We're taking it with us," said Hill.

"We are?" asked Alfonso. "Why?"

Hill cast a sideways glance at Resuza. "I'll explain later," he said.

The four of them continued back toward the Prince Binder in silence. When they arrived at the hotel, Bilblox began unloading the supplies from the donkey cart.

"My vision is goin' again," said Bilblox in a resigned fashion. "But I can see well enough to move some large objects. I guess I'll start with the coffin."

As Bilblox unloaded the coffin from the donkey cart, Alfonso unfurled the Estonian smuggler's map and showed it to Hill. The two of them studied the map together. Soon, Alfonso glanced up to see how Bilblox was doing.

"Oh no!" he exclaimed.

"Holy mackerel!" gasped Hill.

Bilblox was stumbling toward the entrance of the Prince Binder with the coffin balancing on his shoulder. He was weaving back and forth in a manner that made it clear he couldn't see where he was going. He must have been almost completely blind, because he failed to notice the arrival of five Dragoonya soldiers who were standing directly in his path. The soldiers were dressed in the same fashion as the Dragoonya horsemen from the night before. They wore leather armor, lined with eagle feathers, and on their heads they wore shiny metal helmets with long pointy beaks and narrow slits for their eyes.

They all had swords. The soldiers had their backs to Bilblox and didn't see him coming.

"Uncle Hill!" said Alfonso. "Bilblox is headed straight for them. We've got to —"

Bam! It was too late.

Bilblox walked right into one of the soldiers, smacking the back of the soldier's head with the front end of the coffin. The coffin clattered to the ground. Bilblox jumped backwards in fright. An instant later, the five soldiers surrounded Bilblox.

"You idiot!" hissed the largest of the soldiers. He was an enormously tall man with a black feather in his helmet. It appeared as if he was the captain of the group. "Do you realize you assaulted a Dragoonya man-at-arms!"

"He can't see a thing," said another soldier. "He's totally blind—look at his eyes . . . they're white!"

"What happened to your eyes?" demanded the captain.

"None of your business," growled Bilblox.

"Oh, I see," said the captain calmly. "It's none of my business." The captain drew his sword, and in one smooth motion ran his blade across Bilblox's face. Blood gushed from Bilblox's right cheek. Bilblox let out a ferocious cry and struck out with his massive fist, but he merely swung through the air.

"Now," said the captain as calm as ever, "perhaps you would like to tell me how your eyes became totally white."

Bilblox said nothing. His shoulders and fists were coiled to strike, but being blind, he had no target.

"I see," said the captain. "Well in that case, perhaps I can persuade you to talk." The captain lifted his sword again and this time he ran it across Bilblox's chest. Bilblox let out another cry. Blood began seeping through his shirt. "How do you like that, my blind friend?" asked the captain. "Enjoying yourself? Tell me, where shall I cut you next? How about I pluck out one of those eyes?"

A hundred feet away, by the donkey cart, Hill, Alfonso, and Resuza were watching in terror.

"We've got to do something," said Hill frantically.

Alfonso had come to the same conclusion, but he was already in the midst of taking action. He was focusing all of his attention on a lone snowflake that was fluttering its way through one of the holes in the cavern's ceiling. Alfonso concentrated on the hexagonal shape of the snowflake—studying all of its partially melted snow crystals—and watched as the delicate object swirled and sputtered in the drafts of the cavern. Alfonso felt as calm and relaxed as he had ever been. And, before he knew it, he was firmly in hypnogogia.

Alfonso knew he wouldn't be able to stay in this state for long—maybe five or six seconds at most. He had to act quickly. He picked up a sharp, flat stone from the ground and studied it carefully. He estimated the distance between himself and his target, took a deep breath, and then threw the stone with all his might. The stone hurtled through the air like a spinning blade and pierced the right eye-slit of the captain's helmet. Blood shot out of the captain's eye as he shrieked in pain. The other four soldiers pivoted and turned their attention toward Alfonso, whose hands were filled with more stones.

"Get that boy!" shouted the captain. "And slit his throat!"

The four soldiers immediately began to close in on Alfonso. Alfonso leaned up against the donkey cart, exhausted from the effort of entering hypnogogia. Resuza picked up a stone and prepared for battle. Instinctively, Hill reached for his Colt .45, but he didn't have it on him. It was in his bomber jacket, which was buried at the bottom of the donkey cart. The four soldiers closed in rapidly, and they were mere feet away from Alfonso when a chilling and familiar voice called out.

"Don't even think about it," said the raspy, cold voice.

It was Kiril. He was standing next to Bilblox and it seemed as if he had appeared out of thin air. He wore the same fur cloak he had worn when Alfonso had first met him in the Forest of the Obitteroos. His eyes shone ghostly white and he held a sword in each hand.

Upon hearing Kiril's voice, the soldiers abruptly stopped.

"Who in damnation are you?" demanded one of the Dragoonya soldiers.

"I'm the man who is going to kill all four of you in the next five minutes," replied Kiril calmly.

The four Dragoonya soldiers needed no further provocations. All four of them immediately rushed toward Kiril with their swords drawn.

Kiril shot a parting glance at Alfonso. "Run, you half-wits!" yelled Kiril. "The trap is closing around you!"

"He's right—run for it!" gasped Bilblox, who lay in a pool of his own blood. "Leave me!"

"No," said Alfonso. "We've got to help him."

Hill nodded vigorously.

And so, as Kiril fought for his life—wielding his two swords masterfully and keeping his opponents at bay—Alfonso, Hill, and Resuza rushed toward Bilblox, who was gasping for breath. Blood dripped from his chest and face.

"Quickly now," said Hill. "We have to lift him onto the coffin—it has wheels. We can use it like a stretcher."

"He needs a doctor!" gasped Alfonso.

"There is only one," replied Resuza.

"Let's move!" yelled Hill.

CHAPTER 21

ESCAPE

LESS THAN TEN minutes later, Alfonso, Hill, Resuza, and Bilblox were in front of Dr. Van Bambleweep's door. Alfonso banged furiously on it. Half a minute passed and there was no answer. In the distance, Alfonso could still hear Kiril's swords clanging against the armor of his adversaries.

"Doctor!" Alfonso shouted. "It's me—Alfonso! We need your help!" A few seconds later, the door creaked open and the doctor peered out.

"What's going . . . Good GOD!" exclaimed the doctor as he looked down upon Bilblox, who was draped across the loafer's coffin. "What happened to your blind friend?"

"He got into a fight with Dragoonya," said Alfonso. "We need your help. Please!"

The doctor looked them over quickly. Then he glanced at the donkey cart behind them, piled high with their supplies. The sled dogs whimpered nearby.

"Wheel the coffin and this wounded man into my shop!" ordered the doctor. "Then bring your donkey cart down the street! There's a small cavern there, where you can hide it. Go on!"

They followed the doctor's orders in haste. They wheeled Bilblox into Dr. Van Bambleweep's shop and then led the donkey cart, which contained all of their supplies, into an abandoned-looking cavern at the far end of the street. Once everything was hidden, they hustled back to the doctor's office. Van Bambleweep let them in and they gathered in the small sitting area at the rear of the shop.

"This is very upsetting," Van Bambleweep said to Alfonso. "Who in tarnation are all these people?"

Hill and Resuza quickly introduced themselves.

"Idiots!" said the doctor irritably. "Now tell me—what happened?"

Alfonso recounted their confrontation with the Dragoonya as quickly as he could.

"I told you to avoid the Dragoonya," mumbled the doctor. "Now you see what has happened. Here—help me take off his shirt!"

The doctor spent the next thirty minutes attending to Bilblox's wounds. He washed away the blood with pieces of cloth that he had sterilized in boiling water. He then applied generous amounts of a viscous white gel from a bottle labeled "Wheatgrass Wound and Scar-Healing Ointment." Finally, the doctor sewed up Bilblox's wounds with a needle and thread and then bandaged them with a great deal of gauze and cloth.

"I'm feelin' a bit better," said Bilblox weakly as he sat up and looked around the room.

"Your friend is lucky," concluded the doctor. "The cuts he received missed his major blood vessels."

"So he'll be okay?" asked Alfonso.

"For now," said the doctor. "Of course, the problem is that you are trapped. After your attack on a Dragoonya officer, their entire army will be looking for you. Their blood code demands that all of you must die. Fools!"

"Doctor, what about the catacombs?" asked Resuza. Alfonso gave her a confused look. "It is a system of ancient underground tunnels beneath the city," she explained.

"Where do they lead?" Alfonso asked.

"Nowhere," snapped the doctor. "Or, more accurately, the tunnels usually lead to death—especially now that most of them are flooded. The last time I was down there, I ended up in one of the main tunnels and the blasted thing had become a raging river. Is that what you want? I nearly drowned several times. I mean, it is possible to go down there, but not unless you absolutely have to."

"You've been into the catacombs?" asked Resuza with a certain amount of awe. "How brave of you, Dr. Van Bambleweep! How did you find a way in?"

"Why that part is easy, my dear," said the doctor with a mischievous grin. "I have a small hidden stairway in this house that leads directly into the catacombs. You can get in, but leaving is a different story."

"But there must be a way out," persisted Resuza. "I've heard talk of a tunnel that leads from the Trawpoy out to the countryside."

"That's true," said the doctor. "There is such a tunnel, my grandfather spoke of using it when he was a boy, but no one has used it in ages —"

"What was that noise?" Alfonso suddenly asked.

"I didn't hear anything," said the doctor.

"Someone is at your door," said Alfonso.

Moments later, a terrible noise echoed throughout the house, as if someone were pounding on the front door with a sledgehammer. *Bang! Bang! Bang!*

"My goodness," said the doctor nervously. A look of terror crept across his face. "They're here already!"

"Who?" asked Hill.

"Why the Dragoonya of course," said the doctor. His hands were shaking. "They usually leave me alone because of all the free medicines that I give them."

Bang! Bang! Bang! The entire house shook with each bang.

"Wait here," whispered the doctor. "I think I can buy us some time."

Alfonso, Hill, Bilblox, and Resuza all sat and listened intently as the doctor walked down the length of his shop and cracked open his front door.

"What do you want?" asked the doctor curtly.

"Stand back, doctor," boomed a low harsh voice. "We're searching your house!"

"You'll do no such thing," replied Van Bambleweep in a slow but firm tone. "I am seeing a patient right now who is extremely ill. I can't have you barging in and wreaking havoc."

"But we're looking for criminals who have assaulted —"

"I don't care!" retorted the doctor. "I have a patient who is on the verge of death." He lowered his voice. "Please understand: my patient is a close *associate* of Nartam. I know you have little interest in upsetting your king. Give me a few minutes to attend to him, and then you can search all you'd like. Surround the house—no one will leave or enter."

Without waiting for a response, the doctor shut the door and locked it. For the next fifteen seconds there was no noise at all. Then came the sound of the doctor's shuffling footsteps. "I think I bought us a few minutes," said Van Bambleweep as he made his way to the back of the shop. "I'm afraid now there really is only one thing to do: you'll have to go into the catacombs."

"I thought ya said enterin' the catacombs would be certain death," said Bilblox.

"No," said the doctor. "Getting caught by the Dragoonya would be certain death—going into the catacombs is just *likely* death."

"But what about all of our supplies in the donkey cart?" asked Hill. "How will we get them out of the city?"

"I am too old for this," mumbled the doctor softly. "Way too old for this."

"What if we —" began Bilblox.

"Quiet!" said the doctor. He thought for a moment and then announced: "All right—I have an idea, but the idea and my assistance will cost you." He looked at Hill. "Two hundred gold coins. No less."

"That's almost all the money we have left!" protested Alfonso.

"That's the deal—take it or leave it," said the doctor.

Hill nodded.

"Good," replied the doctor. "There *is* a route through the catacombs. Though dangerous, it will get you out of the city. I know the route, mostly, and I'll describe it for you. Alfonso and Bilblox will go that way—they are the ones the Dragoonya will be looking for because they are the ones who provoked the fight. Meanwhile, I'll escort Hill, Resuza, and the donkey cart through the city. I'll bandage Hill up so he isn't recognizable. When we are stopped by the soldiers, I will tell them Hill is a Dragoonya elder who has fallen deathly ill and needs treatment at the Abestine Monastery, which sits just outside the city. I actually take patients there fairly often so this shouldn't seem too far-fetched. Resuza will pass as Hill's devoted daughter. It will make the whole affair more believable. All right?"

"I don't know," said Alfonso. "Can Bilblox really do this in his condition?"

"He doesn't have a choice," snapped the doctor.

For the next five minutes or so, the doctor went back over his plan in detail. He gave Alfonso and Bilblox directions on how to navigate their way through the catacombs. If all went well, they would emerge from the catacombs via a giant river that they would then follow downstream. Eventually, they would come upon a large rock formation known as the Three Fingers, which would serve as the rendezvous point. Meanwhile, Hill and Resuza would head for the Abestine Monastery with the doctor and then proceed on their own to the Three Fingers.

"How far is it from the Three Fingers to Straszydlo Forest?" asked Hill.

"It's just a few days' journey due south," said the doctor. "And once you get to the forest, you should be able to pick up the route on the Estonian smuggler's map."

Hill looked uncertain. "I don't like being split up," he said. "It doesn't sound right."

"It's your decision," the doctor replied curtly.

"All right," replied Hill. He looked sadly at Alfonso. Then he took off the top hat with the bloom nestled inside, placed it in a waterproof sealskin bag, and handed it to Alfonso. The plant had been growing a great deal lately, adding on more leaves and a few spindly branches. Consequently, the bag was quite heavy.

"You should take this," said Hill. "I have a feeling it will be safer with you."

"What about the coffin?" asked Alfonso.

"You should take that with you," interjected the doctor. "It will make an excellent raft."

"Raft?"

"You'll see," replied the doctor. "Now get going!"

CHAPTER 22

JOURNEY INTO THE CATACOMBS

ALFONSO AND BILBLOX followed the doctor down a long, darkened hallway at the back of his shop. The hallway ended at a wall covered with pots and pans hanging from hooks. The doctor pulled down on the uppermost pot and they all heard a click from inside the wall. Van Bambleweep pushed on the wall; it opened like a door and revealed a stairway that spiraled down into an even gloomier darkness.

"Go on!" said the doctor. "The catacombs begin at the bottom of the stairs." Suddenly, he paused and stared at Bilblox through his dark glasses. "What you have stolen is not the ash," he said. "Can I have it back, please?"

"What are ya talkin' about?" Bilblox protested.

"The powder that you took from my shelf just a few minutes ago—while you thought I wasn't looking—contains the ground-up root of a rare mountain mulberry. I use it to treat severe back pain and to help blood clot. If I had any of that purple ash, I certainly wouldn't keep it on an ordinary shelf. Now please, before I get upset, may I have the powder?"

Bilblox's face turned red. He leaned the coffin against the wall and took a vial containing a dark green powder from his pants pocket. "I took it by accident," he gruffly replied.

"Of course," said Van Bambleweep.

"Come on," said Bilblox. "Let's get goin'."

Alfonso was dumbfounded. He remembered Bilblox boasting that he was the only honest longshoreman in Fort Krasnik. And now Bilblox had stolen what he thought was the ash. Alfonso wondered if he should tell Hill, but there was no time. Moments later, he began creeping down the dark staircase, followed by Bilblox.

Both of them took the stairs cautiously. They were in complete darkness, and the wooden stairs creaked in protest. When they finally made it to the bottom, Alfonso was surprised to discover that his face was covered in sweat, despite the cool air.

"Bilblox, you there?" he whispered. "Can you see where you're going?"

"I can see okay," said Bilblox. "But it ain't gonna last."

A second later, Alfonso heard a thud, followed by a pain-filled groan. Bilblox, still weak from the Dragoonya attack, had put down the coffin that contained Spack the loafer. Bilblox had at first refused to take the coffin but reluctantly agreed when Van Bambleweep gave them two old paddles and insisted vehemently that they would need a raft in order to survive the catacombs.

"Are you sure it's not too heavy?" Alfonso asked.

"Nah," replied Bilblox. "The thing has got wheels. Besides, that Spack character don't weigh much. I just hope that yer uncle is right and that she ends up helpin' us. Otherwise I ain't gonna be happy. But don't worry about me. I'm okay—a bit scraped up, but okay. Ya just pay attention to the bloom." Alfonso carried the bloom and a few supplies in a wooden-frame backpack that Van Bambleweep had given them. For added protection, the whole backpack was tightly wrapped in waterproof sealskins.

Bilblox sighed again, and began to rummage around in a sealskin-covered bag slung around his shoulders. After a minute or two of fumbling, he found the waterproof flashlight he had brought from Fort Krasnik and handed it to Alfonso. "It should work," said Bilblox. "I put in new batteries before we left Fort Krasnik." Alfonso clicked it on, and panned the light around them.

They were standing in a tiny cave that looked to be centuries old. The floor, walls, and ceiling were made of stone and packed gray-brown dirt. In front of them was a tunnel about five feet tall by three feet wide. Clearly it had been dug by hand. Alfonso could see indentations in the wall made by pickaxes. Every few feet, old wooden posts lined the walls from floor to ceiling. Most of the posts were cracked and a few had snapped in two. The air here smelled musty and metallic. Thousands of dust particles swirled in the beam of his flashlight. Alfonso shone his flashlight on the ground. He saw a pile of bones with a skull stacked on top.

"Is everythin' okay?" asked Bilblox. "How do my bandages look?"

"They look fine," said Alfonso. "No blood or anything. How do you feel?"

"I've been better," said Bilblox with a grunt. "Come on— let's get goin'."

As they walked into the tight-fitting tunnel, Alfonso recalled Dr. Van Bambleweep's words:

Over the centuries, many have entered looking for treasure, but all return empty-handed, if they return at all. In the catacombs, the careless explorer is easily tricked. Above all, follow the sound of trickling water until you reach an underground river. If in doubt, put your ear to the ground and listen.

For a long time, they heard only the sound of their footsteps and the squeak of the coffin's wheels echoing against the stone walls. Once in a while, they'd stop and listen for water, but heard nothing. Thankfully, there was only one passageway, and so they dutifully followed it. As they wandered through the darkness, Alfonso had time to think—too much time—and he soon found himself wondering what would happen if he and Bilblox got lost in these tunnels. They might die. If this happened, the plant wouldn't reach its destination and a great many people in Somnos would ultimately die as well. Alfonso recalled his uncle's description of the families who had frozen in giant blocks of ice. He shivered. It was a ghoulish thought, but it remained firmly lodged in Alfonso's mind.

They had been walking for more than an hour when Alfonso saw the first trace of water. Running down the tunnel wall was a glistening trail that looked like sweat running down a forehead. Alfonso placed Bilblox's hand on the rock. The burly longshoreman drew a finger across the trail and brought it to his mouth.

"It's water," he announced with a pained smile. "Maybe the river is nearby."

"Maybe," replied Alfonso.

They pressed onward and soon noticed that the tunnel began to slant down. The ground underfoot grew slick with moss and it took great concentration not to slip. Even with the flashlight, Alfonso almost tripped. Bilblox was not as lucky. He crept forward but didn't see a pile of shiny rocks just in front of him. When he stepped onto them, they shot out from under his feet and Bilblox fell down hard.

Alfonso rushed to his side. "Are you okay?" he asked. Bilblox groaned. "My legs are skinned pretty good," he said as he struggled to his feet. When finally standing, he leaned heavily against the wall and buried his face in his hands.

"Bilblox?" asked Alfonso.

"Just a small leaf?" said Bilblox in a low voice. He paused. "Nah, I shouldn't say anythin'."

"What are you talking about?"

"The bloom—I mean, it's in pretty good shape, right?" Bilblox asked. His voice sounded strange. "Well, d-do ya think we could burn just a small leaf? Just enough for me to get out of this underground mess? I can't see *anythin'*. It's so dark—I-I don't know if I can handle it. I'm no help to you like this."

Alfonso felt cold. Suddenly he was very aware of the backpack he was carrying, and of the little sapling nestled inside. "Sorry, Bilblox," replied Alfonso, his voice cracking. "We can't burn anymore."

Bilblox nodded dumbly, as if he had been hit. Suddenly, his clenched right fist smacked into the wall. He was so strong that the wall cracked and a large piece fell away. The whole tunnel seemed to shake. Bilblox howled in pain. "Just a small leaf," he pleaded. *"Ah, fer criminy's sake, I'm blind. Do ya know what that's like!"*

Alfonso's skin crawled as he realized that for the first time, he was scared of Bilblox. "Let's go," he said in what he hoped sounded like a determined voice. "Just a couple more minutes and then I'm sure everything will be just fine." He started walking, his feet loudly smacking against the water.

"All right," came the voice of a defeated-sounding Bilblox. "Let's keep goin'."

Water flowed into rivulets and soon formed a small stream that lapped over their shoes. They splashed forward. The water started to rise, first to their ankles, followed by their legs, knees, and finally, to the waist. The water was quite warm. It had to be the same water that flowed into the Trawpoy's hot springs.

"What do we do?" Bilblox asked.

"I'm not sure," said Alfonso.

"How's the backpack? We can't get it wet," said Bilblox.

"It's fine," replied Alfonso. "The sealskin wraps seem to be working."

They continued on but soon stopped again because the tunnel appeared to end directly in front of them. Yet, as they drew closer, they saw that it wasn't really a dead-end. The tunnel continued, but the ceiling slanted steeply down, so that it hung only a foot or so over the surface of the water. Something else caught their attention as well—the water was moving forward in a strong current, as if something was pulling it forward.

"That underground river has to be just beyond this tunnel," said Alfonso. "We'll have to crawl through."

Bilblox groped his way forward and felt the dimensions of

the space with his free hand. "No way," he said. "There's no way we can get through. It's too tight."

"There's a little space to breathe — in between the water and the ceiling," Alfonso said. "As long as it doesn't narrow any further, we'll make it."

"And what if it narrows?"

Alfonso said nothing.

"I don't like it," said Bilblox.

"Neither do I," said Alfonso. "But we don't have any other options."

Alfonso shoved the flashlight deep into his pocket. "I sure hope this flashlight is waterproof," mumbled Alfonso as he crept deeper into the cave. Water rocked and splashed all around him, but there was just enough space for him to keep his head above the water. Still, it felt awful being in that tiny space, almost completely covered in water, knees and elbows scraping against the sharp rock. Alfonso began to take shallow breaths that left him lightheaded. Behind him, he heard Bilblox struggle to shove the coffin into the tunnel. Rather suddenly, Alfonso was gripped with an overwhelming urge to go back. He tried to turn around but the space was too tight. In any case, the coffin pushed against his back. Alfonso tried to relax, and continued crawling forward.

After about ten feet, the tunnel shrank even more and the water rose above Alfonso's mouth, to just below his nose. His sealskin-covered backpack was now totally submerged. He prayed that the bloom was dry and safe.

"What's goin' on?" Bilblox yelled, his voice muffled by the water. "We're gonna drown!"

"Come on!" sputtered Alfonso. "I can hear the river."

The force of the current around them grew stronger. Alfonso struggled to keep his footing, but it was impossible. His feet were being pulled out from under him as if he were being sucked down a giant drain; and then, quite suddenly, he slipped and was yanked down through the water-filled tunnel. He panicked. Alfonso had always been good at holding his breath, but this was radically different than playing around in a pool. He was trapped underwater and being pulled even deeper! Alfonso thought of his mom, of World's End, Minnesota, and of the bloom that was inside his backpack.

Alfonso's head pounded. His skin crawled. He lost all sense of direction. Then the pressure eased from his ears. His head broke the surface of the water. He had survived!

For a few seconds, Alfonso did nothing but float on the surface of the water and gasp for air. He could see nothing through the darkness. Suddenly, something splashed next to him. Alfonso remembered the flashlight in his pocket. He fished it out and pointed it in the direction of the splash. He flicked on the flashlight and was delighted to find that it worked. He panned it around and saw Bilblox several feet away, floating face-down next to the coffin.

"BILBLOX!" Alfonso yelled. He swam over, grabbed the coffin, and lifted up Bilblox's head. Bilblox coughed and spit up water. He moaned in pain.

"You're alive!" said Alfonso. "I thought we were goners."

"Wh-wh-where are we?" Bilblox weakly sputtered.

"We're still underground," said Alfonso. "We're on a river. I think this is the one Van Bambleweep told us about."

"Yeah," replied Bilblox. "Let's get onto the coffin—it oughta make a good boat."

"What if it sinks?" asked Alfonso. "I don't want Spack to drown."

"This coffin ain't sinkin'," said Bilblox. "Trust me. I was underwater with this thing for a solid minute. It popped right back to the surface like a cork."

After a few minutes of anxious maneuvering, both managed to board the floating coffin. They sat upon it as if it were a big, clunky, wooden surfboard. Alfonso untied the paddles from the side of the coffin and gave one to Bilblox, keeping the other for himself. Then he carefully took off his backpack and tied it to the coffin using the ropes that had tied the paddles together. Alfonso wanted to see if the bloom was okay, but knew that he would have to wait until they reached a safer place.

Bilblox, who was sitting at the front of the coffin, began to paddle with long, powerful strokes. Alfonso, who sat in back, used his paddle as a rudder and navigated them down the river.

The river was moving very swiftly and the roar of the current echoed off the walls and ceiling. Overhead, thousands of stalactites hung like massive stone arrows just waiting to drop. Alfonso's skin itched and he wondered what types of strange minerals were in the water. It seemed like vapors were rising out of the water, but he couldn't be sure. The water itself was quite hot. All in all, the river seemed like it was from another planet.

They gradually noticed that the current of the river was building speed. Bilblox looked concerned. "Did the doctor say anythin' about rapids?" he yelled.

"No," Alfonso yelled back. He was pointing the flashlight down the river. "But I hear something up ahead. Sounds like rapids!"

"Oh brother," muttered Bilblox. "Could it get any worse?"

Just then, the coffin started to rock, and a great pounding sound echoed from within the cavity of the wooden chest: *Bang! Bang! Bang!*

"What's going on?" exclaimed Alfonso.

"By the demons of the *Nyetbezkov!*" yelled Bilblox. "It's that sleepin' fool—Spack. She's finally woken up!"

CHAPTER 23

TRAPPED UNDERGROUND

THE WOODEN lid to the coffin rattled wildly. It appeared to have three panels—one above the occupant's feet, one above her midsection, and one above her head—each of which could be opened separately. All three of them shook. Eventually, the rattling stopped and Alfonso heard the sound of a sliding bolt, as if someone were unlocking the coffin from the inside. A moment later, the middle panel—in between where Alfonso and Bilblox were sitting—swung open. After a great deal of squirming and contorting, a head poked out. The head belonged to a terrified-looking woman with a narrow face, pale skin, and an overwhelming amount of uncombed frizzy hair. It was Spack the loafer and she was dripping wet.

"Got any food?" asked Spack. "I'm starving! Haven't eaten

in days. A bit of pork sausage with some farmer's cheese would be nice. Perhaps a dry red wine as well? But I'll settle for bread crumbs if you have any."

"Now's not the time," yelled Alfonso. "We're in serious trouble!"

"Where are we, anyway?" asked Spack with a yawn.

"There's really no time to explain," replied Alfonso with a nervous smile. "We're in the catacombs beneath Barsh-yin-Binder and I think there are some rapids ahead."

"Only a fool would go into the catacombs!" said Spack. "What's your name, anyway?"

"Alfonso!"

"Never heard of you," said Spack. "And if you haven't got any food, then kindly get off my coffin." With that, Spack extended a wiry arm outside the coffin, and pushed Alfonso into the swirling water. Unprepared for this, Alfonso sank quickly before righting himself and grabbing hold of the coffin with one of his hands. He coughed and spat out water. Spack thought she had taken care of whoever that was, and decided to go back to sleep. She squirmed back into her coffin. This gave Bilblox the chance to crawl up the coffin and slam the middle panel closed. Bilblox then slowed the coffin down with his paddle and helped Alfonso, who was struggling to get back on. Spack started rocking back and forth inside the coffin and pounding against the walls.

"Just ignore her," yelled Bilblox. "There's no time for explanations. We got rapids ahead!"

"Where's the flashlight?" yelled Alfonso. "I can't see a thing."

"I don't know!" yelled Bilblox. "I thought ya had it!"

"Oh no!" said Alfonso. "It must have gone overboard —"

"Heads up!" yelled Bilblox. "Here come the rapids!"

Alfonso knew there was only one option: he had to enter hypnogogia. He closed his eyes halfway, took a deep breath, and pictured sand falling through an hourglass. He envisioned the individual grains falling, one at a time. He controlled his breathing so that with each exhale another grain of sand fell in his mind's eye. Pressure began to build in his ears—everything went silent for a moment—and then his hearing came to life with an incredible sensitivity.

The key was to use the sound and turn it into a visual picture, just like a bat. He listened carefully. Each miniscule bit of sound became a dot in his mind's eye. The countless water drops that made up the river fell into obedient patterns, and in brief flashes he could see what lay ahead. The scene resembled one of those paintings comprised only of tiny dots. He had seen a painting like this once when he had visited the Art Institute of Chicago. The technique was called pointillism, or something like that. When you looked closely at the points you couldn't make sense of them, but when you took a step backwards and took in the wider view, the points formed an incredibly detailed scene. In this case, there were actually millions of dots because the picture in his mind's eye was three-dimensional. The key was not to get overwhelmed. He started by focusing on a single dot and then allowed himself to expand his realm of concentration as if he were zooming out with a camera. Gradually, the entire scene revealed itself to him. He saw a series of twelve massive boulders less than a hundred feet away. Four of them were hidden just beneath the surface of the water, but he could still see them.

"Let's go!" yelled Alfonso. "How do you feel? Can you steer the coffin?"

"I'll do the best I can," said the injured Bilblox.

"I'll tell you which way to go," Alfonso shouted.

"Got it!" yelled Bilblox as the coffin dropped three feet into a pool of foamy water.

"Left!" yelled Alfonso.

Bilblox plunged his oar deep into the water and the coffin jerked to the left. A rock scraped thickly along the bottom and they both heard a muffled yell from within the coffin.

"Right!"

Again Bilblox dug the paddle into the water and the coffin shifted to the right, just missing a jagged, moss-covered rock.

"Right!"

"Left!"

"Left!"

"Left!"

"Right!"

The directions came at a furious pace. Bilblox responded as fast as he could, but still there were moments when they nearly capsized and razor-sharp rocks scraped deep grooves into the coffin.

They dropped headlong into a narrow chute of water surrounded by rock. Ahead was an enormous, spearlike boulder. Alfonso yelled at Bilblox to turn, but it came too late. The coffin hit the boulder head-on, and everyone tumbled forward. Fortunately, however, Alfonso was still in hypnogogia and—without the slightest hesitation—he jumped lightly onto the boulder, pushed the coffin away with a flick of his foot, and jumped back on. The coffin sprang free and shot down a final chute of warm whitewater. Then, as suddenly as it all began, the rapids ended and the roiling whitecaps dissipated into swirls and eddies.

They were through.

Bilblox grinned broadly. "Good job, buddy," he shouted, his voice echoing from wall to wall. "We did it!"

Alfonso nodded wearily. He had managed to stay in the hypnogogic state for five minutes straight, which was a record for him. Now he was utterly exhausted.

"Well I think that Spack has gone back to sleepin'," remarked Bilblox. "And ya know what? Those rapids must-a cleared out some cobwebs in my eyes. I can actually see a little bit now!"

"That's great," Alfonso weakly replied. "Get ready to pull the coffin over in a little bit. I think we're nearing the Great Cavern . . ." Alfonso knew that this would be the trickiest part of their ordeal. He recalled the doctor's words:

Take the river as far as the Great Cavern. You will know that you've entered the Great Cavern when you hear bats chirping and you see a strange glowing blue light. Make sure to get off the river here! Beyond the Great Cavern is a massive two-thousand-foot-high waterfall. You will certainly die if you go over it. Once you enter the cavern, paddle immediately to your right until you reach a pebble beach. Here you will find a giant painting of Prince Binder surrounded by many stone doorways. You should see a stone tablet with writing on it that tells you which doorway to take. The correct doorway should lead you around the falls—at least that's what my grandfather told me. I've never actually been that far, and can only advise you to choose wisely. The wrong doorway will lead back into the maze of the catacombs.

For a while, they floated along in relative silence until they entered an enormous cavern that looked big enough to hold an entire city. A strange, unearthly light with no obvious source caused the water to glow a light blue, as if the sky were below the water. Thousands of bats fluttered and squawked in the murky light. Alfonso looked to his right. Just as the doctor had described, there was a pebble beach; beyond this stood a wall that contained an entire grid of stone doorways. The doorways were stacked vertically and horizontally like a giant tic-tac-toe board. In the center of the grid was a large blank space that contained the remains of a gigantic drawing of a man in an elegant robe. This, presumably, was Prince Binder.

Bilblox thrust his paddle into the water and helped steer the coffin to shore. Soon they were standing on the pebble beach. They walked over to the grid of doorways and the drawing of Prince Binder. At the foot of Prince Binder lay a stone tablet with an inscription that had been written out in four different languages. One language appeared to be English, the second was French, the third was Russian, and the fourth was unrecognizable to Alfonso. The inscription in English read:

I can run,
But cannot walk,
Sometimes sing,
But never talk.

I lack arms,
But have hands.
I've no head,
But do not lack a face.

If you're punctual,
And quite spry,
The door will open,
And let you through.

"It's a riddle," said Alfonso.

Both of them stared at the tablet intently.

"It doesn't make a whole lot of sense," said Bilblox. "I mean, that statue's got arms and a head."

Alfonso walked over and tried opening one of the doors on the grid. It was locked. Nearby, there was a series of toeholds in the wall that enabled a person to climb up with relative ease and Alfonso soon tried every door in the entire grid. They were all locked.

"Now what?" asked Bilblox.

The two of them sat down on the pebble beach and continued to think about the riddle. Eventually, Bilblox broke out a loaf of bread from one of his packs and the two of them devoured it greedily. Finally, Alfonso turned to Bilblox and asked him what time it was. Bilblox showed Alfonso his watch, which indicated that it was now a quarter to three in the morning. Alfonso let out a deep sigh. It was so late. Would they ever get out?

It was so *late.* Alfonso read the tablet again. *Punctual.* Why would they need to be on time? Where did they need to be punctual? "Wait a minute!" cried Alfonso. "The riddle! It's about a clock!"

"Huh?"

"Think about it," said Alfonso. "A clock runs, but doesn't walk. It sings—whenever its bells chime—but it never talks. It has hands, but no arms. And it has a face, but no head."

"Yer right!" exclaimed Bilblox. "So then the rhyme means —"

"It means that the drawing of Prince Binder is actually a clock that's giving us an exact time," said Alfonso. "It's giving us a time when one of the doors will unlock."

"When?"

"It looks like around two fifty-five," said Alfonso. "You see, Prince Binder's short hand is almost pointing at three and his long hand is pointing at five minutes till."

"Holy cow—yer right!" said Bilblox. "But which door will open?"

"It could be the one in the top left corner," said Alfonso. "He seems to be pointing to that one."

Alfonso scrambled back up the beach to the grid of doorways. He climbed his way up to the door in the top left corner and found a narrow ledge directly in front. He inched his way out onto the ledge until he was standing in front of a large brass doorknob. Alfonso glanced at Bilblox's watch, which he had taken with him. It said two fifty-three.

"It's two fifty-three!" yelled Bilblox.

Exactly two minutes later, Alfonso heard a soft click within the brass door handle. He seized the door handle, turned the knob, and the door opened. He stumbled inside.

"Sounds like you opened it!" yelled Bilblox from down below. "Whaddya find?"

"It's a tunnel," yelled Alfonso. "And there's even a few coils of rope on the ground. It ought to help us get the coffin up here."

"Where does the tunnel lead?" yelled Bilblox.

"I have no idea," replied Alfonso.

CHAPTER 24

THE RIVER

THE PITCH-BLACK tunnel led down for almost a mile. At one point, Bilblox stopped and asked if they could rest. He was panting and exhausted. He set down the coffin and then lay on the floor of the tunnel. It was impossible to see anything in the darkness, but Alfonso ran his bare hands across Bilblox's bandages. Bilblox winced. The bandages were wet and sticky. His wounds had likely reopened. Alfonso suggested that they stop for a few hours. Bilblox refused. "We gotta get out of here," he said as he struggled to his feet. "Then we'll rest."

The tunnel ended in a small, circular room lined with red bricks. A very narrow skylight in the ceiling allowed a shaft of moonlight to enter the room. It was their first glimpse of the outside in over a day and they looked up at it hungrily. On the wall they saw what looked to be a piece of rope draped around an old brass ring. Bilblox gave it a curious tug. It tore as easily as tissue.

"I hope we didn't need to use it," Bilblox remarked.

They examined the room by the light of the moon and soon found a wooden trapdoor on the floor. It was covered in dirt but unlocked. Bilblox lifted it and immediately the deafening roar of the waterfall filled the small room. It was unclear where the trapdoor led, since the opening was filled with overgrown ferns and a thick mist. Bilblox fingered a rusted metal ring jutting just below the trapdoor opening. "I betcha that rope was to lower ourselves," he said. "I guess we have to jump."

"No, if we're careful, I think we can just climb down," said Alfonso. "I think I can see a ledge down there."

"Be careful," said Bilblox.

Alfonso nodded and began lowering himself down, brick by brick, through the trapdoor. The bricks were old and thick, and the mortar between them easily crumbled, which gave Alfonso good handholds. Soon he was in the middle of the ferns, covered in mist. About ten feet down, the chimneylike tunnel ended in a mossy ledge, slick with water. Directly in front was a wall of roaring water—the waterfall. The air was filled with thick droplets of water. Alfonso quickly realized that the only way out was to jump through the wall of water. There was no way to tell how far they were from the bottom of the falls, nor what would happen if they jumped through. They would have to leap blindly into the water. Alfonso climbed back up to explain the situation to Bilblox. The longshoreman looked pale and extremely sick. A lump rose in Alfonso's throat.

"What'd the doctor say about this?" Bilblox rasped.

"Nothing," replied Alfonso.

They looked at each other. They both knew their only choice was to jump into the wall of onrushing water.

"I'll go first," said Alfonso.

"Not this time," replied Bilblox with a weak smile. "It's my turn. We longshoremen are as comfortable in water as fish."

Bilblox groped his way through the trapdoor, climbed down slowly, and in a few minutes called for Alfonso to drop the coffin through the trapdoor. Alfonso shoved the coffin down. Bilblox caught it but yelped at the same time. There was no doubt that Van Bambleweep's dressing to the wounds had torn open. Alfonso quickly climbed down and joined Bilblox on the ledge. Bilblox was standing only inches from the wall of water. He weakly lifted his burly arm, shouted, "Longshoremen, ho!" and plunged into the water while holding onto the coffin. In less than a second, he was gone.

Alfonso inched over to the spot where Bilblox had been. He tightened the straps on his sealskin backpack, took a deep breath, and plunged into the wall of water. At first it felt like he was being hit, and his first thought was for Bilblox: could his friend survive this pummeling? Then he had the eerie feeling of being weightless. After what seemed like an extremely long period of falling, he was underwater and being pushed even further down.

He kicked as hard as he could and soon the current released its hold. Alfonso opened his eyes underwater and saw bubbles everywhere rising with him. Less than a minute later, he popped out of the water, gasping. He turned around and saw the magnificent waterfall about a hundred feet away, tumbling, crashing, and roaring in all of its foam-flecked glory.

"Hullo!" called a voice. "Alfonso—are you there?"

Alfonso looked around and saw Bilblox, floating on the coffin, about fifty feet away. Alfonso waved excitedly and swam toward Bilblox. He caught up and clambered aboard the coffin.

"Amazing," said Alfonso. "You know, you could look at the waterfall for a million years and never find the opening that we jumped through."

Bilblox nodded weakly, but said nothing.

Alfonso looked around and breathed in the fresh night air. At last, they were no longer underground! Steam rose from the warm river water, but the riverbanks were covered with snow. They should have been freezing—they were sopping wet and it was midwinter—but the clouds of hot steam from the river kept them surprisingly warm.

Alfonso glanced over at Bilblox and discovered that his friend was lying face-down on the coffin. He was in awful shape. His bandages were torn and tattered and most of his clothes were covered in blood.

Alfonso could barely speak. "B-Bilblox?" he stammered.

"I can't feel my body," said Bilblox quietly.

The coffin traveled down the river quickly and soon they were several miles away from the waterfall. The darkness began to lift and Alfonso stared at his surroundings: they were floating down a steaming river that twisted its way along the bottom of a snow-filled canyon.

"Bilblox—let's pull ashore, okay?" asked Alfonso.

Bilblox didn't reply. Alfonso scooted over and saw that Bilblox was barely conscious. He was shivering uncontrollably and his face was flushed with fever.

Alfonso quickly navigated the coffin toward shore. Once there, he left Bilblox slumped over the coffin and built a fire. With a great deal of coaxing, Alfonso eventually got Bilblox to stand up, limp over to the fire, and take off his wet clothing. Bilblox promptly lay down and closed his eyes.

Alfonso noticed that the coffin had been considerably banged-up during their journey through the catacombs. Although it was still solid enough to float, the wheels that made it easy to transport had snapped off. This wasn't a problem for as long as they floated, but it would make things much harder afterward. Luckily, Alfonso's backpack was in much better shape. The sealskin coverings had worked perfectly. The food, matches, all of their extra clothes, several heavy blankets, and most importantly, the Dormian bloom were safe and dry. In Bilblox's bag, Alfonso also found an extra set of bandages and a jar of Dr. Van Bambleweep's Wheatgrass Wound and Scar-Healing Ointment.

While Bilblox was sleeping, Alfonso unwrapped his bloody bandages and applied a fresh layer of ointment. The longshoreman didn't budge. Miraculously, hardly any of the stitches had ruptured. Alfonso applied fresh bandages, covered Bilblox with several blankets, and then turned his attention back to the Dormian bloom.

Alfonso opened the roof of the top hat. The branches and leaves of the Dormian bloom exploded outward like a puppet from a jack-in-the-box. Quite clearly, it would be impossible to cram the plant back into the top hat. The thing was simply too big. Within the last week or so, the Dormian bloom had been growing by leaps and bounds. It now weighed close to twenty pounds in Alfonso's estimation. He watched as the petals on the plant's flower changed color from yellow to orange to maroon to purple. It seemed to be in fine health. Alfonso was about to put the plant back into the sealskin bag when he was distracted by a noise. It was the sound of someone muttering. Alfonso nervously glanced over his shoulder.

It was Spack.

The loafer was sitting up in her coffin. She wore a dirty painter's smock on top of several tattered shirts, and brightly colored pants tied with a coarse burlap rope. Her chin was covered with dried bits of food. Her frizzy hair was so unkempt that it looked as if she had stuck her finger in an electric socket. At that moment, her green-gray eyes were fixed with a fierce intensity on the Dormian bloom.

"What a stroke of luck . . . It's fallen right into my hands!" muttered Spack.

Alfonso immediately returned the bloom back to the sealskin bag. He looked again at Spack, but the strange woman had fallen back asleep, and the coffin door was locked shut.

Bilblox slept the entire day and that night as well. Alfonso decided to stay put by the side of the river until Bilblox felt better. During this time, Spack kept herself locked inside her coffin and Alfonso worked almost continuously, gathering wood, stoking the fire, cooking food, and dressing Bilblox's wounds.

Throughout the second day Bilblox had a high fever. His forehead and cheeks burned with the heat of a furnace and he moaned pitifully. He was never fully awake, nor completely asleep. Finally, on the third day, Bilblox's fever broke. That evening, he sat up, ate an entire bowl of porridge, and began talking clearly. On the morning of the fourth day, Alfonso awoke and found him eating breakfast.

"Feeling better?" asked Alfonso.

Bilblox smiled. "Yer not kiddin'!" he exclaimed. "I feel like I just woke up from a nightmare. I can even see pretty well. Can ya believe my luck? How long was I sleepin' for?"

"Three days," said Alfonso.

"No kiddin'," said Bilblox.

Looking around, Bilblox declared that this particular place reminded him a little bit of Fort Krasnik. He stopped for a minute and then changed his mind. "There's somethin' weird about this place," he said. "Like it's been empty forever, ya know?" A sudden wind jostled the treetops and made the bare branches clatter against one another. Bilblox shivered and threw the coffee grounds from his cup into the coals of the fire. "Let's get outta here," he said. "This place is givin' me the willies. I don't know, maybe it's because we're travelin' on a coffin."

They looked at each other and laughed.

"You sure you feel up to moving again?" asked Alfonso.

"Let's go," said Bilblox. "The others will be waitin' for us."

"Yeah," said Alfonso quietly. "I just hope they made it out of Barsh-yin-Binder."

For the rest of the day, they floated peacefully down the river. Their destination was a landmark in the river known as the

Three-fingers Gorge. This was the spot where they were to meet up with Hill and Resuza. According to Dr. Van Bambleweep, there was no way they could miss the landmark. The fingers were actually three rock pillars sticking up from the river, each of them approximately two hundred feet tall. A series of wooden bridges ran across the top of the three fingers, allowing travelers to cross from one side of the river to the other. Dr. Van Bambleweep had sketched them a crude diagram:

It was early evening by the time they rounded a bend in the river and came upon the Three Fingers. The sun was beginning to set behind the massive, snow-covered Ural Mountains in the distance, but enough remained to light up the Three Fingers and make them glow. A cool breeze rocked the coffin. Alfonso and Bilblox sat and stared, speechless. From a distance, the Three Fingers looked stark and white, as if they were giant bleached bones sticking up. Bilblox steered the coffin to the shore just before the Three Fingers.

"I guess we oughta climb to the top," said Bilblox. "Hill and Resuza might be there already." He smiled. "Can't wait to see yer uncle and that girl, right?"

"I guess so," Alfonso replied bashfully.

That evening, they set up camp at the top of the gorge, after a long, difficult climb up from the water, especially now that they had to carry the coffin. There were no signs of Hill or Resuza.

For dinner, Bilblox and Alfonso cooked potatoes over the fire. As the scent of roasting potatoes wafted through the air, the lid of Spack's coffin rather suddenly popped open.

"What's for dinner?" came her tired voice.

"Potatoes," said Bilblox. "Want some?"

"Bring them here immediately," said Spack. "I shall have two, well cooked."

"Come and get it yerself," said Bilblox.

"Do you mean to tell me that after kidnapping me, you *now* refuse to feed me?" Spack asked. *"Incredible!"* She lay back down and said nothing.

After dinner, Alfonso and Bilblox were sipping the last of the hot coffee when a lonely howl rose from somewhere in the darkness. In response, more howls came from everywhere, including, it seemed, from someplace very close to the campsite. Alfonso shut his eyes and inched closer to the fire.

"Someone's headed our way!" said Bilblox. "Could be Dragoonya!"

Alfonso leapt to his feet and began kicking snow onto the fire to put it out.

"Get down!" yelled Bilblox. "Get outta sight!"

"Both of you shut up!" hissed Spack.

"It's okay," whispered Alfonso. "I think I know who it is."

Alfonso strained his eyes and saw two sleds being pulled by huskies. It was Hill and Resuza. Alfonso and Bilblox yelled in excitement. Resuza waved back enthusiastically. Hill drove his sled right up to the campsite and parked it next to Spack's coffin. He beamed at Alfonso and picked him up in a massive bear hug. Next was Resuza, who smiled happily and kissed Alfonso on the cheek. He blushed.

"Sorry we're late," said Hill. "Van Bambleweep's plan worked like a charm and we made great time until we got to those bridges by the Three Fingers. We couldn't cross them on the sleds, so we had to go ten miles downstream before we could find a spot to ford the river. Anyway, thank goodness we're fine. Bilblox, you look a little better! Are you recovering?"

Bilblox pointed toward Alfonso. "Thanks to this kid," he growled.

That night, the reunited group huddled around the fire and shared stories. Alfonso regaled them with their rafting adventure on the underground river aboard Spack's coffin, as well as the riddle of Prince Binder. Hill retold the story of their escape from Barsh-yin-Binder. According to Hill, Resuza had played the role of the concerned daughter brilliantly. "This young woman is quite an actress," said Hill. "You should have heard the sob story she gave to those Dragoonya soldiers. I was starting to shed some tears!"

"Ya know," remarked Bilblox, "the only part I can't figure out is why that Kiril fella helped us."

"Indeed, gents," said Resuza. "That was a strange event, and one I hope we shall never repeat." She stared into the campfire. No one said anything. They were all thinking about that terrible moment when Bilblox was almost killed.

Suddenly, out of the darkness, a squeaky voice uttered a single word: "Fools!"

"Who said that?" asked Hill.

"I did," said Spack. She had reemerged from her coffin and was now standing in the darkness, at the very edge of the campfire's glow. Her thin, pale face flickered dimly in and out of the blackness.

"Why did you call us fools?" asked Hill.

A slight smile crept across Spack's face.

"Because you haven't escaped anyone," said Spack slowly. "You're being played like pawns in a game of chess."

"Oh yeah?" said Bilblox. "What makes ya so knowledgeable?"

"My big, blind, dumb friend," said Spack, "I know *more* about *what* you're carrying and *where* you're headed than *any* of you. And let me assure you, it is a very, very, very good thing that you have me here to help."

"Who are you?" asked Hill pointedly.

Spack bowed ever so slightly. "My dear friend, I'm your guide," she replied.

"Guide to where?" asked Hill.

"To Dormia," replied Spack. "My country."

The silence was broken by a far-off but piercing howl.

"Dormia?" said Resuza. "What's Dormia?"

CHAPTER 25

GREAT WANDERING DAY REMEMBERED

SPACK WALKED closer to the campfire and took a seat next to Alfonso. She moved gingerly, as if she had not used her leg muscles in a very long time. She eased her way down to the ground and, as she did, her joints creaked and popped in a very unpleasant way.

"I have urgent business to discuss," said Spack. "But first I have some complaints to lodge with the leader of this expedition, whoever that might be. I can't recall signing up to join this operation, but if and when I did, I neglected to lay down my terms. The food thus far has been poor, the accommodations miserable, and the company wretched! What's more, my coffin has incurred serious bangs, scrapes, water damage, and the wheels have snapped off. I expect some improvements—right away!"

"Ya got some nerve," growled Bilblox. "Why don't ya try walkin' on yer own two legs before ya start askin' for better grub?"

"Tell us what you know and why you claim to be our guide," said Hill. "Then we'll see what we can do for you."

Spack glowered at Bilblox and said nothing.

"Here," said Hill kindly. "Have a cup of cardamom tea. I'm sure you'll be in a better mood afterward. We bought it at a small shop back in Barsh-yin-Binder." Hill grabbed the pot of boiling water dangling above the fire and poured tea into a tin cup. Spack took the cup of tea and grunted appreciatively.

"At last, someone with a bit of humanity," muttered Spack. "You see," she began, "I always knew that I was destined for some great purpose in life . . . destined to play some pivotal role in the fate of Somnos . . . and now it has come to pass."

"What are you saying?" asked Hill. "Something about Somnos? Speak up! You're part Dormian aren't you? I knew I recognized that lullaby! What do you know about Somnos?"

"A great deal," said Spack. "For you see, that place is my home. Let me explain . . ." She took a sip of tea and smiled shyly at Hill.

"I've had a hard life," she began. "Always bullied by other kids and bearing the brunt of practical jokes. Never had any friends. Even my own parents were embarrassed of me . . . Yes, I was diagnosed as a 'tired Dormian,' and that is the worst kind of Dormian to be. We are the freaks of Dormian society because, when we fall asleep, we actually sleep soundly on our backs and do nothing but snore."

"That doesn't sound so awful," said Resuza sympathetically. "Isn't that what most people do?"

"Oh let me assure you, it is awful," said Spack. "I was the only person in my neighborhood who slept like that. It kept me from having friends, going to school, and playing sports. Worst of all, it meant that there was no way that I could fulfill my dream of becoming a Wanderer."

"A Wanderer?" inquired Bilblox.

Wanderers, explained Spack, were the heroes of Dormia. They were charged with the most important task of all: preparing to help the Great Sleeper whenever and wherever he or she might turn up. To do so, they traveled the world and settled into foreign societies. All this because, for strange and mysterious reasons, Great Sleepers and the Dormian blooms they planted always sprouted *outside* Dormia. Therefore, it was crucial that there were Dormians everywhere in the world, ready to help the Great Sleeper and protect the bloom. These Dormians were known as Wanderers because they crisscrossed the globe looking for Great Sleepers. Of course, the vast majority of Wanderers never laid eyes upon a Great Sleeper. Yet there always had to be a steady flow of Wanderers into the 'outside world,' because one never knew *exactly* when a Founding Tree might die, necessitating the emergence of a new Great Sleeper. Those lucky Wanderers who actually helped a Great Sleeper find their way home were idolized and became legends.

"Yes, that's the life!" Spack exclaimed. "Wandering the world: this year China, next year India, the year after that the horn of Africa!"

Even though Spack had always wanted to become a Wanderer, she was never considered for the job because she was a tired Dormian. Still, Spack dreamed. Most of all, she dreamed of participating in Great Wandering Day. On this day, which occurred only once every twelve years, a new generation of Wanderers departed for the outside world.

"The day was one big parade!" recalled Spack. "The city streets were covered with fragrant white and yellow flowers. Banners hung from every window and doorway. Dormians assembled before the city gates in their finest clothes to bid farewell to their wandering heroes. Each Wanderer was given a satchel with a dagger, a slingshot, a pouch of medicinal herbs, a vile of poison, a watch, gold coins, and little toy maracas —"

"Maracas?" inquired Alfonso. "What kind of —"

"Don't interrupt my story!" sniped Spack. "It'll all be clear to you soon enough. Anyway, as I was saying, I wanted to be a Wanderer! And why not? Was it that impossible to imagine that a tired Dormian might be useful? Well, according to the elders, it *was* impossible. They refused, but I showed them. You see, when I was about fifteen years old, there was a Great Wandering Day and I decided to join in, unofficially of course. The Wanderers leave in these great big sleds and, during all the commotion of the parade, I simply darted out of the crowd—as fast as a tired Dormian could move—and hopped into a sled. I hid under a blanket and kept quiet. All around me I could hear cheering and trumpets sounding. Then came a noise that I shall never forget: the rumbling of the great stone doors of Somnos. It was as if the mountainside itself opened up. The very ground shook. Seconds later, howling winds poured in."

Spack paused to have a sip of tea. Every last person, even Bilblox, was hanging on her every word.

"We were brave Wanderers," recounted Spack, her eyes

shining. "It was bitterly cold and the wind was merciless. Everyone was freezing, even me. We slid downhill for two days and I never moved once from my hiding place. Of course, it helped that I could sleep for most of the time. On the third day, though, they discovered me. As you might imagine, they were a bit unhappy but—*overwhelmed* by my bravery—they decided to drop me off in Barsh-yin-Binder, where I was told to go undercover. They never gave me one of their satchels, but what does it matter? There, I was treated like a queen!"

Spack flashed a brief triumphant smile. "And now, here I am leading the Great Sleeper home! I can't wait to see everybody's face. They'll raise a statue in my honor. Everyone will wonder how they could have been so cruel to me."

"Ya haven't led us anywhere yet," said Bilblox. He stood up and looked around the campsite. "I'm not tryin' to sound mean, but how d'we know this ain't made up?"

Hill spoke for the first time in a while. "Spack doesn't need any proof. What she says is true."

"How can you be sure?" asked Alfonso.

"Trust me, I know," replied Hill. "I remember now—I remember what happened." Tears welled up in Hill's eyes and he looked incredibly sad.

"Uncle Hill?" said Alfonso. "What's the matter?"

"The mind is a funny thing," said Hill softly to himself. "All of those years I tried so desperately to dredge those memories from the depths of the past. I tried everything—even hypnosis—but to no avail. Now it's as clear as day. Of course, that's how it happened. Of course! It was Great Wandering Day. What silly boys we were. What silly, silly boys!"

"What in the heck are ya talkin' about?" asked Bilblox.

"I *remember,* Bilblox—I remember it all," said Hill with a dull, faraway look on his face. "That's how Leif and I got lost outside Dormia. It was on Great Wandering Day. The crowds, everyone shouting . . ."

Hill's voice tapered off. "Leif and I had been told to watch each other and be careful," he continued. "But we were curious. So were the other kids. A group of us all ran behind the last sled in the procession. And I just . . . went too far. I didn't turn around with the other kids. Leif ran after me. Then, the next thing we knew, those massive doors slammed shut. I tried to get back in . . . I pounded on the doors but they couldn't hear us. We ran ahead, thinking we'd find the Wanderers, but they had disappeared. It was bitterly cold and all we had were thin jackets."

Hill continued in a low, sorrow-filled voice: "A day later, we found a small band of Wanderers who recognized us. They were very kind, and put us on their sled and gave us food. I remember this one very pretty young woman with long blond hair. She gave Leif a maraca and she gave me the old Dormian watch that I still have. We were crying and I think she wanted to keep us occupied. I don't remember much else, except many days of travel and being so tired I could barely move. And then the terrible howling and snarling began. We must have been attacked. The young woman hid us under the sled, and then left."

He looked at Spack and sighed. "The Wanderers must have died to protect us," he said softly. "Now that I remember, it seems like it happened just yesterday."

"Just like me," said Spack. "And now we're both going home . . ."

Hill turned away from the group and stared into the darkness that surrounded them. No one spoke for a very long time. The only sounds came from the yelps of the huskies as they continued to chew on the bones that Hill had fed them for dinner. A cold wind gusted down from the mountains. Everyone shivered. Finally, Spack broke the silence by directing a question at Alfonso.

"You seem awfully young to be a Great Sleeper," said Spack. "Have you found your weapon yet?"

"Alfonso is too young for weapons," interjected Hill.

"Every Great Sleeper has a unique weapon that he or she masters," replied Spack. "You know, like an Egyptian dagger, or a Japanese *masakari*, or a Chinese meteor hammer, or some kind of magical boomerang. All our history books talk about it . . . You do have one—right?"

"Not exactly," said Alfonso.

"Oh," said Spack with an embarrassed smile. "Well, er, I'm sure you'll find one soon enough. Of course, maybe you're just too young—"

Bilblox interrupted. "You never answered the question," he said. "Why are we such a bunch of fools, and how is it that we haven't escaped? Do you see anyone around us?"

Spack shook her head and then asked, "This fellow you mention by the name of Kiril. Was he, by chance, wearing a ring with the Dragoonya seal on it?"

Alfonso nodded.

"And his eyes were white—suggesting that he has used Dormian ash—and yet it appears that he can see perfectly well, correct?"

Alfonso nodded again.

"Just as I thought," said Spack confidently. "He is a Dormian traitor! Only a Dormian can take the ash and not go blind. Most likely he was a Wanderer whom Nartam corrupted. He has been doing this for the last two thousand years."

"Then why would he help us?" asked Alfonso. "Why would he fight off those Dragoonya soldiers back in Barsh-yin-Binder?"

"It was a ruse," said Spack with a disgusted sigh. "This man isn't helping you—he's following you! He wants you to lead him all the way to Somnos. This is how it works with the Dragoonya. They follow the Great Sleeper back to the city's gates and then— *whammo!*—they sack the city. This is why you cannot be followed! Or perhaps I should say that this is why *we* cannot be followed. Whatever we do, we must be absolutely sure that no one is on our tail. If we lead Nartam back to the gates of Somnos, we will have failed, and the last city of Dormia will be lost. It would be better to destroy the bloom than to allow Nartam in."

Alfonso looked at Resuza. She had been sitting there, looking confused, and finally she spoke. "Wait just a minute," she said. "You're trying to deliver a magical plant to some hidden kingdom in the Urals *and* you're afraid of being followed by a two-thousand-year-old man and his henchman?"

Alfonso, Hill, Bilblox, and Spack all nodded.

"A great secret has been revealed to you," Spack said to Resuza. "I don't know why you and your hulking friend Bilblox have come along—since both of you clearly are not Dormians. And I find it highly suspicious that Bilblox's eyes are white. Highly suspicious indeed! Rest assured, I'll be keeping a close eye on both of you."

Spack turned to Alfonso. "In any case, do you get it now?" she asked pointedly. "Nartam and Kiril never had any desire to capture you, or kill you, or even take your plant. That's why they let you go. They *want* you to find Somnos."

In the silence that followed, Alfonso glanced around and peered into the darkness that surrounded their little campsite. He thought he heard a twig snap, but maybe it was just the fire. A ripple of goose bumps fluttered up his neck. *Was Kiril out there, standing in the gloom, waiting for him?* Alfonso searched the darkness for any sign of Kiril's ghostly white eyes. He saw nothing. After a while, he returned his attention back to the group. As he did, an old suspicion returned. *Could he trust his group? After all, how well did he know them?* Alfonso had just met Resuza and Spack. He really didn't know them at all. And even Hill and Bilblox, both of whom he had come to trust, were not exactly lifelong friends. *Was someone in the group a traitor?* It was an awful thought. Alfonso felt ashamed for even thinking it. And yet, he couldn't stop himself. Although he was brought up to think the best of people, World's End, Minnesota, was far away. Lars's words came back to him: *trust no one.*

Bilblox interrupted Alfonso's thoughts. "So how do we shake these Dragoonya?" he asked Spack. "They probably know this area better than we do."

"Don't worry about that," Spack replied. "In order to get to Somnos, we have to pass through a terrible place called Straszydlo Forest. As your guide, and as an honorary member of the Order of Wanderers, I can assure you that no Dragoonya army would ever, ever, ever enter that place."

"Why's that?" Bilblox asked.

"Well, there's a very good reason for that . . . ," said Spack. Her voice tapered off into a whisper. "Because, well, er . . ." She looked embarrassed. "Sorry. I can't quite remember exactly why. All I know is that no one in their right mind steps foot inside that forest—unless they want to die a miserable death, in which case, walking into that forest is precisely what they should do."

"But we have to cross that forest," said Alfonso.

"Yes," muttered Spack to herself. "That is rather problematic, isn't it?"

"Why can't you remember what's in the forest?" asked Resuza. "Aren't you supposed to be our guide?"

"That's the problem with being a tired Dormian," said Spack with a heavy sigh. "We sleep so deeply that we often miss out on some rather important details."

CHAPTER 26

THE GAHNOS

THE WHISTLING of the wind awoke Alfonso sometime in the middle of the night. It was bitterly cold and he sat up stiffly to see if there was anything else he could use to cover himself and provide a bit of extra warmth. He looked around. A crescent moon hung in the sky. Out of the corner of his eye, Alfonso noticed the faint outline of a man standing twenty feet off in the distance. At first, Alfonso thought it might be Hill—or even Bilblox—but this figure had two long swords slung along his belt, and Alfonso knew immediately that he was staring at Kiril. Alfonso felt oddly calm as he rose to his feet and walked carefully toward Kiril.

"Why are you following us?" asked Alfonso.

"If you were capable of taking care of yourself it wouldn't be necessary for me to follow you," replied Kiril. His white eyes shone brightly in the half moonlight. "Besides, is that all the thanks I get for saving your life yet again?"

"I don't trust you," said Alfonso. "Why were you wearing that Dragoonya ring on your finger?"

"You mean the ring you stole from me back in Fort Krasnik?" said Kiril with a dry laugh. "I've been meaning to ask for that back. It helps me get in and out of Barsh-yin-Binder. That's the only reason I wear it."

"And how come your eyes are white?" asked Alfonso. "That means you're a Dragoonya, doesn't it?"

"No," said Kiril calmly. "It most certainly doesn't. Your friend Bilblox's eyes are white too—is he a Dragoonya?"

"So you're a Dormian?" asked Alfonso skeptically.

"I was a Dormian once," said Kiril. "But not anymore."

"So you're a Dormian traitor?"

"Watch your tongue, lad," snapped Kiril angrily. "You know not what you say. I am not a Dormian or a Dragoonya—I am a *Gahno.*

"A Gahno?"

"Yes—once, many years ago, my family came from the ancient Dormian city of Jasber," explained Kiril. "When I was twelve years old, my older brother, mother, and younger sister traveled to Noctos, another city of Dormia, for a family gathering. During that visit, the city was attacked by the Dragoonya. My brother helped defend the city and, though I was only twelve, I fought by his side. During the battle, part of the Founding Tree burned and many of us—including my entire family—were exposed to the ash as it rained down from the burning tree. We got it into our eyes, which soon turned white.

In the end, we managed to repulse the Dragoonya attack, but afterward—instead of thanking us—the people of Noctos cast everyone with white eyes out into the snow. They called us Gahnos, which means 'untrustworthy' in the ancient Dormian tongue. They hated us—just as they will hate your friend Bilblox when you finally arrive in Somnos."

"What happened to you and your family?" asked Alfonso.

"My five-year-old sister died first," explained Kiril. "She froze to death in the snow. We had no food or blankets. We didn't stand a chance. My mother died two days later. My brother, who had been injured in the battle, died later that night. I managed to wander down into a small ravine and this is where I met the man who became my father. He took me in, warmed me, fed me, and nursed me back to health. He saved my life. I only wish he had found us sooner."

"That's awful," said Alfonso.

"I can stomach a great deal of hypocrisy," continued Kiril, "but I cannot tolerate having my loyalty questioned by you or anyone else. I am a Gahno. We are the embodiment of loyalty—and we have paid dearly for it."

"It still doesn't make sense —" began Alfonso.

"What?" demanded Kiril.

"If you're no longer a Dormian, why are you helping me?"

Kiril said nothing for a moment. Instead, he looked off to the south, where the distant, snow-capped peaks of the Urals shone brightly against the night sky.

"I could tell you some heartwarming tale about how I struggled with my own bitterness and yet still loved Dormia in my heart of hearts," said Kiril with a snort of disgust. "But I see no purpose in lying to you. I don't especially care for you, or your uncle, or your plant, or Dormia. I do this because my father—the man to whom I owe my life—has urged me to take the path of righteousness. It was he who asked me to help you. I told him it was a lost cause, but he insisted. In the end we must obey our fathers—isn't that so?" Kiril shook his head sadly. "But mark my words—in the end, Dormians will regret their treatment of the Gahnos."

"Who is your father?" asked Alfonso. "I think it's time you told me."

"You're in no position to make demands," retorted Kiril. "All in good time."

Alfonso just stood there. He felt paralyzed, as if he and Kiril were replaying their first encounter in the Forest of the Obitteroos.

"I know you don't trust me," said Kiril with a weary sigh. "But the real traitor in our midst is someone within your traveling party—and I assume you know who it is."

CHAPTER 27

THE WOODS ARE HAUNTED

THE FOLLOWING morning, shortly after dawn, Alfonso awoke with a start and looked around anxiously. There were no signs of Kiril anywhere. Alfonso took a sigh of relief. Soon he was busy helping Hill and Bilblox load all of the supplies onto the two dog sleds—including the coffin, with Spack inside of it. The only real packing dilemma involved the Dormian bloom. It had been growing steadily and it was now far too large to be carried in any of their packs. Eventually, they decided to store the plant inside the coffin with Spack. The coffin would protect the growing bloom, and Spack was too awestruck by the bloom to object.

Once the supplies were packed, it was time to go. The huskies barked anxiously as if they too couldn't wait to get going.

"I'll ride with Bilblox," said Hill. "You go with Resuza."

"Resuza is driving the other sled?" Alfonso asked.

"Of course," replied Hill. "She is superb with the dogs."

"I didn't realize you knew how to drive a sled so well," said Alfonso.

"You don't know a lot of things," said Resuza merrily, as she mounted the small standing-board at the back of the sled. "Ready?"

Alfonso rolled his eyes and joined Resuza on the standing-board. Seconds later, Resuza took hold of the sled's whip, snapped it in the air, and yelled, "Yah!" as loudly as she could. Alfonso felt his neck jerk backwards. He quickly lost his balance and almost fell off the sled, but thankfully Resuza grabbed hold of him. The sled whizzed past banks of snow, towering evergreen trees, frozen creeks, giant snowcapped boulders, bushy-tailed foxes, steep cliffs with massive icicles hanging from them, and an endless expanse of frosty blue sky. "Yah!" yelled Resuza as she snapped the whip in the air. "Yah!"

The two sleds headed due south, directly toward the Ural Mountains. Alfonso could see their snowy peaks in the distance. He couldn't believe that the five of them would actually have to navigate their way through these towering masses of ice and rock. But before they did this, they would have to cross Straszydlo Forest. These were the mysterious woods where Vice Admiral Purcheezie had found Hill and Leif all those years ago. These woods also marked the starting point on the Estonian smuggler's map. Alfonso still recalled what the vice admiral had said about these woods: "We came to the edge of a fearsome forest known as Straszydlo. I didn't dare step into the forest but even from the outside, I'd have to say that it's just about the spookiest place I've ever visited."

As far as Alfonso knew, the vice admiral was afraid of almost nothing. So what exactly had managed to spook her in these woods? After all, according to Spack, these woods were so dangerous that not even the Dragoonya entered them . . .

By late afternoon on the second day of steady travel, they reached the edge of Straszydlo Forest and abruptly came to a halt. The sight of these woods immediately gave Alfonso a creepy feeling. The trees, which were all very tall, had branches covered with sharp, curling, silver thorns. The long branches were meshed together so thickly that the forest appeared to be an impenetrable snarl of trunks, branches, vines, and dark shadows. Indeed, the forest was so dense that it was impossible to see more than ten feet into its interior.

The colors of the forest were also quite striking. The bark of the trees was as black as coal and—despite the fact that it was midwinter—fiery red leaves dangled from the branches. Alfonso mustered his courage and walked directly up to the edge of the forest itself. There, he saw the most alarming sight of all: a series of enormous footprints, each of which bore the imprints of seven long, slender claws.

"What kind of footprints are those?" asked Alfonso.

"No idea," said Resuza. "And I hope never to find out." She sniffed the air. "Smoke," she said. "There is a fire nearby."

"It's coming from over there," said Hill as he pointed off into the distance. "It looks like there's some kind of house by those evergreen bushes."

Everyone looked toward the spot where Hill was pointing. There, nestled amid a small grove of evergreen bushes, was a house built entirely of stone except for a bright-red front door, which was made of wood. The structure was just one story high, although at the rear of the house stood a narrow, extremely tall stone tower. The tower looked so thin and tall that it seemed as if a wind or even a breeze might topple it.

"I wonder who lives there," said Alfonso. "Should we go knock?"

Before anyone could answer this question, however, a rumbling noise came from inside the coffin. The coffin's door swung open and Spack poked her head out and looked around. "Well, well, look at those trees. If I didn't know better, I would say we've arrived at Straszydlo Forest."

"That's exactly where we are," said Hill. "And something tells me that it's not wise to stay near these woods at night."

"Why not?" asked Alfonso.

"It just seems like a bad idea," said Hill somewhat testily. He seemed unusually uneasy and this, in turn, put Alfonso and Bilblox on edge. "I can't quite put my finger on it," mumbled Hill. "But these woods seem —"

"Haunted," finished Spack.

"Haunted by what?" asked Alfonso.

"Your guess is as good as mine," replied Spack with a yawn. "But those woods are clearly . . ." This sentence tapered off into a snore. Once again, Spack was sleeping.

"Well," said Hill slowly, "let's not get too close. Evening is upon us . . ." A lonely howl rose from the forest.

"City folk often say that nature is haunted," said Resuza. "Maybe they're just not used to the fresh air."

"Maybe," said Hill. "But all the same, let's not try the woods now. Perhaps someone is home at that little house. We could all use some sleep under a roof."

Hill looked at Resuza. She had a concerned expression on her face. He asked her what was wrong.

"I think someone ought to stay outside tonight and keep an eye on things. Just to make sure," she said. She looked at Alfonso. "It's probably nothing," she continued. "But over the last day, I've had this strange sensation, as if I'm being watched. Of course, I've never seen anyone, but . . ."

"I'll stay outside," said Alfonso.

"Forget about it," said Hill. "We need to keep you and the bloom hidden."

"I'd do it," said Bilblox, "but I can barely see a thing."

"Let me do it," said Resuza. "I'm accustomed to living outside and, after all, you chaps are paying me for my services."

"I don't know . . . ," began Alfonso.

"Don't worry, yer girlfriend will be fine," said Bilblox teasingly.

"Much obliged for your concern," said Resuza with a smile at Alfonso. "It's sweet of you—it really is—but I'll be fine."

"Okay," said Hill. "But be careful."

Resuza nodded, smiled at the group, and walked off into the murky twilight.

CHAPTER 28

THE RULES OF THE FOREST

THEY APPROACHED the stone house. Hill walked up to the red door and rapped his knuckles on it. There was no reply. He tried again, this time using his entire fist to pound on the wood. Moments later, the door swung open, and a frail, gray-haired woman in a dark red cloak appeared in front of them. She leaned heavily on a gnarled piece of wood that she used as a cane. Her arms were thin, bony, and covered with a thicket of white hairs. She had a long, angular, and sad-looking face, and her eyes looked oddly red.

"Why do strangers trouble me as night draws near?" asked the woman in a scratchy voice.

"Good evening, madam," said Hill with a slight bow. "We

are gentle travelers, in search of food and shelter. We can pay, of course."

"Why would I want to help you?" asked the woman. Her voice creaked like an unoiled hinge. "'Tis strange indeed to be wandering around these woods. What is your business?"

"Our business is a private affair," replied Hill with a smile. "But do not worry—we are only passing through. Tomorrow, we intend to cross this forest."

The old woman cackled heartily.

"Well," she said, "in that case, I'll never deny a man his last meal. And I suppose that we can provide some shelter as well. Come follow me. My name is Rosalina and I will introduce you to the other members of our household. You can let your huskies roam outside. They'll be scared enough of the forest not to wander too far."

Hill, Alfonso, and Bilblox—who was carrying the coffin that contained both Spack and the Dormian bloom—followed Rosalina down a long, drafty hallway and into a large kitchen that smelled of freshly cut herbs and chicken broth. The smell was coming from a cast-iron pot that hung above a crackling fireplace. The walls of the kitchen were lined with shelves containing jars of pickled vegetables and fruit. Lying on the floor were several wooden crates filled with all manner of vegetables, including carrots, beans, and cabbage. The ceiling was lined with long wooden rafters from which hung burlap bags filled with dried and salted meats. In the center of the room was an old wooden table with benches, and on one of these benches sat a woman wearing a dark blue cloak who looked identical to Rosalina.

"The woman sitting there is my twin sister, Masha," explained Rosalina. "And the adorable little kitty sitting by the fireplace is our cat, Sam."

They turned their attention toward a low-slung chair perched directly in front of the fireplace, where the fattest cat that any of them had ever seen was sitting. It had to weigh at least a hundred pounds. Sam was so heavy that it was doubtful that he could, even in the most extreme of circumstances, use his small legs to move himself. His head rested limply on a half-eaten loaf of bread.

"These foolish travelers need a place to sleep and I have invited them to stay for the night," explained Rosalina. "Sam, do you think that my sister will object?"

Alfonso, Hill, and Bilblox glanced at the cat, as if expecting him to reply. He looked up, yawned, and began eating the loaf of bread.

Masha cleared her throat and declared, "Sam, my sweet fluffy kitten, if my younger sister has decided to welcome guests to our house, then I have no objection, unless you do."

Sam, who was licking the air with his splotchy pink tongue, did not reply.

"Good," replied Rosalina. "Then we shall have dinner together. Sam, do you think that my sister would agree to serving her chicken broth?"

"Sam," replied Masha, "please tell my sister that I am happy to do so."

"Oh good," said Rosalina. "If you will, Sam, please extend our sincerest thanks to my sister."

Bilblox, who was thoroughly confused by this back and forth, set down the coffin and inquired, "Don't you two ladies ever talk to each other—or do ya always talk to that cat first?"

"We find it much easier to talk to Sam," explained Masha politely. "He's very polite, and it helps *all of us* get along better. Plus, it keeps Sam's spirits up. He hasn't been eating well lately."

Bilblox looked confused, but nodded anyway.

They all sat down on the benches around the old wooden table and enjoyed a dinner of chicken broth and freshly made bread. After many nights of camping in the snow, it felt very good to be inside, near a crackling fire, sipping warm soup. Alfonso thought about Resuza, and hoped she was all right. It was terrible to miss such a wonderful meal.

Meanwhile, Rosalina was in the midst of a lengthy complaint about her nephew, Wenceslaus, and the infrequency of his visits. "It gets very lonely here," griped Rosalina. "If it weren't for Sam, I don't know what we would have done."

"So you haven't seen anyone besides us in quite a while?" inquired Hill.

"It's been years since I laid eyes on a man as handsome as yourself," said Rosalina with a suggestive smile.

Hill coughed on his soup.

"So you haven't seen any Dragoonya?" interjected Alfonso.

"Oh goodness no," replied Rosalina. "Like everyone else, they avoid the forest."

"What's the big deal with that forest anyway?" asked Bilblox. "Why is everyone so worked up over a bunch of trees?"

Masha—who had said very little up until this point—cleared her throat and declared solemnly, "It is dangerous, but you can survive as long as you follow the rules."

"What rules?" asked Hill.

The two sisters both looked at Sam nervously. The cat, perhaps sensing their gaze, yawned and then moved his head in a way that looked remarkably like a nod. With this approval, Rosalina began telling them about the forest.

"Straszydlo is a funny place," she began in a serious tone. "I always tell people who wish to enter that they must be *very careful.* A group of hunters once passed through here and we tried to tell them about the rules, but they paid no mind. The next day, one of the hunters—only one—pounded on our door. His clothing was tattered and soaked in blood. He wouldn't say what happened. Instead, he started weeping like a child . . ."

"I got no problems followin' rules," said Bilblox. "I'm a longshoreman—a union man—and you should see the stuff we gotta sign. Import, export, bills of ladin', insurance . . . I can follow rules with the best of 'em and I'll make sure everyone else does the same."

Again the sisters looked at Sam rather nervously; and again the cat nodded as if he somehow was following the conversation.

"Well . . . ," said Rosalina. "Shall we move to the fireplace and talk this over?" The two old ladies stood up and walked over to the large, overstuffed leather chair where Sam was sitting. Each of them perched delicately on an arm of the chair and began petting Sam's head. Alfonso and the others followed them and sat down on various dusty pillows scattered across the floor. Rosalina withdrew an old wooden flask from her coat.

"Perhaps you gentlemen would enjoy a sip of our homebrewed spirit, finklegrog," she said. "It has a most pleasing aftereffect." Rosalina took a healthy gulp from the flask, smiled strangely, and then burped into the fire. Her burp caught fire, giving off the appearance that she had just breathed fire like a dragon. "Any takers?" asked Rosalina.

"Yes please!" said Bilblox excitedly. He grabbed the flask eagerly and filled his mouth with the liquid. Instead of swallowing it and burping, he spit it into the fire. A massive plume of fire shot out from his mouth.

Rosalina and Masha tittered with laughter.

Hill shot Bilblox an annoyed look and pressed Rosalina to tell them more about the rules of the forest.

"All right," began Rosalina, "the first rule is the simplest: never, ever, *ever* set foot in the forest at night."

"That's right," added Masha. "At night the forest belongs to the Straszydlo. That's what I tried to tell those hunters, isn't that right, Sam?"

Sam looked up for a moment, as if he actually might say something, but instead he coughed up a good-size fur ball.

"Straszydlo?" inquired Alfonso. "Who are they?"

"They're the ones who live in the forest," explained Masha. Then she added in a hushed whisper: "They're the ones you don't want to *upset*." She looked severely at Alfonso.

"The second rule is that you must always go alone," said Rosalina. "The Straszydlo have a fear of groups of people."

"I warned those hunters about that as well," added Masha. "But they paid me no mind."

"And then comes the third and final rule," said Rosalina. "And it is—by far—the hardest to follow."

"Quite true," added Masha. "This is the rule that usually gets people in trouble. And, the funny thing is, it's almost as simple as the other rules—"

"What is it?" demanded Bilblox.

"*Never* look back," both Rosalina and Masha said at once.

"That doesn't sound like such a big deal," said Bilblox.

"That's what they all say," replied Rosalina with a dark chuckle. "But just you wait until you have a Straszydlo right on your heels—so close that you can feel its steamy breath on the back of your neck. It happened to me once—never again!" Rosalina took another swig of finklegrog. Her eyes blazed with the heat of the fire.

"The worst is when they start talking to you," added Masha. "The Straszydlo can mimic the sounds that they hear, like parrots. Sometimes what they say is just harmless nonsense like, *What time is it?* But often what they mimic are people's last words—you know, what they said just before the Straszydlo finish them off. You can imagine the kind of awfully desperate things people say before they die . . . Once I was in the forest, and a Straszydlo was following me, repeating all the while in a high-pitched woman's voice: *You aren't going to hurt me, are you? Please don't hurt me. Just one more moment, I beg you!*"

The entire group fell silent.

"What do these Straszydlo look like?" asked Alfonso finally. "How big are they?"

"Your guess is as good as mine," said Rosalina. "Anyone who has ever turned around to look hasn't lived to speak of it. But I can tell you this, from the size of the footprints that they leave, they appear to be quite large."

"How large are we talkin'?" asked Bilblox.

"Fifteen feet tall," said Rosalina. "If not taller. But they will leave you alone *if* you follow the rules."

"For us it will really come down to timing, won't it?" asked

Hill. "I mean, if we are not allowed in the forest at night then I presume we have to cross the forest within the span of a single day—between dawn and dusk."

"That's correct," said Rosalina.

"Is this possible?" asked Hill.

"Yes," said Rosalina. "I did it many decades ago, when I was a young girl. Back then, at least, the trail was clearly marked. It starts not far from here, near the place where the three boulders rest. From there, it travels quite some distance through rolling terrain. The trail is fairly straight. At one point, there is a stream crossing, but that shouldn't pose too much of a problem unless there's a heavy snowfall the night before. If you leave at the crack of dawn, you should be able to make it easily by sundown—and if not—well then, heaven help you."

"And do you recall what's on the other side of the forest?" asked Hill.

"Yes, of course," replied Rosalina. "On the other side are the High Peaks of the Urals—the most amazing mountains that you've ever seen. In fact, if you want to catch a glimpse of them, you can take the ladder up to the top of our lookout. There is still a bit of daylight left."

"I'd like to do that," said Hill.

"All you have to do is shimmy up the ladder," said Rosalina as she pointed toward the chimney above the fireplace. "Just keep going up."

Hill inspected the chimney more closely and noticed that the stones on an exterior wall of the chimney formed a ladder that led up to a trapdoor in the ceiling.

"I'll just take a look," Hill announced.

"Can I come with you?" asked Alfonso.

"Sure," said Hill. "Let's go."

Hill and Alfonso climbed up the wall of the chimney, opened the trapdoor, and continued up the darkened inner spine of the tower itself. After a few minutes, they reached a tiny perch at the top that was barely big enough for both of them to squeeze into. The view was breathtaking. Together they looked west—out across the dark expanse of Straszydlo Forest—toward the last traces of pink and purple that were quickly sinking into the High Peaks of the Urals. The mountains were spectacular: wild, craggy, jagged, serrated, snowcapped peaks that jutted into the clouds. The view electrified Alfonso. Somewhere, nestled amid these peaks, was Somnos.

"Look," Alfonso said, pointing. "That must be the start of the trail through the forest!"

Hill saw the spot immediately. Just as Rosalina had described it, three large boulders sat in a row by the edge of the woods. From there a small, white, snow-covered trail cut its way through the woods in a relatively straight line and soon disappeared into the thick forest.

"My gosh," said Hill under his breath. "That will be a long journey." He looked at Alfonso. "I'll set out tomorrow at dawn and—assuming that I make it across—I'll camp out on the far side of the forest. Then, the following morning, I'll head back."

"Why would you bother to do that?" asked Alfonso.

"Because," said Hill gravely, "someone has to see if this journey can be done. Otherwise, we could all be walking to our deaths."

"What about time?" said Alfonso. "How many days do we have left on the date wheel?"

"Eleven," replied Hill. "I have it all figured out. It will take me two days to cross the forest and return. Then it will take another five days for all of us to cross individually. That leaves us four days to find Somnos."

Alfonso whistled but said nothing.

"I know," said Hill. "It's going to be very close."

CHAPTER 29

AVALANCHE

SHORTLY before bedtime, the two sisters sat down to play a game of cards at the kitchen table. They mumbled quietly, sipped their tea, and stroked Sam's purring head. The others sat around the fireplace, also sipping tea. Resuza was there too, slurping down some soup. She had come in from the cold to get some food and warmth before venturing back outside for the night. Her cheeks and eyes glowed with excitement as she described the incredible northern lights putting on a show across the entire sky.

Hill then outlined his plan for crossing Straszydlo Forest. He would cross the forest first, spend the night on the other side, and would return the next day. If all went well, they would then cross the forest one at a time over the course of the next few days. Although Hill seemed confident, Alfonso had a bad feeling about the forest.

Later that night, after Resuza had left and the others had gone to bed, Alfonso lay awake. He could not sleep. He was certainly comfortable enough. Rosalina and Masha had provided heavy woolen mats and soft cotton blankets for everyone to sleep on. Alfonso had placed his mat by the fire, where it was warm and quite cozy. The night was quiet, except for the low, deep-throated rumble of Sam snoring, which actually sounded very pleasant. Still, Alfonso couldn't fall asleep.

For the first time in a few days, Alfonso thought of his mom and Pappy back in Fort Krasnik. He had always assumed that he'd make his way back to them, but now, in the depths of the night, he could not avoid the fear that he might never see them again. Eventually, his thoughts drifted to Resuza. Alfonso pictured her huddling outside in the snow, keeping watch over the house. He had never known a girl like her—brave, confident, pretty in an unkempt way. As tough as she was, however, Alfonso was worried about her. It occurred to him that he should poke his head out the door and check on her. Wearily, he got up from his mat and walked down the long, drafty corridor to the front door. He unlocked the door, pushed it open, and stuck his head out. A light snow was falling. It was deathly quiet.

"Hey, Resuza," he whispered urgently.

No response.

"Resuza!" he called.

Nothing. He took a step outside, closed the door behind him, and took a deep breath. "Resuza!" he bellowed as loudly as he could.

Still nothing. Alfonso looked around. The northern lights

had disappeared, and the darkness, without the moon, was total. He shivered. What should he do? A minute later, his teeth chattering, he returned to his warm place near the fire. He shook Hill awake to tell him of Resuza's apparent absence. Hill seemed totally unconcerned.

"Go back to bed," he mumbled sleepily. "Of all people, that girl can definitely take care of herself."

The next morning, everyone in the house rose before dawn to see Hill off. Even Spack woke up, vigorously rubbed her eyes, smoothed her crazy hair into a thick ponytail, and stumbled along with the others. Rosalina and Masha led the way down to the path's entrance by the three boulders. They all stared at the small, lonely path that headed directly into the forest and waited for the first glimmer of dawn to squeak its way over the horizon. When it finally did, Rosalina pounded her walking stick against the ground impatiently and hissed, "All right, it's daylight. You can enter. Go now and whatever you do, never look back!" Hill nodded, smiled one last time at his nephew, and hustled into the woods.

After Hill's departure they all returned to Rosalina and Masha's home for a breakfast of raisins and porridge. Resuza hadn't yet returned, but no one except Alfonso seemed concerned. They all ate quietly. No one stirred except Sam, who was meowing to himself contentedly as if he were enjoying a secret. Eventually, the silence was broken by Spack's loud grunts. She had stood up and begun to pace back and forth across the room. From the look on her face, she was in great pain.

"What in blazes are ya doin'?" asked Bilblox.

"What does it look like I'm doing?" replied Spack. "I am exercising my leg muscles in order to revive them from their long hibernation. To my dismay, I will have to *walk* through this Straszydlo Forest, which means that I need to get in shape."

"Will you be able to make it?" asked Alfonso.

"I certainly hope so," replied Spack. "It has been years, perhaps decades, since I walked more than a few blocks on my own, but someone must lead this expedition onward to the gates of Dormia . . ."

"Oh, please," said Bilblox as he rolled his eyes.

"Yes, it shall be the fight of my life," continued Spack in a dramatic tone of voice. Her eyes flashed with excitement. "But realizing full well that everything rests on my slender but capable shoulders, I will not give up!"

Her mood suddenly changed. "I hope that uncle of yours will be careful," she said to Alfonso. "It must be terrible to walk through that forest, all alone. Of course, like me, he is a brave Dormian . . ."

Around midmorning, there was a knock on the front door. Alfonso scurried past Rosalina and opened the door. It was Resuza. She looked exhausted. Resuza announced that she was tired and very hungry, but happy to report that she hadn't seen anyone snooping around the house all night. She explained that she had spent the entire night, and much of the morning, hiding in a snowbank not far from the house. Everyone welcomed this news and greeted Resuza warmly. Alfonso wondered why Resuza hadn't heard him when he called out the night before, but said nothing.

Rosalina fed Resuza three bowls of soup and then insisted that she take a bath. "It is not proper for a young girl to appear so filthy in polite company," said Rosalina in a scolding tone. It was true that Resuza was quite dirty. She was wearing the same rags and overcoat that she had been wearing in Barsh-yin-Binder and they had only gotten dirtier with time.

"Masha and I will prepare some hot water for your bath," said Rosalina. "Then we will give you a clean set of clothes and a cloak."

"Meanwhile," added Masha, "we will examine these wounds of yours, Mr. Bilblox. The bandages are soiled and in need of cleaning. My goodness, you people are as dirty as worms!"

And so, while Resuza was taking her bath, Masha inspected Bilblox's wounds and changed his bandages. The crisscross of the Dragoonya blades on his skin had scabbed over, and turned a dark red. Masha clucked like a worried hen, but eventually nodded and declared that Bilblox was healing nicely.

An hour or so later, when Resuza emerged from her bath, she looked like an entirely different person. She wore black wool pants and a blue wool sweater. Her blond hair, once grimy and matted, was now curly and lustrous. Her skin, which had been caked with dirt and dried sweat, now gleamed a healthy pink. Alfonso wanted to say something, but no words came to his mouth.

"Wow, ya clean up nice!" said Bilblox. "Who woulda thought?"

"You're not kidding," mumbled Alfonso. "You're really, quite, er . . ."

Fortunately for Alfonso, this awkward moment was interrupted by a great rumbling that sounded like thunder—only deeper—almost like a small earthquake.

"What was that?" asked Bilblox.

"Just an avalanche," replied Masha in an unconcerned manner. "This late in the winter, the snow is heavy and avalanching all the time."

"I'm going to take a look," said Alfonso. "Anyone else want to come?"

"I shall accompany you," replied Resuza with a smile. "Someone experienced needs to make sure you do not fall into trouble."

Alfonso shrugged, but secretly he was pleased. They walked outside into the snow and saw that the sleds and the dogs were fine. In the distance they could see where an avalanche had rolled down the side of a nearby mountain and uncovered a long smear of bare earth and rocks.

"Wow, do you see that?" asked Alfonso.

"Indeed," replied Resuza. "Do you fancy investigating it?"

Alfonso knew that this probably wasn't a good idea. The mountain looked far away and it was already early afternoon. His uncle would never have agreed to let him go. But Hill wasn't here, the bloom was safe inside the house, and Resuza was looking at him expectantly.

"Sure," said Alfonso as casually as he could. "Let's do it."

Alfonso tied the dogs into their harnesses and then connected the harnesses to the sled. They got on the sled; Resuza took the reins, snapped a whip, and yelled, "Yah!" The dogs leapt to their feet and began bounding through the snow. Without the weight of their packs—or large adults like Bilblox—

the sled moved very quickly across the snow-covered fields. In an hour they had reached the avalanche spot. The ground was scattered with enormous pieces of snow—some of which were bigger than entire houses—and intermixed with the snow were boulders, chunks of mud, and entire trees. They had clearly rolled down the mountain and taken out everything in their way.

"We used to have avalanches like this every spring in the little mountain town where I grew up," said Resuza. "Once I was walking with my parents—I couldn't have been more than five or six years old—and this massive avalanche came down just behind us. No one was hurt, but the noise . . ." Her voice tapered off into nothing.

This was the first time that Resuza had mentioned her family. Alfonso looked at her with surprise.

"It's one of the only memories I still have of my parents," confessed Resuza. She had a sad, faraway look in her eyes. "My mum I remember better—she had these big green eyes—but my father . . ." There was a long silence. "Ah well," she said with a slight sniffle, "what does it matter anyway?"

"What happened to them?" asked Alfonso.

"They both died when I was little," she replied wearily. "Early one morning—midsummer perhaps—I woke up to the screams of my little sister, Naomi. I looked up and the ceiling was on fire, with smoke as black as night pouring out the windows. We both started coughing as the smoke filled our lungs. Naomi wanted to go outside, but I wouldn't let her, because I could hear them . . ."

"Who did you hear?" asked Alfonso.

"The horsemen," replied Resuza.

"Dragoonya?"

"Of course," said Resuza, who was looking strangely at the palms of her hands. "They were riding down the streets, wielding their swords, and setting the town on fire. Eventually, Naomi and I had to go outside and that's when I found Mum and Dad, lying on the ground, not breathing or anything, just lying there . . . Naomi starting bawling . . . I tried to get her to run . . . I begged her . . . Begged her and begged her . . . But she wouldn't budge . . . And so I . . . I left her . . . left her standing in the middle of the road."

"Where did you go?" asked Alfonso quietly, so quietly that for a moment he wondered whether Resuza had even heard him.

"Hid by the river," said Resuza. "Hid among the reeds and, days later, when I finally came back to town, there was no one left—not a soul. Only ghosts . . ." Her voice tapered off. "But enough of this," she said quite suddenly. "I hate talking about the past—it's nothing but misery."

"Do you know what happened to Naomi?" asked Alfonso. "I mean did she . . ."

"Die?" asked Resuza.

Alfonso nodded sheepishly.

"I don't believe so," said Resuza. "The Dragoonya usually take their captives to Dargora. It's their capital, somewhere north of here. No one knows anything about it. Apparently, it's impossible to find because the city is only visible at twilight."

"Still, you might be able to find her."

"Not a chance," said Resuza. "No one enters or exits Dargora freely except the Dragoonya. And besides, everyone knows that the Dragoonya work their slaves to death. Everyone says they use the bones of their slaves to build their homes." Her eyes filled with tears.

Alfonso could think of nothing to say, and stared awkwardly at his feet.

"Hey!" said Resuza suddenly. "Look at that."

Resuza pointed up to a large, perfectly square-shaped opening or cave that had been exposed during the avalanche. Steam was pouring out of the cave. The sight of the steam against the snow reminded Alfonso of a hot spring in wintertime.

"That's so weird," said Resuza. "That cave looks perfectly square."

"Yeah," said Alfonso. "And what's with all that steam? Let's go check it out."

It took them several minutes of climbing to reach the spot. The mouth of the cave was indeed shaped like a perfect square, although it didn't appear to be man-made. The rock had simply broken off in this manner. The truly amazing thing, however, was that the cave turned into a kind of square-shaped tunnel, which was at least thirty feet in height and width. Both Alfonso and Resuza peered into it. The tunnel burrowed down into the mountain at a steep angle. The walls of the tunnel were dark green and soft to the touch, as if covered with moss. The floor was dotted with chunks of rapidly melting ice. The melt from these ice chunks was draining down the tunnel and into the depths of the mountain.

"What on earth do you suppose this is?" asked Resuza.

"I don't know," said Alfonso. "It looks like a giant pipe of some kind—only the walls appear to be covered with algae or moss. Maybe it's a Uralian hot spring! I'm going to check—"

"For heaven's sakes, no!" said Resuza. She clutched his shoulder to hold him back. "It doesn't look safe."

"I'll just take a peek," he said as he shrugged off her hand and stepped deeper into the cave. A moment later, however, his feet slipped on the water and he began sliding down. Alfonso struck frantically at the wall to try to grab hold of something. At last, his feet stopped at a tiny ledge.

"ALFONSO! Are you all right?" yelled Resuza.

"Yes," yelled Alfonso. He looked back up at Resuza. He had slipped about twenty feet. "I'm on a little ledge but I don't know how stable it is," he yelled. "Can you get some rope?"

"There's some in the sled," yelled Resuza. "Hold on, I'll be right back!"

"Hurry!" he yelled to her. Alfonso felt his grip slipping, while small pieces of ice slid down and hit his head. Finally, Resuza reappeared at the mouth of the cave. "The rope!" she yelled. "Climb up—the rope is tied to the sled."

She tossed the rope down to Alfonso. He grabbed it with his free hand and began to pull himself up. Resuza saw that he was holding on, and she commanded the huskies to pull. They strained forward and slowly lifted up Alfonso. He emerged covered in snow and ice-cold water. Resuza's face had gone white.

"That was incredibly stupid!" she said angrily. "Who knows where you could have fallen! These mountains are no place for childish games."

"I know," said Alfonso bashfully. "I'm sorry."

They stood there, staring at each other. "What do you suppose it is?" Resuza eventually asked. "I've never seen anything like it."

"I don't know," said Alfonso. His voice was still trembling. "But it looks like it just keeps going down forever and ever."

"Perhaps Masha or Rosalina will know what this is," said Resuza.

"We can't tell them or anyone else about this!" blurted out Alfonso. "Uncle Hill would kill me if he hears what I did."

Resuza nodded.

"Okay," she said, "I'll keep your secret if you keep a secret of mine."

"What's your secret?" asked Alfonso.

"Well, it's not exactly a secret, it's more like something I overheard," said Resuza. "It's really quite silly —"

"What is it?" asked Alfonso impatiently.

"Last night, before I left to sleep outside, do you remember how the sisters were playing a game of cards?"

Alfonso nodded.

"Well they weren't actually playing a game," said Resuza. "They were reading tarot cards and talking in their village dialect, Tagolosh, which is quite similar to my native tongue. Anyway, do you remember how they kept on mumbling and acting strange? It was because Rosalina kept on drawing the death card. They said that when we cross the forest, one of us will die."

CHAPTER 30

BLIND IN THE FOREST

THE FOLLOWING day there was nothing to do but wait. Everyone in the little stone house was thinking the same thing: would Hill reemerge from the woods at the end of the day? To be sure, Hill was in excellent shape. Throughout the entire journey he had never complained of getting tired or sore. But the trail through the forest was long and Hill had to finish it twice in two consecutive days. And then, of course, there was the added challenge of not looking backwards. This sounded easy enough, but in practice, it was actually quite tricky. Alfonso knew full well that when a branch cracks behind you, it is only natural to glance backwards. When he was tramping around in the pine forests near World's End, Minnesota, he looked around all the time without even thinking. Just one such glance would ensure Hill's doom.

They were sitting in the kitchen, just before sunset, when Bilblox called for Alfonso, who came over to his blind friend. Bilblox asked if they could go outside for a second.

Alfonso nodded, grabbed his jacket, and led his friend out into the cold.

"What is it?" he asked.

"I'm worried," Bilblox replied softly. His white eyes gleamed. "I ain't been able to see more than shadows for almost two days. How am I gonna make it through the forest?"

"Everything will be fine," Alfonso replied reassuringly. "The path through the forest seems to be easy—you just have to go straight. Plus, it looks like there are stones or some kind of gravel on the path. If you veer off, you'll feel the ground change under your feet. And we'll make it as easy as possible for you. Maybe you shouldn't carry anything."

"Maybe," replied Bilblox doubtfully. "But I still gotta carry the bloom! Ya know how heavy that thing has gotten?"

Alfonso frowned. Bilblox was right. The plant had been growing at an astounding rate. Earlier in the day, Rosalina had given him a large terracotta pot, and then, with Bilblox's help, he had re-potted the bloom into it. The whole thing weighed close to fifty pounds, and the only person who could carry it with any ease was Bilblox. But could they really trust him to carry the bloom?

"Come on," said Alfonso. "We'll figure all of this out when Hill returns. Let's go to the edge of the woods and wait for him."

The two of them walked down to the spot where the three boulders sat by the edge of the woods. The sun was dropping rapidly now. Alfonso fixed his eyes on the opening. He could still see Hill's footprints in the snow from the day before. A stiff gust of wind blasted through the woods, pushing loose bits of snow this way and that. The sky darkened to a deep sapphire blue. And then, quite suddenly, Hill appeared. He was walking briskly, his spine ramrod straight, and whistling a tune. He walked up to the spot where Alfonso was standing and embraced him tiredly. "My dear nephew," he said. "It is so good to see you again."

Alfonso hugged him back. "How was the journey?" he asked.

"Long," said Hill. "But I'm confident it can be done by any of us."

"Any problems with the Straszydlo?" asked Bilblox.

"None at all," said Hill. "Once I heard something walking behind me, but that was it. I went quickly and certainly never glanced backwards. Maybe the old ladies are exaggerating."

That night, over dinner, Hill recounted his journey. The path itself, Hill confirmed, was perfectly straight. Midway down the trail, there was a stream but the water was frozen solid and easy to cross. At the far end of the woods, Hill had found a small cave where he built a fire and slept very well. That cave would be their meeting point on the other side. Taking the dogs was impossible, so they made arrangements to leave them with Rosalina and Masha. The two sisters were very pleased with this arrangement, since the dogs would make excellent companions for Sam.

Next, they discussed the order in which they would make the journey. They soon decided that Resuza would go first, since she had already proven that she knew how to sleep out in the wild at this time of year. Next would be Bilblox, then Alfonso, then Hill, and—finally—Spack. This order would give Hill time to rest and Spack time to get in shape. If all went well, they would all be on the other side of the forest in five days' time.

"So," said Hill happily, "the only matter left to decide is who will carry the Dormian bloom. Obviously, in his state, Bilblox cannot do it. So I will volunteer for the task."

"Wait a minute," said Bilblox indignantly. "I've been doin' a pretty good job so far!"

"You misunderstood me," said Hill. "We all know that you have done an excellent job of carrying the bloom—and we are deeply indebted to you—but you *are* blind and it will be hard enough to cross the forest on your own, let alone cross it with a very heavy plant."

"Maybe I could do it," said Alfonso hopefully. "There's a wheelbarrow in the front yard. Maybe we could put the bloom in the wheelbarrow and I could push the thing across the forest?"

"Hmm," said Hill. "I don't know."

"It's a complete mystery to me why you're lugging that odd-looking plant through the forest," said Rosalina with a slight chuckle. "Who ever heard of such a thing? Where are you taking it anyway? And why?"

"Yes," chimed in Masha. "I'd like to know that as well."

"Well," began Hill, "I'm afraid we can't—"

"Trust you!" finished Bilblox. "They don't trust anyone—even their own friends!"

Alfonso let out a sigh of frustration, but said nothing.

"Let's sleep on this," said Hill finally. "Hopefully, in the morning, we'll all agree on a solution."

While everyone prepared for bed, Rosalina poured Hill a

steaming cup of finklegrog and asked if he had, by chance, come across the statue of the one-eyed man.

Hill clapped his knees. "Of course!" he said. "I almost forgot about that." He described the statue to the others: "It was most curious. Just after the stream crossing there was a large, stone statue of a man with just one eye. And beneath it, there was an engraving of some kind."

"Yes, yes, yes," squawked Rosalina. "That is the statue of the cyclops. He used to roam these parts, hundreds of years ago, or so the legend goes."

"What does the inscription say?" asked Hill. "I couldn't read whatever language it was in."

"It is written in the ancient language of Mezscrit, which is no longer spoken, of course," said Rosalina. "My grandfather said it was a poem:

This old sphere may be pried.
Many a clever person has tried.
Remember how the cyclops died.
Through the ear and not the eye.

What exactly does the future hold?
Its many secrets remain untold.
Hidden in the burning hot and biting cold.
Is the key to a future foretold."

"What does that mean?" asked Alfonso.

"I have no idea," replied Rosalina. "I suppose it is a riddle, but who has time to experiment with such foolishness when crossing through Straszydlo Forest?"

"I bet there are more clues on the statue," said Alfonso eagerly.

"Don't get any ideas, boy," chirped Rosalina. "When you cross the forest you don't dilly-dally for any reason. You just get across."

"Yes," said Hill sternly. "Don't even think about wasting time on that statue."

"Fine," said Alfonso testily. "I won't."

"Good," said Hill. "Now let's all go to bed."

Resuza set out for the forest at first light the following morning. Alfonso was there to see her off. She was quiet on the way to the three boulders and at the departure point, she turned and gave Alfonso a firm handshake. "Don't worry," she said confidently. "No matter what, I'll be fine."

"I know," replied Alfonso. "Just go as fast as you can."

With that, she turned and strode into the forest. Within a hundred feet, she had disappeared from view.

After a hearty breakfast of wild-grass bread and freshly churned butter, Alfonso, Hill, Bilblox, and Spack gathered in the front yard to inspect the sisters' wheelbarrow. It was a rickety, old, wooden device with a squeaky metal wheel. For the rest of the morning, Alfonso and Hill practiced rolling the wheelbarrow, which was loaded with both the Dormian bloom and Spack's coffin. The load was extremely top-heavy and neither Alfonso nor Hill could maneuver it with any success. The wheelbarrow lurched from side to side, and proved extremely difficult to keep balanced.

"I first pushed around a wheelbarrow at the age of five," Bilblox proclaimed. "Ya oughta let me do it."

"By all rights, the Great Sleeper should carry the bloom," said Spack, who up until now had remained silent on this subject. "Especially since Bilblox is blind. I won't ask how it happened, but I have my suspicions . . ." She stood there awkwardly, her arms folded. "Wanderers must take risks, and for the sake of the group I am willing to make the following gesture: if it's too much trouble, we don't need to take the coffin, especially since it is in such terrible shape."

"Good," said Hill. "That should make the load much easier to push."

They removed the bloom from the coffin, and placed it in one of the large sealskin packs that Hill had bought in Barshyin-Binder. They then placed the pack in the wheelbarrow and secured it tightly so it wouldn't move around. Unfortunately, even with the coffin removed, the wheelbarrow was still both heavy and unstable. Alfonso and Hill were able to maneuver it, but neither of them felt confident that they could push it all the way across the forest. Indeed, Alfonso felt exhausted after pushing it for just fifteen minutes, and Hill couldn't go much more than an hour.

"Look," said Bilblox finally. "Whether ya like it or not, yer gonna have to let me push that wheelbarrow."

Alfonso nodded wearily.

"I'm afraid Bilblox is right," said Hill. "That seems to be our only option."

"No!" hissed Spack. "That giant oaf burned a leaf of the bloom, didn't he? Whether or not you admit it, I know that's what happened! He shouldn't even be on this trip, much less anywhere near the bloom."

"Bilblox's been with us longer than you have," replied Alfonso angrily. "And he's the bravest, most reliable person I've ever known."

"You'll regret this," said Spack. "Our—your—only priority should be getting the bloom to Somnos. This is not some boyish game! Your loyalty to your friend comes a distant second. Don't you see—people's lives are hanging in the balance! I simply cannot accept this!"

"You don't have to come," retorted Alfonso.

Spack stared angrily at Alfonso, Hill, and Bilblox. "Fools!" she said. "You obviously won't listen to reason. Suit yourselves. But mark my words: you'll need me before this journey is through. I'm a *Wanderer.*"

At sunrise the next morning, Bilblox grimly set off through the forest. He had been blind for three days straight, and before that, he had been able to see for only a few minutes at a time. He was doubtful his sight would ever return.

But he tried to forget about this as he set off on the path. Luckily, it was just as straight as Hill said it would be. There were a few occasions when he began to stray a little from one side or another, but he simply felt around with his feet and confirmed he was still on the snow-covered path. An hour passed, then two and three, and Bilblox continued his fast pace. It was actually quite easy. And the one good thing about being blind was that there was no temptation for him to look back over his shoulder. Once, he thought he heard footsteps behind him, but he couldn't be sure because the wheelbarrow was in need of an oiling and its wheels were squeaky and loud. In any case, he didn't look back.

Eventually, around what felt like midday, Bilblox reached the stream crossing. He felt the crunch of the icy surface underneath his feet. All he had to do was make it across without falling, slipping, or getting turned around. This, he realized, would be the trickiest part of his journey. The key was to do it slowly and carefully. Very cautiously, he rolled the wheelbarrow onto the ice. Then he placed one foot onto the ice followed slowly by the other. The ice didn't crack or budge. It was frozen solid. Hill had told him that the stream was roughly ten paces in width. That was nothing—just ten confident steps.

Bilblox took his first step and counted out loud to himself, "One." He took another step and said, "Two." He took yet another step and said, "Three." Everything was going quite well. On his fifth step, Bilblox smiled with confidence, thinking it would be easy. Unfortunately, he couldn't see that below him was a patch of ice swept clean of snow. It gleamed with a brilliant shine, and it was by far the slipperiest piece of ice around. In his confidence, Bilblox put his foot down a little too hard. It slipped and in a split-second, his legs came out from under him and he hit the ice with a monstrous *thunk!* His head cracked against the ice and he passed out for a second. When he came to, he had no idea what direction he was facing. Even worse, he had lost his grip on the wheelbarrow.

Bilblox struggled to regain his composure. The wheelbarrow had to be nearby. It simply had to be! He groped around in every direction, but felt nothing. He was reluctant to move because then he would lose his sense of where he was. He knew, for example, that he was in the middle of the stream somewhere near the path. And if he had turned around by mistake, would the Straszydlos attack? Maybe they wouldn't attack a blind man. Regardless, he had to find the wheelbarrow without moving. But how?

After a few anxious minutes, he realized that the answer was sitting underneath him. He grabbed at the snow around him and quickly made four, firmly packed snowballs. He would throw one in each direction. Hopefully one of them would hit the wheelbarrow and make a noise. Perhaps the Straszydlos wouldn't notice his plight.

Bilblox tossed the first snowball, but it landed silently in the snow. He turned ninety degrees and tossed the second. Nothing. He turned again and tossed the third. *Thunk!* It was the sound of the snowball hitting the wooden frame of the wheelbarrow. He'd found it! On his second stride in the direction, he found the wheelbarrow.

Bilblox grabbed it, spun around, and reversed his steps, but on the way back the wheelbarrow ran smack into a tree. He grimaced and realized that despite his best efforts, he was completely turned around. For a few minutes, he walked around wildly until a sudden wind bit into his cheeks and he realized the situation was getting desperate. He had to make it to the other side of the forest by sundown, but he was currently stuck in the middle of a stream with no ability to see. And to make matters worse he had the bloom with him. If he couldn't figure a way out, he would die. And then what would happen to the bloom? More importantly, what would happen to all of those people in Somnos who were counting on them to arrive with the plant?

At that very moment, Bilblox heard the unmistakable sound of a branch snapping somewhere behind him. Another branch snapped. He heard the sound of breathing. Then came the panicky whisper of an older man's voice: *Which way is it? I think we're lost. We never should have come into these woods.*

"Who's there?" yelled Bilblox.

Immediately his question was echoed back at him. *Who's there?* Bilblox shuddered. It was his voice being mimicked back at him. The Straszydlos had arrived.

A moment passed. Then the older man's voice repeated itself: *Which way is it? I think we're lost. We never should have come into these woods.*

Seconds later, Bilblox heard a deep growl, followed by a man's voice quavering in fear: *My wife! My children! Please don't!*

At least one Straszydlo was nearby, maybe more. Bilblox had to return to the trail and start moving. But how?

He knew the answer. It was in the sealskin pack. He remembered that awful moment in the catacombs below Barsh-yin-Binder, when he had frightened Alfonso by demanding to have just a pinch of the powder. He'd do anything for Alfonso, and his friend trusted him with the most important thing in the world, the bloom. But now he was alone.

Bilblox knelt on the ice, opened the sealskin bag, and pulled out the bloom. Tenderly, even lovingly, he ran his hands across the leaves of the plant. He remembered his pledge aboard the *Success Story* never to touch the plant again. But what choice did he have? If he couldn't get out of the forest, the bloom would never make it to Dormia.

It had to be done.

Just then, a scream tore through the silent forest. *Not my leg! Please God, not my leg!*

Bilblox cringed and bit his lip. His hands shook as he took hold of the smallest leaf at the bottom of the stem, tore it away cleanly, and placed it in a small depression in the ice. He gulped down the lump in his throat, reached into his inner coat pocket, and pulled out a book of matches. He struck the first match to the leaf, but its flame died instantly in the wind. He struck another, moved its flame quickly to the leaf of the plant, and the leaf caught fire. A moment later, it was done and Bilblox felt sick to his stomach.

He delicately placed a moist index finger where he had burned the leaf, picked up a few granules, and placed his finger directly onto his wide-open white eyes. His whole body shuddered in complete and utter pleasure. In a flash, he could see again—only it was telescopic vision. He glanced up, through the clouds, up toward a patch of blue where two hawks were passing overhead. He could see their individual feathers vibrating against the wind. The hawk's talons held a dead mouse. He could even see the mouse's black, beady eyes. A moment later, the telescopic vision was gone. He felt strong, even stronger than on the *Success Story.* He felt invincible. The wounds across his shoulders and chest disappeared, and he felt as healthy as ever.

Next came the moment of prescience—the brief window when he could glimpse into the future. He saw Alfonso resting at a campsite on a snowy mountainside. Hill was making breakfast. Spack was just getting up. A teakettle was clanking. Bilblox knew instinctively that he must remember all of these details. Much like the flying fish that he had seen last time, these clues would help him place this vision. High above the encampment a large piece of ice suddenly broke loose. It hurdled down the mountainside with enormous speed and, before anyone could react, it crushed the entire camp. Everyone was buried, and they would soon suffocate to death. The vision ended—everything went black—and then Bilblox's vision returned. For the first time in days, he could see! He shivered at the thought of what he had just foreseen. But there was no time to think of this. First he had to make it through the forest. Before returning to the trail, he knelt down and carefully checked the area for the ash. He found a few small granules. With his heart beating in excitement, he took the ash and placed it carefully in the breast pocket of his heavy jacket. He wouldn't take the ash anymore, he told himself, but just in case, he'd have a little bit. There was no reason to leave it behind.

Bilblox glanced up the frozen-over stream and saw that the trail was about twenty feet away. He packed up the bloom, returned it to the sealskin pack, and strapped it back onto the wheelbarrow. Within seconds, he was back on the trail, running toward the setting sun. With his vision working perfectly he was soon making excellent time. Though he was sick with worry about the bloom, Bilblox couldn't help feeling ecstatic. He could see! Everything was beautiful—the gloomy trees, the snow underfoot, the dark blue sky, everything. For the next three hours or so he practically ran down the trail. After his encounter with the Straszydlos at the river, the forest was silent. Only when sundown approached did his vision ebb. It felt like his eyes were a TV with bad reception. He wanted to thump his head but he knew it would do no good.

As the sun started its descent toward the horizon, he emerged at the far end of the forest. His vision was blurry, but he soon found the cave. There was no sign of Resuza.

"Resuza!" yelled Bilblox. "RESUZA!"

Silence.

He kept yelling for another ten minutes until his voice was hoarse. The sun had disappeared beneath the horizon, and Bilblox shivered in the dark. He buried his head in his jacket. "Oh, Resuza," mumbled Bilblox. "I hope you're okay."

CHAPTER 31

THE CYCLOPS

By the next morning, when Alfonso set out across the forest, the path was well beaten down. He had been walking down the path for roughly a mile when he came upon a heavy red cloak lying across the trail. It was Resuza's and it was torn badly. Alfonso picked up the cloak. Beneath it, someone—presumably Resuza—had neatly carved a series of numbers and a message into the snow.

1, 4, 9, 16, 25, 36, 49, 64, 81, 100

WARN THEM!

Was this message meant for Alfonso? What did these numbers mean? And whom, exactly, was Alfonso supposed to warn? None of this made any sense. Alfonso stared at the drawings. Suddenly, another thought occurred to him: what if it wasn't Resuza who had done this? Could it be a trick of the Straszydlo? Alfonso glanced around to his left and right. He was very careful not to look backwards. He saw nothing, but he sensed that someone—or something—was standing directly behind him.

Excuse me, sir, said a gentlemanly voice.

Alfonso's head jerked, as if to glance backwards, but at the last moment he stopped himself.

Excuse me, sir, said the voice again.

Alfonso wanted to keep walking, but he felt bound to stick around and see if anything bad had happened to Resuza. Quite plainly, a Straszydlo was standing directly behind him. Alfonso was trying to plan his next move when he heard the voice of a frightened girl.

I'm so sorry, Alfonso!

The voice was almost a shriek, but it sounded vaguely familiar. It sounded like Resuza.

I'm so sorry, Alfonso!

"Resuza, is that you?" asked Alfonso without turning around.

I'm so sorry, Alfonso!

Alfonso felt a shiver twitch its way up his spine. He had an awful thought: were these Resuza's last words?

I'm so sorry, Alfonso! The voice was much closer.

Alfonso dropped Resuza's cloak, broke into a run, and started sprinting up the path. He ran and ran and ran until he was completely winded. At one point he stumbled and almost fell. Tears fell down his cheeks. He wondered if he should retrace his steps and return to where he had found Resuza's cloak and the strange message. He couldn't just keep going. Could he?

Sometime around midday, Alfonso came to the stream crossing. A thin coating of snow sat upon the icy surface. It was covered with footprints and wheelbarrow tracks. They led all over the place as if—for some strange reason—Bilblox had decided to walk in circles. Had he become turned around or lost? Alfonso grew worried but then he noticed the wheelbarrow tracks continuing on the far side of the stream. He sighed with relief and continued on his way.

Less than five minutes after crossing the stream, Alfonso saw the twenty-foot-tall stone statue of the cyclops just off the trail but semihidden by a number of trees. The statue depicted a figure, dressed in heavy robes, who looked just like a normal man—except that he had only one eye squarely in the middle of his forehead. The eye was the only part of the statue not made of stone. It looked like a dark blue glass or crystal. Alfonso glanced at the inscription at the foot of the statue. He could not read it, because it was written in Mezscrit—a strange-looking language with lots of dots and swirls—but he remembered Rosalina's translation of the first stanza: *"This old sphere may be pried / Many a clever person has tried / Remember how the cyclops died / Through the ear and not the eye."*

Alfonso knew he should keep moving, but he couldn't resist

the urge to stop for a minute or two in order to inspect the statue. What did it mean, "This old sphere may be pried?" Alfonso supposed it meant that the eye could somehow be removed. But how? "It has to be related to how the cyclops died," he said to himself. "*'Through the ear and not the eye'*—but what does that mean?"

Alfonso walked around the side of the statue to get a better glimpse of the cyclops's ear. He moved very carefully so that he never once allowed himself to look backwards. To his surprise, Alfonso noticed that the ear of the statue was badly damaged, as if someone had repeatedly hit it with a hammer or a pick. Then Alfonso glanced down at his feet and saw that the ground was littered with wooden arrows, almost all of which were broken. It was as if someone—and perhaps many people—had been shooting at the statue's ear with a bow and arrow. Where were they shooting from? Alfonso glanced momentarily off into the woods—directly to his right—and then he saw it: about fifty feet away, deep in the forest, stood a second statue. It was an archer holding a giant bow.

Alfonso was paralyzed with indecision. He knew deep in his gut that he shouldn't waste anymore time. But the discovery of the second statue had him burning with curiosity. He had to look.

Alfonso scurried through the woods to the spot where the second statue was standing. He sidestepped the whole way—again making certain not to look backwards. The statue was of a large man, dressed in light chain-mail armor, holding a bow that was pointed directly at the cyclops. The bow, like the statue itself, was made of stone; but the bow itself had hinges, so that it could swivel, and the cord on the bow was made of real string.

Clearly, the bow could be used, and it appeared that several people had done so, in an attempt to hit the cyclops in the ear and perhaps dislodge the sphere. The shot looked nearly impossible. The arrow had to travel fifty feet through dense forest and hit the statue's ear—a target that was roughly the size of a large coin.

Alfonso felt certain he could do it if he entered hypnogogia. He looked around the base of the archer statue until he found an arrow that looked intact. He climbed on top of the statue and balanced precariously on one of the archer's arms. Alfonso placed one hand on the bow and immediately it bent backwards toward him. All he had to do was aim it properly. Alfonso loaded the arrow into the archer's bow and pulled the string taut. There was only one last thing to do. He closed his eyes halfway and imagined a large hourglass with thousands of grains of sand falling swiftly down. He allowed himself to picture a single grain as it shifted in the upper chamber of the hourglass and then slowly made its way down to the narrow part where it broke through and fell into the lower chamber. The familiar rush flooded his mind. He was firmly in hypnogogia and aware of everything around him: the wind, the movement of the trees, the tautness of the string, the slight imperfections of the arrowhead, and the impossible trajectory that the arrow itself would have to make. Then he let go. *Twang!* The arrow flew through the air at an incredible speed and struck the statue squarely in the ear. *Ping!* A moment later he heard the gentle thud of something falling to the forest floor.

Alfonso scrambled down and sidestepped back to the cyclops statue. There on the ground, beneath the statue, lay the dark blue sphere. With his heart thudding in excitement, Alfonso picked it up and examined it. It was roughly the size of a grapefruit, and despite the fact that it appeared to be made of solid glass or crystal, it weighed no more than a Ping-Pong ball. "Why is it so light?" he asked himself.

Alfonso gently tossed the sphere to test how it moved through the air. To his astonishment, the sphere exploded up with the force of a cannonball, tearing through massive tree branches as it went. The ball flew a hundred or maybe even two hundred feet—it was impossible to tell because it moved so quickly—and then it shot down with the same incredible speed and hurtled back into Alfonso's hand. Alfonso flinched, but the sphere didn't hurt him at all. It landed in his hand quite softly, as if it had traveled only a few inches. A moment later, giant tree branches that had been struck by the sphere began to crash down to the ground all around him. Alfonso ran for cover and cowered at the base of the statue. Suddenly he recalled Spack's words: "Every Great Sleeper always finds a unique weapon."

"I think I've just found mine," Alfonso said to himself.

He placed the sphere securely into the pocket of his coat. Although unsure of what exactly he had found, Alfonso was certain of three things. First, he was definitely holding on to this sphere. Second, he would tell absolutely no one about it—after all, Hill would be furious if he knew that Alfonso had dilly-dallied in the forest. Third, he had to get going right away. He had wasted almost a half-hour at the statue and he had no time to spare. He set off down the trail at a sprint and he ran steadily for the next forty-five minutes. Eventually, he reduced his speed to a fast walk and held that pace for the remainder of the day.

Around twilight, Alfonso saw the opening in the woods that

marked the end of the trail. And there, standing in the receding afternoon light, was Bilblox. Alfonso ran the last leg of the trail as quickly as he could. It didn't take long for him to realize that something was wrong. Bilblox looked wretched—tired, muddy, and disheveled.

"Alfonso," said Bilblox wearily, "is that ya?"

"Yeah," said Alfonso. "What happened to you? You look awful."

"I-I've been lookin' everywhere outside the forest," said Bilblox in a strange stammer. "Sh-sh-she's gone." His round red cheeks glistened with tears. "I don't know how to say this, b-but I d-don't think R-Resuza made it. She's *gone*."

CHAPTER 32

A BITTER DEPARTURE

THE NEXT day, Hill made it through the forest with great speed. He arrived in the early evening, with a walking stick in hand, whistling a melody to himself as if he were out for a leisurely stroll. In his hand, Hill held Resuza's red cloak.

Hill strode up to the spot where Alfonso and Bilblox were waiting for him. "Nasty animals, those Straszydlo. They harassed me nonstop this time, but the secret is to keep walking at a good clip. Eventually they get tired of following you if they know you're aware of the rules . . . Still, I'm glad to be finished with that place." He looked at Bilblox. "Well, you got through fine, didn't you? In fact, you look positively healthy. You're a fast healer!"

Bilblox couldn't stop a hot flash of shame from coloring his cheeks. "Everythin's fine for me," he muttered. "It's Resuza we're worried about."

"Yes indeed, she left her coat on the trail," replied Hill as he showed them the red cloak. "Where is she?"

"We don't know," said Alfonso grimly.

"What do you mean?" demanded Hill.

"We think she didn't make it," said Bilblox.

Hill turned white. He looked at the red cloak in his hands. "It's not possible," he said. "Could it be just a mistake? Maybe she's off hiding, to see if anyone is following us."

"Maybe," replied Alfonso. He didn't know what to say and turned away to look back at the forest. He thought back to Resuza telling him about Rosalina and Masha and the death card. It didn't make sense. He could imagine himself or Bilblox or even Hill falling prey to the Straszydlo, but Resuza? It seemed impossible. She was so hardy—so tough.

That night, the three of them crowded into the cave that Hill had first discovered during his initial crossing. It was no bigger than a one-car garage, but it was clean, dry, and rather cozy. During the day, Alfonso had collected several dozen mushrooms from nearby fields and that evening Hill made a large pot of mushroom soup. They ate in silence. Everyone's mind was on Resuza. The only logical conclusion was that the Straszydlo had in fact gotten her. This hunch, this increasingly undeniable reality, hung over the group like the darkest of clouds.

"Maybe she'll show up," said Bilblox hopefully. "You never know."

No one replied to this.

"For the time being, we must think of Spack," said Hill

gravely. "I suspect it will be a terrible journey for her. The Straszydlo can sense weakness."

ೞ

Almost from the moment she dragged herself into the forest, Spack could sense that she was being followed. She could hear the footsteps—*thump, thump, thump*—just a little ways behind her. Clearly something large was following her. Spack knew this not only by the loudness of its footsteps, but because it was taking just one step to her five. The stride of this particular Straszydlo had to be almost fifteen feet long, which meant that its legs had to be enormous. The footsteps terrified Spack. To calm herself, she tried to remain focused on the task at hand. "I just have to keep going forward," she whispered. "If I just keep walking, I'll make it." But this, she knew, was not entirely true. It wasn't enough simply to keep walking—she had to keep walking at a certain speed—and if she failed to do this, she wouldn't reach the other end of the forest by sundown.

As if all of this weren't unnerving enough, the Straszydlo behind her was mimicking the voice of a young man, who had quite clearly been frightened to death when he uttered his last words. *I love you, Mother,* came the hysterical, sobbing voice. *I love you, Mother. I love you, Mother.*

"Shut up!" yelled Spack.

But it was no use. The Straszydlo continued with its massive footsteps—*thump, thump, thump*—and its incessant banter of *I love you, Mother.* It was as if this particular Straszydlo knew that Spack was not going to live and it was staking its claim to her from the outset.

"The Straszydlo know when a person *isn't* going to make it," Rosalina had explained the night before. "They can sense when someone is weak. They're like vultures—when they spot someone who is straggling or not following the rules, they just keep circling and circling, until finally, they decide to attack."

By the time Spack reached the frozen stream in the middle of the forest, she sensed that there were at least three or four Straszydlo following her. She scurried across the stream as quickly as she could and, almost directly behind her, she could hear the ice cracking under the massive weight of the Straszydlo's legs. She could hear the voices that each of them were mimicking in rapid succession.

I see a black light, moaned a quavering old man's voice.

Night is coming, oh heavens, night is coming, screeched a woman's voice.

I would have liked to see my wife one last time, gasped a young man's voice.

I can't go any faster, Father, whined a boy's voice. *I can't go any faster!*

These voices persisted through much of the afternoon until they were eventually replaced by much deeper growling noises. The growling grew louder and louder as the afternoon progressed and, at one point, Spack could hear two of the Straszydlo gnashing their teeth and fighting with each other. It was a horrible sound. "What are you beasts fighting over?" Spack whispered hoarsely to herself. And then, rather grimly, she realized that they were fighting over her. She would be a tasty meal and none of them were in the mood to share. Panic swept through her body and she had to fight to control her breathing.

Spack stumbled along in the deep forest. Her legs felt like weights and her muscles screamed with pain. Every time Spack took a step, a shot of burning agony tore through her calves and up into her thighs. The sun began to set through the trees, making the forest even gloomier than before. As sundown drew near, Spack knew she still had a ways to go. She had been slowing down gradually over the last few hours and the Straszydlo were getting closer. She could now feel their hot, steamy breath on the back of her neck. She willed herself to go faster, but it didn't work. She had walked farther in the last day than in the previous ten years.

At that very moment, on the far side of the forest, Alfonso, Bilblox, and Hill gathered at the end of the path to wait for Spack. They waited, and waited, and waited. The sun slowly sank into the woods. The sky turned dark blue, then violet, then purple. The moon began to rise and the first stars appeared. The sun disappeared. Sunset. Alfonso's heart sank. Would Spack share Resuza's terrible end?

"Wait a minute!" Alfonso yelled. "I think I see something."

They strained their eyes to see through the darkness.

"It's some kind of light," said Hill. "And it's coming toward us."

The light drew nearer.

"That's definitely Spack's lantern," said Hill.

"Come on, Spack!" yelled Alfonso at the top of his voice. "You're almost there. Hurry up! HURRY UP!"

Now Spack was only about a hundred feet away. They could see her clearly, carrying a small lantern. She was limping heavily and they could hear her grunting as she walked. She sounded exhausted and in terrible pain.

"There's something behind her," said Alfonso. "Do you see it?"

"Yes," said Hill. "It's hiding in the shadows directly behind her. I can't really make it out."

"It has to be a Straszydlo," said Bilblox.

Spack was now less then fifty feet away.

"I think I see two Straszydlo," said Hill. "One on her left and one on her right. It's hard to tell."

"Spack, run for it!" yelled Bilblox. "They're right behind you!"

Spack dropped her lantern and broke into a strange but surprisingly fast run. Her legs kicked out into a wild spastic motion—as if someone had prodded her with a hot poker. She ran just past the edge of the forest and then crumpled to the ground.

"They followed me the whole way," gasped Spack. "But I kept going. I always kept going."

Hill grabbed her tenderly and helped her stand up. "You made it," he said. "You did great. We're very, very proud of you."

"Thank you," murmured Spack. "Thank you."

The group woke at sunrise the next morning and got their first up-close look at the High Peaks of the Ural Mountains. Now that they had crossed the forest, they had a perfectly clear view. The mountains looked like massive walls of snow and ice and it seemed unimaginable that they would attempt to cross these behemoths without dogs or sleds. Spack eyed the mountains wearily.

"We ought to get going," said Spack. "We don't have that much food and we'll have to make our supplies last."

Hill took out his old pocket watch and glanced at the date wheel, which showed the numeral four.

"Yeah," Bilblox gruffly agreed. "And don't forget that Vice Admiral Purcheezie's boat is settin' sail in less than three weeks. We gotta get back to Barsh-yin-Binder before then. So there really ain't a lot of time."

"You're absolutely right," said Hill. "But before we go, I think we should do something for Resuza. To remember her."

"You mean a funeral?" asked Alfonso.

Hill looked with sorrow at Alfonso. "Something like that," he said.

"I don't know," said Alfonso. "I mean, we don't know for sure if she's dead." Alfonso recalled the sight of Resuza's cloak draped across the trail and the cryptic scrawling underneath.

"Still," insisted Hill, "we should do something. We'll build a cairn."

"A what?" asked Bilblox.

"It's a memorial," said Hill. "A pile of stones stacked together to honor someone. To honor Resuza."

Without another word, they spent the rest of the morning building a large rock pile in front of Straszydlo Forest. When they were finished, the pile stood almost six feet tall.

Just before they set off into the High Urals, Alfonso, Hill, Bilblox, and Spack gathered in front of the cairn to say a final goodbye.

"Resuza, I'm truly sorry," said Bilblox. His white eyes lent a particular ferocity to his words.

Hill approached the cairn and lightly touched it.

"She was so young," Spack said.

Alfonso said nothing. He stared at the dark, moss-speckled rocks and his eyes filled with tears. They all stood there, staring at the rocks and listening to the bitter wind howl in the distance.

Bilblox was the first to break the silence. "Let's go," he said roughly. "Nothin' we can do for her now. We're wastin' our time." He picked up the sealskin pack that held the bloom, and began stumbling awkwardly up the narrow path, one searching step at a time.

"All right, Bilblox," Hill softly replied. He, Alfonso, and Spack shouldered their packs and followed their blind friend into the foothills of the High Urals.

CHAPTER 33

INTO THE HIGH PEAKS OF THE URAL MOUNTAINS

ALFONSO had seen mountains before, but none as grim as these. When they had flown to Fort Krasnik in their seaplane, they had crossed over the Rockies, yet the High Peaks of the Urals were entirely different. These mountains had a dark, empty, foreboding feeling about them. There were no trees to be seen anywhere on their slopes—just endless expanses of snow that climbed up to black, stony peaks. Heavy clouds shrouded the mountains in mist, as if storms were a permanent fixture.

Alfonso, Hill, and Bilblox trudged through the snow and up the rising slopes that led to the High Peaks. It was tough-going, but at least they wore sturdy snowshoes that Hill had purchased for them back in Barsh-yin-Binder.

Hill served as their navigator. He continually consulted the Estonian smuggler's map as he led the way past massive clumps of snow that were just waiting to become avalanches, past exposed rocks that howled with a cold, stinging wind, and into a world so filled with swirling snow that at times it was impossible to see more than a few feet.

They continued plodding forward in this manner for the next three days. Each day they'd get up early and spend all the daylight hours in a slow and steady climb. For Bilblox, it was especially difficult. He was blind most of the time, and had to rely on Alfonso's guidance. He had a few moments of vision after burning the leaf, but these moments left him feeling guilty. Every so often, he'd secretly check the bloom to see if it was fine. It looked normal, but what did he know about plants? He'd glance sideways at Alfonso and wonder if his friend somehow sensed that he had betrayed their pledge not to harm the plant. Bilblox was afraid that almost any conversation might lead to talking about the bloom, nestled inside the sealskin pack that he was carrying over his shoulder. So he kept quiet, and when anyone asked him a question, he grunted as short a reply as possible.

Alfonso and the others didn't sense Bilblox's inner torment, partly because the hiking was so exhausting, and partly because everyone was amazed by Spack. Since leaving behind the coffin and struggling through Straszydlo Forest, she was a changed person. She walked by herself and stayed awake just as long as they did. In the evening, she helped set up camp and in the morning, she even helped pack up.

On the third day after leaving Straszydlo Forest, the group encountered its first real mountain storm. A screaming wind poured down from the High Peaks above them, blasting them from all sides. Snow swirled everywhere and the sun disappeared in a cloud of white. Thousands of tiny shards of ice flew about in the wind, cutting their faces and stinging their eyes. The temperature dropped to the point where Alfonso could no longer feel his feet. Everyone needed to stop and rest, but they couldn't find a place protected from the wind. They pressed onward through the storm until finally they came upon a possible shelter — a slab of dark, volcanic rock flanked by several massive pieces of ice. It provided just enough protection from the wind for them to set up camp and build a fire. They all huddled around the fire as Hill prepared a thin stew. When dinner was ready, they all ate ravenously and then tried to fall asleep.

Alfonso lay on his back with Hill to his left and Bilblox to his right. His body ached fiercely from the cold and from their long, tough journey. He was overwhelmingly tired, but he couldn't sleep because he kept thinking of all the steps that had brought them to this forgotten, lifeless area: the Dormian bloom, *McBridge's Book of Mythical Plants,* the ticking coordinates of Hill's watch, and the mysterious Estonian smuggler's map. Would it all add up to something? Most worrisome of all, the date wheel on Hill's watch was at one. They had less than twenty-four hours to find Somnos. It seemed impossible. Alfonso looked at his uncle. Hill's face was drawn and weary, as if the strain of leading them through the high mountains had taken its inevitable toll. He looked like an old man. Alfonso wanted to say something, but at that moment, a powerful wave of tiredness washed over him. He fell into a deep but restless sleep.

Alfonso was the first to wake up the next morning. The storm had passed. Alfonso investigated the area around their campsite in the morning light but found nothing remarkable. The area contained only snow, ice, and rock. It was as desolate a place as he had ever seen. It seemed impossible that anybody or anything, even the smallest piece of moss, could live in such an extreme place.

Upon returning to the campsite, Alfonso found Hill scrutinizing the Estonian smuggler's map and muttering to himself. "This makes no sense," Hill said. "It just can't be right."

"What's that?" asked Alfonso.

"Well," said Hill with a frown, "according to this map, and to my calculations, we have arrived at the coordinates sixty-four degrees north latitude by sixty-two degrees east longitude."

"Really?" asked Bilblox excitedly.

"That's the problem," said Hill. "I don't see any cliffs, or mountains walls, or rock outcroppings where the gates to Somnos might appear."

"I agree," said Spack, who was tending to a teakettle dangling over the campfire. "This doesn't look like the right place at all."

Hill sighed heavily.

Spack began pouring everyone cups of tea.

At that very moment Bilblox rose to his feet and cocked his head to one side. "Wait a minute . . ." he mumbled. He was overcome with a very strange feeling. It was nothing easily described, except to say that the atmosphere at that moment—the scent of burning wood, the bite of the cold wind, and the sound of the rattling teakettle—felt familiar. But how? Why?

"Hey," said Bilblox, "does this place look familiar to any of you?"

"Not at all," replied Spack. "In fact, that's exactly the point that I was just making. We're *nowhere.*"

"Strange," said Bilblox. He looked around, but his eyes were barely working. He could tell it was morning, but everything seemed foggy, like white mist on white snow. There was no reason for any of this to be familiar.

Nearby, a few soft chunks of snow fell from above and pattered lightly against the ground. It was an almost imperceptible sound, but it struck fear in Bilblox's heart. Suddenly, he realized where he had heard that sound before. It was in Straszydlo Forest—just after putting the ash in his eyes.

"MOVE!" yelled Bilblox. "GET OUT!"

Hill, Alfonso, and Spack exchanged confused looks.

"A little early for that kind of excitement, eh Bilblox?" Spack said.

Bilblox stood up. His big cheeks, perpetually red, gleamed a pale white. "You don't understand!" he shouted. "The ice above us is gonna come crashin' down. We'll all die. *Please* believe me, I know. Come on!" For a second, everyone was too shocked to move. Another small bit of snow pattered down from above. This did the trick. Alfonso and Hill stood up, followed a second later by Spack.

Bilblox pushed them roughly. "Hurry!" he shouted, and picked up the sealskin pack and its precious cargo. Bilblox half-stumbled, half-ran down the path they had trudged up the night before, and stopped about thirty feet away. Behind him followed the rest of the group. When they reached Bilblox's position, they stopped and listened, but heard nothing. Alfonso was about to accuse Bilblox of playing a very bad joke on them when a sudden roar made him turn around. In the next instant, their camp disappeared in a storm of white. It was an avalanche, and the full brunt of its fury landed on the exact spot where they had been sleeping only moments before. For a full two minutes, the avalanche raged. It was a terrifying sight, especially when they were so close that ice pellets from the falling snow rained on them.

Finally, the avalanche stopped and the snowy mist cleared away. Their camp and all their gear lay buried under thirty feet of snow. The small, hollowed-out place where they slept had become part of the mountain wall, indistinguishable from any other steep incline.

With an astonished look in his eyes, Hill turned toward Bilblox. "How did you know?" he asked. "*How?*"

Bilblox shrugged. "I guess I got a sense for these things," he replied. "Longshoreman's instinct."

Alfonso looked at Bilblox with surprise and confusion. "I can't believe you predicted that," he said.

Bilblox just smiled, and hoped they'd fall for his explanation. Everyone stood there for a minute or two, not knowing exactly what to say or how to react. Hill, however, continued to look at Bilblox.

Bilblox ignored him.

"You know," Hill slowly said to Bilblox, "the last time you had that type of 'sense' was on the *Success Story*. Right?"

"Don't remember," said Bilblox nervously.

Alfonso knew what Hill meant. On the boat, after he had rubbed the ash into his eyes, Bilblox had predicted the arrival of the flying fish and the iceberg. And now, in a very similar manner, he had predicted the avalanche.

"Did you do it?" Alfonso asked Bilblox. "Did you burn another leaf?"

"What are ya talkin' about?" Bilblox protested.

Everyone was silent.

"Sorry," said Alfonso. "I had to ask."

Bilblox said nothing for a moment, then sighed and buried his head in his hands. His huge shoulders hung low and he looked terribly sad. "I'm so sorry," he said. "I-I-I got turned around on that iced-over stream and I just knew those blasted Straszydlos were everywhere. I *heard* 'em! I thought I'd be killed, and then what would happen to that little plant? The wheelbarrow had slipped away and then, when I found it, I didn't know where I was and so —" He stopped and looked at everyone.

"So you burned *two* leaves from this plant?" asked an astonished Spack.

Bilblox nodded.

Spack shook her head grimly. "Of all the terrible things you could have done . . ." she said.

"But does it really matter?" asked Bilblox. "I mean I just saved us *and* the bloom."

"We'll see about that," Hill replied. He opened the pack and carefully reached in for the Dormian bloom. It looked the same, except for the obvious spot where Bilblox had broken off another leaf.

"Bilblox," Hill began. "I don't know what to say."

"I'm not surprised," declared Spack. "I bet he'd slit our throats for a pinch of that ash! Didn't I tell you? Leaf-burners are the worst scum on earth."

"It's not like that," Alfonso protested. "Bilblox is a loyal friend."

"That's not the point," yelled Spack. "Even if he was a loyal friend in the past, it no longer matters. Don't you see? He's burned the sacred Dormian bloom and used its ash—not once, but twice. I *told* you before we entered the forest that he can't be trusted. Any Dormian would tell you the exact same thing. Bilblox *must* leave. Now."

"I dunno what to say," mumbled Bilblox. He slumped to the snow, head and hands uncovered, and sat there dully, as if punched. "I'm sorry, I'm sorry, I'm sorry," he repeated. After a few minutes, he said in a soft voice, "I'll leave."

Bilblox stood up, waved his hand feebly, and turned to weave back down the trail. He walked carefully, like a cat, and held his hands outstretched for balance.

"It's a sad business," said Spack, shaking her head. "But this was the right thing for him to do."

"It's a pity," said Hill. "Such a pity. We trusted Bilblox."

"Wait," said Alfonso.

"Let him go!" snapped Spack. "There's no other choice. Even if he was a good man, that's finished now. He will keep burning the bloom until there is nothing left. I've read about this. He's no longer human—he doesn't know right from wrong."

"I'm afraid Spack is right," said Hill, his voice low and sad. "Bilblox is a good man, but he's a danger to us now. We have to let him go."

Alfonso said nothing but continued to watch Bilblox as he stumbled his way down the mountainside.

"No," said Alfonso as he stared at his snow-covered boots. He was tired and rundown, and it was about the worst he had ever felt in his life. His cheeks burned with the cold and he was shivering violently. Still, none of that compared with how sick he felt when he looked at his friend Bilblox shuffling down the mountain, perhaps to his death. It wasn't right.

"No!" declared Alfonso. "That bloom is mine—I grew it and I'm taking it to Somnos. It's my call and I say that Bilblox stays with us."

"A true Great Sleeper wouldn't take that chance," sniped Spack. "His only goal would be to return the bloom. Don't be foolish! You'll bring ruin to all of us. You'll be responsible for the destruction of Somnos and its people! Don't make this mistake!"

The wind was beginning to pick up again. All of them felt miserably cold, on top of their hunger and general lack of sleep. Alfonso turned to Spack and looked at her steadily. "Spack, I *am* the Great Sleeper," said Alfonso. "And Bilblox stays."

Hill saw in Alfonso's eyes a determination he had never seen before. "All right," Hill concluded. "It's your decision to make. I hope you made the right one."

CHAPTER 34

THE FALCON'S CAVE

THE GROUP quietly took stock of their situation. The avalanche had buried their gear under many feet of hard-packed snow. They had only what was in Hill's backpack: his map and compass, a little firewood, dried food enough for one more meal, and a heavy wool blanket. Everything else was gone. Worst of all, they had arrived at the coordinates of sixty-four degrees north latitude by sixty-two degrees east longitude and there was no sign of Somnos. None at all.

The group looked around at the remains of their camp dejectedly.

"I'm not sure what we should do," said Hill. "Let's investigate the area. Maybe we'll find something to help us find our way. I wonder what time it is . . . Where's my watch?" Hill reached into his pocket for his Dormian pocket watch, but came up empty-handed. "Hey," he said, with a slightly alarmed look on his face, "has anyone seen my watch?"

"No," said Spack.

"Me neither," said Alfonso. Soon after, though, he realized that there was something clunky and unfamiliar in his pants pocket. He fished it out and discovered, to his great surprise, that it was Hill's watch.

"What's my watch doing in your pocket?" asked Hill.

"I don't know," said Alfonso. "It wasn't there yesterday. I guess my sleeping-self grabbed it. Sorry."

Alfonso inspected the watch quickly before giving it back to Hill. His heart sank as he realized that the date wheel was at zero. Reluctantly, he gave it to Hill.

Hill stared at the watch but said nothing. While closing it, he noticed a jagged line and an arrow scratched onto the watch front's intricate filigree. The filigree was a series of squiggly lines that looked like magnified fingerprints.

"Who did this?" Hill asked.

Alfonso shrugged. "I don't know," he said.

"You must have done this in your sleep," said Hill.

"I don't think so," said Alfonso, though, truth be told, he wasn't quite sure what he had done while asleep.

Hill stared at the deep scratch.

"Why would your sleeping-self do this?" he muttered. Hill turned the watch over and over. His fingertip rubbed the scratch. "Your sleeping-self is usually more careful. It always does things for a reason."

"Let me see that," said Spack, who had just joined the conversation. She examined the watch closely. "Interesting—the front looks exactly like a contour map."

Hill looked at her in shock. "What? Let me see." He examined the watch front. Spack was right. The lines shifted and shimmied just like on a contour map. And Alfonso's sleeping-self had just scratched a line through it.

Spack took the watch back and asked Hill for the Estonian smuggler's map. Hill pulled it out and they all leaned over and stared at it in the bright morning light. Spack crinkled her brow, and muttered to herself as she glanced at the map, then at the watch front, and then back to the map.

"The Great Sleeper has done it," she announced matter-of-factly. "And now I understand why those Wanderers were so focused on teaching map skills. The front of Hill's watch isn't ornamental: it's a contour map of this area. Alfonso just traced a path through that map to another location less than a day's march away. And I'll bet a good night's sleep that this new location is *Somnos.* I'll lead us there—it should be easy enough to find."

"You're sure this is only a few hours away?" said Hill.

"Trust me," replied Spack. "I'm a Wanderer. It should be less than a day. In any case, it'll have to be, because all our supplies are buried under thirty feet of snow. We won't last much longer than a day." She touched Hill's hand and smiled. "Trust me, old boy—I want to get home as much as you do."

They headed uphill at a steady march with Spack in the lead. No one said anything. They heard only the wind and the squeak of their snowshoes on the snow. Although it was nice not to be carrying anything, it also made them all too aware of their vulnerability. They were in the middle of the desolate High Peaks of the Urals without gear or food. Alfonso kept glancing at the sky, which had filled with heavy, low-lying clouds. *If we are caught in another blizzard . . .* He was reluctant to finish the thought.

It wasn't long before everyone was ravenously hungry and thinking of the meager handfuls of food in Hill's backpack. However, Spack refused to stop or even turn around. She shook her head no, and continued through the snow in her strange half-lurch, half-walk. She led them along a mountain ridge, down the other side and smack into a brief but intense snowstorm. Only during the storm did Spack grudgingly stop for a minute. They huddled in a circle, as snow dusted across their faces and covered every inch of their jackets and hoods. Alfonso stared blankly at the white ground. His mind shut down and refused to think.

He was brought back to his senses by an unexpected feeling of warmth. Alfonso looked up and noticed that Hill was building a small fire with a handful of sticks that he had apparently stowed away in his bag. Seconds later, Spack jumped to her feet and stomped out the flames with her boots.

"What on earth are you trying to do—give away our location?" demanded Spack. "What if someone is following us? You'd be helping them. There can be no fires. It's too risky at this point in the journey."

"I was just so cold . . ." muttered Hill.

"You know better than that," said Spack. "What were you thinking?"

Hill shrugged sheepishly. He didn't seem himself. He was tired, weary, and chattering with cold.

"Don't worry, my friend," said Spack with a bit of tenderness in her voice. "You remember Somnos, don't you? It's a tropical paradise. Green plants, colorful songbirds, ripe mangoes, humid air, soil so ripe you could practically eat it—we're almost there."

By midafternoon, they reached a snowy plateau roughly the size of a soccer field. It was hemmed in on three sides by walls of sheer rock and the only way in was the route they had just taken. The wind began to howl. There were no signs of life—anywhere.

Spack looked concerned. She looked at the Estonian smuggler's map and then at Hill's watch. "Something's wrong," she said. "This is nothing like Somnos. Everything is covered in snow and the only sign of life are those vultures circling above us, just waiting for us to drop dead so they can eat our flesh and crack open our bones. Disgusting."

They looked up and saw at least three, maybe four birds circling lazily above them.

"Strange that vultures would be in the high mountains like this," said Hill. "They must be well adapted to the altitude."

"Those aren't vultures," said Alfonso. "They're falcons. Eurasian gray falcons, I think. I read about them in my falconeering books. They're the biggest falcons alive: twelve-foot wingspan, beaks like steel razors, talons that will rip apart a mountain goat with one thrust, and gray feathers that turn a burnt orange in the summer. They'll eat anything, but I've never heard of them attacking humans."

"Well, they seem to be interested in us," said Spack.

They stared at the falcons for a while longer.

"Alfonso, was it your sleeping-self or your waking-self that was most interested in falcons?" Hill asked.

"Both, actually," replied Alfonso.

Frozen and tired to the bone, Alfonso stared up at the magnificent Eurasian falcons and sensed somehow that they were important. He glanced over at Hill and it was clear from the expression on Hill's face that his uncle was thinking the same thing.

The falcons abruptly lost interest in the group below them and flew off toward one of the sheer cliffs that surrounded the plateau. Hill took out a monoscope, which he kept tucked into his jacket at all times. "Looks like they've got a nest in that cliff," he said. "It's hard to see, but I think it's a cave. That would make sense. Any nest exposed to this weather would be blown off in a second."

Alfonso took the monoscope from Hill and looked at the small opening in the cliff. It looked empty but then he saw a slight movement from just inside. At least one of the falcons was there.

"Well, that's interesting and all," Spack said, "but this doesn't help us much, does it? I guess we'd better take a look around and hope we find something."

For the next two hours, until the sun dipped below the horizon, the group combed every inch of the plateau. They found nothing but snow and sharp rock. The temperature began plummeting and the situation was desperate. They had no equipment to survive in that environment. Alfonso looked at Bilblox, Spack, and Hill, and saw by their drawn faces and shaking hands that they were just as cold and concerned as him.

"We can't be wrong," muttered Spack. "Somnos must be nearby."

"If we're wrong, we die," said Hill. His voice quavered and his eyes were blood-shot. They could barely hear him above the ferocious, snow-filled wind. He looked at Alfonso, who was staring up at the cliffs.

"Alfonso?" he said.

Alfonso turned and looked at Hill. "I'll be back," he said. "I have to climb the cliff and see that falcons' nest." He nodded gravely and then, without another word, began walking toward the sheer rock face.

The others looked at one another, confused.

"Are you crazy?" Spack shouted after him. "Those cliffs are straight up! You'll kill yourself!"

Alfonso soon reached the cliff wall. He paused to look for a good route, which gave Hill time to catch up.

"Stop," gasped Hill, his whole body shaking from the effort of breathing. "Tell me exactly what you're thinking."

"It can't be a coincidence," explained Alfonso. "I've been taking care of falcons in my sleep ever since I was eight years old and here we are—just outside Somnos—and what do we find? Falcons! It all makes sense. Don't you see? My sleeping-self must have been preparing for this moment for years."

"But preparing for what exactly?" asked Hill.

"I'm not sure," said Alfonso. "But I know that I have to see what's in that nest."

Hill stared into Alfonso's serious eyes. "All right," Hill said. "We're desperate. Give it a go." He reached into his backpack, took out a coil of rope, and handed it to Alfonso. "Put this in your backpack," said Hill. "Just in case you need some help."

With night falling, Alfonso began to climb toward the falcons' cave. Despite the bitter winds that tore at his exposed hands and face, Alfonso climbed steadily. The wall rose almost straight up, but it had many holds and crags, like the bark of the Great Obitteroos back in Minnesota. Alfonso was thrilled at his success in climbing. It was something he knew how to do, although usually he was only comfortable doing it while asleep. This time, he wasn't asleep or even in hypnogogia. It was just him—normal, awake Alfonso doing the climbing.

Only toward the end of his climb did he begin to slow down. The ligaments in his fingers ached dully and his shoulders began to cramp. Shooting stars burst across his eyes and he wondered what was happening to him. He couldn't feel the tips of his fingers. Once, his hands slipped off the rock, but he had learned long ago that balance in the legs is the most important part of climbing. That lesson saved him, and he was able to teeter on the rock face without falling, and seconds later his fingers again gripped the rock. A cold sweat broke out and trickled down into his eyes. It was so cold that seconds later the sweat froze on his skin. Still, Alfonso kept climbing, because to stop would mean wasting the last dregs of his strength. He only looked up, and slowly, minute by minute, his destination drew nearer.

Alfonso's mind was in a complete fog when he dragged himself onto the wind-swept ledge in front of the cave. He lay there motionless for a full minute before his head began to clear and he started creeping toward the cave opening. At that moment, an enraged mother falcon emerged from inside. He could tell it was a female by the marking on her enormous wings. She was, in fact, the largest bird that Alfonso had ever seen—standing at least five feet tall. Her beak alone was almost the size of Alfonso's head.

The mother falcon let out a piercing shriek and lunged at Alfonso. Instinctively, Alfonso rolled away, back toward the edge of the cliff. The falcon lunged again and, an instant later, Alfonso screamed. His right shoulder throbbed with pain. The falcon had slashed him with her razor-sharp beak. Alfonso touched his shoulder with the palm of his left hand, and it came away covered in glistening blood. He looked up and saw the falcon towering over him and eyeing him angrily. She snapped her beak and screeched. It was obvious that she was getting ready to strike again.

"Kee-aw, Kee-aw, Sqrook!" Alfonso yelled.

The falcon paused and cocked her head.

"Kee-aw, Kee-aw, Sqrook!" Alfonso yelled again.

The mother falcon seemed confused.

"Kee-aw, Kee-aw, Sqrook!" Alfonso yelled yet again.

This time, the mother falcon took several steps backwards, retreating into the darkened recesses of the cave. For the moment, at least, Alfonso appeared to be safe. He promptly curled in a tight ball, the way he had seen the baby falcons do, and tried to resist touching his right shoulder. He stayed this way for several minutes. The mother falcon did not return. Alfonso rose gingerly to his knees, again repeated the baby falcon call, and crept deeper into the cave.

The smell of the cave was overpowering—a mixture of wet underbrush and rotten meat. Long-dead rabbits and mice lay everywhere, their insides smeared across the dirt and rock. Alfonso could sense that the mother falcon was somewhere nearby in the darkness. He could hear her rustling her feathers and cooing gently. She didn't sound angry. Alfonso crept still farther into the cave. Then he saw it. On the floor in front of him sat a thick bramble of twigs and branches, carefully smoothed down in the middle. It was the falcons' nest. In the center, barely visible in the dim light, was a large egg.

Alfonso inched his way toward the nest. The mother falcon didn't seem to react. Alfonso drew closer still, until he was less than a foot away from the nest. He stared at the egg. It was, without a doubt, the strangest-looking egg that Alfonso had ever seen. Its shell was rough, almost like the bark on a tree, and it was carved with lines that curved and squiggled. Very cautiously, Alfonso reached out and touched it. Immediately, he knew it wasn't a real egg. It was far too heavy, as if perhaps it were made out of metal or even steel. Alfonso glanced back over his shoulder again. The mother falcon was still cooing peacefully. He returned his attention to the egg, and this time he picked it up and inspected it very closely.

The egg was split across the middle by a thick black line. Alfonso soon discovered that the egg could be twisted so that the top part of the egg rotated to the right and the bottom part of the egg rotated to the left. For a moment, Alfonso thought he could simply unscrew the top of the egg, but this wasn't the case. Whoever made this egg, and Alfonso suspected that he or she was a Dormian, had designed it far more cleverly than this. In some fashion or another, the egg was locked. *So how did it open?* Alfonso suspected that the answer had something to do with the intricate bark that covered the shell. Suddenly, it hit him. He had to align the bark on the top half of the egg with that on the bottom so that all the lines and squiggles matched up perfectly.

Alfonso took hold of the egg and began twisting it very slowly in an attempt to make both sides match up. He twisted, and twisted, and twisted. Nothing. He couldn't find a position where it all came together. There had to be such a position, but Alfonso couldn't find it. The problem was that the pattern on the egg was so finely detailed that it would take a microscope or a high-powered computer to find the exact point where all the lines matched.

The only solution was for him to enter hypnogogia.

Alfonso swiveled his head so that he was looking back toward the mouth of the cave. A shaft of light was pouring inward and it was illuminating thousands of small dust particles that were hanging in the air. Alfonso locked his attention onto one of these particles. He watched it flutter for a few seconds. He studied the way that it collided with other particles and he almost felt as if he knew which way it was going to bounce and swirl ahead of time. Moments later, Alfonso was firmly in hypnogogia.

Alfonso immediately turned his attention back to the egg. His hyperaware eyes examined all the different lines and squiggles that covered the barklike outer layer of the egg. There were thousands of these markings—perhaps tens of thousands—and Alfonso focused on all of them. He slowly rotated the top of the egg a quarter turn to the right. Then, very delicately, he moved it another sixteenth of an inch. He tried moving it just a little bit more, but his fingers were too big and clumsy to make the final adjustments needed to line up both halves of the egg. He needed a very small tool.

What could he use? Time was of the essence—he could feel himself quickly tiring of the hypnogogic state. Quickly, he plucked a solitary hair from his eyebrow. He then used the thicker end of the hair to nudge the top half of the egg ever so slightly into position. Perfect! The two halves of the egg blended together seamlessly. Alfonso pulled on the two halves, and they came apart. Something metallic fell out and clattered against the floor of the cave. It was a brass skeleton key.

Alfonso left hypnogogia and grabbed the key. Now he had to find the keyhole. He glanced around the cave. It could be anywhere! He sat down and thought about this.

If the key was in the bird's nest, the keyhole would probably be nearby. Alfonso inspected the bird's nest and discovered that it moved around easily. He lifted one end off the ground and found a small, circular trapdoor with a keyhole on top. The brass skeleton key fit into the keyhole. Alfonso opened the trapdoor. There was just enough light to reveal a ladder descending into a narrow hole.

He sighed. The whole thing reminded him of the catacombs.

Very wearily, Alfonso grabbed hold of the rickety wooden ladder and started down. The ladder was only about ten feet long. Alfonso found himself standing in a dark and narrow space, no more than three feet across. He was standing on something slippery and crunchy. It was probably ice, but he wanted to make sure. He reached into his pocket and pulled out a book of matches.

He struck the match, and in the flare of the light he saw an ice-covered floor beneath him. Just before the match went out, he noticed what appeared to be a wall painting directly in front of him. He lit another match and stared at the strange image: it was an old key, but the handle was a tree:

Alfonso lit another match. It lasted a few seconds and, during this time, he got another good look at the strange image. *What did it mean?* He thought about this for a few seconds, and then his eyes lit up in excitement.

"Of course!" he exclaimed. "That must be it!"

He scrambled back up the ladder and into the cave. He looked about cautiously. The mother falcon was still cooing in her corner. Alfonso darted over to the mouth of the cave and stared down to the landscape below. He could see Hill, Bilblox, and Spack.

"HEY!" yelled Alfonso as loudly as he could. "Hey, down there!"

His three friends looked up.

"Bilblox!" he yelled. "Climb up with the bloom!"

"What? Why?" yelled Bilblox.

"Because," yelled Alfonso, "the bloom is a key!"

CHAPTER 35

THE GATES OF SOMNOS

THOUGH BLIND, Bilblox had lost none of his famed agility. It took him a bit longer to find holds on the rock face, but still, he made it up to the cave in just over a half-hour. Climbing while blind actually wasn't that tough. At least he knew that he was going in the right direction—up. There was only one tricky moment when he almost slipped off the rock, but as he dangled precariously he remembered the ash in the breast pocket of his jacket. Knowing that he had it—just in case—helped him climb with confidence. By the time he arrived, twilight had turned to evening, and the sky was dark.

On the ledge, Alfonso thanked Bilblox and told him to wait outside so he wouldn't interfere with the falcons. He then took the bloom inside. The plant was heavy—very heavy. It now weighed so much that Alfonso really had to grunt and strain himself whenever he picked it up. As carefully as he could, Alfonso lugged the Dormian bloom into the cave and then down the ladder. He placed the bloom onto the small icy floor at the bottom.

Suddenly, the entire cave shook and pieces of rock dislodged from the ceiling. Small rocks hit Alfonso on the head. In his weakened, post-hypnogogia state, they were enough to knock him out. He slumped to the ground, unconscious.

Down below, Hill and Spack were running for their lives away from the cliff and toward the middle of the plateau. As soon as the rumbling began, boulder-size chunks of snow had begun falling all around them.

Boom! Smash! Kaboom!

When the rumbling stopped, and the cloud of snow had cleared, they discovered a gaping hole in the cliff face about thirty feet high and twenty feet wide directly beneath the falcon's nest. The hole revealed a simple but massive stone gate that looked quite different from the cliff. It was blue-gray and very smooth, as if polished. The only marking of any kind on the gate was the carving of a serpent whose body formed a giant *S*.

"What just happened?" yelled Spack frantically.

"I'm not sure," mumbled Hill. "Some kind of avalanche . . ." His voice tapered off—his mind was elsewhere. In a tired panic, he scanned the cliff for the falcons' nest. He could think of only one thing: Alfonso.

"Well, well," said Spack in a gleeful tone. "This has to be it—that serpent is the insignia of Somnos. We've made it—we'll be sipping tea in Somnos in no time!"

"No," replied Hill. "First we find Alfonso and Bilblox."

Moments later, a deep grinding noise rose above the sound of the howling wind. The gate was opening. The massive stone door swung wide and a lone horse-drawn sled emerged. The sled was entirely black and pulled by a team of eight dazzling black stallions. The horses and sled stood out brilliantly against the backdrop of snow and ice.

Hill and Spack were speechless. They strained to see past the gates for a glimpse of Somnos, but it was too dark. In fact, it looked like a tunnel.

As the sled drew nearer, hundreds of soldiers poured out the stone gate. They were dressed in brown fur pants and matching fur coats. They marched in a strange formation—like an arrowhead, with only a few soldiers at the front. The rest were bunched tightly behind them. After an initial burst out of the gate, the formation smoothly pivoted and followed the path that the black sled had taken through the snow and rock-strewn plateau. In no time at all, the sled came to a stop directly in front of Hill and Spack. The soldiers encircled Hill, Spack, and the sled. A frigid wind gusted down off the mountains. The soldiers stood totally still. In fact, the only body parts that the soldiers moved were their eyelids. In unison, all of them opened and then closed their eyes every several seconds. It appeared as if they were all taking short, two-second naps together. They jumped back and forth between waking and sleeping, waking and sleeping, waking and sleeping—and their weird sleep cycle was perfectly synchronized.

"Dormian knights," Spack whispered in amazement. "The elite. Well, it's time to introduce ourselves."

She stood as tall as she could and coolly examined the hundreds of soldiers who surrounded them. She began speaking in a strange-sounding tongue. It was a mix of low, guttural sounds followed by high-pitched noises that sounded like the yelps of puppies when their ears are pulled. At first, Hill found Spack's speech to be totally foreign-sounding.

He closed his eyes to concentrate on the individual words. Gradually, they began to sound more and more familiar. Suddenly, Hill was overcome with memories of his mother. He could see her standing in the kitchen of their old home in Somnos talking to him in this very language. The language was Dormian. He had not spoken it, nor heard it spoken, in many decades—and he no longer understood what any of the words meant—but he felt certain that this was his native tongue.

Spack spoke for several minutes and ended with a burst of yelps so high-pitched that the others had to block their ears. In response, one of the soldiers stepped forward, uttered several quick yelps, and then bowed. This soldier was the same height as the others but his heavy fur coat was entirely white and he wore a bright green cap with the feather of a falcon sticking out of it.

"This is General Loxoc," explained Spack. "He's the leader of the Dormian knights, and he welcomes us. He says to follow his orders completely and without question."

"We'll do nothing until Alfonso is safely down from those cliffs," said Hill sternly. "This man may be a general, but we carry the Dormian bloom. I am far more concerned with my nephew's safety than I am in following orders."

The soldiers obviously understood English, because in reaction to Hill's declaration, they drew long, glitteringly sharp daggers from sheaths around their waists.

"That was *not* a good answer," replied General Loxoc in an icy-cold voice. His dark eyes stared intently at Hill. He spoke English with a strange Dormian accent. His words squeaked harshly, as if they were rusty and in need of oil. "Find the two in the cave and search the plateau and cliffs for any others," he loudly ordered. "We shall remain here and observe the foreigners." The soldiers broke apart like a light bulb smashed to the floor. They formed into groups of three and scattered across the plateau, running across the snow as easily as deer. Several groups began to scale the cliff that Alfonso and Bilblox had climbed. They were obviously experienced, because they climbed swiftly and soon disappeared from view.

"Now listen carefully, General," Hill said. "If your soldiers so much as harm a hair on Alfonso's head —"

"Don't be an imbecile," said General Loxoc coolly. "If he is the Great Sleeper, I am bound by sacred honor to protect him with my life."

When Alfonso finally came to, he found himself sitting in the backseat of the elegant black sled. Next to him was his uncle Hill. Across from him were Bilblox and Spack. Instinctively, Alfonso glanced around in search of the Dormian bloom.

"Don't worry," said Hill reassuringly. "It's tied to the back of the sled. But the soldiers searched you and found a dagger with a Dormian symbol on it. Where on earth did you get that?" He paused. "Did Kiril give it to you?"

Alfonso nodded, a bit embarrassed.

"I'm sorry—I should have told you . . " began Alfonso.

"Never mind," said Hill. "We're all safe and that's what matters. The soldiers carried you down from the cave. They carried Bilblox too, as if he were a small child. What a sight that was!"

"I think they know I'm blind," whispered Bilblox nervously. "The soldiers were mutterin' to each other when they carried me. I know they saw my white eyes!"

"Don't worry about that now," said Hill.

"Where are we?" asked Alfonso.

"In a tunnel of some sorts," said Hill. "They're taking us through the mountains to Somnos."

Alfonso looked around. The sled was making its way through a large passage with high vaulted ceilings and a stone floor covered in ice. The sled was surrounded on all sides by Dormian soldiers. There were no lights, other than the torches that some of the Dormian soldiers carried, and so it was nearly impossible to see much more than this.

"We'll be in Somnos soon," said Spack with a smile. "And I'll be welcomed—I mean, we'll *all* be welcomed—like heroes. Well, not this big oaf of a leaf-burner, Bilblox. You'll see what Dormians think of leaf-burners . . ."

"Noo," replied a still-woozy Alfonso. "There'll be no mention of leaf-burning—not a single bad word about Bilblox—or I'll see to it that there isn't so much as a park bench erected in your honor."

Spack sighed indignantly, but said nothing.

Alfonso kept quiet. He was too woozy to speak. In the

distance, through the gloom of the tunnel, he could see a small patch of the night sky and the glow of moonlight.

"We're almost there!" exclaimed Spack. "At long last, I'm back—this time as a hero!"

"Don't toast yourselves just yet," said General Loxoc, who was suddenly riding alongside their sled on a beautiful white stallion. He seemed less than pleased.

"But the date wheel on the watch just turned zero," protested Hill.

"Yes," replied the general curtly. "You have cut it very, very close. Far too close for our comfort. Do you realize just how dire our situation is?"

"Is it too late?" asked Spack nervously.

"That remains to be seen," replied the general. "Today the tree has begun to die and, within three days' time, its death will be complete. It's not clear whether we will be able to get the Dormian bloom planted in time. I'm sorry to say that our fate is in a most precarious situation. So the answer is that you may indeed be too late. Time will shortly tell."

The group continued onward in silence.

Eventually, the tunnel ended at a broad stone ledge. They saw before them a vast valley, in the middle of which stood the city of Somnos. It was all illuminated in moonlight. Spack gasped. "I-it's a-all wrong," she cried out. "What happened?"

The scene before them was terrifying. Instead of a green valley with lush vegetation and chirping birds, as Spack had previously described, snow and ice almost completely covered the ground. It was as if the glaciers from the mountains were creeping toward the city from all sides to strangle it in an icy chokehold. They could clearly see that Somnos had been a land filled with bounty. Palm trees dotted the landscape, but they were topped with tufts of snow. Mangoes still hung from their trees, but they were covered in frost. Icicles hung from thick jungle vines. Patches of tropical giant bamboo lay half-buried in massive snowbanks. Waterfalls, which once must have sprayed warm mist, were now frozen solid.

"It started a few months ago," explained General Loxoc. "We're down to our last reserves. Only the city is free of snow, but the temperature has been dropping the last few days. As I said, the tree is almost entirely dead. We are a city on the brink of extinction."

They stared blankly at the view. For the last few days, the thought of a warm, sunshine-filled day had spurred them on, and to be faced with more cold seemed cruel beyond words. Alfonso thought of Lars, alone at the top of his iceberg, dreaming of a warm Somnos. That dream was almost extinguished. The sapling needed to be planted—quickly.

Alfonso turned his attention to Somnos. It was surrounded by six enormous stone towers. These towers, which formed the perimeter of the city, were all evenly spaced about a mile apart. The towers were connected by a series of high city walls and, together, these walls formed a perfectly symmetrical hexagon. In the middle of the city stood an enormous tree. It was the Founding Tree of Somnos, and it was dying. More skeleton than tree, perhaps a fifth of its leaves still remained.

"Halt!" yelled General Loxoc. "We stop here for a few minutes."

The general rode his horse around the entire party and then returned to the sled, where he stopped and fixed his eyes on Alfonso.

"Your strong friend—Bilblox—how did he become blind?" the general asked pointedly.

"He was born that way," said Alfonso with as much confidence as he could muster.

General Loxoc said nothing. Eventually, he spoke again. "We will be in Somnos within an hour. We expected the Great Sleeper weeks ago but because of your late arrival, we will be forced to speed up our investigations of you and your party. Perhaps that was your plan all along?"

"What are you talking about?" protested Alfonso. "We came as fast as we could!"

"Oh, really?" asked the general. He stared harshly at a dead songbird nestled in a corner of the ledge. Obviously it had tried to protect itself from the cold, but to no avail. It was frozen in a sheath of ice.

CHAPTER 36

A PECULIAR DREAM

THEY HURTLED down a steep road to the valley below. The sled dashed across the frozen floor of the valley. Moonlight glistened off the ice. An hour or so passed. Eventually they heard the clanking of a gate as it opened. They were entering the city. The sled came to a halt and then it heaved up and down in a strange manner. Only when they started moving again did they understand why—the sled runners had been replaced with wheels, since the snow did not appear to have entered the city.

With the wheels securely attached, they rode into Somnos and headed directly for one of the six towers. They approached a stone road that curled its way up around the tower the way a snake might wind its way up a tree. When the carriage rolled onto the road, the vehicle began to shake terribly, as if the wheels were coming off. The road immediately slanted up so steeply that those facing backwards—Bilblox and Spack—tumbled off their seats and crashed into Alfonso and Hill. They could all hear the horses panting and straining to keep their forward momentum. The driver yelled harshly and cracked his whip.

Alfonso could not imagine how the horses could keep climbing up this road, but the animals plodded on, dragging themselves and the carriage around every turn. Everybody felt dizzy as the carriage circled up and up. After ten minutes, the horses came to an abrupt stop. The general appeared at the side of the carriage.

"Welcome to the foreigners' guesthouse," said the general. "It is situated at the very top of the city's northernmost tower. In the morning you'll see that you have quite a view. This is where you will be staying. It is specially equipped for those not accustomed to Dormian life. It has bedrooms with actual beds in it so that foreigners can lounge about and do nothing in their sleep."

"Do you get many visitors?" asked Hill.

"Not recently," replied the general. The tone in his voice discouraged them from asking any more questions.

The guesthouse was a beautiful, spacious home with more rooms than Alfonso, Hill, Spack, and Bilblox could possibly use. There was a dining room with a massive table holding a jug of greenish-colored liquid and a solitary bowl containing dried fruits and nuts; apparently, this was all the food that the

Dormians could spare in these dark times. The guesthouse also had a bedroom for each of them—each furnished with a massive king-size bed draped with thick blankets. In the middle of the house was a courtyard with a large earthen pot.

"Put the bloom there," ordered the general. "It will be well-protected."

Alfonso withdrew the bloom from its sealskin pack and placed it inside the pot. Though General Loxoc had seen it briefly when the soldiers had found Alfonso, he now stood riveted. He approached the bloom cautiously, saying nothing and stopping about two feet away. Then he snapped out of his spell and turned to leave without saying goodbye. He ordered the soldiers nearby to stand guard outside. "No one leaves," he commanded, with a last glance at Alfonso.

After the Dormian soldiers withdrew, Alfonso, Hill, Spack, and Bilblox sat down at a wooden table and devoured all the nuts and berries. In their starving conditions, it felt like a feast.

"I must say," said Hill with a mouthful of nuts. He looked around and slowly raised his glass, filled with the liquid that shimmered green. "I-I just want to say how proud I am to have traveled this road with all of you. We made it."

The others stopped chewing and swallowed quickly. They raised their glasses.

"To the bloom, and to Resuza," said Hill. They solemnly clinked glasses.

Alfonso gulped hard. His eyes stung with tears as the awful truth of Resuza's death came back to him.

They ate in silence for a few minutes.

Spack cleared her throat and looked at Hill. "I assume you'll be wanting to find your family?" she asked. "You said you came from Somnos, right?"

Hill nodded and looked at Alfonso. "I don't know what we'll find," he confessed. "It's been an awful long time since I left. I'm afraid I —"

"Don't worry, Uncle Hill," interrupted Alfonso. "We'll ask around first thing tomorrow."

After eating, they all retired to their bedrooms. Alfonso undressed quietly and readied himself for bed. As he took off his winter parka, Alfonso reached into the front pocket and removed the dark blue sphere that he had found in Straszydlo Forest. It had been such a difficult journey after Straszydlo Forest that he had almost forgotten about it. Besides, he never had a moment alone to play with it.

Alfonso couldn't help but smile rather mischievously as he tossed the sphere lightly into the air and watched it zoom up, almost hitting the ceiling. Alfonso then walked to an open window and threw it again. The sphere sailed out the window about two hundred feet and then hurtled back to his outstretched hand. Without even thinking, Alfonso closed his eyes, concentrated intensely on the sphere, and threw it just as he entered hypnogogia. This time the sphere sailed out a mile and then turned back toward his hand and shot backwards with such tremendous speed that it was back in his grip within a second or two. Over the next five minutes, Alfonso played with the sphere while in hypnogogia. He discovered that, in this state, he was able to exert a much greater degree of control over the sphere itself. He learned, for example, that very subtle movements in his fingertips could affect how far, fast, and forcefully the sphere traveled. What's more, very slight adjustments in how he held his wrist greatly altered the direction in which the sphere would travel.

Alfonso spun the sphere in his palm, like a top. It glowed briefly, spun quite fast, and then abruptly stopped. A light flickered from within the sphere, and suddenly images of a man appeared in the glass. He was a bald monk with only one eye set high into his forehead. Astonished, Alfonso hunched over to get a better look. The monk was working in what appeared to be an orchard. He carefully pruned branches and picked oversize yellow fruit. After about five minutes of this, the images grew faint and then disappeared.

Dazed and tired, Alfonso shoved the sphere back into his parka and wearily climbed into bed. He leaned over to a nearby side table to turn off a lantern, but noticed just underneath an elegant book that gleamed in the light. Alfonso's eyes grew wide as he read the title. Quickly, he got out of his bed, picked up the book, and sat down in an old rocking chair in a corner of the room. He cracked open the cover and began reading:

THE GREAT SLEEPERS OF DORMIA: A COMPLETE HISTORY

by Doctor Katarzyna Lipska

Chapter I

The First Great Sleeper

Thousands of years ago, when humans were few and scattered across the earth, a small group of Siberian nomads were separated by a winter storm from their prized possession, a herd of reindeer. They searched for these animals everywhere, and wandered deep into the mountains.

After many terrible frost-bit months, the starving nomads stumbled upon a small valley free of snow and filled with all manner of tropical life. In the middle of the valley stood the Founding Tree. The nomads settled there and became the people of Dormia.

It was a beautiful but strange tree. The swaying of the enormous leaves made them tired, but when they slept, they did so fitfully. At first, they thought it was their location: they were in the far north. In the wintertime, darkness fell over them like a thick blanket, and in the summer, the sun shone all day and all night. But soon they realized that it was the tree that caused such strangeness when they slept. It was something in the way that the leaves swayed and the branches swished in the wind.

Over the years, the elders and scholars of Dormia investigated the tree. They analyzed its power to transform barren land into fertile soil. They also noticed the effect of the tree on their people and they discovered that it unlocked within each of them the capacity of wakeful or active sleeping. The great Dormian scholar Nazanin Moghbeli has described this as "a state of deep concentration, somewhat like meditation, that allows one to perform feats of amazing precision."

In time, the Dormian knowledge of sleep grew deeper and more intricate. They learned when to accomplish tasks while asleep, and when to remain awake. They became expert defenders, and trained the first of the Dormian knights, who were particularly skilled in sleep warfare.

Along with the study of sleep, Dormian elders undertook rigorous study of their lifeblood — the Founding Tree. They began by attempting to grow new Founding Trees, but they failed. This disturbed them greatly. How would they survive if the Founding Tree died?

Their questions were answered when the first Founding Tree began to fail. A stranger — an old woman bent over like a blade of grass — arrived at the Dormian city. She presented the anxious Dormians with an unbelievable gift, a sapling of the Founding Tree. She lived in the floodplain of the Yangtze River, and told a fantastic story of sleep-walking for many nights to a nearby gorge, where her sleeping-self carefully tended a few seeds. They were the seeds of the Founding Tree, and she was the first Great Sleeper.

Confused, the Dormians wondered how this could have happened. And then they remembered: many centuries before, one of the Dormians refused to stay in the valley, and had left heading due south. He had heard stories of the famous Yangtze River, and wanted to see it. As a memory of Dormia, he took with him a few of the seeds that no one had successfully germinated. And thus the Dormians made two epic realizations. The first was that a Founding Tree could be born only outside Dormia. The second — and more profound — was that the fate of the Dormians and their Founding Trees were intertwined. Dormians depended on the Founding Tree for life; and the Founding Tree depended on Dormians to spread its seeds throughout the world, where they could be germinated, and then eventually returned to their indigenous soils, deep in the Ural Mountains.

The ancient scholars eventually discovered that only Dormians who grew up in Dormia — under the canopy of a Founding Tree — could develop the powers of active sleeping. The one notable exception to this rule were the Great Sleepers. These very special people, who often were born in distant lands, developed extraordinary sleeping powers. Typically, a Great Sleeper will emerge whenever a Founding Tree is dying, and that Great Sleeper will not rest until he or she has hatched a new tree and delivered it to Dormia. The connection between the Great Sleep-

ers and the Founding Trees is powerful, fascinating, and wholly mysterious.

Under the protection of the first Founding Tree, the people of Dormia grew prosperous. Over successive generations, they explored the valleys and peaks of the Urals, and found ten more trees, each as beautiful and mysterious as the original. They settled under each of the trees, and these settlements became the eleven cities of Dormia.

After reading this first chapter, Alfonso skimmed over the ensuing pages until he came to a chapter heading that seized his attention. He began reading again, very astutely.

Chapter XXVI
The Rise of Nartam

At the height of Dormia's power, there were a total of eleven cities, yet one by one these majestic cities vanished from the face of the earth. Four were lost because the Great Sleeper failed to arrive in a timely fashion. Five were ravaged by Dormia's ancient and eternal enemy — the Dragoonya. One city's fate, the ancient capital of Jasber, remains uncertain, but it too has likely vanished. Now only Somnos exists.

The only hope we Dormians have in fighting the Dragoonya

lies in what precious little we know about them. "Know thy enemy," the ancient sages tell us. Tragically, the Dragoonya leader — Nartam — is Dormian. He was born Milos Brutinov Nartam in the city of Dragoo in the year 2365. By all accounts, he was a brilliant child and excelled in math, physics, and poetry. He was particularly skilled with the use of a short-sword and was a gifted harpsichordist.

At the age of just sixteen, Nartam became a member of the Dragoo Society of Sages and Scholars. Here he devoted himself to the Scorial Sciences, which study the uses and properties of the purple ash that is produced in very small quantities when a Founding Tree is burned. At the age of nineteen, Nartam authored the book Scorial Science & the Future of Dormia, *which argued that Dormians should occasionally burn portions of their Founding Trees and use the powers of the ash to their advantage. This was the only way, he concluded, that Dormia could survive in the face of other competing civilizations. Many people denounced this book, and it was even banned in several Dormian cities. Others, however, hailed Nartam as a hero who possessed the courage to challenge the sacred rules of the past.*

By the age of twenty, Nartam had become a leading political figure in Dragoo. Before long, he demanded that the city's

Grand Vizier — Cecil Cyrus — burn at least one leaf from the city's Founding Tree. When Cyrus refused, as he was obligated to do by ancient Dormian law, Nartam accused him of being both weak and a coward. Nartam then threatened to burn a leaf himself. Cyrus decided to move against Nartam, but this proved problematic. A band of armed thugs — who called themselves the Dragoonya — had sworn their loyalty to Nartam and promised to deliver "hellish retribution" if anyone came after their leader. Defiant in the face of this threat, Cyrus gave the orders for Nartam to be arrested. The plan failed. Nartam went into hiding and, a day later, a gang of Dragoonya thugs set fire to Cyrus's house, creating a terrible inferno that consumed much of the city. The death toll included Cyrus, his family, and several hundred other residents of Dragoo as well. During this fire, three leaves from the Founding Tree of Dragoo were burned and the powder fell into the hands of the Dragoonya.

Within a week, Nartam had seized control of the city. Over the following months, Nartam burned several large limbs from that magnificent Founding Tree of Dragoo. He and his men grew addicted to the Founding Tree's purple ash, which led them to burn the entire tree within a year's time. By the year 2386, Nartam — at the age of twenty-one — had destroyed the city of Dragoo and named himself Prince of the Dragoonya. Eventually, he and his men wandered far to the north and founded Dargora, which means "city of twilight" in the ancient tongue.

Alfonso tried to keep reading, but his eyes had become too heavy. It didn't matter—he had a good sense for what happened next. Nartam and his Dragoonya legions would constantly search for the remaining Dormian cities; and, as *McBridge's Book of Mythical Plants* had described, the Dragoonya would conquer huge areas of the Asian landmass. The only limit to their lust for power and violence was their supply of ash.

Alfonso yawned again. He laid the book on the floor and slid under the bed's luxurious covers. He would read more in the morning. Sleep came very quickly, but it was not peaceful. In fact, it was one of the strangest spells of sleep that Alfonso ever had because—for the first time in his entire life—he had a dream. The dream was set in a valley covered with snow, much like many of the valleys that Alfonso had crossed during his trek through the Urals. Directly in front of Alfonso stood a boy of his own age. The boy's face looked oddly familiar, though Alfonso couldn't recall who the boy was or how he knew him. The boy's eyes were firmly shut, as if he were sleeping.

"Excuse me," said Alfonso. "I'm sorry to wake you, but I feel certain that I know you."

The boy's eyes flicked open and, to Alfonso's surprise, they were entirely white.

"My name is Kiril," replied the boy calmly.

"Oh," said Alfonso rather dumbly. "What are you doing out here?"

"The heartless wretches kicked us out of the city—*after we fought for them*—and now my family members have all died in the snow," he replied softly as a lone tear ran down his cheek. "Are you a Gahno too?"

"No," replied Alfonso.

"That's good for you," said the boy. "I should have known. Your eyes aren't white like ours. You should be glad for that. After the battle, they said we couldn't be trusted. They said that we had become addicted to the purple ash and that in time we would become traitors. Some said we already were traitors."

"So you're all by yourself now?" asked Alfonso. "What will you do?"

"Oh, thankfully, I'm not alone," replied the boy. His voice suddenly had an eerie calmness about it. "I have met a man who saved my life. He wants to be my father."

"And who is that?" asked Alfonso.

The boy laughed suddenly.

"Why, that's a silly question, Alfonso," replied the boy. This gave Alfonso a start because he had not yet introduced himself by name. "I think you know perfectly well who he is. As a matter of fact, my father is someone you know."

"I see," replied Alfonso. "Well, in that case, can you take me to him? I would like to know who he is for certain."

"Oh, don't worry," said the boy. "You'll meet him again soon enough."

Alfonso awoke from his dream with a start. It was the middle of the night. He was breathing rapidly; sweat covered his forehead and stung his eyes. It took him a moment to realize that he had been dreaming. He tried to remember every detail. One particular sentence echoed in his mind: *My father is someone you know.*

CHAPTER 37

A SURPRISE FOR HILL

DESPITE his extreme exhaustion, Alfonso couldn't sleep much that night. At first it was because of the dream. Then he was awakened by a great flapping noise that sounded like a ship's sail fluttering in the wind. At dawn, he crept out of bed to investigate. His bedroom opened directly onto a large stone patio that wrapped all the way around the guesthouse. Once outside, he looked up and gasped in amazement. Directly above him hung the largest leaf he had ever seen. It had to be at least two hundred feet long and fifty feet wide and, as it rocked back and forth in the heavy morning wind, it made a great deal of noise—*thwap, thwap, thwap.* It was a leaf from the Founding Tree of Somnos.

Alfonso dashed over to the stone railing at the edge of the

patio. He now had a perfect view of the entire city of Somnos and his eyes focused immediately on the city's centerpiece: the Founding Tree. Its trunk rose from the center of the city, traveling high up into the sky, and then exploding into a giant tangle of branches. Despite the fact that the tree was near death, there were still a few dozen leaves left, each of them as big as the one flapping directly over the guesthouse. It was impossible to tell exactly how tall the Founding Tree was. The marble towers were quite tall, at least twenty stories in Alfonso's estimation, and the Founding Tree was roughly three times taller than these towers. More impressive than the height of the Founding Tree, however, was the size of its canopy. Indeed, the tree's many branches covered much of the city like an enormous umbrella.

Alfonso noticed that in certain sections the trunk of the tree was gleaming. It was hard to see from this distance, but it looked as if tendrils of ice were creeping their way up the tree. Several of the Founding Tree's branches were entirely bare and looked as if they were already dead. Alfonso could see teams of workers, standing on various limbs of the tree, cutting or pruning its deadened branches with giant hacksaws. Other teams were using ropes, nets, and pulleys to make sure that the severed limbs didn't crash down to the ground below. Alfonso shivered as an icy wind blew across the patio.

Alfonso turned his attention to the city's six marble towers. The towers were connected to one another by a series of walls that formed a hexagon. The towers themselves were made of a light pink marble and were decorated with beautifully detailed carvings. Armies of stonemasons must have labored to turn these giant slabs of rock into beautiful works of architecture, complete with windows, doors, columns, terraces, ladders, and stairways. The nicest homes appeared to be the ones, like his guesthouse, which were built on the flat tops of the towers. He noticed that the sturdy roads that coiled up the sides of the towers were congested with a great deal of traffic—hundreds of men and women on donkeys, in horse-drawn chariots, and on foot.

Within the city walls, the buildings were also made of pink marble, and while they were much smaller in height than the towers, they were equally beautiful. Their roofs were mostly domed and, from this perch, they looked like bubbles waiting to be popped. The streets were narrow and winding, but all of them converged at the center of the city, where the Founding Tree rose from the ground.

"Amazing!" Alfonso said to himself. "I just can't believe it."

"Believe it," said a voice from behind him. "Welcome to Somnos—the last city of Dormia."

Alfonso spun around and discovered that the voice belonged to General Loxoc. It was as if he had appeared out of thin air. He was clothed in his dress uniform. He wore knee-high leather boots, a black wool shirt and pants, a dark green velvet hat, and a matching velvet cape. Around his waist was a heavy belt made of silver chainlinks that held two throwing daggers and a full-length sword. Several medals glittered on to his shirt. The general was a big man, almost as large as Bilblox, with neatly combed silver hair and a pronounced forehead and chin. His face was expressionless and his eyes were firmly shut.

"I didn't know you were here," said Alfonso.

"Oh, I am an early riser," said the general stiffly. His eyes snapped open as he became fully awake.

"How is it that you speak English so well?" asked Alfonso.

"I learned to speak Wanderer when I was a boy," explained the general. "It is taught in all of our schools, thanks to our last Great Sleeper, Aldwyn Blodeuwedd. He was a schoolteacher from the Isle of Man in the Irish Sea. He arrived in Dormia roughly three hundred years ago with a Dormian bloom, a collection of William Shakespeare's plays, and a great love of the English language. You see, it is customary that all Dormians learn a second language, which we call the 'Wanderer dialect.' It is crucial that our Wanderers know how to communicate with others when they venture into the outside world—otherwise they would have little chance of surviving. Prior to Blodeuwedd's arrival, our Wanderer dialect was the language of the Romans. Blodeuwedd said that English was the language of the future and he convinced the Grand Vizier at the time. You'll find that most Dormians speak English reasonably well and a few—those who hope to become Wanderers—speak it exceptionally well. It's almost become something of a problem with the younger generations. Many of them speak Wanderer better than Dormian."

"Well, I guess he was right about English, or Wanderer as you call it," said Alfonso. "It is a pretty popular language in the outside world."

"Tell me," said the general, "What's it like being a Dormian in the outside world—never belonging—always being so fundamentally different from everybody else?"

"I don't know," replied Alfonso, "I didn't have a choice. I mean, I didn't even know there was a Dormia. I just had to make the best of it."

"I could never do it," said the general with a resolute nod of his head. "Never. In any case, enough chitchatting, I've come to tell you that you'll be facing your challenge today."

"My challenge?"

"That's correct," said the general solemnly. "I will be taking you to a place called the Iron Pillow. Normally, the Great Sleeper's arrival ushers in a two-week period of investigation known as Fortnight. However, because the tree's death is so imminent, we are forced to speed things up. You will face your challenge today. Then, of course, there will be a great many questions to be answered. Hopefully, if all goes well, we can get the bloom in the ground within the next seventy-two hours."

"Why can't we plant the bloom right now?" Alfonso asked. "You said that the situation was dire."

"That is true," replied the general. "But we cannot rush, even though our people are starving. There are certain precautions that we always must follow. Just because you and your party have arrived in such a suspiciously late fashion, we will not compromise our safety."

"But people will freeze if we don't hurry up," said Alfonso impatiently.

"Funny you should say that," replied the general with a dark smile. "You are not the first Great Sleeper to arrive late and then suggest that we abandon our safety protocols. The other to do so was a man named Noel Cranlost, who arrived at the gates of Loptos in the year 3408 and turned out to be a Dragoonya in disguise. He arrived very late, much as you have, and then demanded that he be led directly into the city's inner sanctum so that he could plant his bloom with all due speed. Shortly thereafter, he burned the city of Loptos to the ground."

"I understand that you don't trust me," replied Alfonso with a sigh of exasperation. "But that shouldn't stop you from planting the bloom. You can put us all in jail for the time being if you like, but for goodness sake, why don't you just put the bloom in the ground now and end the city's suffering?"

"We may have to do just that," replied the general. "But for now, we will follow protocol. First, you and your party must be tested and questioned. Then the bloom will be planted. Understood? In any case, we can't plant the bloom just yet because, apparently, it has been damaged and I want our scientists to inspect it before we go forward. So, as you can see, there is much to do and little time to waste."

"Yeah," muttered Alfonso. He was frustrated and it was difficult to suppress his feelings. "At the very least, can you tell me a bit more about this place . . . the Iron Pillow?"

"Oh you'll see soon enough," said the general rather mysteriously. "I'll be back in a few hours and tell you more. Why don't you just relax until then?"

"All right," replied Alfonso. "Can I bring my uncle Hill along? He's Dormian, you know, originally from Somnos. His—our—family might still be around."

"Not to worry," replied the general. "We have already begun to investigate whether your uncle really is who he claims to be."

Around midday, Alfonso and Hill were waiting patiently at the front door of the guesthouse when a magnificent silver-colored chariot arrived. The chariot had plush leather seats and a white silky awning. It was pulled by a team of six shimmering white stallions. The chariot's driver was a small bearded man who nodded hello, introduced himself simply as Ivan, and then continued with what appeared to be a very deep and restful sleeping trance. The chariot's one passenger was General Loxoc, who sat in back. He beckoned for Alfonso and Hill to get in.

It took roughly ten minutes for the chariot to make its way back down the tower, around and around, and all the way to the street below. From this perspective, on the ground, the Founding Tree looked even bigger. Many of the tree's uppermost branches actually disappeared into the billowy white clouds passing above. Alfonso could now see that a man in a horse-drawn cart was actually driving down one of the tree's lowermost branches. The branch was so wide that it could apparently be used as a road. And, a little bit farther down this same branch, a team of thirty or so men appeared to be working on one of the tree's giant leaves. Some of these men were climbing up and down a series of rope ladders that dangled above the leaf. Others were actually standing on the leaf and sweeping it.

"What are those men doing up there?" asked Alfonso.

"They are leaf-sweepers," explained the general. "They perform essential maintenance of the tree, although now that it is dying, I'm afraid their work has become nearly impossible. They must devote all their time to picking up the falling leaves. Given their size and weight, it is a twenty-four-hour operation just to avoid chaos in the streets of Somnos."

"Excuse me," mumbled Ivan sleepily. "I don't mean to interrupt, but they are about to light the urns. Shall we stop and watch?"

"What is it?" asked Alfonso.

"The lighting of the urns is a daily tradition," said the general. "In the summer the urns are lit only at night, but during the winter—when the sky turns dark so early—we light them each afternoon. You arrived too late last night to witness it."

They stopped at the side of the street and got out. On the other side of the street was the massive wall that protected the city. Alfonso looked up and saw a shiny metal urn, at least ten feet in diameter, sitting in the curve of the wall. Ivan yelled. Alfonso looked up and saw a streak of red light shooting from the Founding Tree. It hit the urn squarely in the middle and it immediately burst into blood-red flames.

"That was incredible," gasped Alfonso. "Where did the arrow come from?"

"From the tree," replied General Loxoc proudly. "We have five urns that light up the walls of the city. Every evening, just at dusk, the five best archers fall asleep and aim for the urns. It's not hitting the urns that's difficult, it's the distance. You have to shoot the arrow over half the city."

"Do the archers ever shoot while awake?" Alfonso asked.

"Of course not," replied the general with a slight chuckle.

"I remember the urns," said Hill softly. "Aren't they a warning system of some sort?"

The general nodded.

"Wait—isn't there a rhyme?" asked Hill. "Wait—don't tell me. I believe it goes: *If the urns are red / You can rest your head / If the urns are green / Wake from your dream.*"

"Yes, indeed," said the general. "That's the English version, though the Dormian version is far more pleasing to the ear. It's one of the first things we teach our Dormian youth." He looked at Alfonso and explained, "You see, every archer in the Dormian army is given a few green-tipped arrows, and if the city is ever attacked, that archer can shoot the green-tipped arrow into any of the urns. This causes a special green flame to burn. And, every Dormian knows, green flame means danger lurks near."

After explaining this, the general gave a hand signal to Ivan and, seconds later, the chariot was speeding down a narrow and extremely windy road that snaked its way through the city. A large sign stood alongside the road:

"It means there is a dangerous road up ahead," said the general. "You must drive it while soundly asleep."

Alfonso glanced at Ivan.

"Don't worry about Ivan," said the general, who apparently sensed Alfonso's concern. "He is the best sleep-driver in Somnos."

"Does anyone do anything in this city while they're awake?" asked Alfonso.

"Of course!" said the general. "Some tasks are best done when you're asleep and others are best completed when you're awake. For example, it is always best to be fast asleep when you do something that requires great dexterity or concentration—like racing a chariot, or shooting an arrow, or wielding a sword, or even playing sports. On the other hand, it's always best to be awake if you're doing something that requires creativity or decision making. So if you were playing chess or painting you'd definitely want to be awake. People are either awake or asleep depending on what they're doing. People in the outside world fall asleep only if they're tired, but we think that's terribly foolish."

Ivan steered their chariot onto a wider thoroughfare lined on both sides with restaurants whose names were written both in English and Dormian hieroglyphs on intricately carved wooden signboards. There was the Naptime Tearoom, the Sweet Dreams Pub, the Sonorous Snorer's Bistro, and to Alfonso's delight, the Great Sleeper Café. In front of each of these businesses were stacks of fresh towels and several large oak barrels filled with water. Alfonso observed that, before entering a restaurant, a patron would always dunk his or her head into a barrel and then dry off with a towel.

"What's with the head dunking?" asked Alfonso.

"That's how people wake up before they have a meal," explained the general. "It is considered rude to eat in your sleep in Somnos—at least at the good restaurants—and so the owners provide the barrels. Unfortunately, there is not much in the way of food these days in Somnos. Most restaurants are just serving water and bread."

As they continued to speed along, Alfonso witnessed many other curiosities. In each instance, the general provided an explanation. For example, Alfonso noticed that every house in Somnos had two doorknockers—one made of brass and the other made of cork. "You always use the cork knocker first because it is very quiet and, if the household is asleep, their hearing is quite sensitive," explained the general. "Then, if no one answers the first knock, it means the household is awake and you can use the loud brass knocker." When the chariot pulled past a weaver's shop, the general pointed out that all of the assistant weavers, who were mechanically and mindlessly weaving many strands of thread, were asleep. Meanwhile, the master weaver, who was deciding what pattern each assistant should use, was very much awake. A short while later, they drove past city hall, which consisted of two identical buildings: one housed the Waking Mayor and the other housed the Sleeping Mayor. When they passed a large three-story building with a red roof, the general explained that this was the Somnos Hospital for Problem Sleepers. This was where you went if your sleeping-self and your waking-self didn't get along.

"There are times when I would have liked to pay that place a visit," said Alfonso with a smile.

Eventually, the chariot turned off onto a side street and came to a halt in front of a ramshackle one-story home with a front door painted sky blue. Despite the fact that it looked perfectly ordinary, Hill stared at the house and scratched his head. "Strange. This place looks familiar," said Hill.

"Indeed," said General Loxoc. "According to the records found at city hall, this is the home where you and your brother, Leif, were born. Thus far it appears that you are indeed who you claim to be."

"Oh my . . ." gasped Hill. "I never thought I'd live to see it again . . . *this* is the place! My mother painted the front door and my father . . . My father used to grow tomatoes on the roof!"

"The building now belongs to a local shoe cobbler," explained the general. "He's not home right now, but I met with him earlier today, and he gave me a key so we could take a peek inside."

"What?" asked Hill. His voice had choked down to a whisper. "What about my parents? The *grandparents* to the Great Sleeper! Where do they live now?"

The general cleared his throat and looked at the ground.

"I'm afraid they both passed away—it was just a few months ago," said the general. "I'm very sorry. Your mother died of pneumonia once Somnos turned cold and we began to run out of food." He sighed. "I didn't want to tell you this, but here it is: apparently, your father died shortly thereafter. I am very sorry indeed."

Hill stared at the house. His eyes had a wild, red sheen to them, as if they had been rubbed with sand. He turned to look at Alfonso. "Were they still alive when we met in World's End? Maybe if we had gone faster. I thought of taking the plane straight to Barsh-yin-Binder, but I just didn't think it was possible . . ." Hill buried his face in his hands. His shoulders heaved and a low moan, terrible in its intensity, wracked his body.

Alfonso couldn't look. At that moment, he was overcome with thoughts of Judy and Pappy. How awful it would be to return home and discover that your closest relatives had died in your absence. The thought was terrifying and at that very moment Alfonso said a silent prayer for his mother and grandfather.

"One other thing," said General Loxoc. "You have a sister, Elisa, who was born after you left Somnos. She became a Wanderer. I'm told she promised her parents to search the world for you and Leif. We believe she might be in Tasmania. We're looking for more information."

"Well that's good news, isn't it?" asked Alfonso.

Hill said nothing. He stared blankly at the blue front door.

"Would you like to take a look inside the house?" asked the general. "I have the key."

"No, thank you," said Hill hoarsely. "I'm not quite feeling up to it." Still, he stepped down out of the chariot and walked slowly to the blue front door. He placed his left hand on the faded paint. He whispered something intelligible, and then returned to the chariot. He looked at Loxoc. "Her name is Elisa?"

The general nodded. "Elisa Persplexy."

CHAPTER 38

THE IRON PILLOW

THE IRON PILLOW sat on a narrow street in the Trunk District, which was what most people called the very upscale neighborhood that surrounded the base or trunk of the Founding Tree. From the outside, the Iron Pillow didn't look particularly impressive. It was a small building made of white stone with a low-slung slate roof. A sign hung in front, with the following diagram on it:

"What is this place?" asked Alfonso.

"It's called the Iron Pillow, the official meeting hall for the Royal Order of Sleeping Knights," explained the general matter-of-factly. "You'll see."

The general opened the door and strode inside. Alfonso and Hill hurried to keep up with him. Inside, the Iron Pillow was grand and imposing. It was a cavernous room with high, vaulted ceilings, and illuminated by many flickering candelabras. In the dim light, Alfonso could see dozens of men and women dressed much like the general. They wore knee-high leather boots, black wool shirts and pants, dark green velvet hats, and matching velvet capes. As soon as the general entered the room, someone yelled, "On your feet!" Instantly, everyone stood at attention and saluted the general.

"As you were," said the general.

Slowly, the knights in the room returned to their activities. Most of them were playing strange games that involved incredible levels of skill and concentration. In one game, a young knight with red hair was throwing small darts through a keyhole at a distance of twenty feet. Alfonso watched as the knight hit his target six times in a row. In another game, two older knights were stacking toothpicks on top of one another vertically—pointy-end to pointy-end. Currently, their skinny tower of toothpicks appeared to be almost ten feet high. Yet another game was being played by a group of five knights who each took turns sifting through an enormous pile of hay. Alfonso eventually learned that this game was called needle in the haystack and the object was to find a small needle that was buried within the haystack as quickly as possible. Most of the knights were able to do this in less than five seconds.

"This place is unbelievable!" said Alfonso.

The general nodded proudly and led Alfonso and Hill to the far end of the room, by a long wooden bar. Here three different bartenders were busy pouring frothy mugs of Dormian grog. Right away, a bartender handed the general three mugs. "Drink up," said the general as he handed one mug to Hill and another to Alfonso. "This stuff will make you sleep like a baby tonight."

Alfonso took a small sip and examined his environs more closely. All along the entire back wall of the room there were dozens of long wooden shelves containing hundreds of slender glass tubes that appeared to be empty. Each tube was marked with an inscription and a date written both in English and in Dormian hieroglyphs. One read: *Meganka Craiglovskov—October of 1278—five points.* A second read: *Konrad Grumäller—December of 2776—seven points.* A third read: *Johno Loxoc—May of 4901—nine points.* One glass tube, which was on a shelf of its own, stood out. Its inscription read: **Aldwyn Blodeuwedd (G. S.)—January 4523—twenty-one points.*

"What's with all those empty tubes?" asked Alfonso.

"Oh they're not empty," replied the general with a smile. "Each tube contains a collection of split hairs. You see, the ultimate game here at the Iron Pillow is called splitting hairs. It's quite a simple game actually. The contestant is given a case containing eight daggers. Meanwhile, each of the three bartenders plucks exactly eight hairs from his head. Then, all at once, the three bartenders toss their plucked hairs up into the air so that there are twenty-four different wisps of hair spinning about. We do this in a special room, which is equipped with a very large fan, and this causes the hairs to hover or float in the air. And as these hairs float about, the contestant must toss his or her eight daggers and try to split as many hairs as possible. The hairs must be split lengthwise, from top to bottom, otherwise it doesn't count. The record belongs to Aldwyn Blodeuwedd, the last Great Sleeper to arrive in Somnos. He scored twenty-one points by splitting twenty-one different hairs."

"Wait a minute," said Alfonso. "How could he split twenty-one hairs if he had only eight daggers?"

"A good question," replied the general. "He did this by doing double and triple splits. Basically, he split multiple hairs in a single throw. It is very difficult to do. You have to wait until two or three hairs line up perfectly and then throw the dagger in such a way that it splits all the hairs in the course of its trajectory. It's incredibly rare that someone is able to pull this off. In my lifetime I saw only one person pull it off —"

"Who was that?" interjected Alfonso.

"It was my younger brother, Johno Loxoc," explained the general. "He scored nine points, which means he achieved seven single splits and one double split. He did that almost twenty years ago, just before he left Somnos to become a Wanderer. Johno was very good with a knife. The only people who've beaten his score are Great Sleepers."

"You mean like Aldwyn Blodeuwedd?" inquired Alfonso.

"Yes," said the general. "Blodeuwedd scored three triple splits. He also scored a quadruple split, which is the only one ever recorded in history. You can see for yourself. His score card is up on the wall."

Alfonso turned around and noticed a wooden plaque commemorating Blodeuwedd's achievement.

Aldwyn Blodeuwedd

1st Dagger	*Double Split*
2nd Dagger	*Double Split*
3rd Dagger	*Double Split*
4th Dagger	*Triple Split*
5th Dagger	*Triple Split*
6th Dagger	*Quadruple Split*
7th Dagger	*Double Split*
8th Dagger	*Triple Split*
TOTAL	*Twenty-one Points*

The general set down his mug of Dormian grog and called out to the bartender. "Barkeeps," said the General, "I want each of you to pluck eight hairs—this young lad is going to have a go at it."

The oldest of the three bartenders, who was nearly bald, began grumbling in Dormian.

"He's unhappy because he says that he's barely got eight hairs left," explained the general with a laugh. "But I told him to cheer up—his hairs might become part of history!"

"They're falling out anyway," quipped another bartender who was busy plucking his hairs.

Eventually, all three bartenders did as they were told and stood waiting behind the bar. Meanwhile, as onlookers noticed what was going on, excitement began to build. A shout rang out from the far side of the room.

"Excuse me, General Loxoc!" yelled a tall, skinny knight. "Excuse me, sir!"

The entire room fell silent.

"Yes?" said the general.

"Is it true that the young guest is the Great Sleeper?"

"Well," said the general with a slight smile, "we are here to resolve that question."

"I knew it!" hollered the skinny knight excitedly. "Will he try to break Blodeuwedd's record?"

"Yes," said the general. He addressed the group in a loud voice: "As you all know, our last Great Sleeper—Aldwyn Blodeuwedd—managed to achieve twenty-one points back in January of 4523, almost four hundred years ago. Of course, his case was exceptional because he was a Great Sleeper. The record for a Dormian knight belongs to my brother, Johno Loxoc, who scored nine points. If this young lad is indeed the Great Sleeper, the ancient laws say that he will be able to match or even exceed the feat of the previous Great Sleeper. After all, the only person who can outdo a Great Sleeper is another Great Sleeper."

"That doesn't seem quite fair," interjected a young lady knight, who was standing nearby. "Blodeuwedd was exceptionally good—even as Great Sleepers go."

"I'm afraid, my dear, it is not a question of fair," replied the general. "Rules are rules and customs are customs—they must be followed. I don't envy Alfonso's task. Yet somehow, in the past, Great Sleepers have always risen to the occasion and equaled or outdone their predecessors—and so too will Alfonso if he is the real thing."

The room erupted with noise. The knights were suddenly cheering, arguing, laughing, snorting, betting, and hoisting their mugs of Dormian grog into the air.

"This is ridiculous," said Hill. He looked angry. "My nephew arrived with a Dormian bloom! What more proof does he need? This is a bush-league operation, if you ask me. I'm his uncle Hill Persplexy, US Air Force, retired, and you've got my word that this boy here is the Great Sleeper!"

"Just because he carried the bloom doesn't prove that he is the Great Sleeper," replied the general sternly. "Once, many centuries ago, a man posing as a Great Sleeper found his way into Loptos and then burned the city to the ground. I've already told you the particulars of this story so I won't repeat myself. The point is, the arrival of a Great Sleeper is a time of considerable danger for Dormians. It is one of the few times we open our mountain gates and allow a stranger to enter. The danger, of course, is not only that the Great Sleeper may have been followed but that he or she may in fact be an imposter. You understand, then, that we have no choice but to test Alfonso. I profoundly hope that he succeeds."

By the time that the general had finished explaining this piece of history, the knights had all migrated into an adjoining room. Hill, Alfonso, the general, and the three bartenders all followed them. This room was quite long and its walls, floor, and ceiling were all made of soft wood that was scarred with thousands and thousands of dents and grooves that had been made by thrown daggers. In the corner, two knights began operating a large, hand-cranked fan that blew air up toward the ceiling. The fan creaked and groaned as it blew. The general placed his arm around Alfonso and led him out into the center of the room. As they walked, the general whispered into his ear: "I want you to take your time and be very careful. It is crucial that you pass this test. Failure to do so will result in immediate expulsion from Dormia. Do you understand?" Alfonso nodded soberly. Seconds later, one of the knights emerged from the crowd carrying an old wooden box, which he presented to Alfonso. Alfonso opened the box and discovered a set of eight long, elegant, silver daggers.

"Barkeeps!" yelled the general. "Do you have your hairs ready?"

The bartenders nodded and held up their right hands, each of which was bunched in a tight fist.

"Well then, I formally authorize you to launch them!"

In one perfectly synchronized movement, all three bartenders unclenched their fists and shook loose their plucked hairs. Twenty-four tiny hairs wafted up toward the ceiling. The hairs were so light that they simply dangled and fluttered about in the air like particles of dust. And, indeed, they were so incredibly thin that it was possible to see them only when they were directly under the light of one of the candelabras that hung overhead.

Alfonso threw his first three daggers so quickly that hardly anyone had a chance to enjoy a sip of grog or even take a breath of air. The daggers shot through the air with tremendous speed and then—*twangggggg!*—lodged themselves firmly into the soft wood of the ceiling. There was a gasp from the crowd. Hill watched on with great nervousness. He knew, from the look on Alfonso's face, that his nephew was firmly in the hypnogogic state. "Take your time, dear boy," muttered Hill. "Take your time. You've passed all those tests before—remember Fort Krasnik?" Alfonso squinted his eyes fiercely and then, an instant later, he threw another four daggers.

"Wait!" yelled the general. "We should inspect the blades to see how many hairs he has split before we go on. That is the custom after the seventh throw."

One of the bartenders emerged with a folding ladder. He propped it against the wall, and then scurried up to the top rung. The bartender then reached into his vest pocket, produced a magnifying glass, and inspected each of the seven blades stuck in the ceiling.

"Well?" yelled the general.

"The lad has done well," yelled the bartender as he scurried down the ladder. He walked over to the wall at the far end of the room where a small chalkboard hung. The bartender picked up a small piece of chalk and wrote Alfonso's score on the board.

Score

1st Dagger	*Double Split*
2nd Dagger	*Double Split*
3rd Dagger	*Double Split*

4th Dagger	*Triple Split*
5th Dagger	*Double Split*
6th Dagger	*Triple Split*
7th Dagger	*Double Split*
8th Dagger	*?*
Total thus far	*Sixteen Points*

"He needs a quintuple split!" yelled one of the knights excitedly.

"What do you mean?"

"He needs to split five more hairs and earn five more points in order to tie Blodeuwedd's record and he has only one dagger left," explained another knight.

"A quintuple split—that's impossible!"

"It's never been done!"

"That's enough," said the general. "Let him give it a try."

Alfonso picked up the eighth and final dagger. He then began to creep around the floor of the Iron Pillow like a mongoose stalking its prey. He stepped ever so softly and always kept his head cocked up, looking for five separate hairs, and waiting for that moment when they would align themselves perfectly. His timing would have to be just right. He continued to creep along the floor and gradually the knights began to clap their hands in unison—*clap, clap, clap*—so that the whole room throbbed with a great pulsating beat.

In a dazzling burst of speed, Alfonso flung his dagger across the room. It shot through the air so quickly that not a single knight saw its flight. The only thing that anyone noticed was the sound that the dagger made—*twangggggg!*—as it stuck into the wall directly behind the general.

Immediately, the bartender rushed over, retrieved the dagger, and presented the weapon to General Loxoc, who inspected it. The evidence was there for him to see—ten incredibly small hairs pressed flat against the blade of the dagger.

"He's done it!" yelled the general as he thrust the dagger into the air. "He's made a quintuple split! All hail the Great Sleeper! All hail the leader of the Dormian knights!"

A chorus of knights sang back to him: "All hail the Great Sleeper! All hail the leader of the Dormian knights!"

The noise level in the Iron Pillow became deafeningly loud as the knights cheered and clanked their mugs of grog.

"Wait just a minute!" boomed the general. "Before we get carried away, everyone would do well to remember that even though Alfonso is the Great Sleeper, there are others who must question him before we can proceed to the planting of the bloom."

The room quickly fell silent.

"Later this afternoon the Royal Dormian Tribunal will convene and they will conduct their own investigation," said the general. "Until then, we should probably keep our celebrations under control."

With a great deal of grumbling, the knights quieted down and returned silently to their mugs of grog.

"General Loxoc," said Alfonso, "what *exactly* will the tribunal investigate?"

"Well, my boy," said the general with a kindly smile, "first let me say that I am sorry for any lack of courtesy that I have shown you or your traveling party thus far. I meant no offense. I was only following my solemn duty. But now I can say without any hesitation that you have my loyalty. I will gladly lay down my life to protect you—as will any of the knights in this room. And as for this tribunal, well . . . they'll ask you a few questions, in order to make sure that you weren't followed, and then they'll inspect the plant. Just to make sure it's in good shape."

"Inspect the plant?" asked Alfonso nervously.

The general placed his arm around the boy's shoulder and whispered, "Yes, that is my concern as well. I noticed that it has been damaged and I suspect that it probably has something to do with the whiteness of your friend Bilblox's eyes. I myself am not a fanatic about such matters. I am not one to make absolute judgments about what the purple ash does to a man's heart or his soul. Such judgments are rash and foolhardy if you ask me. But others do not see it this way—others on the tribunal that is. We could have problems later tonight—serious problems that may place your friend Bilblox in an unfortunate predicament—but we will face these problems together. Come, my boy, let's find your uncle Hill and get you home. I'll tell you a bit more about the tribunal when we're in the chariot."

Later that afternoon, upon returning to their guesthouse, they met Bilblox and Spack, who were eager to hear what happened.

Alfonso related all of the events of the day, including the final bit of news that they would be summoned that evening to the Royal Dormian Tribunal.

"They're gonna question us and bully us some more?" asked Bilblox angrily. "What kind of homecomin' is this?"

"Now now," began Hill, but Bilblox cut him off.

"And what happens when they ask about the plant and its missin' leaves?" asked Bilblox.

"Maybe they won't notice," ventured Hill.

"Yeah, right," said Bilblox. "One look at me stumblin' around all over and my white eyes, and they'll put two and two together . . ."

"Look, old boy," said Spack, who up until now had been silent. "If they notice what *you* did, then you'll just have to face the consequences. That's all there is to it."

"No," said Alfonso. "We won't abandon Bilblox. If there is a problem, I'll handle it."

CHAPTER 39

THE ROYAL DORMIAN TRIBUNAL

THE ROYAL Dormian Tribunal assembled at a place known as the Tree Palace, in the heart of the Trunk District. The palace, made of gleaming white marble, was a large, circular complex built around the base of the Founding Tree. In fact, it was impossible to touch the bark of the Founding Tree without first passing through the palace gates. In this way, the palace had two purposes: it was a place for important Dormians to meet and it also served as a giant fence that kept people away from the tree itself.

Most of the palace was roofless, since the Founding Tree's leaves shielded the entire complex from the open sky. The central gathering place at the palace was a large outdoor arena, or amphitheater, with several hundred seats and a small stage. It was here that Alfonso, Hill, Bilblox, and Spack were summoned to meet the Royal Dormian Tribunal. The group was escorted from the guesthouse to the palace by a dozen or so Dormian knights dressed in silver ceremonial armor. They were then paraded down the center aisle of the amphitheater and given seats together in the front row. Every seat in the amphitheater, and almost every available inch of standing room, was occupied by Dormians who had packed in to catch their first glimpse of the Great Sleeper. The crowd was noisy, excited, and nervous. Alfonso could tell that Somnos was on edge. Archers patrolled the walls of the Tree Palace, and quite a few Dormians appeared to be wrapped in heavy blankets to keep them warm from the frigid temperature, which seemed to be dropping steadily. Many had drawn, strained faces that clearly showed how little they had recently eaten.

Up on stage sat three figures all dressed in green robes. On the far left was the general. Above his chair hung a wooden sign engraved both with Dormian hieroglyphs and English lettering. The first sign read: GENERAL GILLIAD LOXOC, SUPREME COMMANDER OF THE DORMIAN ARMY OF SOMNOS. Next to the general sat an elderly woman with chestnut-colored skin, a long prominent nose, and elegantly braided hair. Above her, a sign read: HONORABLE SOFIA PERZEPOL, GRAND VIZIER OF DORMIA. And on the far right was a short pudgy man with bright red cheeks, a sweaty forehead, and a pug nose. Above him, a sign read: DR. NORD NOSTRITE, CHIEF SCIENTIST & KEEPER OF THE FOUNDING TREE.

Fortunately for Alfonso, earlier that same day the general had given him a quick rundown on how the tribunal would operate. To begin with, the general would introduce Alfonso and announce that he had proven himself at the Iron Pillow, confirming that he was in fact the Great Sleeper. At this point, Grand Vizier Perzepol would take over. The general said that she was the most important Dormian alive. Historically, the grand vizier of Dormia ruled over all eleven cities of Dormia. In the old days, it was the job of the grand vizier to oversee the entire kingdom of Dormia by traveling through a system of underground passageways—known as the fault roads—which burrowed beneath the mountains and connected the eleven cities. Over the years, as the cities of Dormia were sacked, the fault roads were deliberately destroyed, and the grand vizier was left with just one city to govern: Somnos. According to the general, the grand vizier was a tough but very fair woman. She would try to determine whether Alfonso and his party had been followed. "She won't try to trick you or make you look bad," the general had said. "She just wants to make sure that the city is safe." Unfortunately, said the general, the same could not be said for Dr. Nostrite. Technically, his job was simply to make sure that the plant was healthy and to nurse it back to health if it were in poor condition. But, apparently, he saw his role as much more than this. "Be wary of him," the general had warned. "He likes to make trouble, if given the chance. He fancies himself the true protector of the Dormian bloom and he may consider you a threat."

Alfonso and the others sat uncomfortably in their seats, knowing full well that hundreds of people were staring at them. They glanced at one another and at the three members of the tribunal. Finally, General Loxoc rose slowly to his feet. Alfonso's heart raced.

"I hereby call this session of the Royal Dormian Tribunal to order," announced the general. "As a courtesy to our visitors, I will speak in Wanderer, as will the other presiding officials. I am happy to report that yesterday I greeted a party of travelers at the Mountain Gate of our kingdom. The party included a young man named Alfonso Perplexon who was carrying a Dormian bloom. This young man has since proven himself at the Iron Pillow by tying Aldwyn Blodeuwedd's record. I can vouch for the fact that he is, without a doubt, the *Great Sleeper.*" A huge cheer rose from the people in the amphitheater and, for a very brief moment, the general allowed himself to smile. "And so, in accordance with ancient Dormian tradition, I now hand this ceremony over to the grand vizier." The general then took his seat. Moments later the grand vizier rose.

"Thank you, General Loxoc," she said. Her voice was loud and yet very calm and even soothing. She turned to look at Alfonso and the others. "And our most heartfelt thanks to the Great Sleeper and his traveling party." She paused and sighed deeply. "Our Founding Tree, which has sheltered and protected us for so many years, is nearly dead. It began to die yesterday morning, and it will be completely withered and desiccated within two days' time. However, before we can proceed with the planting ceremony of the new bloom, two final inquiries must be made. I realize that it must seem like little thanks for us to question you so thoroughly after your long journey, but we have no choice. The safety of our world demands that we do this. It is no coincidence that our kingdom has survived through the millennia. We have survived by following our ancient customs and safeguards. So please, we ask you kindly, give us your patience."

This short introduction was followed by a period of silence.

Hill then rose to his feet and declared, "My name is Hill Persplexy, a Dormian by birth, and uncle to the Great Sleeper. All of us are pleased to answer your questions, whatever they may be."

"Thank you kindly, Mr. Persplexy," said the grand vizier with a smile. "And welcome home."

For the next four hours, the grand vizier questioned every single member of the group and went over all the details of their journey. She was especially interested in all the people whom they had met along the way, including Dusty Magrewski, Vice Admiral Purcheezie, Hellen, Shamus, Lars, Dr. Van Bambleweep, Resuza—including her likely death in Straszydlo Forest—Kiril, and the two sisters Masha and Rosalina. The grand vizier asked dozens of questions about how they looked and acted. She focused on Kiril, and had Alfonso describe, in great detail, his encounters with him in Minnesota, Fort Krasnik, Barsh-yin-Binder, and on the journey to Straszydlo Forest.

"This is most worrying," she announced. "If Kiril has white eyes but can still see, then he is a Dormian who has taken the powder." She looked steadily at Alfonso. "If his story is true, and he is a Gahno, then his is a very sad tale indeed. As you may know, originally the Gahnos were a group of Dormians who accidentally got ash into their eyes during the Battle of Noctos. Let me be the first to admit, the Gahnos were treated shamefully by our ancestors and words cannot remove that stain from our history. They should *never* have been cast out into the snow to die. If this was the fate of Kiril's family, then I grieve for him, and feel no small measure of shame. However, it must be said, if Kiril did indeed fight in the Battle of Noctos—which happened over six hundred years ago—then it confirms that he is alive only because he still uses the ash on a regular basis. After all, the immortality conferred by the ash is one of its greatest lures and, in order for it to work, it must be taken once every few years . . . If Kiril has done this, then there is no question that he is now in league with the Dragoonya. They are the only ones who have the stuff.

"What's more, Nartam knows about the Gahnos. In fact, we know from our historians that Nartam personally rescued several Gahno children from the freezing snow outside Noctos. It seems clear to me that when Kiril speaks of his 'father,' he is referring to Nartam. The sad truth, however, is that Nartam has used these tragic people as his pawns, caring for them and nurturing them so long as they remain absolutely loyal, and depriving them of the ash—effectively killing them or ending their immortality—as soon as they step out of line." She sighed deeply, and it was clear that she was gravely worried.

The grand vizier looked at General Loxoc. "I'm afraid I have some more disturbing news involving Kiril," she continued. "The dagger that Kiril gave to the Great Sleeper in Barsh-yin-Binder has been traced." She paused and her stern features softened. "You see, each Wanderer is given a unique hand-forged dagger for close combat. These daggers are always inscribed with special markers so that we can identify to whom they belong. Wanderers prize these weapons greatly. They would never part with one unless . . . unless they were killed. Over the years, the Dragoonya have targeted Wanderers in order to track Great Sleepers and to learn more about Dormia. We believe that Kiril must have killed the owner of this dagger—an esteemed Wanderer named Johno Loxoc, who was the younger brother of General Loxoc. We will mourn his loss."

All eyes turned to General Loxoc. It was clear from the look on his face that he had already been told of this news and he now wore a sad, stoic expression of mourning.

After a few seconds, the grand vizier began again. "We must reluctantly conclude that Kiril followed the group for quite a while, perhaps as far as Straszydlo Forest, which is too close for my comfort. And yet, from the group's description of Straszydlo Forest, it also seems clear that the forest is in excellent condition. For millennia the Straszydlo have served us well by preventing Dragoonya armies from crossing through their forest and getting near our city. We owe them a great debt of thanks." She looked at General Loxoc. "But the best news is this: our Dormian scouts, who have been perched in their mountain lookouts since the arrival of the Great Sleeper, have reported back to General Loxoc that no army has been sighted in our vicinity." At this, Loxoc nodded sternly. "In short," continued the grand vizier, "despite all the close calls that the Great Sleeper has had, it does *not* appear that he has been followed."

A great cheer erupted from the amphitheater once again. Everyone was on their feet, shaking hands and exchanging hugs. Throngs of Dormian men and women swarmed Alfonso and the other members of the group.

No one in the group enjoyed this more than Spack. "I led the group here personally," she told a gang of adoring elderly men. She glanced at Hill, who was standing nearby. With a sly grin, she put her arm through his. "Well, perhaps that's not completely true. We couldn't have done it without this handsome Dormian. I suppose they'll erect a statue in our honor. Of course, a bronze statue would be nice, especially a large one somewhere in the Trunk District. Wouldn't you gents agree?"

"We will build you two statues," cried one of the old men enthusiastically. "There will be one in the Trunk District and another in my backyard."

The only person who did not seem very pleased was Dr. Nostrite, who remained in his seat with a slight scowl on his face.

"Excuse me!" yelled the grand vizier. "Excuse me!"

Gradually, the crowd settled down.

"I have concluded my formal inquiry into the matter of whether the Great Sleeper was followed," announced the grand vizier. "At this point, I would like to hand the third and final portion of our inquiry over to Dr. Nostrite."

The crowd sighed. Many of them took this moment to leave, although more than half returned to their seats. When everyone was settled, Dr. Nostrite rose to his feet and began to pace back and forth on the stage. He was sweating a great deal, but the scowl was now gone; in its place was a smile that looked more like a sneer.

"Greetings and salutations," proclaimed Dr. Nostrite in his thin nasal voice. "I am the chief scientist and keeper of the Founding Tree. My offices are located on the first major branch of the Founding Tree." Dr. Nostrite paused and gestured skyward, up the trunk of the Founding Tree, to an enormous tree house that sat perched on its lowermost branch. "It is there that I have studied this magnificent tree and come to know it so well. It is my job to look after this arboreal wonder and, rest assured, I will do so!

"I would like to invite all members of the Great Sleeper's party to make their way onto the stage with the Dormian bloom," continued Dr. Nostrite. "And let's be quick about it, we have a lot to do."

Alfonso, Hill, Bilblox, and Spack stood up and made their way onto the stage. Bilblox carried the Dormian bloom with his right hand and clasped Alfonso's shoulder — for guidance — with his left hand. Bilblox set the plant down on center stage and then backed away. Dr. Nostrite glared at Bilblox's eyes, but said nothing.

For the most part, the plant appeared to be in excellent shape. Its stem stood tall and straight. Its leaves were large and healthy-looking. Even the soil in the plant's pot looked perfectly moist and fertile. In Alfonso's estimation, whatever that counted for, the bloom was ready to be planted. Upon seeing all of this, Alfonso hoped that the inspection might go well.

Dr. Nostrite began examining the plant carefully. "At first glance, the Dormian bloom appears to be in moderate condition, but there are a number of worrisome signs on the stem of the plant," he said in his nasal voice. As he spoke, an assistant named Philliam — who also turned out to be Dr. Nostrite's son — took notes, nodded constantly, and, at every convenient moment, said, "Yes indeed, quite right, dearest father, quite right!"

"The stem shows wear and tear from exposure to extreme altitude," muttered Dr. Nostrite.

"Well we did fly in an old seaplane . . ." began Alfonso.

"Uh-huh," said Dr. Nostrite.

"Quite an astute observation, my dearest father, quite right!" said Philliam eagerly.

"Shut up, Philliam," said Dr. Nostrite.

"Yes sir," said Philliam.

"I also see that the plant's growth was somewhat stunted because it was confined to a narrow space," said Dr. Nostrite.

"We transported it in a hat and then a coffin when it grew too big for the hat," explained Alfonso.

"Why am I not surprised?" asked Dr. Nostrite with a roll of his eyes.

"We had to carry the plant in somethin'!" protested Bilblox.

"Silence!" snapped Dr. Nostrite. "Now what do I see here? It looks as if someone actually broke off two leaves from the plant. The scars are obvious. I'll want to take a closer look of course . . . *Philliam:* get me a magnifying glass!"

Philliam scurried across the stage and returned a moment later with a magnifying glass. Alfonso's heart beat furiously and he felt his palms go wet. Bilblox shifted about uneasily. Dr. Nostrite grabbed the magnifying glass and held it closely to the bottom part of the plant, where the two leaves had been broken off. He inspected the plant with exacting detail for almost ten excruciating minutes. At long last, he stood up and flashed a triumphant and yet malevolent grin.

"What do you see, dearest father?" asked Philliam excitedly.

"If you look long enough and carefully enough, it's amazing what you can find," said Dr. Nostrite calmly. "In this case, I have found a lone speck of purple ash—otherwise known as Dormian ash. Someone has broken off two leaves from the Bloom and *burned* them!"

A giant collective gasp resonated from the crowd.

"Burned?" Philliam asked in a horrified tone.

"I can explain everything —" began Alfonso.

"Did you burn them?" snapped Dr. Nostrite. "Are you—honored Great Sleeper—using the Dormian ash? Do we have another Nartam in our midst? Perhaps you didn't realize how little ash you can get from it. Are you and your blind friend looking to destroy more, just like Nartam? First a few leaves, then a branch, then the entire tree!"

"No!" shouted Bilblox. "I'm the only one who did it. Alfonso had no part in this. I'm the one to blame."

"He's not to blame," pleaded Alfonso. He looked at Hill. "We didn't know it was bad to burn it—it was just an experiment! It's not Bilblox's fault!"

"Guards!" yelled Dr. Nostrite at the top of his lungs. "I order you to seize that man called Bilblox. He is an enemy of Dormia!"

Several guards began walking toward Bilblox. Before they could get any closer, however, Alfonso darted in between them and Bilblox. "Stay back!" yelled Alfonso defiantly. "He is a friend of mine and of Dormia."

The guards stood frozen in place. Clearly, none of them wanted to make trouble with the Great Sleeper.

"Seize that man!" yelled Dr. Nostrite. "He committed the gravest crime imaginable: he burned the bloom! If you do not arrest him I will bring you up on charges of treason!"

The guards nodded off to sleep, readying themselves for a fight, and then stepped forward. Alfonso reached into his pocket and clasped his blue sphere. Perhaps the time had finally come for him to use it. Everyone in the amphitheater tensed for the battle that was about to ensue.

"Enough!" yelled General Loxoc. "This has gone far enough! Have we lost all sense of dignity?"

"Dr. Nostrite," said the grand vizier, "in your professional opinion, has any real harm been done to the Dormian bloom?"

"Miraculously, the bloom appears to be quite healthy," replied Dr. Nostrite. "No thanks to these incompetent fools!"

"If the bloom is healthy then what's the harm?" asked Alfonso. "Can't we just forget about this?"

"I'm afraid not," said the grand vizier. "Burning anything, even the smallest leaf or root or bark from a Founding Tree or a Dormian bloom is the most serious offense that anyone can commit. Don't you see? That is *precisely* what separates us from the Dragoonya. The temptation is always there to burn just a single leaf. After all, who among us would not enjoy having a quick glimpse into the future? And for Dormians the temptation is even greater. As I am sure you've been told, a Dormian who uses the ash can prolong his or her life by centuries. We believe that's how Nartam has lived as long as he has. But we can't go down this path. We cannot sacrifice the Founding Tree for our own selfish needs. It is the tree—and only the tree—that sustains our people. Without it, we are nothing."

"I understand," said Alfonso. "But Bilblox didn't burn the plant to enjoy its powers. It's not his fault. It's *mine.* Can't you make an exception?"

The grand vizier shook her head sadly. "I wish I could," she said. "But, you see, once someone puts the ash into his or her eyes, that person can no longer be trusted."

"I tried to tell them that," interjected Spack. "I told them that even a good person like Bilblox would be corrupted once he put the ash into his eyes."

"And I still don't believe it!" said Alfonso angrily. "Are you going to treat Bilblox as badly as you treated the Gahnos?"

"Whether you believe in it or not, we Dormians have certain basic laws that cannot be put aside, not even at the request of a Great Sleeper," said the grand vizier. "Rest assured, Bilblox will be treated humanely. He will not suffer the fate of the Gahnos.

I give you my word on that. In the meantime, I will take this matter up with my advisors."

"I think some kind of punishment is required," snorted Dr. Nostrite. "We must shackle him and imprison him at once. And I demand that we search him for any incriminating evidence."

The soldiers looked at General Loxoc, who nodded in agreement.

Bilblox tensed his fists. "Don't," said Alfonso. "We don't have anything to hide anymore." Bilblox knew what was about to happen. His shoulders sagged, as if all his strength had left him. The soldiers searched his pants and then his jacket.

"General!" cried one of the soldiers. With one hand he was holding Bilblox's jacket and in the other sat a few glittering granules of purple ash.

Alfonso looked at Bilblox in shock. "Bilblox?" he said. "Where did you get that ash?"

Bilblox stared at the ground. "I didn't use it," he said in a low voice.

"Take the bloom and the ash and lock it securely in my office at the palace," General Loxoc said in a firm voice. "And take this man to prison."

"For how long?" asked Alfonso.

General Loxoc stared hard at Alfonso. "Somnos law is clear: all leaf-burners face life in prison."

CHAPTER 40

THE SOMNOS PRISON

BILBLOX SAT in the back of a horse-drawn sled, his arms and legs bound with cut iron chains. His head felt unbearably heavy. Dr. Nostrite's biting words still rung in his ears. It had all happened so quickly and now, as his sled rattled on toward the Somnos prison, Bilblox's despair took on a dreamlike quality. All of his recent memories jumbled together. For a second, he wondered if he were dead and, instead of being taken to prison, he was actually in a coffin on the way to being buried. "It's the same thing," he said to himself drearily. "I might as well be dead if I'm going to spend the rest of my life behind bars." Bilblox imagined his beard becoming thick and matted, his fingernails growing long and yellow, and his hair lengthening out and flowing down past his shoulders. He'd be the insane blind man—hated by all because he burned two leaves from the Founding Tree. And it all happened because he had been trying to do the right thing.

The sled slowed and Bilblox heard a long, rusty screech. It was the iron gate of the prison opening. The sled inched forward another hundred feet or so and then stopped. Another voice, heavy and angry, called, "Attention, leaf-burner, take it slow and easy. No quick moves—we know all about you!"

Bilblox climbed out of the sled and hesitated on the top step. He could see nothing, but he could hear guards moving all around him. Immediately, a pair of hands grabbed his leg chains and began yanking on them. "Come on," barked the guard. "Out of the sled!" Bilblox stepped down slowly, each foot searching for the rung below. The rungs were evenly spaced, but he couldn't see that the distance between the last rung and the ground was much greater than the others. Bilblox, champion of Ballast and widely recognized as the strongest longshoreman in Fort Krasnik, searched blindly with his foot for the ground, found nothing, and toppled forward to fall heavily onto the snow. Everyone laughed. Bilblox groaned and rested his head on the ground.

Several guards picked him up and half-dragged him to his cell. Bilblox inched across the wall of the jail cell until he bumped into a mattress. He immediately lay on it and uttered a mournful sigh.

"Oh come on," said a nearby voice. "It's just prison, after all."

Bilblox sat up quickly. "Who's that?" he growled. "I'm blind but I'll crush ya with one fist."

The voice, half-scratchy, half-squeaky—like many Dormian voices—just laughed. "Oh, I'm sure you can," came the reply.

"But don't do it now. I'm your cellmate and probably your only friend. The name is Clink."

"That's a strange name," Bilblox said with a trace of the growl still in his voice.

"True," replied Clink as he sat up in his bed. "But when you've been in jail eleven times, you tend to get strange nicknames like that. You're the leaf-burner, aren't you? That's why you're blind. I may just call you Leafy for short."

Bilblox said nothing.

"Don't worry," Clink continued. "I don't care what you did, *Leafy*. The rules in this crazy city are useless, anyway. As it so happens, I'm in the process of leaving Somnos. I'm just looking for a way out—then I'll be on my way."

Now it was Bilblox's turn to laugh. "Are ya serious?" asked Bilblox with a chuckle. "Yer in prison and, as if that ain't bad enough, yer in a walled-in valley. Heck, yer in a prison within a prison. Trust me, fella, I know. We only barely made it into this place. There's nothin' around this valley for days in every direction except snow and ice. Believe me when I tell ya that yer trapped and ya ain't gettin' out."

"Now don't so be negative, Leafy—you're just feeling depressed," said Clink sympathetically. "You'll see, I'll hatch a good escape plan for us. In the meantime, tell me about the outside world. Tell me everything you remember. Spare me no details, no matter how boring or seemingly inconsequential. If the water tastes different in the outside world or if the air has a different color, I want to know!"

"Not much to tell," said Bilblox with a sigh. "The outside world is a lot like here, only bigger. Of course, there are a whole lot more people, and those folks sleep properly, but otherwise it ain't all that different."

"Excellent!" said Clink. "I plan to see it all. I'll visit Shanghai, then Paris, then Jerusalem, then Atlantis —"

"Atlantis is underwater, I think," interjected Bilblox.

"Don't be negative!" said Clink excitedly. "If the place is underwater then I shall swim there. I aim to see the world and no one can stop me!"

"Be my guest," said Bilblox. "But first, ya mind tellin' me how come ya been in jail eleven times?"

"Easy," said Clink. "I was born disreputable, and I guess I've just been going strong in that direction ever since." Bilblox could hear him walking back and forth. "My mother, Esmelexia, sewed clothes for everyone in the neighborhood. And when that didn't pay the bills, she was a pickpocket. Being a pickpocket turned out to be a very hard line of work in this city. As you can imagine, it's very hard to rob people when they are asleep. They usually hear you coming a mile away. And those who are awake know better than to carry a wallet on them because they'd just be sitting ducks. You know how it is — most people are awful clumsy when they're awake. But my dear old mother tried her best."

"A pickpocket?" asked Bilblox. "In Somnos?"

"She was the only one," said Clink. "I helped her when I was a kid, so moving into picking locks was easy. I'm the world's best picklock. Ask anyone. That's why they call me Clink."

"Well then how'd you get caught eleven times?" Bilblox asked.

Clink sounded annoyed. "When you live in a place where it's

impossible to leave, eventually you get caught," he said. "There are only so many hiding places. As you pointed out: Somnos is one big prison. But I'm telling you Leafy, you and me, we're busting out of this place. With my knack for escaping places, and your knowledge of the outside world, we'll be unstoppable."

Clink approached Bilblox's bed and began to whisper: "I can escape any time I want, but the hard part is leaving Somnos. Tell you what: I'll get you out of here, no questions asked. But *you* have to promise to get me out of Somnos. Do we have a deal?"

"I told ya already," said Bilblox with a sigh of exasperation, "I don't know how to get outta Somnos."

"Well can you at least point me in the right direction?" asked Clink hopefully.

Bilblox thought about this. Though he had been in prison for only a very short period of time, the idea of escaping was irresistible. But then he imagined Alfonso getting the news that he had escaped. Typical behavior for a leaf-burner, everyone would say.

Bilblox shook his head. "No," he finally said. "I ain't escapin'."

"Why not?" said Clink.

Bilblox said nothing.

"Suit yourself," replied his cellmate. "But I'm leaving tonight. I can escape whenever I want, you know. It's just that Somnos is a small place. Escaping this jail is the only fun I get."

The day dragged on. It grew colder, and Bilblox could hear Clink muttering to himself and blowing on his hands. Bilblox was too numb to be cold. He lay on his mattress and tried unsuccessfully to sleep. His mind journeyed back in time to Fort

Krasnik and to the *Success Story.* Over and over, he returned to that moment on the *Success Story* when he touched the powder and rolled it curiously in his hands. He had been tired, that much he remembered. And so it was perfectly normal for him to yawn and to rub his tired eyes with his hands. In that small moment, his life had changed forever. Now he was blind and facing life in prison. The sadness of it all overwhelmed him. He sighed heavily. Then, completely unexpectedly, he saw a flash of bright light. A moment later, his vision returned.

Bilblox leapt to his feet and shouted with joy. He knew that this spell of vision wouldn't last. Although he still experienced brief moments of sight, in recent days they had hardly come at all. However, when they did, he could see perfectly for a few precious minutes.

"Wh-wh-what happened?" asked Clink excitedly.

"My eyes can see again," said Bilblox happily. "Really, it's true. I can see."

He quickly walked over to the cell's thickly barred window and stood there, drinking in the sight of the sky and the landscape, which was bathed in moonlight. He couldn't remember seeing a more beautiful sight in his entire life.

"Not a bad view, eh?" asked Clink.

Bilblox nodded and turned back. He saw Clink for the first time; he was a tall, skinny man with a wild mane of scraggly hair. Clink reminded Bilblox of a paintbrush, with his narrow body and a thick bushy top. He was so skinny that Bilblox could make out most of his bones. The cell looked grim. The floor was muddy and the roughly cut stone walls were covered with a slick-looking green moss that was flecked with specks of ice. He turned back, grabbed the iron bars of the window, and felt the rust flake off in his hands. The feel of the bars in his hands should have depressed him, but it didn't. At that moment Bilblox felt surprisingly happy. In fact, he wondered if he'd ever been happier. It was so good to see again! For a few minutes, he stood there, staring out. He marveled at the movements of the clouds and the incredible Ural Mountains looming above everything else. Their snow-covered flanks slowly turned a phosphorescent gray in the moonlight.

Bilblox tried to keep his eyes open as much as possible. He was afraid that if he closed them—even to blink—his vision would disappear. He swiveled his head back and forth, trying to see everything. Everything looked normal; in other words, beautiful. Only one thing struck him as odd: just beyond the prison wall he could see someone walking alone in the snow-covered landscape, as if out for an evening stroll. It was an older man. His back bowed heavily to the ground and he staggered forward, leaning on an old cane for support. There was something familiar about that walk.

"Clink," said Bilblox.

"Yes?"

"Do ya know all the guards here?"

"I guess so," Clink replied. "I've been here eleven times, you know."

"Yeah, I know," said Bilblox. "How about that old guy outside the prison walls? Ain't he too old to be a guard?"

"Maybe he's not a guard," said Clink. He walked to the window and looked at the old man. "Strange. He's not wearing a prison guard uniform, and he's certainly no prisoner. Maybe he's lost. Sometimes these elderly Dormians, well, they get a little confused. *Especially* if they're awake."

"He looks very familiar . . . ," said Bilblox, his voice trailing away. But who exactly? The old man stopped and looked in Bilblox's direction. At that point, the moon retreated behind some clouds, and Bilblox couldn't see the old man's face. Still, an unmistakable chill ran down the longshoreman's spine. After a long pause, the old man continued walking and soon disappeared from sight.

Bilblox's rare moments of vision usually lasted only three or four minutes, and unfortunately, this was no exception. His vision disappeared moments later and the awful blank whiteness in his eyes returned. Bilblox moved away from the window and the gentle breezes and shuffled to his mattress. He sat down.

"What happened?" asked Clink.

"What do ya think happened?" said Bilblox. "I'm blind again." He recalled what Dr. Van Bambleweep had told him back in Barsh-yin-Binder: *your blindness is irreversible and it's only going to get worse.*

As he recalled those words, Bilblox froze.

"Van Bambleweep—that's who it is!" he shouted. Bilblox stood up, walked over to the window, and stared blankly outside. "But what would *he* be doing here? It doesn't make sense . . ."

"What are you talking about?" asked Clink.

"Clink!" exclaimed Bilblox. "I've changed my mind. Can ya get us outta here?"

Clink sprang up from his mattress, his eyes shining with excitement. "I'm only the most famous escape artist in Somnos!" he proclaimed. "Let's go!"

CHAPTER 41

AN ANCIENT MYSTERY

THAT NIGHT, Alfonso tossed and turned. The knowledge that Bilblox was sitting in a prison cell made him feel both angry and guilty. The following morning, he tiredly joined Hill and Spack for breakfast, although it was soon interrupted by a loud knock.

"Who could that be?" asked Hill.

"I'll get it," said Spack. She stood up and headed for the front door of the guesthouse. Moments later, she returned with an elderly man at her side. He was completely bald except for a few specks of curly white hair that stuck up from his head. He had a long white beard that reached down to his waist, and was dressed in a spotless white robe.

"This is Josephus," explained Spack. "He says he's some kind of historian or something."

"I am the royal scribe of Somnos, which is just a fancy way of saying that I take a lot of notes," explained Josephus with a hearty laugh. "It is my job to write your story for the history books. As you know, the Dormian bloom is scheduled to be planted either later today or tomorrow morning, and I would like to conduct this interview before then. That would be in keeping with custom of course. You see, every time a Great Sleeper arrives, the royal scribe records his or her story —"

"Can't we do this later?" Alfonso interrupted.

Josephus looked at Alfonso with total bewilderment.

"Alfonso," said Hill. "Let's go with him. It would do us good to get out of here for a while."

"Excellent!" declared Josephus. "I'm also interested to hear about the outside world. We've had no news in some four hundred years. I'm most curious to know whether the British ever confronted the Spanish armada."

A few minutes later, the entire group—Josephus, Alfonso, Hill, and Spack—climbed into Josephus's carriage. It jerked forward and within seconds they were hurtling down the steep, spiraling road that connected their guesthouse with the city below. Soon they arrived at the Somnos library. It was an imposing five-story building made of the same marble as the six towers. A long rectangular slab of stone with an inscription on it adorned the front of the building. Josephus explained that the inscription was Dormian hieroglyphs.

"What does it say?" asked Hill.

"Ahh yes," said Josephus excitedly. "A very good question. The inscription comes from the ancient Story of the Tree and, interestingly enough, it pertains directly to Alfonso."

"To me?" inquired Alfonso. "What do you mean?"

"Well," said Josephus, "the inscription says, roughly translated, 'Study the path of the Great Sleeper and all will be well.'"

"What's that supposed to mean?" asked Alfonso.

"Simple," replied Josephus. "We learn to better protect ourselves by examining how Great Sleepers either succeed or fail. That's how all the rituals developed. For example, we had to make sure that you were not an imposter, because—as you know—a Dragoonya soldier once posed as a Great Sleeper, entered the city of Loptos, and then burned it to the ground. That's why you were tested. We are also interested in how exactly a Great Sleeper gets his or her hands on Dormian seeds. I believe you got yours from a maraca. We have used other devices to send seeds out into the world—including necklaces, belts, and even earrings—but have found, from interviewing previous Great Sleepers, that maracas work best.

"That's also how we developed the Wanderer's watch that you used to get here. Aldwyn Blodeuwedd helped us develop it. Believe it or not, there is actually a Dormian seed from the current Founding Tree of Somnos implanted within that Wanderer's watch. For reasons that we still don't fully understand, Dormian seeds typically shed their seed coat, or outermost shell, roughly one hundred and forty three days before the death of the Founding Tree from which they came. This gives the Great Sleeper a five-month period to germinate the seed and then get the plant to Dormia. We built the Wanderer's watch in such a way that the date wheel starts ticking backwards as soon as the coat seed erodes. In any case, we're always trying to improve our techniques."

Josephus beamed and clapped Alfonso on the shoulder. "All

this brings us to today's Transcription of the Tale," he said. "I can assure you, we're *very* excited."

Upon their arrival at the library, Alfonso discovered that the front steps of the building were mobbed with librarians pushing one another and angling to get a look at the Great Sleeper. When they saw Alfonso walking toward them — with Hill and Spack trailing behind — the librarians let out a huge cheer and clapped wildly. Alfonso blushed. Walking just in front of him, Josephus beamed and slowed down to allow more time for cheers.

"Notice how they're all awake?" asked Josephus. "Ordinarily, most of these employees are asleep, filing and cataloguing. But I gave them special permission to be awake for your arrival, so that they could enjoy the moment to its fullest!"

Once inside, they walked down a long marble corridor known as the Hall of Great Sleepers. The walls contained a number of oil paintings with ornately carved gold frames. Each painting, explained Josephus, was a portrait of a Great Sleeper from Dormia's past. Beneath each portrait was a plaque that provided a name and historical information. Three in particular caught Alfonso's eye:

One showed a man in a toga who appeared to be Roman. His plaque read:

MARCUS DOLORIUS — BORN IN 3034 (122 A.D.) IN THE ROMAN CITY OF CAESARIA. HE AND HIS SEVEN BROTHERS ARRIVED IN SOMNOS IN 3068 (156 A.D.) RIDING ON A PROCESSION OF ELEPHANTS. HIS JOURNEY WAS A LONG ONE. HE WANDERED THROUGH THE URAL MOUNTAINS FOR

ALMOST SEVEN YEARS BUT, ALONG THE WAY,
HE MADE A SERIES OF VERY CAREFUL MAPS.
THOSE MAPS, NOW KNOWN AS THE DOLORIUS MAPS,
ARE STILL IN USE TO THIS DAY.

Another painting showed a tall, imposing man dressed in a bright red robe. His plaque read:

ONERO MITIMBU—BORN IN THE WEST AFRICAN KINGDOM
OF ATANGA IN 2092 (820 B.C.). HE ARRIVED IN
SOMNOS IN 2177 (735 B.C.) AT THE AGE OF
EIGHTY-FIVE, PURSUED BY A PACK OF
SNOW LEOPARDS AND DRAGOONYA.

Yet another painting showed a barefoot woman in a dark green robe with a herd of goats behind her. Her plaque read:

MOLLY FINNEGAN'S DATE OF BIRTH IS UNKNOWN,
BUT SHE LEFT HER HOMELAND OF IRELAND AS A CHILD
AND SPENT THE NEXT SEVERAL DECADES WALKING
TOWARD SOMNOS. SHE ARRIVED AT THE GATES OF SOMNOS
IN 4060 (1148 A.D.) BUT, FOR SOME REASON, HER ARRIVAL
WENT UNDETECTED AND SHE SPENT ALMOST THREE YEARS
WAITING IN THE SNOW FOR THE GATES TO OPEN.
EVENTUALLY, AFTER SHE FINALLY MADE IT INTO
THE CITY, FINNEGAN HELPED INVENT THE CURRENT SYSTEM
WHEREBY THE GATES OF THE CITY OPEN AUTOMATICALLY
WHENEVER A DORMIAN BLOOM IS PLACED IN THE
KEYHOLE LOCATED IN THE FALCONS' CAVE.

The group spent several minutes perusing these paintings and then continued onward to Josephus's office, a spacious, high-ceilinged room filled with strange-looking books and maps. In the center of the room was a massive wooden desk. Josephus walked over to the desk and sat down on a chair behind it. A stack of blank paper, four quill pens, and an oversize bottle of black ink rested in front of him. The group sat down in a row of high-backed cushioned chairs that faced Josephus. He looked at them eagerly. Alfonso could see his feet dangling like a boy's about a foot above the creaky wooden floor.

"And now," said Josephus in a solemn, formal voice, "please begin with your story. Spare no detail." Josephus took a sheet of paper from the pile in front of him, dipped his quill pen into the ink well, and smiled expectantly.

"Before we begin," said Alfonso, "there's something I wanted to ask."

"By all means, go ahead," replied Josephus with a kindly smile.

"Is there any connection between Morvan's syndrome and the Dormians' ability to do crazy things in their sleep?"

"Morvan's syndrome?" asked Josephus. "I'm afraid I don't know what you're talking about."

"*Quiesco coruscus,*" interjected Hill. "Sleep shaking."

Josephus laughed. "Of course not," he replied. "Sleep shaking was a terrible illness many hundreds of years ago, but Dormia was never affected. The history books are filled with Dormians worrying that somehow they'd get that disease, but we're much too isolated for catching any nasty bugs. Is the outside world still worried about that?"

Alfonso shook his head. "So the Dormian sleeping ability comes only from Dormia," he said.

"That's right," replied Josephus. "You have to be born here. Simple as that. The only exception is someone like you, a Great Sleeper."

"And how is a Great Sleeper chosen?"

Josephus hooted. "You may as well ask how many stars there are in the sky! Some things we just can't answer . . . All we know for sure is that a Great Sleeper must come from the outside world, while also having some connection to Dormia. Even a drop of Dormian blood may do the trick. Why we once had a Great Sleeper from Mongolia who was only one-sixteenth Dormian." He cleared his throat. "Are you ready?" he asked.

Alfonso and the others were tired of telling and retelling the story, but soon they were caught up again in the memory of their adventure, beginning as it did many months ago in Minnesota. Josephus wrote furiously, never seeming to tire. The sheets of paper filled up with his elegant writing as the story took them to Fort Krasnik, to Lars's iceberg, across the polar icecap into Barsh-yin-Binder, and after many harrowing days, to the doorstep of Somnos.

Hours passed. Library workers brought in trays of strongly scented herbal tea. After a while, Alfonso noticed a wall hanging that intrigued him. It was an intricately drawn map of Dormia, with the eleven major cities and a number of outposts scattered among the mighty peaks of the High Urals. Josephus saw Alfonso looking at it, and he nodded sadly. "Yes, Dormia was once a mighty kingdom," he remarked. "As I'm sure you know by now, there were once eleven cities of Dormia. We were a loose but patriotic grouping of city-states, but mistrust and suspicion followed Nartam's actions, and Dormia was never the same after the city of Dragoo fell. After a second city, Iopode, was destroyed by Nartam and his gang, the ties that bound the Dormians together were torn, in a tragic event called the Splintering."

Josephus sighed and rummaged on his desk and found a chart that he showed Alfonso. "Here it is," he said. "This shows the fate of the eleven cities. Yes, we were once powerful and respected far beyond this tiny corner of the Urals. And now only Somnos is left."

The Eleven Cities of Dormia
Current Date 4920

Dormian history starts with 0—
the year Jasber was founded.

City	*Year Destroyed*	*Cause of Destruction*
Prenjuk	984	*The Great Sleeper failed.*
Majlom	2114	*The G. S. failed.*
	**Order of the Wanderers founded* 2116	
Dragoo	2386	*Nartam burned his own city to the ground.*
Iopode	2429	*Dragoonya followed G. S. and sacked city.*
	**Splintering occurs* 2430	
Zuydhoek	3111	*The G. S. murdered by Dragoonya.*

Loptos	3408	*Dragoonya impersonated G. S. and sacked city.*
Quartin	3776	*The G. S. failed.*
Ribilinos	4131	*Dragoonya sacked city.*
Noctos	4318	*Dragoonya sacked city.*

**The fault roads are closed 4319*

Jasber	*Date unknown*	*Exact fate unknown.*
Somnos	*Still in existence*	

"Why don't you just rebuild the cities?" asked Alfonso.

"Not without a Founding Tree," replied Josephus. He stood up, looked out the window, and gestured broadly out the window at the thin layer of snow that now covered much of the city. "You see what happens when a Founding Tree dies? Winter takes over. When burned, the change is much more rapid: the roots shrivel up, the fields disappear, and the ground freezes. All that is alive and growing dies. Without the Founding Tree, there is no life. In the past, we Dormians have tried to regrow a Founding Tree in the place where one once stood, but it has never worked. As far as we know, the only person who can hatch a seed from the Founding Tree is a Great Sleeper like you. What's more, a Great Sleeper is summoned only when a Founding Tree is at the very end of its natural life. So when a Founding Tree dies prematurely—because someone has burned it—no Great Sleeper is summoned and no replacement is delivered. This is why our cities have perished, one by one, and have never been rebuilt. Once a Founding Tree is burned, the city surrounding it is doomed."

"Why have the Dragoonya been so successful?" Alfonso asked. "Didn't the Dormians fight?"

"Of course!" replied Josephus. He seemed offended. "Dormians are formidable fighters, some say the best in the world. But the Dragoonya can overwhelm anybody with their vast numbers—especially when they have some Dormian ash to rub into their eyes. The ash gives their archers spectacular vision and it also allows their generals to see briefly into the future. Imagine, if you will, a Dragoonya army that knows your key plans at the same time you do! And what's more, over the centuries, they have maintained one crucial advantage . . ."

"What is it?" asked Alfonso. "What do they have?"

"I'll show you," replied Josephus.

Josephus sprang from his seat, walked to a nearby bookcase, extracted a massive book—thicker than the thickest dictionary—and staggered with it back to his desk. The book was bound in leather and its cover was emblazoned with the following title in big, block letters: THE DRAGOONYA, A COMPLETE HISTORY.

"This book contains all that we know about the Dragoonya and the destruction of the Dormian cities," explained Josephus. "Although it describes our battles with the Dragoonya in varying fashions, I've noticed that the battles always seem to turn in their favor when a certain person emerges." He looked at Alfonso. "I'm sure you know who I mean."

"Nartam," whispered Hill. "Tell me, are there other Dormians from Dragoo who are still alive and fighting at his side?"

"Very few," replied Josephus sternly. "Over the years Nartam has killed off most of them."

"Why?" asked Alfonso.

"Because he doesn't want to share any of his Dormian ash with them," explained Josephus matter-of-factly. "Of course, Nartam still has a few of his original conspirators from Dragoo at his side—and a few Gahnos as well—but the rest of his men are non-Dormians who work as mercenaries. And I'm afraid these men are incredibly loyal to him because he provides them with loot and he always leads the charge in battle."

Josephus flipped through a few pages of the massive, leather-bound book. The book's binding squeaked and dust rose thickly in the air.

"Here's a famous passage written by the great scribe of Noctos, Maxso Minter," said Josephus. He put his glasses on and began to read:

The army of horsemen came from the north, pouring out of their ice-built pit of damnation, the city of the polar wastes—Dargora. Clad in feathers and yowling like possessed beasts, they fell upon our fair city. Their leader rode at the front, and though he was blind, and wore only a thin black shawl for armor, he was a powerful fighter who smote many Dormians. The hair of this cursed man shone white against the black smoke of our fair city's destruction. His men called him Nartam.

"The descriptions of Nartam are always the same," Josephus continued. "And the few drawings we have of him highlight the same profile—a bit crooked along the spine, shoulders that hunch and yet ripple with muscles, a long chin, and ears that run flat against the head. Of course, his face is always covered by the cloak, and all we have are a few drawings, done in the heat of battle, but still . . ." His voice trailed away. A few seconds later, Josephus returned to his subject with renewed passion. "It's *always* the same story: each time the Dragoonya attack, the battle is tightly contested until a man appears, wearing the same black cloak, and at that moment the battle turns against us. When he emerges the Dragoonya become like rabid dogs."

"Can I see the drawings?" Alfonso asked. Josephus nodded and motioned for Alfonso to approach the desk. Josephus turned the heavy book around to face Alfonso, and then joined him on the other side of the desk.

"Here," said Josephus, pointing to a carefully drawn picture of a pitched battle. In the left corner lurked a tall man covered entirely in a black cloak. Only the contours of his face were visible: a long chin, hunched shoulders, and prominent, raised cheekbones.

"This is from the infamous sacking of Noctos," explained Josephus. "It took place six hundred years ago. Maxso Minter made this drawing and wrote the entire account. He was a keen scholar with a tremendous eye for detail. If anyone can be trusted to describe what happened on that fateful day, it would be Minter. Now, let's fast-forward to the destruction of Loptos." Josephus flipped carefully through the large, brittle pages until he came to another drawing. This one was less carefully drawn, and obviously done under great strain. The lines were wavy and weak, and trailed off into blank space.

"An unknown Dormian, probably a simple foot soldier, drew

this," said Josephus in a solemn voice. "It was discovered many months after the destruction of Loptos. From the looks of it, the drawing was the last thing he did before he died."

Alfonso looked carefully at the drawing and stared at the faint lines. The only clear picture was in the middle, of a tall, hunched-over man wearing a cloak. It was exactly like the picture from Ribilinos, except for one incredible detail. The body-covering cloak had slipped in one area and exposed a hand.

Alfonso felt a sudden pressure in his chest and head, as if he were being smothered. He opened his mouth, but air wouldn't enter. He gripped the table and began to cough.

"What's the matter?" Josephus asked, his bushy eyebrows twitching with concern. "Yes, it's a terrible picture. But an important one, because it's the only picture that shows at least a part of Nartam's body. That hand is disgusting, isn't it? And the fingernails are positively revolting."

Alfonso felt the blood rush to his face, coloring it a deep red. He recognized the man in the drawing.

"Uncle Hill," said Alfonso. "Come over here—you need to see this."

Hill had been sitting on the other side of the desk and had been—rather absent-mindedly—staring at some maps on the wall. Now, suddenly, Hill knew something was wrong. He dashed over to his nephew's side and examined the drawing.

"Oh my goodness," said Hill. "That can't be —"

"It is," said Alfonso in a surprised, suddenly nervous voice. "Look at his whole body and then focus on his hand—with those long curling fingernails. Who does that look like?"

"Yes, yes, yes," stammered Hill. "That's the spitting image of Dr. Van Bambleweep from Barsh-yin-Binder."

Before anyone could process this alarming realization, however, one of Josephus's assistants rushed into the room and cleared his throat loudly.

"What is it?" asked Josephus irritably.

"I bring some upsetting news," said the assistant nervously. "I just received a dispatch from the Somnos prison. Apparently the leaf-burner—the one they call Bilblox—has escaped."

CHAPTER 42

RETURN OF THE LONGSHOREMAN

THAT EVENING, Alfonso sat alone, shivering, on the outdoor terrace. Just enough light remained so that he could see the white-cloaked Urals in the distance. Darkness was falling rapidly and there was still no word of what had happened to Bilblox. Where was he? And, more importantly, why had he broken out of jail?

For the moment, he could only sit and wait. Hill had gone to the Iron Pillow, at the invitation of several knights, and wouldn't return for a few hours. Most importantly, nothing could be done until General Loxoc returned. The general was currently in the countryside inspecting Somnos's outermost defenses and making some last-minute preparations before the bloom was planted. Upon his return, the general would learn two bits of unwelcome news: first, Bilblox the leaf-burner had escaped; and second, Nartam was alive and living in Barsh-yin-Binder. What's more, he had actually brushed shoulders with Alfonso. Inevitably, this would raise a new set of suspicions about Alfonso and his party.

Alfonso continued to sit by himself on the terrace of the guesthouse, trying to relax, when he heard a sound floating up from below—as if someone or something was scratching the marble walls of the tower. Curious to see what was going on, Alfonso walked closer to the edge and peered over. At first he saw nothing, but then, not more than five feet below, he saw a snow-streaked head of hair. It belonged to a man whose face was pressed flush against the wall of the tower. His fingers were searching the marble for an outcropping or a crack or anything that might help him hoist his body up. Alfonso's heart began to pound. It was Bilblox, and he was only feet away from reaching the top of the tower!

Alfonso looked around. The terrace was empty. Everyone else was inside, probably getting ready for bed. Moments later, Bilblox pulled himself up over the railing and onto the terrace.

"Bilblox!" whispered Alfonso excitedly. "I can't believe it! What are you doing here? Did you climb all the way up the tower?"

Bilblox weakly raised his head and nodded. "All in a day's work," he said hoarsely. "Just thought I'd drop in and pay ya a visit." He coughed and slowly stood up.

Alfonso gave his longshoreman friend a hug. Bilblox was drenched in sweat and his muscles were quivering from the strain of the climb.

"Are you all right?" asked Alfonso. "How'd you get here?

"There's so much to tell ya," gasped Bilblox. He began to tell Alfonso about Clink and their escape from prison. Clink had agreed to guide his blind cellmate to the base of the tower, where Bilblox could use a fire escape ladder to climb up and avoid being seen. In return, Bilblox vowed that if he ever left Somnos—which seemed highly unlikely—then he would take Clink with him. At this point, the two of them parted ways and Bilblox began climbing the ladder. "The only problem was that the fire escape ended a third of the way up the tower," Bilblox explained. "So then I just had to climb straight up." He laughed. "I just did a whole lot of groping."

"Incredible," said Alfonso. "We've got to find some place to hide you."

"Ya ain't gonna hide me anywhere," vowed Bilblox. "In fact, I'm gonna turn myself in. But not until I tell ya what I saw in prison. It was durin' a moment when I could see again. Do ya know who I saw? Ya'll never believe it."

"Who?" asked Alfonso.

"That nutty old quack from Barsh-yin-Binder," replied Bilblox. "Ya know, Dr. Van Bambleweep."

Alfonso turned pale. "Are you sure?" he asked.

"Yeah," said Bilblox. "How do ya think he got here?"

ര

Alfonso summoned a messenger and sent word that General Loxoc should return to Somnos immediately—the enemy had been sighted. He and Bilblox waited nearly an hour in the dark until they heard the heavy clatter of the general's chariot pulling up to the front of the guesthouse. The general hopped out of his chariot, dunked his head in a bucket of cold water that was attached to the back of the vehicle, and exclaimed, "Arrrgh—I really hate waking up this way!" Then, with his head dripping wet, he knocked on the front door of the guesthouse.

Alfonso and Bilblox met him in the entranceway. The general looked at Bilblox and shook his head in disgust. "We were wondering where you were," the general said coldly. He turned to his driver. "Return to the barracks immediately and bring ten soldiers. We've found the blind leaf-burner."

"Bilblox escaped for a good reason, General," Alfonso said. "There's something we have to tell you. Somnos is in danger." Alfonso quickly outlined their suspicions that Dr. Van Bambleweep was actually Nartam, and then, Bilblox's discovery of Van Bambleweep walking near the prison the night before.

Loxoc listened intently. After Alfonso finished explaining, Loxoc nodded slowly but said nothing. "Sounds fishy to me," he finally said. "Bilblox regains his sight for a few minutes, and by chance he sees this Van Bambleweep character? Sounds like an excuse to escape. It's not that I believe Bilblox is a bad person or servant of Nartam or any of that hysterical, moralistic nonsense. That kind of talk is utter rubbish in my opinion. Still, I don't trust Bilblox. It's not his fault. It is what the purple ash has done to him. I simply don't trust him and I never will."

Alfonso sighed with frustration. "If he just wanted to escape or deceive you why would he insist on delivering this news directly to you?"

Loxoc said nothing.

"General Loxoc," Alfonso continued, "a mistake or two does not destroy a person."

"It depends on the mistake," said the general.

"We have to go to the prison," Alfonso said. "Maybe we can find a trace of Nartam before the trail goes cold."

The general's face was a stony mask. Finally he nodded at Alfonso and said, "All right. You and Bilblox will accompany me to the prison." He looked at Bilblox. "I hope that you are right. I would like to believe you, Bilblox—I truly would—but I remain highly skeptical."

Bilblox remained defiant. "Ya may not trust me because my eyes are white," he said in a voice quivering with emotion, "but Dr. Van Bambleweep—Nartam—is here in Somnos. There's a battle comin', whether ya like it or not."

CHAPTER 43

THE UNDERGROUND ARMADA

THE RIDE to the jailhouse was a quick one. Alfonso and Bilblox followed General Loxoc into his chariot and all three of them held on to their seats with tightly clenched fingers as Ivan—the general's sleeping charioteer—drove them speedily through the night. They stopped only to switch the chariot's wheels with skis, and then flew through the darkened, snow-covered countryside toward the large and gloomy stone prison. It was a perfectly clear night and the moon cast a pale light on the building. In front, two guards were sitting on wooden stools, warming their hands in front of a small fire and chatting quietly. As soon as they saw the general, they rose to their feet and offered a salute. "Welcome, General Loxoc," said one of them nervously. "What brings you here?"

"What brings me here are two prisoners who recently escaped under your watch!" said the general angrily as he stormed out of his chariot. "Maybe if you had done your jobs—and stayed fast asleep as you were supposed to do—these prisoners wouldn't have gotten out!"

"Sorry, sir," muttered the guards.

"All right, now get to sleep!" barked the general. "You can wake up when you get off work." Upon hearing this, both of the guards promptly closed their eyes and commenced snoring.

As soon as they had all clambered out of the sled, one of the now-sleeping guards led the way to the jail cell where Bilblox had been imprisoned. They all walked through a large stone entranceway that narrowed into a long corridor lined with torches whose flames cast a flickering glow against the dank, moss-covered walls. The ground was soft and muddy and more than a few rats scurried underfoot as they made their way deeper into the prison. Eventually, they came to a large cell whose door was wide open. The entire group entered the space. Bilblox groped his way over to the prison cell's window and gripped the rusting iron bars, just as he had done the day before.

"We saw the doctor—uh, Nartam—right through this window," said Bilblox. "He was about fifty feet outside the prison wall. It looked like he was just walkin' around."

"Wait," said Alfonso. "I think I hear something." He paused. "It almost sounds like it's coming from the ground." Alfonso entered the hypnogogic state and put his ear to the ground to listen. At first he was overwhelmed by countless different sounds—earthworms squirming through the soil, the pitter-patter of rats scurrying to and fro, and even the sound of water particles crystallizing into ice. Suddenly he realized that something was missing. The soil seemed too thin.

A thought struck him: the ground beneath was hollow. There must be some kind of cave or cavern directly below them. Then, just as he figured this out, there came another noise. Alfonso heard a dull, rhythmic thumping followed by a slight splashing. *Thunk! Kirsplish! Thunk! Kirsplish! Thunk! Kirsplish!* Where had he heard this sound before? It seemed so familiar. Suddenly, he found himself thinking of Minnesota in the summertime. Why had this memory come to mind? *Thunk! Kirsplish! Thunk! Kirsplish!* He knew this sound well. He was certain that he had heard it somewhere near the lake by his house. Why the lake? Of course, thought Alfonso, it's the sound of oars paddling through water. Someone far beneath him was rowing a boat through the water. But this made absolutely no sense. What was going on?

"Is there some kind of sewer pipe or tunnel beneath this room?" Alfonso asked quickly.

"No, I doubt it," replied the general. "The ground in this part of the countryside is too muddy and soft for tunnels."

"Well there is something down there," said Alfonso. "Will you help me dig?"

"Dig?" said the general curiously. "Well, I suppose we can." He looked at the prison guard and ordered him to return immediately with shovels.

The guard ran off and soon returned with a few shovels. In no time, the entire group was breaking up the ice-flecked soil on the floor of the jail cell and burrowing down into the earth. They worked steadily for fifteen minutes until they reached a depth of about four feet, at which point, they unearthed what appeared to be a shiny green board. Alfonso pressed his fingers against it and discovered that it was soft and moist to the touch.

"What's that?" asked Alfonso.

"It's a root of the Founding Tree," whispered the general. "We can dig no further."

Alfonso hopped down into the hole and ran his hand across the root. He looked up at Loxoc.

"I've got to get a glimpse into that root," said Alfonso. "Something is happening inside. I'm certain of it."

"Impossible!" replied Loxoc. "No one is allowed into the Founding Tree's root system. What's more, it is strictly forbidden to tear or cut open any portion of its roots."

"How could somethin' be happenin' inside a tree?" Bilblox asked incredulously. "These are roots we're talkin' about, not tunnels."

"The tree's root system is massive," explained the general. "They can grow to be hundreds of feet wide and, sometimes, the roots take on strange geometric shapes. I once saw a picture of a gigantic triangular root. And they're long. I remember Dr. Nostrite saying that the longest root they ever found was just under a thousand miles in length. It makes sense, doesn't it? The tree itself is the largest living thing in this world and it needs a massive root system to sustain itself."

"General, please," said Alfonso. "We need to take a look down there."

"We could all be banished from Somnos for considering something like this," said Loxoc angrily.

"The hole will be very small," said Alfonso. *"Please."*

The general sighed heavily. "This will be the end of me. Go ahead and be quick about it."

For the next several minutes, Alfonso used a pickax to cut through the outer wall of the root. He worked the blade of the ax carefully until he had made a hole that was roughly three feet across. A faint light radiated up from this hole. A very loud thumping sound was now audible to everyone. The entire group peered down into the enormous root and together they discovered an astounding scene: a river flowed along the bottom of the root as far as the eye could see, and on this river floated a string of small wooden ships filled with soldiers. The ships were laden with wagons, chariots, catapults, battering rams, cannons, cannonballs, bales of hay, enormous stacks of wood, goats, dogs, and what looked to be giant vats of oil. Some of the boats were large enough to carry dozens of armed horsemen. These horsemen were dressed in armor covered with feathers and metal helmets with pointy beaks. Some of the soldiers pushed the boats forward with long wooden sticks, while others carried torches in both hands to light the way.

"Holy cow!" exclaimed Alfonso. "Those soldiers are —"

"Dragoonya," finished the general. His voice trembled and his eyes were wild with alarm. "I can't believe it — they've infiltrated the Founding Tree's root system."

CHAPTER 44

THE SQUARE ROOT

GENERAL LOXOC stood up. "Let's go," he said grimly. "Somnos must prepare for battle."

"Wait," replied Alfonso. "Let me go down there—I'll see what they're up to."

"Are ya crazy?" asked Bilblox. "Ya can't go down there!"

The general considered this. "It might be worth a try," he said. "But be careful! As you know, the Founding Tree is dying. Soon, the root system itself will collapse. The roots' ceilings and walls will simply cave in. It could happen at any time. Be very, very careful!"

Alfonso nodded and slithered through the hole. Only once he was fully inside did Alfonso realize the seriousness of his situation. He was basically clinging to the ceiling of a giant tube and several hundred feet beneath him was a river of icy water. If he fell, and did not die from the impact, the Dragoonya knights would waste no time in killing him. The key, he told himself, was to use his hands and feet to dig into the soft, dark green walls of the root. The strange texture of these walls felt oddly familiar. Alfonso had a quick moment of déjà vu—as if he had been in this very root before—but he knew that this couldn't be the case.

Alfonso crawled like a spider down the wall of the root. Halfway down, he came across a wet, slimy patch about ten feet wide. It was crumbly to the touch and smelled strange, like mold. Alfonso remembered General Loxoc's warning, and cut a wide path around the area. Finally, he came to a stop near the waterline, where he crouched in a small crevice and watched several boats of soldiers float by.

Alfonso crept downstream for several minutes until he came upon what appeared to be a giant construction site. It was dark enough inside the root that Alfonso was able to move without being seen. As poor as the visibility was, however, Alfonso could see that the Dragoonya had just finished building a giant wooden ramp. Indeed, hundreds of foot soldiers and horsemen were already marching up the steep incline of the ramp in order to reach the top of the root. There, another work crew had burrowed a tunnel through the ceiling of the root and up through the soil to the surface above. All in all, this appeared to be an incredibly well-organized operation. Clearly, the entire Dragoonya army would soon be above ground.

Time was of the essence. Alfonso had to scurry back to the top of the root, reenter the prison, and warn General Loxoc as quickly as possible. Alfonso turned to leave, but just then, he noticed something out of the corner of his eye. It was a head of long blond hair. He looked more closely and there, standing near the base of the giant wooden ramp, was the last person he had expected to see: Resuza.

The very moment that Alfonso saw her, it all came together. His head swirled with dizziness at the realization that Resuza had betrayed them. The moment of betrayal had occurred back on the other side of Straszydlo Forest on the day of the avalanche. That was when Alfonso and Resuza had discovered the mysterious square tunnel on the side of the mountain. Alfonso had nearly fallen in. At the time, Alfonso had been too scared and confused to see this tunnel for what it was—a root of the Founding Tree of Somnos. This was why the texture of the tunnel's walls felt so familiar! He had been in this very root system once before! Normally, roots of the Founding Tree were probably buried deep beneath the ice, but this one had been sheared off by the avalanche. Resuza had either figured this out or simply reported it to the Dragoonya. In any case, Nartam had been given an opportunity—an actual opening into the Founding Tree's root system—and he had seized upon it!

Alfonso was so angry that he almost felt lightheaded. He grabbed a thick portion of the wall of the root and held on, as if seasick. Suddenly, he heard a new sound. It was the light patter of footsteps, and they were coming toward him. He looked up—Resuza was only a few feet away and drawing closer. Her attention was focused on the river. Only seconds remained before she discovered him.

He whirled to one side of the path and waited for her to arrive. When she did, he grabbed her leg and pulled her to the ground. She fell with a muffled thud. Although she tried to scream, Alfonso had placed his hand over her mouth. Her eyes widened with shock when she saw him.

"Traitor!" Alfonso hissed. "How could you do it?"

Resuza's eyes were wild with panic, and she struggled against him.

"What happened to you?" asked Alfonso. "We thought you were *dead.*"

"I wish I were dead," said Resuza bitterly as she pried Alfonso's fingers away from her mouth.

"Why'd you do it?" demanded Alfonso.

Resuza said nothing.

"Why?" he repeated.

"I didn't have a choice," she replied.

"What's that supposed to mean?"

"Don't look so surprised," whispered Resuza. "If you knew anything at all about Barsh-yin-Binder you would have guessed that I was a Dragoonya slave. For goodness sakes, Barsh-yin-Binder is a city of slaves."

"You're a slave?"

"Of course," said Resuza. "I have been a slave since the day that the Dragoonya killed my parents and captured my sister and me." A tear rolled down her cheek. "And Naomi is still a slave, in their capital of Dargora."

"What about Straszydlo Forest?" asked Alfonso. "How did you survive?"

"I didn't go very far," said Resuza. "I just walked in, threw off my cape, and then reversed my steps, walking out backwards."

"We thought you were dead!"

"I know," said Resuza dejectedly. "That's what *he* told me to do."

"Who?"

"Kiril," said Resuza. "Don't you see? Kiril was telling me what to do from the beginning. He knew you would be coming through Barsh-yin-Binder. I waited by those docks for you every day for a month."

Alfonso shook his head. "So it was all a setup?"

"I am sorry," said Resuza. "I wanted to tell you, but Kiril was always there, hiding in the shadows, watching. The only time I knew for certain that I was alone was in Straszydlo Forest. Only then could I warn you—by carving the list of perfect squares into the snow. Did you see it?"

"Perfect squares?"

"You know—one, four, nine, sixteen, twenty-five—all are numbers that have perfect square roots," said Resuza. "I was positive that you would figure it out. After all, you solved the riddle of Prince Binder in the catacombs. You love riddles!"

Alfonso looked confused.

"Don't you remember?" asked Resuza exasperatedly. "We found that perfectly square-shaped tunnel that was actually a root—*a square root!* I even wrote "Warn them!" in the snow. I wanted you to warn the Dormians! Didn't you get it?"

Alfonso shook his head in frustration. He hadn't figured it out. Now it made sense. She had tried to warn him and the Dormians about the severed root! Suddenly, Alfonso also remembered the words that the Straszydlo had uttered: *I'm so sorry, Alfonso!* These were words that she had said—not in the anguish of death—but in a spell of regret. He stared at Resuza and didn't know what to do.

"There were other moments when you could've warned us," insisted Alfonso. "You could've told Hill on the way out of Barsh-yin-Binder, or you could've whispered it to me. Kiril couldn't have been watching the whole time."

Resuza shook her head. "You don't know him," she said. "He sees everything."

At that moment, a gruff voice interrupted their conversation.

"Who's there?" asked the voice. Alfonso looked up. Two Dragoonya soldiers were standing less than five feet away. One of them had his sword drawn.

"Come out of the shadows," demanded the soldier whose sword was drawn. "Show your faces."

Alfonso reached into his coat pocket and slipped his fingers around the cool surface of the blue sphere. He could not see the sphere, of course, but he pictured it; and he pictured exactly what he had to do with it.

"It's just me, kind sirs—the slave girl," said Resuza nervously. "Give me a second."

"You'll come out right now or I'll cut you to pieces!" barked the soldier. "I'll give you three seconds: one, two . . ."

But the soldier never finished counting. Before he could say the word *three,* he had fallen to the ground and was unconscious. An instant later, the other soldier lay knocked out beside him. Neither soldier would have any memory of being smacked directly in the forehead with a darting blue sphere.

"How did you do that?" asked Resuza.

"Nevermind," said Alfonso. "We've got to get out of here."

"What?"

"Come," said Alfonso. "It's not too late to atone for what you've done. Besides, if you stay here, you'll be killed. After all, we just attacked two Dragoonya soldiers."

Resuza said nothing.

"Are you coming?" asked Alfonso.

CHAPTER 45

TWO GREEN-TIPPED ARROWS

SEVERAL minutes later, General Loxoc was flabbergasted to see Alfonso emerge from the root of the Founding Tree with a young blond-haired girl in tow. "What's the meaning of this?" asked the general. "Wh-who is she?"

"This is Resuza," explained Alfonso hastily. "She's a Dragoonya slave, but she's going to help us."

"Resuza!" boomed Bilblox. "Are ya kiddin'? She's alive?" His tone turned suspicious. "Wait—what was she doin' with the Dragoonya?"

"Don't worry about it," gasped Alfonso. "I'll explain later. Resuza, tell the general what you know."

"Something happened last night," explained Resuza. "The Dragoonya were planning to wait in the tunnel until their full army had arrived, but Nartam went up to the surface, and then rushed back with the order that the attack was to proceed today. It's strange, because their full force has not yet arrived."

"Can this girl be trusted?" asked the general.

Alfonso hesitated for a fraction of a second and then nodded.

"It makes sense," replied General Loxoc. "Only the ash from burning a living tree gives them what they want. From his reconnaissance, Nartam undoubtedly realizes that the Founding Tree is dying. If it dies before he burns it, he will lose any chance of getting the purple ash."

"The advance guard is exiting the root about a quarter-mile south of here," continued Resuza. "But there's another group, with about thirty men, including Nartam. They're continuing deeper into the root."

"So it's a two-pronged attack," said the general. "The Dragoonya force will strike the city from the north. And as for that second group with Nartam, they must be heading for the main chamber. We've caught a break—Nartam's army won't hit us with its full force. Let's hope our defense is strong enough." He looked at Alfonso and shook his head. "We have no time to waste—let's go!"

The general dashed out of the cell and sprinted back toward the entrance to the jail. Alfonso followed, and just behind him was Bilblox, clutching fiercely to his shoulder. Resuza brought up the rear.

"Wait!" yelled Alfonso. "What's the main chamber?"

"It's where all the roots converge at the base of the tree," yelled the general without looking back. "It's the best place to go if you want to burn down the whole tree."

"Why is that?" asked Alfonso as he hurried after the general.

"Because," yelled the general impatiently, "the roots of the tree aren't flammable but the trunk is—and the main chamber is where the trunk starts—it's like the fuse on a giant firecracker."

"Oh boy," grunted Bilblox.

"Shouldn't we go back into the root system and stop them?" yelled Alfonso.

"No!" yelled the general. "There's a faster way to get to the main chamber—but we have to hurry!"

Their only hope was speed. As they boarded the chariot sled at the prison, General Loxoc pointed to a cloud of snow lit up by the moon and rising from the ground in the distance. It was the Dragoonya army emerging from the root. Clearly, they were under instructions to make for Somnos immediately, since the Dragoonya on the ground appeared to be galloping at full speed toward the city.

The race was on.

Alfonso, Bilblox, Resuza, and General Loxoc were soon experiencing the ride of their life as Ivan snapped his whip and goaded the horses back toward Somnos at breakneck speed. "Yahhhhhhh!" screamed Ivan. "Yahhhhhhh!" The only other sounds that Ivan let out were snoring grunts. With each grunt, he raised his right arm in the air and snapped his long whip. Fortunately, the horses needed little encouragement. They galloped mightily in a cloud of pounding hooves and billowing snow. Inside the sled, the wind rushed against their faces and flattened back their hair. The bumps in the road were so numerous that everyone was popping out of their seats like kernels of corn in a hot frying pan.

"It's going to be close!" yelled the general, who was riding in the front with Ivan. "We'll beat them back to the city gates, but I won't have much time to gather my men and warn the rest of the city. In this darkness, the Dragoonya won't be noticed until it's too late. We must try to light the urns with the green flame right now!"

He looked at Alfonso. "Reach under your seat," ordered the general. "Hand me my crossbow."

Alfonso crouched on the floor and pulled out a giant crossbow, which weighed close to fifty pounds and stood almost four feet in height. Attached to it was a quiver with some twenty arrows—almost all of them had red tips except for two that had green tips. Alfonso remembered the ceremony that he had witnessed in which the Dormian archers had shot the flaming arrows into the urns. He realized what had to be done: they had to shoot a green-tipped arrow into one of the urns. This would cause a special green flame to erupt and, if all went according to plan, the people of Somnos would realize that they were about to be attacked.

"It's going to be a very difficult shot!" yelled the general. "We're still a good distance from the city. Alfonso, you take the shot! You're the only one who could do it from this distance."

Alfonso nodded. "Help me load the crossbow," he yelled. "The cord is very stiff." Indeed, it was wound so tightly that both Bilblox and Resuza had to help Alfonso pull it back and snap it into the crossbow's trigger mechanism. Alfonso then took out a green-tipped arrow and loaded it. The general lit the arrow, and it began to sizzle. "Okay," Alfonso said to himself. "Nice and easy." He looked up at the night sky, concentrated on a single star, and then allowed himself to see all of the other stars around it. Bam! He was in the hypnogogic state. He peered out of the sled and out through the darkness toward the distant city wall of Somnos. He trained his concentration on a large urn that sat in plain sight at the highest point of the northern gate. Alfonso took a deep breath—sucked in the air, let it out—then swiftly took hold of the crossbow and fired. But just as his finger squeezed the trigger the sled hit another bump and his arm jerked involuntarily. The shot was spoiled. The arrow veered violently off course and sailed into a faraway field.

"Don't worry," yelled the general. "There should be one more green-tip."

Alfonso said nothing in reply. He simply reached into the quiver and pulled out the one remaining green-tipped arrow. Bilblox and Resuza helped him pull back the cord once more. When this was done, Alfonso loaded the arrow into the crossbow and shifted his focus to the large urn. He had to hit it. He took a long steady breath—sucked in a gulp of air, slowly let it seep out—then swiftly grabbed the crossbow, aimed it, and clutched the trigger. *Twangggggggg!* The shot came off cleanly—sailing straight and true into the night sky, arching high into the glare of the moon, then slowly tilting down and plummeting toward the large stone silhouette of the northern gate. The arrow disappeared into the darkness. For a good long moment there was nothing. Then there was a sudden eruption, an enormous flame burst from above the gate, and the entire area was bathed in an eerie, flickering green light. Seconds later, other flaming arrows flew out from the Founding Tree—the archers there had been trained well, and responded immediately. Soon urns around the city were lit with large green flames. Trumpets sounded. The city sprang to life.

"What a shot!" yelled the general exuberantly. "What a spectacular shot!"

"I knew you'd do it!" whooped Resuza. "I knew it!"

"Unbelievable," murmured Ivan sleepily. "Simply unbelievable."

Unfortunately, this celebration was extremely short-lived.

"Oh boy," mumbled Ivan. "Have you looked behind us?"

"I can't see a thing," said Bilblox.

Alfonso set down the crossbow and craned his neck so that he could get a glimpse backward. "Holy cow!" he said. "Where did they come from?"

Now everyone looked back and saw a sight that they would not soon forget—a vast cavalry of at least five hundred Dragoonya horsemen were pursuing them in a wild, stampeding charge. Behind these horsemen were thousands of foot soldiers who had fanned out in a giant line that was steadily advancing on Somnos. For those in the sled it was now, quite literally, a race for their lives to the city gates. The lead horsemen were less than a few hundred yards away. Some of these horsemen were carrying crossbows of their own and soon a barrage of arrows began to rain in and around the sled. Arrows hit the sides, the seats, the floor, the horses, and the passengers themselves. All except Ivan hit the floor. Soon there were so many arrows sticking out of the sled itself that it looked like a giant porcupine on skis.

In the midst of another barrage of arrows, one struck Ivan in the buttocks. He let out a yelp, promptly woke up, and began to tug on the reins. "We're going too fast!" yelled Ivan hysterically. His cool demeanor had vanished. "This is insanity!"

"No we're not!" snapped General Loxoc, who instantly grabbed the reins. "You've just woken up, Ivan. Don't worry. I'll take over." The general then cocked back his head, as he often did before nodding off, and then fell asleep. Moments later, the general was snapping the whip and snoring at a furious pace.

"Yahhhhhhh!" he yelled. "Yahhhhhhh!"

They were now less than a quarter-mile from the northern gate. Alfonso could see the Dormian soldiers near the gate furiously turning a large crank, which hoisted the iron portcullis within the gate. The general snapped his whip. The portcullis continued to lift. Alfonso glanced up ahead and saw a line of Dormian soldiers at the ready.

General Loxoc unsheathed his sword. As the sled sped through the gate itself, the general raised his sword and—in one incredibly swift motion—sliced his blade through the rope that held the portcullis in place. The portcullis rattled down to close securely behind them. They had made it! They were safely inside the city! The general pulled back hard on the reins and the horses clattered to a stop. He looked up, his half-closed eyes blazing and shouted a series of high-pitched orders in Dormian. Then, perhaps for Alfonso's benefit, he added in English: "Soldiers! Prepare for the fight of your lives! We must defend Somnos, the Founding Tree, and the kingdom of Dormia!"

CHAPTER 46

DEFEND THE CITY!

INSIDE THE city walls, the atmosphere was utterly frantic. Dormian knights were mounting their horses and switching from awake to asleep and back again. Swordsmen were struggling to put on their armor. Shopkeepers were frantically locking up their storefronts. The Sleeping Mayor of Somnos was on hand, standing atop the northern gate, urging people to compose themselves and fall asleep. Next to the mayor was a gray long-haired woman playing the harpsichord. "Everyone hush now," exhorted the mayor in a calm voice as the harpsichordist played a soft, melodious tune. "Hush now and allow yourselves to grow sleepy. You are feeling sleepier, and sleepier, and sleepier!" His advice didn't seem to be working. Swarms of people continued to run about in a mad frenzy—all of them wide awake. Meanwhile, the preparations for battle continued. In the marble towers, hundreds of archers ran to preassigned firing positions that looked down upon the oncoming tide of Dragoonya soldiers. Far off in the Trunk District, hundreds of leaf-sweepers were at work with hoses, pumping water onto the Founding Tree, presumably to help keep it from burning down. It seemed as if every last person in Somnos was rushing to do one thing or another.

Meanwhile, a small crowd had gathered around the general's sled. Among those in the crowd was Hill. "What on earth happened?" yelled Hill frantically. "Where did all those Dragoonya soldiers come from?" He stopped short and stared dumbfounded at Resuza. "What on earth . . ." he began.

"Do you see Resuza? She's a traitor!" announced Bilblox.

"I found her with the Dragoonya," explained Alfonso.

"I don't get it," said Hill, who seemed utterly bewildered.

"She was a slave," said Alfonso. "But it's okay—she's helping us out now."

"Yeah sure," said Hill. "Until she decides to betray us again."

"Exactly!" said Bilblox angrily. "She should be tried for treachery. She's the one that ought to be in jail—not me!"

"Enough of this," interrupted the general. "We have other matters to attend to right now!"

Two Dormian officers stepped forward, saluted the general, and yelped out some information in Dormian. Then they both turned, saluted Alfonso, and addressed him in English.

"Colonel Pissaro reporting for duty," announced a short, balding, bullnecked man.

"Major Hornslight reporting," announced the second officer, who was quite tall and lanky.

"Okay," replied the general. "Hornslight, reinforce the archers in the towers and all along the city walls. Send all able-bodied volunteers to the Founding Tree to assist the leaf-sweepers. I want all three regiments of Dormian knights to gather here at the northern gate. We'll launch our counterattack and the knights will lead the charge. Brigadier General Hill Persplexy will lead the effort to protect the bloom. He will take a dozen men and proceed directly to my office at the Tree Palace where the bloom is being kept."

"Very well, but who is this Brigadier General Hill Persplexy, sir?" asked Major Hornslight quizzically. "I've never heard of him."

"That's me," said Hill with a surprised—but very proud—look on his face.

"Who are you?" asked Colonel Pissaro in an extremely skeptical tone.

"He is the army's new brigadier general and you will address him as 'sir,'" said General Loxoc. "He is an accomplished soldier."

"Former captain in the United States Air Force," interjected Hill proudly.

"What's the United States?" asked Colonel Pissaro.

"And what's an 'air force'?" asked Major Hornslight.

"Nevermind that!" yelled the general who was more irritable than ever. "Just obey your orders!"

"Yes sir—nice to meet you, Brigadier General Persplexy—sir!" barked both Colonel Pissaro and Major Hornslight at once.

"Good," said General Loxoc. "Next, I want the Great Sleeper, Resuza, Bilblox, Colonel Pissaro, and a dozen Dormian knights to head directly to the main chamber of the Founding Tree in order to intercept Nartam." He looked around. "MOVE!" he shouted.

They followed Ivan to a chariot nearby that had been abandoned in the swirl of confusion. Hill scrambled in last. "Can someone please tell me what's going on?" he asked. "You can start by telling me where Resuza came from."

"Yeah," said Bilblox. "I'd like to hear this too."

And so, as Ivan snapped his whip and drove the chariot toward the Tree Palace, Alfonso and Resuza took turns explaining everything that had happened since they had last been together in Straszydlo Forest. Bilblox and Hill were amazed.

"So you're on our side now?" asked Hill in a bitter tone.

"I am," said Resuza. "I swear it."

"Hmm," said Hill. "We'll see about that."

Conversation was soon cut short as Ivan continued to press the horses to go faster and faster. Behind them, a convoy of ten other chariots—carrying Colonel Pissaro and a contingent of Dormian knights—struggled to keep up. The plan was for the entire convoy to travel to the Tree Palace together, for safety and because their destinations were nearby. Once there, Hill would lead his group to General Luxoc's office in order to protect the Dormian bloom; meanwhile, Alfonso and Colonel Pissaro would lead their group into the main chamber of the Founding Tree in order to intercept Nartam.

As the convoy of chariots tore through the twisty, cobblestone streets of Somnos, the scene that unfolded was utterly topsy-turvy. Everywhere people were running around in a panic—locking doors, boarding up windows, hiding valuables, chasing after children, sharpening swords, putting on battle helmets—and everyone seemed to be wide awake. Somnos usually had a calm, quiet air about it because most of its inhabitants were blissfully asleep. But now hysteria swept over the city. It seemed that no one could fall asleep.

The most immediate reason for this was an incredibly loud noise that was getting closer. It sounded like thunder, but was too regular to be the approach of a storm. *Boom! Boom! Boom! Boom!* The noise was so loud that Alfonso and the others could feel and hear it. The vibrations from the booms reverberated across the city, through its marble buildings, down its cobblestone streets, up the wheel of the chariots, and into all of their bodies until their fingertips felt numb with tingling. "That's the sound of the Dragoonya drums of war," mumbled Ivan sleepily. "'Course these drums seem louder than usual. You can really hear and feel 'em right into your teeth. Luckily I can sleep anywhere, anyhow. That's why I'm the general's driver!"

"No kiddin'," said Bilblox with a slight whistle to show that he was impressed, or scared, or both. "Well, I'm glad Ivan can sleep through this racket, but for everyone else's sake I hope General Loxoc has a plan for —"

Bilblox was interrupted by the sound of a small explosion overhead. Everyone looked up and saw several large balls smash into the front of a nearby building and then clatter to the ground. At first glance, Alfonso assumed that these objects were cannonballs or simply rocks that had been hurled over the city walls by Dragoonya catapults. But then something very curious happened. As soon as the balls had come to rest on the street, they opened up like flower petals on a tightly clamped bud and began to scurry along the ground. One of these curious specimens was now running directly at them. It was moving quickly and it appeared to be using its roots almost like legs. As it drew closer, Alfonso noticed that this *thing* had a mouth with a great many sharp teeth. He had seen them before, in Minnesota. He was staring at a Dragoonya plant of war.

"Watch out!" yelled Alfonso. "They're firing Dragoonya plants of war into the city. We've got one coming at us!"

Ivan nodded vigorously and steered the chariot to the right so that one of its front wheels ran directly over the plant of war. The chariot lurched forward, there was a loud popping sound, and instantly the plant of war withered into a pool of greenish slime. Several more explosions sounded overhead and five new plants of war fell from the sky. Two of them crashed through open windows and disappeared. A third landed in a blazing urn and immediately burst into flames. A fourth landed on the chariot at the very end of the convoy. The horses in this chariot panicked and, before the driver could react, the entire chariot toppled over into the street. The fifth and final plant of war landed on the street directly in front of Alfonso's chariot. Ivan tried to run the thing over with his front wheels, but he missed, and instead the plant of war managed to latch one of its roots onto the side of the chariot. In the next instant, the plant had climbed into the chariot and was snapping its teeth ferociously.

Resuza let out a terrible yell. The plant lunged at her, but Alfonso tugged her away. Ivan steered the chariot violently to the left, in order to throw the plant off balance. The plan worked—the Dragoonya plant toppled heavily onto its side—but it also threw Alfonso, Hill, and Resuza off balance. Hill was hit the worst. He lost his equilibrium completely and toppled backwards out of the chariot. Alfonso jumped up onto his seat in order to see what had become of his uncle. He was relieved to find Hill holding onto the wooden fender of the speeding chariot with just one hand. Alfonso grabbed both of his arms and helped him back onboard. When the two of them turned their attention back to the plant of war, they saw that it had its teeth locked around Bilblox's right leg. "Get it off! GET IT OFF!" Bilblox was yelling. In a flash, Hill grabbed the Colt .45 revolver from its belt holster, aimed it squarely at the plant's head, and fired several times. The plant wilted and fell back into the street.

"Thanks," said Bilblox. "That bugger was makin' minced meat of my leg."

"You're quite the brigadier general," added Resuza admiringly.

"Oh it was nothing," said Hill with a dismissive wave of his hand. But it was clear to everyone that he was quite pleased. "Just doing my duty."

"Hey look," said Alfonso. "We're here!"

They were rapidly approaching the Tree Palace. High above, dozens of plants of war were now hurtling through the air, and a good number of them seemed to be landing inside the Tree Palace. Hill hurriedly began reloading his Colt .45 revolver. He looked at everyone else. "Be ready," he said. "It looks like we'll have more plants of war to deal with."

"Yeah," said Alfonso. "We'll have to keep our eyes open. There are a lot of nooks where those plants can hide."

The palace itself, which had been so bright and inviting in the warm glow of day, was dark and quite strange in the dead of night. In the background, they all heard the beating in the distance of the Dragoonya war drums: *Boom! Boom! Boom! Boom!* The Founding Tree, which rose up from the palace like an enormous plant from a tiny pot, was also darkened and foreboding against the night sky. Water dripped onto them, probably from the leaf-sweepers up on the tree, using their hoses to spray down the leaves. Soon all of the nine remaining chariots in the convoy pulled up to the front steps of the Tree Palace. Hill hopped out of his chariot and bounded up the steps. "We have no time to lose!" yelled Hill. "My team should follow me. The rest of you, follow the Great Sleeper!"

"Yes sir!" called the Dormian soldiers as they poured out of their chariots. "Long live the Great Sleeper. Long live Somnos!"

Hill paused, glanced over at Alfonso, and said in a hoarse voice, "Good luck, my nephew. I'll see you soon. Fight bravely and Godspeed!"

CHAPTER 47

INTO THE FOUNDING TREE

AFTER PARTING ways with his uncle, Alfonso set out for the main chamber of the Founding Tree. According to Colonel Pissaro, the only way to enter the main chamber was through a secret doorway situated in Dr. Nostrite's tree office. "It's hard to describe," explained Colonel Pissaro. "I only hope you're not afraid of heights!"

Colonel Pissaro hurried onward and the rest of the group followed. Upon arriving at the base of the Founding Tree, Pissaro led them up a narrow flight of stairs that ended at a large platform. He whistled loudly and looked up into the canopy of the Founding Tree. Alfonso and everyone else looked up as well and saw a large wooden box descending from the sky. As the box drew closer, Alfonso realized that it was actually an elevator, suspended on a series of ropes that hung from a branch of the Founding Tree. Once the entire group was inside the elevator, Colonel Pissaro whistled once again and the elevator shot up. The elevator had large openings on each side, offering them a spectacular view of Somnos.

They could see a massive battle raging at the northern gate of the city. Thousands of Dragoonya soldiers were assaulting the city. Some were using catapults to launch plants of war into the city, some were climbing their way over the city walls with ladders, and still others were preparing to bash in the gate with a giant battering ram. In response, the Dormian archers were unleashing a torrent of arrows on the attacking army. At this point, it was impossible to say who had the upper hand, but Alfonso knew that if Nartam succeeded in burning down the Founding Tree, the outcome of the battle below would hardly matter.

After a minute or two of climbing up, the elevator came to an abrupt halt. Colonel Pissaro exited the elevator and walked out onto the biggest tree branch that Alfonso had ever seen. It was at least twenty feet across. The top of the branch was also remarkably flat so it was as easy to walk on as a road.

"This way," said Colonel Pissaro as he directed them around the back of the elevator and into a large wooden tree house attached to the trunk of the Founding Tree. The tree house itself was quite large. It appeared to have many spacious rooms and several balconies that looked out onto the city. Colonel Pissaro proceeded directly to the back of the tree house, where they found a small door marked CHUTE. Here, they found Dr. Nostrite guarding the way with a dagger in each hand. His face was covered with sweat and his arms were shaking with fright.

"What is the meaning of this!" asked Dr. Nostrite angrily.

His high-pitched Dormian voice sounded even squeakier than normal. "These are my private offices and I did not give you permission to enter. Especially since the criminal leaf-burner is here! Trying to get to the tree's source, eh? Need more powder now that your Dragoonya friends are here?"

Alfonso placed a cautioning hand on Bilblox's shoulder. "Dr. Nostrite," he replied in a soothing tone, "please understand: we need to get into the main chamber right away. These are direct orders from General Loxoc. We are trying to save the tree."

"The Great Sleeper is correct," added Colonel Pissaro.

"I don't care who issued your orders," growled Dr. Nostrite. "I don't trust this Great Sleeper—I never have—and I refuse to let any of you enter."

"Now be reasonable . . . ," began Colonel Pissaro. But before he could utter another word, Bilblox stepped forward toward Nostrite's voice, raised his fist into the air, and swiftly hit the doctor over the head. Instantly, Dr. Nostrite collapsed to the ground.

"I'm sorry," said Bilblox. "But it had to be done."

"Don't be sorry, old boy," said Colonel Pissaro. "That man is an insufferable fool and it was about time someone knocked some sense into him."

"Come on," said Alfonso with a slight smile. "Let's have a look at what this chute is all about." He walked over to the round door and opened it. On the other side was a small room the size of a closet with a perfectly round hole in the floor. Just to the side of the hole stood an official-looking sign marked in English and Dormian heiroglyphs. Alfonso read it aloud for everyone's benefit:

WARNING: This chute leads directly to the main chamber of the Founding Tree. Only authorized personnel are allowed to use it. Those who ride the chute should be prepared for a very, very, very quick ride. Pregnant women, young children, senior citizens, those afraid of heights, and anyone who has just eaten a large meal should avoid using this device. Keep your legs together and your arms tucked in tightly at your sides as you descend. Above all, no flammable objects are allowed beyond this point!

"Oh boy," said Colonel Pissaro with a heavy sigh. "I have a cousin who rode this thing once. He is a big fat fellow who works in the grand vizier's office. He got to ride this thing on some official occasion and has never been the same since. Nowadays, he is so scared of heights he won't even go near a flight of stairs. He says that this chute was the ruin of him."

"Hogwash," replied Resuza. She boldly stepped forward, and before anyone could object, jumped feet-first into the darkened hole. "Yoweeeeee!" she yelled as she plummeted down. Her voice tapered off into nothing. Alfonso, Bilblox, Colonel Pissaro, and the twelve Dormian knights said nothing for a good long moment.

"Well," said Bilblox awkwardly. "It is good manners to let the lady go first—even if she is a traitor."

"I guess I'll go next," said Alfonso. "See you guys at the bottom."

Alfonso took a deep breath, tucked his hands into his pockets, and then hopped feet-first into the darkened hole. He felt his stomach shooting up into his throat and his eyes rolling back into his head. He couldn't see or hear anything. Wind pounded against his face. It felt as if he were spiraling down like an airplane about to crash. Slowly, he realized that he was riding a spiral slide that kept curving steeply down, like a giant corkscrew. Around and around and around he went. After what seemed like several minutes of near free-falling, the chute spit Alfonso out into a large pile of soft, cold powder. Groggily, Alfonso opened his eyes and saw that he was lying in a bank of snow.

"Whoa," he said with a sickly groan. "That was intense."

"I loved it!" said Resuza, who was standing several feet away. "I would do that all day if I could. How do *you* feel? You look rather ill."

"Don't rub it in," said Alfonso weakly. "Where are we?"

"I suppose we are in the main chamber," said Resuza. "Isn't this place amazing?"

Alfonso looked around. They were in an enormous cavern that appeared big enough to fit a football stadium. Heavy fog hugged the ground and it felt as if they were inside a cloud. The cavern floor was blanketed with perfectly white snow and in several places the snow had accumulated into banks that were twenty feet high. The walls of the main chamber, by contrast, appeared to be made of a soft, sticky, green covering. This green covering must have been quite hot to the touch because it was giving off a great deal of steam. It was an odd environment in the main chamber—both hot and cold at once—and the feel of it reminded Alfonso of late spring in Minnesota when he could cross-country ski in his shorts.

Alfonso noticed several large holes in the wall that opened into giant tunnels. The room reminded him of a giant subway station with tunnels arriving from all parts of the city. But these tunnels, Alfonso realized, were actually the roots of the Founding Tree. It all began to make sense. Chunks of ice from the High Urals around Somnos floated along the root system into the main chamber. Once the chunks of ice arrived here, the warm walls of the main chamber melted them into water, and the Founding Tree quenched its thirst.

As if all this wasn't strange enough, Alfonso suddenly realized that it was snowing. He was in the main chamber of a massive tree, presumably hundreds of feet underground, and yet there was no doubt that soft and full snowflakes were peacefully floating to the ground.

"How . . ."

"Is it snowing?" Resuza finished his thought. "I am not positive, but I believe it comes from the same place as this fog. This cavern has its own weather system! I thought it would be some dreary, dark place, but this is even stranger and more amazing. Where is the light coming from?"

Alfonso looked up and soon noticed that the ceiling of the main chamber was lined with thousands of small glass lanterns, each of which was filled with fireflies. This made perfect sense, thought Alfonso, because the fireflies gave off light without creating any fire hazards. Resuza was right. This place *was* amazing!

Suddenly, Alfonso heard a loud rattling noise coming from directly above him. It sounded as if a large portion of the ceiling was about to cave in.

"Get moving!" said Resuza. "Someone else is coming down the chute!"

Alfonso sprang to his feet and got out of the way. A moment later, Bilblox shot out of a small black hole in the ceiling and dropped down into a nearby snowbank. Bilblox hit the ground with a tremendous thud and there he lay—utterly motionless. Alfonso was afraid that his big, blind friend was seriously injured. But then Bilblox raised his head and smiled like a big kid. "Fantastic!" groaned Bilblox. "That was the most fun I've had in weeks!"

Resuza hurried over to where Bilblox was lying and extended her hand. "Let me help you," she said.

"I don't need any help from a traitor," snarled Bilblox.

"Come on," said Alfonso. "We all deserve a second chance. You should know that better than anyone. Why don't you give her a break?"

"Why do ya trust her?" asked Bilblox.

"Same reason I trust you," replied Alfonso. "Sometimes you just have hunches about people."

"No one ever gave me a break," muttered Bilblox. "But what does that matter?"

Over the course of the next fifteen minutes, Colonel Pissaro and all twelve of his Dormian knights followed this same trajectory—shooting out of the small hole in the ceiling and landing in the snowbanks. As this was happening, Alfonso and Resuza explored the fog-filled main chamber. To their enormous relief, they quickly discovered that there were no signs of Nartam or his men anywhere. Apparently, the Dormians had succeeded in beating the Dragoonya in the race to the main chamber. Now all they had to do was wait and ready themselves for the enemy to arrive.

Colonel Pissaro posted one of his Dormian knights just inside each of the ten different roots that led into the main chamber. The rest of the group hid in between two snowbanks and waited. Ten minutes passed and nothing happened. Then, a few minutes later, one of the Dormian knights gave a low whistle. Alfonso and the others all looked up and directed their attention toward the tunnel from which the whistle had come.

Soon they heard a distant crunching—the way ice sounds when it is being stepped on. *Crunch. Crunch. Crunch.* Something was definitely moving through that tunnel toward the main chamber. They saw one faint speck of light, then a few more. Soon they saw approximately thirty specks of light bobbing and weaving gently through the fog as if carried by a faint breeze. The Dormian knights who had been stationed in each of the ten different roots quietly rejoined the rest of the group hidden behind the tall snowbanks. The fog seemed to get thicker, and all of them shivered in the chilly conditions. All they saw were hazy pinpricks of light that became more ominous the closer they came. Alfonso gulped and for a second wished that he was blind like Bilblox—the scene would haunt him for years to come.

The procession of lights drew nearer, and it soon became clear that these lights were torches—torches being held by Dragoonya soldiers. The Dragoonya were dressed in full battle gear. They wore pointy steel-tipped boots, chain mail armor covered with feathers, and battle helmets with protruding metal beaks. Four of these soldiers were carrying an old man on a large chair. He wore heavy gray robes. His face was haggard and shriveled and his long bony hands quivered uncontrollably. Nartam! He appeared to have aged thirty years since they had seen him in his disguise as Dr. Van Bambleweep. Clearly, from the looks of him, Nartam had run out of Dormian ash, and now the last signs of life were oozing out of him.

Alfonso felt his heart pounding in his chest like a wrecking ball. It all came down to this moment. He and his men were outnumbered roughly three-to-one. They had estimated that Nartam was traveling with just a dozen men. That had been a miscalculation; there were at least three dozen. But there was no turning back now. The fate of Somnos rested in their hands. The only advantage that they had now was the element of surprise. "Steady," Pissaro whispered to the group. "We'll wait until they go right past us and then we'll ambush them from behind."

Slowly, the procession drew nearer. As the group entered the main chamber, the Dragoonya soldiers came to a halt and stood at attention, waiting for further orders. Nartam rapped his knuckles against the wooden arm of his chair. The knights who were carrying him set his chair down. Shakily, Nartam rose to his feet and looked around. "Draw your swords," he said in a deep, hoarse voice that quivered with fatigue. Instantly, all thirty Dragoonya unsheathed their swords. The sound was enough to raise the hairs on the back of Alfonso's neck.

"Fan out and search the chamber," said Nartam calmly. "Kill any leaf-sweepers or anyone else that you find."

All of the Dragoonya soldiers grunted and nodded in unison.

"Now's the time—we can't wait any longer," whispered Alfonso to Colonel Pissaro. "Have your men fire at them while they're still in a tight group."

The colonel gave a discreet hand gesture. The four of his men who were archers loaded their crossbows, nodded off to sleep, and took aim. "Now!" whispered the colonel. *Twang! Twang! Twang! Twang!* Four arrows shot through the air with perfectly accurate precision and immediately four Dragoonya knights fell to the ground. "Attaaaaaaaaaack!" yelled Colonel Pissaro as he rose to his feet. "Fight for Somnos!"

The ambush had worked! Nartam hadn't foreseen this. They had surprised him! Alfonso's heart raced with hope and excitement. This couldn't have happened if Nartam still possessed the purple ash. Nartam and the Dragoonya were beatable!

Alfonso and the entire group of Dormians let out a wild, raging war cry and then charged directly at the band of Dragoonya. To his surprise, Alfonso felt totally ready for this moment; and, as he sprinted toward the enemy, he effortlessly slipped into the hypnogogic state. The first thing that Alfonso noticed was that a Dragoonya archer was pointing his crossbow directly at Colonel Pissaro. Without the slightest hesitation, Alfonso reached into his pocket, pulled out his blue sphere, and threw it directly at the archer. *Swoosh!* The sphere shot through the air like a cannonball and hit the Dragoonya archer smack in the chest, causing him to fly backwards a good fifteen feet. In the blink of an eye, the blue sphere was back in Alfonso's hand. A second later, Alfonso sensed that a spear was coming through the air in his direction, so he ducked, rolled, sprang to his feet, and continued his charge. An enormous Dragoonya knight, who had to be almost seven feet tall, spotted Alfonso and attempted to slice him in two with his enormous battle sword. Alfonso jumped, leapt over the sword, and dove back toward the ground. As soon as he landed, Alfonso threw his sphere and—an instant later—the knight crumpled to the ground.

Alfonso looked around. The air was filled with hoarse shouts and the sound of steel clashing against steel. Colonel Pissaro was dueling with two Dragoonya soldiers. Resuza was throwing daggers and leaping around as if springs were attached to her feet. Bilblox was swinging his fists with such incredible intensity that it compensated for the fact that he couldn't see a thing. The Dormian knights were fast asleep and expertly wielding their swords. Only one question loomed in Alfonso's mind: where was Nartam? Then, out of the corner of his eye, Alfonso saw Nartam disappear around a snowbank at the far corner of the main chamber. He had a flickering torch in his hand and Alfonso knew what he was up to—he was going to burn down the Founding Tree!

Alfonso broke into a sprint. As fast as he could, he ran across the deep, snowy floor of the main chamber. At one point, he heard footsteps behind him. He turned his head and saw Resuza. "I'm coming with you!" she gasped. Alfonso nodded and kept sprinting.

By the time the two of them reached Nartam it was too late. He had already used his torch to light a small portion of one of the main chamber's walls. Despite the fact that the wall itself was very moist—and giving off a great deal of steam—it was burning. Small rivers of red flames made their way up the walls of the main chamber. As this happened, a few specks of bright purple powder began to waft down toward Nartam. He looked up and the powder settled lightly like snow onto his face, in his hair, and on his wide-open eyes. He wept—wept and moaned to himself. "I am saved," he said in between sobs. Purple tears ran down his face. "I am saved, I am saved! *Once again!* I am saved!"

Rather suddenly, Nartam sensed that he was not alone. He tensed, spun around, and saw Alfonso and Resuza approaching with their weapons drawn. Alfonso held his blue sphere and Resuza had a throwing dagger in each hand. Nartam didn't flinch or show any signs of fear. He looked much healthier and stronger than just seconds before. The powder was miraculous: he had become a much younger man. His face, which had been drawn and gaunt, now looked full. His chest, which had been measly and sunken, now seemed strapping. His spine, which had been slouched, was ramrod straight. And his arms, which had been almost twiglike, had grown wide and muscular. Even his skin had changed. Instead of pockmarked and sagging, it was smooth and firm

"You fools!" hissed Nartam. "You are late. Again, too late. Just like every other Great Sleeper for all these thousands of years. As you can see, I have already set fire to the Founding Tree. If you had any sense at all, you would run while you still can."

"This fire can still be put out and I'm going to—" began Alfonso.

"You'll do nothing," sneered Nartam as he blinked furiously, allowing the purple ash to dissolve into a moist film over his eyes. "Don't you see, little boy? It's all over. As we speak my men are taking the city. The only thing left to do is let this tree burn, so if you don't mind . . ."

"*No,*" said Alfonso, hoping he sounded determined. He took a step closer to Nartam, as if to grab him. "I won't let you."

"You won't let me?" cackled Nartam. "You and this little runaway slave? Ha! You may be the most incompetent Great Sleeper I have ever destroyed. You and your uncle allowed Kiril to follow you halfway around the globe and then you led us right into the heart of Somnos. You have *let* me do everything I wanted to do and more. And when this city burns, which it soon will, it will have little to do with me, or my soldiers, or even your Dormian knights. It will burn because you—in your callowness—have let it burn. Destiny is at work here. It was both inevitable and ill-fated that the Dormians entrusted the fate of their last city to such a foolish boy. Now step aside," he growled. "Your role in all of this is done."

"Resuza," said Alfonso. "Put out the fire and I'll take care of Nartam."

A puzzled and slightly amused look crept across Nartam's face as if he knew some humorous little secret. Alfonso ignored this; instead, he took a deep breath and a split-second later, hurled the blue sphere through the air. Nartam dove to his left and avoided it with ease. Alfonso had thrown the sphere faster than a bullet, and yet for Nartam it was child's play to step aside.

Alfonso threw the sphere again and, once more, Nartam skillfully dove out of the way. This time, however, Nartam hurtled toward Alfonso, did a quick somersault, popped back on to his feet with lightning speed, and smashed Alfonso in the chest. He flew twenty feet in the air, dropped the blue sphere, and landed in a nearby bank of snow. Alfonso struggled to get up, but before he could even get to his feet, Nartam had darted across the snow and retrieved the sphere. It was as if Nartam knew *exactly* where the sphere was going to land ahead of time. Alfonso looked about helplessly. He was weaponless.

"Don't you get it?" sneered Nartam. "I can foresee your every move before you even think about making it. I have enough ash in my eyes to foresee all of your feeble attempts to fight. It's hopeless."

Alfonso said nothing.

Meanwhile, Resuza was working furiously to put out the fire by throwing chunks of wet snow on the portion of the wall that was now ablaze. It didn't appear to be working; the fire was slowly spreading up. What's more, the specks of ash mixed with steam from the melting snow created a cloud of purple.

"Resuza, get away from there," yelled Alfonso as he sprang back to his feet. "Don't let that stuff get in your eyes or you'll go blind like Bilblox."

"What do you want me to do?" screamed Resuza. "The tree is going to burn!"

"Yes, children," replied Nartam calmly. "Yes it will."

CHAPTER 48

DRAW YOUR SWORDS!

MEANWHILE, HILL LED a group of ten Dormian soldiers to the top floor of the Tree Palace, which contained General Loxoc's spacious office. They ran up the palace's main staircase and, upon reaching the top floor, crept along a darkened corridor until they reached their destination, two massive marble doors intricately carved with famous battle scenes from Dormian history. The doors were slightly ajar—and a thin sliver of light shone through.

"That door is supposed to be locked!" whispered one of the soldiers. "The enemy is already here—they've taken the bloom!"

"Draw your swords!" commanded Hill.

They silently drew their weapons. Hill cocked his Colt .45

revolver, took a deep breath, and shoved open the door. They all rushed inside.

Instead of surprising a horde of Dragoonya, they found only one person: he was slender but sported a bushy mane of hair, like a paintbrush. A faded leather satchel hung over his shoulder.

"Clink! What are you doing here?" yelled one of the soldiers. "And why have you unlocked General Loxoc's safe?"

"You know this guy?" asked Hill.

"Everyone does," replied the solider. "He's the city's most famous pickpocket."

Clink spun around nervously. He was standing in a far corner of the general's office, next to a massive walk-in safe whose door reached from floor to ceiling. The safe was open. The Dormian bloom sat inside, healthy and untouched. Clink, however, was holding an ornate, jewel-encrusted sundial.

"Clink?" said Hill. "That name sounds familiar . . . You're the one that helped Bilblox break out of prison."

"He's stealing the Dolorius sundial!" said the soldier. "The Great Sleeper Marcus Dolorius used it to make his famous maps of the Urals. It's nearly two thousand years old."

Clink immediately returned the sundial to its resting place within the safe. "Not so," he protested. "I heard the commotion by the gates and came here to safeguard everything." He smiled weakly.

"Your city is in mortal danger, and all you can think of is stealing," muttered the soldier. He advanced toward Clink. "You'll pay for this, *thief.*"

At that moment, Hill heard a scurrying noise coming from the hallway. It sounded familiar. A sudden memory appeared in

Hill's mind: upon entering the greenhouse back in World's End, Minnesota, they had heard the same noise.

"Close the door!" Hill yelled. "We've got company—Dragoonya plants of war are here!"

Four soldiers immediately closed the massive marble doors and locked them shut.

"That won't hold them," said Clink. "It took me ten seconds to pick that lock from the outside. It's a lot flimsier than it looks."

"Brace yourselves," shouted Hill. "Clink, do something about that door!"

"Easy enough," replied Clink. He shut the safe, vaulted over Loxoc's long desk, and approached the marble doors. The scurrying noise outside was growing louder. Clearly, more plants of war had arrived. Clink put his eye to the keyhole and peered through. Just at that moment, a delicate brown root made its way into the keyhole from the other side of the door. One of the Dragoonya plants of war was using its roots to pick the lock.

"One of the plants is already at the lock!" Clink shouted. He immediately whipped out a thinly tapered metal rod from his satchel and inserted it into the lock mechanism. He twisted it back and forth so that more than half of the rod was pushed inside the lock. He then bent the rod toward the floor. It snapped in half, leaving the rest jammed inside the lock mechanism.

"They won't get in now—the lock is completely jammed," said Clink with a smile. "Unless they can break down this door, we'll be fine."

For the next ten minutes, Clink, Hill, and the ten Dormian soldiers listened to the Dragoonya plants of war in the hallway trying to find a way inside. Roots slithered underneath the door but found nothing to help them. The plants took turns hurtling their hard shells against the marble doors, but the doors didn't even shake.

Hill smiled at Clink. "Good job!" he exclaimed. "I think we've managed to outwit those beasts."

"Yeah," replied Clink. "It's a good thing I came along to help sa —"

Crash!

The room filled with the sound of breaking glass. They whirled around and saw plants of war entering the room through two shattered windows.

"We must guard the safe!" roared Hill. He looked at Clink. "Please tell me you locked it!"

Clink appeared terrified, but nodded.

They dashed to the safe and formed a protective semicircle around it. In front were two rows of Dormian soldiers, who fell asleep at once. Behind them, and closest to the safe, were Hill and Clink. Hill immediately began firing his Colt .45 with pinpoint accuracy. Clink withdrew a glittering, razor-sharp dagger from his satchel, unsheathed it, and cut away plant of war roots that were creeping toward them. They all defended their ground with incredible ferocity and bravery. Dozens of Dragoonya plants were immediately destroyed. However, they poured through the windows, as thick as locusts.

Hill soon ran out of bullets. He threw aside his revolver and picked up the sword of a Dormian soldier who had just been killed. Despite the skill of the Dormians, the Dragoonya plants of war never stopped coming. Their hard shells littered the floor and began to pile up around the small band of defenders.

One by one, the Dormian soldiers fell, overcome by the sheer number facing them. The battle raged for more than an hour and by the end, only Hill, Clink, and one Dormian soldier were left. Their swords were broken but they used the snapped-off handles as daggers and kept fighting. All the furniture was destroyed. The candles lighting up the room had been extinguished. Darkness filled the room.

Hill, Clink, and the Dormian soldier stood with their backs to one another, breathing heavily, exhausted. They were covered in scratches and bruises. Hill leaned sideways against the safe; his right leg had been gouged by a plant of war, and he could no longer stand on both feet. For the moment, however, they paid no attention to these injuries. They were waiting for the next attack.

"Are there any more?" whispered the Dormian soldier.

"Probably," gasped Hill. "But they won't get the bloom. Not as long as we're alive. We fight to the death, gentlemen—to the death!"

CHAPTER 49

THE BATTLE FOR DORMIA

BACK AT THE northern Somnos gate, the situation was grim. After barely failing to capture General Loxoc during the race to the gate, the Dragoonya had regrouped and were massed a few hundred feet from the walls. In front were the infantry, several thousand strong, protected from Dormian arrows by thick shields placed in front and above them.

Directly behind this first line of soldiers were several hundred Dragoonya archers. About a hundred of them had long, seven-foot crossbows loaded with heavy iron arrows. Burly men, probably criminals drafted from the dregs of Barsh-yin-Binder society, dragged forward huge vats of burning oil. It smelled terrible, like a combination of sulfur and burnt flesh. The archers dipped the tips of their arrows into this repulsive stew and once lit, fired them a great distance. Their target was the Founding Tree. Each time a flaming arrow hit, the leaf sparked and sometimes caught fire. In response, Dormian leaf-sweepers ran and leapt from branch to branch, trying to stamp out the flames and prevent a fire from spreading.

The other archers held shorter bows, for more precise aiming. They too dipped the tips of their arrows into the burning oil and aimed for the Dormians massing on the wall. They picked off anyone who dared show himself or herself for longer than a second. The foul-smelling fire burned clothes and sizzled leather. These arrows spread death to the masses of Dormian soldiers at the base of the wall, who were huddled together and trying desperately to fall asleep.

The overwhelming *boom-boom-boom* of the Dragoonya drums made any attempt at sleeping extremely difficult. The drummers and their instruments were positioned directly behind the archers, easily out of the range of Dormian arrows. The drums were at least six feet wide, and some looked to be even larger. The heavy bass of the drums seemed to burrow into the earth and make it shake on their command. It wasn't just the size of the drums but also their number. The Dragoonya had obviously thought about this part of their invasion. About a hundred drums beat together, and all that noise silenced everything else, even thoughts inside the head.

General Loxoc, who considered himself the toughest Dormian alive, felt a small curlicue of panic light deep within his stomach. The noise was too loud! They hadn't trained for this—you weren't supposed to feel sound, but these new Dragoonya drums were a physical presence. Of course, every Dormian soldier had gone through the basic drills: half a squad shouting at the top of their lungs while the other half fell asleep on command. However, the reality of this was too much. Loxoc could tell by the scared looks of his soldiers that the noise was beyond anything they had imagined. It was enough to encourage terrible thoughts, like running away or even surrender.

Still, the walls held, even after the initial charge and the pinpoint flaming arrows of the Dragoonya. Somnos was the queen of Dormian cities, their people's most treasured place. The walls were six feet thick and forty feet high. And of course, they still had the bloom . . . Loxoc thought of Alfonso and the others, bravely defending the dying Founding Tree from the inside. He shook his head. How was it possible that Nartam and the Dragoonya had penetrated Somnos so easily? He and his fellow Dormians had taken *every* precaution. And yet the city—and indeed Dormian civilization—stood on the brink of extinction. And all this had happened on Loxoc's watch. The general felt deeply ashamed.

As this thought crossed his mind, the thick ramparts next to him burst into rubble. Dormian soldiers, screaming in pain and terror, hurtled to the ground below. Even with the thump of the drums, General Loxoc heard the sickening thud of their bodies as they hit the ground. Another nearby rampart exploded. What were the Dragoonya doing?

Loxoc peered into the smoke that rose up from whatever the Dragoonya had used to destroy portions of the rampart. "Major!" he yelled.

Major Hornslight appeared at Loxoc's side. His helmet was covered with dust and a long bloody scrape ran from his scalp to his chin. He snapped to attention. "Yes sir!"

"What happened?" Loxoc yelled. "Damage report?"

"Unclear," replied Major Hornslight. "Some sort of new Dragoonya technology. We'll bounce back, though. As soon as our soldiers fall asleep." Both of them glanced below, where hundreds of Dormian soldiers were forcibly closing their eyes, trying to will themselves to sleep.

A voice filled with authority spoke up: "Those are gunpowder charges, sir. They were brought recently to Barsh-yin-Binder by modern traders. The Dragoonya have had them for almost three years now. 'Tis an evil instrument." Loxoc and the major turned in shock to see Spack, decked out in Dormian battle gear meant for an officer, standing next to them.

"You're that lazy Dormian that Alfonso found in Barsh-yin-Binder," said Loxoc.

"Not so lazy anymore," replied Spack. "I'm here to help. I've helped the Great Sleeper, and now it appears that you lads are in need of assistance as well. By the way, you wouldn't know where a tall, dashing friend of mine has gone off to? He goes by the name of Hill."

"He's off on other business," growled Loxoc. "But he's safe, for now."

"Excellent news!" replied Spack. "Now let's —"

She was interrupted by a whistling noise that grew louder and louder. Loxoc realized it was another Dragoonya bomb—filled with gunpowder—and it was heading straight toward them.

"Jump!" yelled Spack. All three of them dove onto the ground. Above them, the wall exploded from the force of a direct hit. Huge chunks of stone erupted and the wall split in two, crumbling into a pile of rubble. The same smoke appeared. Everyone gasped and rubbed their reddened eyes.

When the smoke cleared a minute later, Loxoc jumped to the

top of the rubble pile and tried to spot the Dragoonya army. He knew it should be several hundred feet in front of them.

He stood on the rubble, peering into the smoke, and suddenly realized something was different. The noise—that awful pounding of the drums—had vanished. What happened? Of course the Dragoonya hadn't left, but what were they doing?

From nearby, perhaps only fifty feet away, he heard a bugle sound for only a second. It was answered by the roar of thousands of bloodthirsty Dragoonya. This was quickly followed by the sound of horses beginning to gallop. Then the drums began again, and it seemed as if the world was swallowed up by noise.

Loxoc turned to face his men. He shook his head. "Fall asleep!" he shouted. "The wall is breached! Make way to defend—the Dragoonya cavalry are coming." He paused and realized no one could hear him. The drums were too loud. "If you don't fall asleep," he said, more to himself than anyone else, "we'll all die here."

As all of this was happening, General Loxoc recalled a memory from his youth. It was the funeral of his grandfather Milo Loxoc, who had also been a general. At the end of the funeral, a lone voice from among the crowd began to sing. At first it was almost too low to understand, but slowly the voice grew stronger, and was joined by other voices in the crowd. Loxoc remembered looking up at his mother and watching in great surprise as tears rolled down her face. "Why are you crying?" he remembered asking her. She had smiled and hoisted him up. "It's an old Dormian song," she had explained in a soft voice. "It's a song my parents used to sing to me when I was just your age. Some say it's a children's song. But others say the ancient

Dormians sang it to bring on sleep before battle. It's called the 'Warrior's Lullaby.'" And then she joined the crowd and began to sing as well.

This sudden memory sent Loxoc into a type of trance. His body relaxed and he lowered his sword. He began to sing in a voice that—like many years ago, in a different era and for different reasons—started low and steadily grew stronger. He walked among his fellow Dormians. Despite the overwhelming noise coming from the Dragoonya side, they all heard Loxoc's increasingly strong and emotion-filled voice as he sang in Dormian.

While the general sang, the breached wall filled with Dragoonya horsemen. The first wave had arrived. Dormian knights, held in reserve several hundred feet behind the wall, rushed to confront them. At first they were awake but as they approached, they joined General Loxoc in singing the lullaby, and fell asleep just as they met the Dragoonya swords and spears. Ordinary Dormian soldiers witnessed this, and joined the general and the knights until several hundred Dormians were all singing in one overpowering chant.

In what seemed like the blink of an eye, an amazing transformation took place. Ordinary Dormian soldiers who had been close to panicking fell into a sleeping trance, and turned smartly to join the knights in facing the onrushing Dragoonya. The ground thundered with the bass of the drums and the hooves of the iron-clad Dragoonya horses. And yet the sleeping Dormians maintained their positions. They raised their swords and, at impact, weaved and floated like butterflies.

In the middle of this phalanx of Dormian soldiers, a fast-asleep Loxoc and Spack wielded their swords high above their heads, and drove them down with the force of giants into the onrushing Dragoonya horsemen. The battle was so packed with sound that it drove out the air. The noises were deafening—the sharp whistling of arrows, the thunderous reports of gunpowder, and the deep, subterranean bass of the Dragoonya drums. And yet General Loxoc's song had worked. The Dormians were asleep and calm. They defended their city and battled as if their entire lives were spent preparing for this one moment.

"We're driving them back!" yelled the general triumphantly. "Prepare to counterattack!"

At that moment, a tall Dragoonya officer dressed in a fur cloak appeared in front of Loxoc. He was wielding a long bloody sword and his eyes gleamed white. It was highly unusual for an officer to be on the front lines like this—and an officer with white eyes . . .

"You!" yelled the general accusingly. "Are you the one they call Kiril?"

A dark smile crept across the face of the Dragoonya officer.

"You killed Johno!" shouted the general.

"You seem surprised," replied Kiril calmly. His voice was so conversational and unassuming that General Loxoc could barely hear it over the din of the battle. "But I assure you that killing Johno was not a difficult feat. I cut him down quickly enough—though, unfortunately, he took his time before dying. It's a shame isn't it, that sword wounds so often make for such drawn-out, pitiful deaths?"

General Loxoc yelled and lunged at Kiril. He slashed his sword down across Kiril's body, but Kiril narrowly avoided the sword and spun out of the way. Loxoc's face flushed and he charged Kiril in raging fury. In one incredibly swift motion, Loxoc threw down his heavy broadsword and pulled out a dagger from a sling around his shoulder. Before Kiril had time to blink, Loxoc plunged the dagger into Kiril's shoulder. It sank to the hilt. Kiril screamed, clutched his shoulder, and wrenched the dagger from his own body. With the bloody dagger in hand, Kiril attempted to slash at Loxoc, but Loxoc was too quick and he knocked the dagger away. It clattered to the ground.

Kiril lunged for General Loxoc and the two of them—both without weapons—searched for any advantage. They punched and kicked and scratched, as if possessed. At one point, Kiril began grasping the ground, as if in search of something. An instant later, Loxoc gasped sharply. A trickle of blood appeared on his lips and ran down his chin. The dagger, which Kiril had managed to snatch up off the ground, was now firmly lodged in the general's chest. A look of surprise and great sadness came over the general's face. He tried to speak but could not.

Kiril shoved General Loxoc's dying body to the ground. With his face spattered in blood, Kiril stood above Loxoc and smiled. "Join your brother, wherever he is," Kiril spat. "And know this: before the sun begins to rise, Somnos will die with you. I *will* have my revenge."

Kiril leaned over and yanked the general's dagger from his body. He wiped it on his own clothing and then rejoined the battle.

"General Loxoc is dead!" called a nearby Dormian knight.

Officially, Major Hornslight was now in command, but he appeared to be in a state of shock. Spack, who was now at Major Hornslight's side, spoke up. "Major, we need to launch a counterattack," yelled Spack. "We still have the upper hand!"

"But we Dormians don't attack," said Major Hornslight wearily. "We are a defensive people."

"You're right," replied Spack. "Everyone knows we defend, especially the Dragoonya. They're counting on us just staying right here." A high whistling sound interrupted them. It was a cannon round, angling down toward them. It exploded just a few feet away.

"Major, there's no time!" Spack urged. "You know who I am, the lazy Dormian from Barsh-yin-Binder. You know I'd never do anything if I didn't have to. Well, I have to do this." With that, Spack raised her sword, yelled loudly, and began running toward the Dragoonya lines. It looked awkward, this mixture of sleep-walking and running, but there was no hiding Spack's determination.

Major Hornslight watched her for a few seconds. The other Dormians stared at Spack. Major Hornslight heard the high-pitched whistle from another cannon round. "Run!" he yelled. "Run foward! Follow the lazy Dormian from Barsh-yin-Binder!" With that, the major raised his sword and began to sleep-run after Spack. The entire Dormian army followed behind, led by what remained of the knights.

The Dragoonya were surprised by the Dormian counterattack, but they regrouped quickly. The cannons were cut out of the battle, but the archers swiftly aimed at the onrushing Dormian army. Wave after wave of fire-tipped arrows slashed into the Dormians. Since she was in the front, Spack was cut down first. Dozens of arrows pierced her shield and body armor. She lunged forward and fell to her knees. Her eyes rolled back into her head, and she pitched forward, dead.

Major Hornslight witnessed this from only feet away. He

roared like a wounded tiger and rushed into the Dragoonya lines, followed closely by the entire Dormian army. The battle raged with a ferocity never witnessed before. At first, the Dragoonya withstood the Dormian charge, but they could not overcome the constant, calm pressure of the sleeping Dormians. The Dragoonya wavered and began to shuffle back. Men on the front lines turned and ran. Moments later, a chorus of Dragoonya bugles sounded, calling for a retreat. Major Hornslight and his army pursued them through the fields. Retreat turned to panic, and the Dragoonya stripped off their armor and threw away their weapons to focus on running away as quickly as possible.

Eventually, the retreating Dormian army reached the giant wooden ramp they had used to exit the Founding Tree's root system. In a wild rush, thousands of Dragoonya soldiers descended the ramp into the murky darkness below. At the bottom of the ramp, the Dragoonya scrambled into their boats and paddled back upstream in the hopes of escaping Dormia with their lives. This chaotic stampede only further weakened the already decaying walls of the root system. Soon enormous chunks of the roots' ceiling were breaking off, falling down, and crushing the Dragoonya below. The root had finally begun to collapse and the walls began to cave in, as if the earth itself were swallowing up the entire Dragoonya army.

One of the last of the Dragoonya to descend into the collapsing root was Kiril. During the Dragoonya army's retreat from Somnos, he galloped among his men, yelling at them to stop and fight. For those unlucky enough to be within the reach of his sword, he killed them for disobedience. Still, he could not convince them to turn back. The remains of the Dragoonya army fled underground. Kiril roared in frustration as he stood at the mouth of the ramp. "Cowards!" he yelled. "Filthy cowards!" Arrows from the pursuing Dormians fell around him. Kiril jumped into the tunnel and disappeared into the darkness.

CHAPTER 50

ALFONSO AND NARTAM

INSIDE THE Founding Tree, on the foggy, snow-filled floor of the main chamber, the battle raged on. Bilblox, Colonel Pissaro, and the band of Dormian knights continued to hold off the Dragoonya soldiers. Thanks to the handiwork of the Dormian archers, who had managed to pick off quite a few of the enemy, the contest was now almost evenly matched. "Hold your ground, men," yelled Colonel Pissaro. "They're losing heart!"

"I wish I could see," muttered Bilblox as he continued to swing his fists wildly.

"Bilblox, watch out!" yelled Colonel Pissaro. "You almost hit me. Make a quarter-turn to your right—and be quick about it—you've got a Dragoonya coming at you."

Bilblox quickly pivoted and thrust his fist outward just in time to strike down a large, grunting Dragoonya.

"Well done!" yelled Colonel Pissaro. "Now, quarter-turn back to your left, we've got three more Dragoonya headed our way. We'll take 'em together."

On the other side of the main chamber, Resuza worked frantically to fight the growing flames. She kept her eyes clenched shut—to protect herself from the purple clouds of Dormian ash—and used her bare hands to throw snow into the fire. She wasn't able to put the fire out, but she was able to keep it from spreading. Her main problem was that she was getting tired. She would have to rest soon and, when she did, the fire would almost certainly spread. She needed some reinforcements, but none appeared to be coming. Colonel Pissaro and his Dormian knights had their hands full while Alfonso and Nartam had disappeared from sight.

Alfonso had left the main chamber altogether. He was deep in one of the tree's many roots where, at that moment, he was running for his life. This wasn't simply because he had no weapons to use. Alfonso also knew that as long as Nartam could foresee his every move, there was no beating him in battle. There was just one thing that gave Alfonso hope: he had to keep Nartam away from any more ash. Alfonso knew that one of the powers that the ash bestowed—the ability to see into the future—never lasted very long. Bilblox's vision into the future didn't last more than a few minutes. Who knew exactly how long Nartam's vision would last? Perhaps ten minutes. Perhaps thirty minutes. Perhaps it was an hour, because of the extra powder that covered Nartam's face. He would have to wait. As soon as Nartam lost his ability to see into the future, Alfonso could turn and fight him. But until then, he ran away from Nartam as fast as he could.

"Look at the Great Sleeper on the run," cackled Nartam as he chased after Alfonso. "The great hope of Somnos fleeing like a cowardly child!" Nartam was holding Alfonso's blue sphere in his hand. He gripped the sphere tightly and then hurled it at Alfonso. Alfonso jumped to avoid getting hit by the mighty force of his own weapon, but it was no use. Nartam had foreseen Alfonso's jump and had thrown the sphere so that it would strike Alfonso in midair. The sphere nailed Alfonso in the lower back—*bam!*—and caused him to topple backwards off a chunk of ice that he had been climbing. Alfonso landed with a heavy thud. His back was in excruciating pain, but there was no time to wallow. He scrambled to his feet and continued running as best he could.

Nartam continued to hurl the blue sphere at Alfonso as he ran. Ice exploded everywhere around Alfonso as he scrambled deeper into the root. The situation was growing increasingly desperate. As quickly as he could, Alfonso crawled up an enormous piece of ice that looked like a pyramid, except that the very top was flattened. Upon reaching the top of this pyramid, Alfonso made two very troubling realizations. The first was that the ice under his feet didn't feel stable at all. Using his powers of hypnogogia, he could sense that there were hundreds of cracks within this pyramid of ice, and that it was only a matter of time before the whole thing fell apart. The second and far more troubling realization was that there was no way down from here. The other walls of the pyramid, which Alfonso had not seen until now, were much steeper than the one that he had just climbed. If he fell off, he'd likely slide to his death. He was trapped. A moment later, Nartam appeared. Snow swirled around him, making him look like a ghost. The two of them stood poised atop the pyramid, no more than ten feet apart, staring fiercely at each other.

"My young friend," said Nartam softly. "I'm tired of running after you. In fact, I'm simply tired of you altogether. Goodbye."

Nartam clutched the blue sphere, looked at it thoughtfully for a moment, and then threw it at Alfonso. Alfonso dove and cringed for the expected blow. Much to his surprise, and relief, Alfonso realized that the sphere had missed him. How was this possible? Nartam had been standing so close to him. How had he not foreseen which way Alfonso was going to dive? Suddenly he realized why. The powder covering Nartam's face had washed away by the snow and the dampness of his own sweat. He no longer had the ability to see into the future.

Nartam looked surprised and the entire pyramid began to tremble. The sphere, after it missed Alfonso, slammed into the pyramid with enormous force and burrowed deep inside. The sphere returned back to Nartam's hand while several massive cracks began to work their way up from the base of the pyramid. There was a giant rumbling sound. Huge chunks of ice began to break away all around them. The pyramid itself began to dissolve. A moment later, what was left of the pyramid split apart into two pieces and then into four separate pieces. All four of the pieces teetered unsteadily like bowling pins in the wind. Nartam stood atop one of these pins. Alfonso stood on another.

Alfonso closed his eyes and let himself feel the trembling of the ice. In his mind's eye he could see every single crack and fissure that was working its way through the four legs that once made up the pyramid. He could also feel the torque, bend, and sway of the ice. And then he knew: all but one of the pieces of ice were about to fall. The piece directly to his right, on which no one was perched, would remain standing. Alfonso took a deep breath and leapt across the chasm onto the piece of ice to his right. A moment later, the other three pieces of ice clattered to the ground in an overwhelming cataclysm of sound. Alfonso saw Nartam toppling down into the abyss, but then he disappeared from view, buried beneath the avalanche of ice.

It took Alfonso the better part of an hour to climb down from the ice and make his way back to the main chamber. He was in considerable pain and he limped much of the way. He was also quite cold. His fingers were so frigid and frostbitten that he could barely control them. But he did his best because, in his hands, he held his blue sphere. He had found the sphere near the spot where the pyramid had disintegrated. At the time, Alfonso had been searching for Nartam. He wanted to make sure that his enemy was dead. He used his powers of hypnogogia to search every last crevice. He found nothing and concluded that Nartam was buried somewhere at the very bottom of the avalanche, dead underneath tons of fallen ice. This thought didn't exactly cheer Alfonso. In a way, it actually saddened him, though he couldn't say why. His spirits, however, were soon lifted when he found his blue sphere lying in a nearby pile of crushed ice. Alfonso snatched it up, smiled for a brief moment, and then headed back down the root toward the faint glow of the fireflies.

By the time he reached the main chamber, Alfonso saw a most welcome sight: Colonel Pissaro and his Dormian knights were putting out the last of the flames. The purple Dormian ash was still fluttering in the air—which required Colonel Pissaro and his men to keep their eyes firmly shut as they worked—and this meant that none of them spotted Alfonso as he limped back into the main chamber.

The only person to see him was Resuza. She was resting on a nearby pile of snow and, as soon as she spotted Alfonso, she ran toward him, hugged him, and began talking so rapidly that Alfonso could barely understand her. It didn't matter. He quickly got the gist of it: the Dragoonya had been defeated and the last embers of the fire were now being put out. Alfonso then relayed the news that Nartam was dead. Resuza let out a cheer and she, in turn, shouted the news to Colonel Pissaro and his men. Soon everyone was cheering wildly. Everyone but Alfonso. He still was preoccupied with another thought. Where was Bilblox? What had happened to him? Then Alfonso spotted his large friend, standing on the far side of the main chamber with his arms crossed, looking rather pleased with himself.

"Hey, Bilblox!" called out Alfonso. "What are you doing over there?"

"I won't go anywhere near that purple ash," yelled Bilblox. "Besides, our work here is done."

"Yes it is," replied Alfonso softly—so softly that it almost seemed as if he were talking to himself.

CHAPTER 51

AN ANCIENT CEREMONY

THE BATTLE for Somnos, as it came to be known, ended just before dawn. It had raged for almost twelve hours and suddenly it was over. There were no immediate victory celebrations because, just minutes after the battle ended, a raging blizzard swept over the city of Somnos. Bitterly cold wind shook the buildings, while snow fell almost horizontally, forming massive drifts that threatened to overwhelm the battered city walls. It was clear that the Founding Tree was essentially dead and no longer offered any protection to the Dormians. Citizens of Somnos plodded along over snowdrifts, taking stock of their badly damaged city. After many months of little food, Somnos's supplies were exhausted. Everyone was starving. Given their desperate situation, the grand vizier decided that the planting ceremony would be held that very morning. It would have none of the pomp and finery Dormians associated with such an important event.

Still, the Dormians themselves were in high spirits, especially the children, who ran around the snow, screaming with delight. They had good reason to be happy. After all, the people of Somnos had defeated an invading army and vanquished their age-old enemy, Nartam. Of course, all this had come at a price. It would take months, and perhaps even a few years, for them to rebuild Somnos and restore the city to its former glory. It would also take some time, after the planting ceremony, for the new Founding Tree to sink its roots into the soil and beat back the encroaching cold of winter. For the time being, however, all anyone in Somnos could think about was how good it felt to be alive—and perhaps none felt this more keenly than Hill Persplexy.

"This is a day I will never forget as long as I live," declared Hill as they rode to the Tree Palace for the planting ceremony in a sled, surrounded by cheering citizens. Hill was clothed in his Somnos military dress uniform, which included a black velvet cape, a feathered cap, and a shirt full of gleaming gold medals. Snow fell steadily, turning his uniform white. "Please slow down the sled," added Hill. "I want this moment to last as long as it possibly can."

"Yeah," added Bilblox in a gruff but happy voice. "Let's enjoy this. We've earned it." A hurriedly fashioned medal was pinned onto Bilblox's heavy jacket. In ancient Dormian script, it declared that Paks Bilblox was pardoned of his sins and declared an honorary citizen of Somnos.

"Of course, gracious sirs," replied the driver who, of course, was none other than Ivan, although this time he had been given permission to be awake to fully enjoy the event. "Enjoy it all you can, sir," said Ivan. "But why don't you show them the bloom? That's what they really want to see. They're hungry, they're cold, they're miserably tired—but they have hope because of that little tree that you've dragged halfway around the world."

"Yes, that's a fine idea," said Josephus who was sitting next to Ivan, with paper and pen in hand. Josephus was there, of course, to document the planting ceremony. "You have to show them the bloom," continued Josephus. "That's what this is all about." The other passengers in the sled—Alfonso, Resuza, and Bilblox—all agreed and urged Hill to show off the plant. The bloom, which was sitting in a pot on the floor of the sled, was in excellent health. The people of Somnos had Hill to thank for this, since he led the small band that had protected the bloom. Word had spread quickly of his heroics—very quickly—and every last person in Somnos knew of his deeds. Now they all chanted his name in unison. "Hill, Hill, Hill, Hill, Hill," called the crowd.

"Go on," said Alfonso with a smile. "There's no sense in being shy, Uncle Hill. Show them the bloom."

Hill nodded obligingly, picked the bloom up off the floor, and held it high over his head. The crowd exploded with delight as the snow swirled around them. Children, parents, grandparents, policemen, soldiers, teachers, even Dr. Nostrite—who was riding in a sled directly behind them—began to holler with unstoppable joy. They cheered, not only because the bloom was alive and well, but because very soon it would be placed in the ground. The planting ceremony marked the start of an incredible year in which the bloom would grow three feet each day for twelve consecutive months. By this time next year, the small plant that was currently resting in Hill's hands would stand over one thousand feet tall. Meanwhile, the current Founding Tree of Somnos would quickly wither away. Crews of leaf-sweepers would work around the clock to help take down the old tree and make sure that it didn't accidentally topple over and crush a large section of the Trunk District. Within a year, explained Josephus, Somnos would return to being paradise. Alfonso wished Spack was there to witness the rebirth of the paradise she always described and remembered so fondly.

Ivan drove the sled right up to the Tree Palace. Here, the entire group came upon a most unexpected sight. Standing by the front gates of the palace were two large, freshly carved ice sculptures of Dormian soldiers dressed in full battle gear. Clearly, several artisans had done some quick work. The faces on the sculptures looked familiar—very familiar. One belonged to General Loxoc and the other to Spack. In fact, at the base of the sculptures were two blocks of ice with engravings both in Dormian hieroglyphs and in English. The English engravings read:

GENERAL GILLIAD LOXOC

SUPREME COMMANDER OF THE ARMY OF DORMIA—
HERO OF THE GREAT BATTLE OF SOMNOS. HE WAS,
INDISPUTABLY, THE BRAVEST SON OF SOMNOS
EVER TO HOLD THE RANK OF GENERAL.

SPACK OF BARSH-YIN-BINDER

RENOWNED NAPPER, PROCRASTINATOR,
PROFESSIONAL BEGGAR, MOOCH, SCROUNGER, BORROWER,
FREELOADER, HITCHHIKER, WANDERER, DEVOTED
PATRIOT, AND MOST COURAGEOUS HERO OF WAR.
IN THE GREAT BATTLE OF SOMNOS, SHE LED THE
CHARGE THAT SAVED OUR FAIR CITY.

Everyone stepped out of the sled and stood silently for a moment as they paid their respects to Spack and General Loxoc. Josephus unsheathed a ceremonial sword and left it at the base of the sculptures. The others watched on reverently.

"Well," Hill hoarsely said. "Spack got what she wanted—a statue in her honor right in the heart of Somnos. I just wish she was here to enjoy it."

"You're right," said Alfonso with a sad smile. "She would've been very happy."

"Rest in peace, General," said Bilblox as a tear ran down his cheek. "And as for you, Spack, we all cursed your laziness more than once on the trip here, but when it counted, you came through—you saved us all, old gal."

"Come," said Josephus finally. "It is time to plant the bloom."

Josephus, Hill, Alfonso, Bilblox, and Resuza trudged through the snow and made their way into the Tree Palace. Today the palace was completely empty. No spectators were allowed in. Tomorrow, and in the coming days, every citizen of Somnos would be allowed to see the new Founding Tree of Somnos for themselves. But during the planting ceremony, only the Great Sleeper and his traveling party were allowed to enter. This was the custom—the way it had always been—and the way it always would be.

Inside the palace, the group was greeted by the grand vizier, who was dressed in an elegant but simple green velvet robe. She was, as custom dictated, fast asleep. The grand vizier nodded politely to the group, yawned, and then drowsily shuffled down a long marble hallway that eventually opened up into an intimate courtyard. Snow lay everywhere, in the cracks in the wall and piled on the floor. The courtyard, however, had been shoveled clean of snow, although more snow kept falling and the ground was quickly being covered with a new layer of white. In the center of the space was a small hole recently dug into the dark, frozen soil. Directly to the right of this hole stood a lone violinist, dressed in a heavy fur coat, who was the only other person there. The grand vizier nodded once, just slightly, and the violinist began to play. He played a slow, sad ballad that sent shivers up Alfonso's spine. It was a haunting melody whose notes conjured up images of Dormians from ages past. It was also somehow familiar. Alfonso looked at Hill, who was singing along in a soft voice:

Bitter cold, pounding snow
Dying with no place to go
As we wandered through the empty wasteland
Young and old did weep
Then one day, like the sun
Lives of green had just begun
For our people finally found a place to sleep
Founding Tree, guiding light
Dormia sleeps tonight

Neath your leaves
We can live our lives in peace
Proud and true
We protect and cherish you

"What was that?" asked Alfonso when the violinist had finished.

"The national anthem of Dormia," whispered Hill. "It's one of the few things I never forgot. With a little coaxing I think I could even sing it in Dormian."

"My dad used to whistle that tune when he took me on walks in the forests back in Minnesota," said Alfonso.

Without saying a word, Hill placed his arm around his nephew and gently squeezed his shoulder. The violinist started to play another tune. It was a faster-paced melody, the sort that almost made you want to get up and dance, and it seemed to restore a sense of relief and happiness to the event. The grand vizier nodded once more and Josephus explained that it was time for the Great Sleeper to put the bloom into the ground.

"If it's all right," said Alfonso, "I would like Bilblox to do the planting."

"Me?" said Bilblox curiously. "But besides bein' blind, I ain't even a Dormian."

"A noble idea," interjected Hill. He turned to look at Bilblox. "Your devotion to this quest is all the more praiseworthy because you *aren't* a Dormian. You risked your life again and again for a land that wasn't even your home. I think you've more than earned the right."

"Well it's highly unorthodox," mumbled the grand vizier sleepily. "But then again, everything about this process has been unorthodox, so I don't have any objection."

Hill promptly handed the bloom to Bilblox, who took hold of it in his large callused hands.

"Just keep walking forward," instructed Hill. "We'll tell you where to go." Bilblox walked about thirty paces, until Hill told him to stop. "It's right in front of you," explained Hill. "You're all set." Bilblox nodded appreciatively and then dropped to his knee and lowered the bloom into the small hole in the ground. When this was done, he scooped up several handfuls of dirt and spread them around the base of the plant.

"It's all done," called out Bilblox, his loud voice cracking with pent-up emotion. "She's in the ground. Alfonso, she's in the ground."

They listened to the heavy snowfall. It sounded like a long, drawn-out sigh of relief. Everyone stood there and watched the little Dormian bloom as snow thickly covered its leaves and branches.

Resuza gasped and grabbed Alfonso's arm. "Do you see that?" she exclaimed, and pointed at the frozen ground surrounding the bloom. It glistened in the morning light. It was melting. In less than a minute, the bloom had begun to melt an area of several feet around it. After another minute, the circle of melting snow had expanded ten more feet. Next to the bloom, the melting snow revealed brown and bent-over grass that immediately turned a brilliant, luscious green.

"The seeds of tomato and cucumber plants are buried nearby," said the grand vizier. "They'll be ready for eating by tomorrow."

Alfonso turned to look at Hill. Despite the fact that they had expected this, it was still astonishing. His uncle's eyes brimmed with tears.

"I could stand a good fresh tomato salad," said Hill. "Yes indeed."

CHAPTER 52

A SAD FAREWELL

TRADITION held that the gates of Somnos opened only once every twelve years on the occasion of Great Wandering Day. This was the day when Hill and Leif had accidentally gotten caught up in the crowd and been forced out of the city. This was also the day, some twelve years later, when Spack had managed to escape. This tradition, great and honored though it was, now posed an immediate problem for Alfonso and his group. The next Great Wandering Day was still three years away. This meant that, according to the rules, Alfonso, Bilblox, Resuza, and Hill would have to wait until then before they could begin their journey home. Luckily, however, Josephus found a note in his history books saying that special exceptions could and should be made for visiting parties that included at least one non-Dormian.

And so it was arranged that, in two days' time, the gates of Somnos would be opened so that Alfonso and the others could head home. This would give them exactly two weeks to return to Barsh-yin-Binder, where they hoped Vice Admiral Purcheezie would still be waiting for them. She had promised to wait only five weeks, and none of them wanted to test her patience. According to their calculations, they would arrive in Barsh-yin-Binder the day before the vice admiral set sail. They'd make it, vowed Alfonso. It was time for him to return home—Pappy and his mom would be sick with worry.

Resuza would return to Barsh-yin-Binder; Bilblox would go as far as Fort Krasnik; and Alfonso and Hill would go all the way back to World's End, Minnesota. Or at least that's what Alfonso thought. But, the night before their departure, Hill pulled Alfonso aside after dinner in the guesthouse and asked to talk with him in private. There was a peculiar and rather sad look on Hill's face. It took a moment for Alfonso to sense what was coming, but suddenly he knew, and he felt a hollowness in his stomach.

"You're not coming home with us, are you?" asked Alfonso.

"No," said Hill. "I'm afraid not."

"Why?" asked Alfonso.

"Because this *is* my home," said Hill. "I've spent too much of my life away from here. This is the place where I want to grow old. I feel comfortable here, as if I really belong, which is a feeling that I've never really had anywhere else. I feel like I could truly settle down here on one of these sleepy streets. I could help rebuild the city. I've always been good at fixing things."

"What about me?" asked Alfonso weakly. "You're my only uncle and we've practically just met."

Hill clapped him on the shoulders and enveloped him in a massive hug. "I have every confidence in you, my dear nephew," said Hill. "You and Bilblox know the way back—you'll be just fine. There isn't another lad in all the world with your abilities."

"What about Resuza?" asked Alfonso.

"She wants to stay here," replied Hill. "She has nothing in Barsh-yin-Binder and her sister is lost. I told her that she could live with me. I've talked to the grand vizier about it and she has given her conditional approval."

"I see," said Alfonso.

"This was a tough decision, and just three months ago, when I first met you, I never would have left you on your own," said Hill. "But things have changed. You're different now. Older and wiser. You're going to be all right. More than all right. And who knows? Maybe you'll find your way back here someday."

"Yeah," said Alfonso as he struggled to hold back a sob. "I guess the gates will open again in three years for Great Wandering Day."

"They will indeed," said Hill. "And I'll be here waiting for you."

The following morning, under the cover of a heavy fog, Alfonso, Hill, Bilblox, and Resuza headed for the giant stone gateway. The party traveled with Josephus in his sled. A garrison of Dormian knights accompanied them.

Everywhere snow was melting and icicles were shrinking. The water from this epic melt was seeping into the earth and feeding a massive blossoming of life, the likes of which Alfonso had never seen before. Thousands of wild flowers were emerging through the frost. Insects were crawling out of the earth in droves. In places, fresh green grass was sprouting and giving off a thick, ripe steam. The Founding Tree had taken hold. Part of Alfonso longed to stay and see the end result—the complete return of tropical warmth—but he knew that this was not meant to be.

When the sled reached the mouth to the long darkened cave that burrowed through the mountains and led to the outside world, everyone stepped out. There was a final round of goodbyes. Alfonso gave his uncle and Resuza long hugs. Then, with great sadness, Alfonso turned and headed into the darkness of the cave. Bilblox followed, helped along by a Dormian knight. In the distance, they heard a low, rumbling sound as the gates of Somnos opened.

Josephus turned to Hill and looked at him appraisingly. It was clear that Hill was quite sad. "That nephew of yours is a good lad," said Josephus softly.

"I know," said Hill.

"Don't worry," added Josephus. "Someday I suspect that he'll come back."

EPILOGUE

It was late evening in the middle of the North Pacific. The *Success Story* pushed forward through choppy water, on its way back to North America. Bilblox was in the windmill, already asleep. The deck was empty except for Alfonso, who was lying on an old blanket and looking up at the stars. He wasn't tired that evening—something about sleeping in the windmill had made him anxious to get out. Maybe it was the memory of staying in there with Hill. Alfonso wondered for the thousandth time since he had left Somnos: would he ever see Uncle Hill again? His other worry concerned Bilblox. Alfonso doubted that there would be much use for a blind longshoreman back in Fort Krasnik. Poor Bilblox. This journey had taken its greatest toll on him. It didn't seem fair.

Alfonso let out a heavy sigh and then looked up. Above him, the stars of the Northern Hemisphere glittered and sparkled. They were a brilliant white and they seemed much brighter than normal. There was Orion, surrounded by other admiring constellations. Just below was the Big Dipper, low in the evening sky. The same stars hung over Somnos, and perhaps Uncle Hill and Resuza were looking at them too.

The *Success Story* churned through the cold waters. The wind was picking up and the growing waves made the icebreaker seem tiny. Alfonso shivered and wrapped the blanket tightly around himself. He closed his eyes, and replayed in his head the battle with Nartam, and of course, the parade, and the planting of the bloom. And now, after all that, he was returning home to World's End, Minnesota. Sure, it'd be great to see Pappy and his mom. But how could he really return to World's End and go back to school as if none of this had ever happened?

Alfonso thought back to the very first time he had met Uncle Hill. It was in the evening; he remembered that much. Hill had told them an amazing story about Dormia that seemed too crazy to be true. Alfonso smiled to himself. Back then, he hated his sleeping-self and his heart sank every time Pappy fussed at him about his tomfooleries or someone told him, "I can't believe what you just did in your sleep!" However, none of this seemed to bother him anymore. Truth be told, ever since leaving Somnos, Alfonso had been sleeping peacefully, without doing anything strange in his sleep.

The wind of the North Pacific blew harder across the deck. Alfonso shivered and felt his eyes grow heavy. He suddenly felt tired. Tomorrow, if all went well, they'd catch their first glimpse of North America and later that day, they'd drop anchor outside Fort Krasnik. Alfonso stared ahead and saw the moon being reflected in a small puddle of seawater that accumulated on the deck. He focused on the moon's reflection in the puddle and effortlessly entered into hypnogogia. The familiar rush swept over him. He heard Bilblox's heart beating as his trusty friend slept nearby. He heard Vice Admiral Purcheezie muttering to herself in her cabin. Underneath the icebreaker, he heard every ripple of underwater current, the swish of fins pushing through the water, and the sonar ping of two dolphins calling to each other from miles away. Alfonso shifted his focus outward, toward land hundreds of miles away. A late-night breeze swayed the pine trees along the shore. On the ground below, chipmunks rustled through piles of dead leaves. Alfonso sniffed the air and caught a hint of smoke from a small campfire somewhere near Fort Krasnik.

A few seconds later, he returned to his normal state and yawned again. Alfonso stood up and felt the deck roll beneath his legs. He thought again of Pappy and his mom, and hurried to the windmill. He'd see them soon enough, but first he had to sleep.

Selected Dormian Hieroglyphs

ALL WILL BE WELL

STUDY HARD

EEP EEP KEE (THE GREAT SLEEPER)

THE IRON PILLOW, EST. 2394

DIFFICULT ROAD AHEAD

DRIVE ONLY WHILE ASLEEP

NATIONAL ANTHEM OF DORMIA

Translated from ancient Dormian by Frank Kujawinski

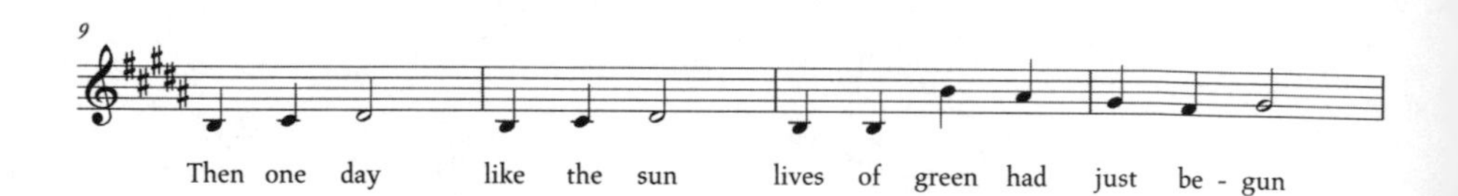

ACKNOWLEDGMENTS

We'd like to start by thanking our families, who believed in Dormia long before it ever existed in print. Our wives, Nancy and Kasia, indulged us and allowed us to be boys when—by all reasonable standards—we ought to have been spending our time doing something far less whimsical and far more grown up. Special thanks to Tamar Halpern, of Somnos Press, for her editing and endless moral support! You kindled the spark, and we'll never forget it. We also give thanks to those in the mighty Kujawinski clan—Frank Kujawinski, Jo Kujawinski, Arlene Weinsier, Adele Prince, Dan "Znimber Palace" Kujawinski, Mark Behn, Liza Kujawinski-Behn, and Alex the Boy Wonder. In the Tribe of Halpern, we first thank Stephen "Big Shanty" Halpern, for always picking up the phone, listening, and believing. Also thanks go to Greg Halpern, Elizabeth Stanton, Paul Zuydhoek, Barbara Lipska, Mirek Gorski, the original Alfonso (Jan Czerminski), and, of course, Sebastian Mistephold Halpern—the magic of Dormia twinkles in your eyes.

To our superhuman literary agent, Tina Bennett, we say thanks for going out on a limb for this one. To her assistant, Svetlana Katz: you must truly be part Dormian (and work in your sleep) to be as helpful and responsive as you always are. Kate Schafer gave us our first break and some wonderful insights that brought the book to another level. Finally, to Sally Willcox at CAA: thanks for your support and hard work on the movie front.

This book would not exist if it weren't for Julia Richardson, our editor extraordinaire and good friend. It's hard to imagine working with a smarter, warmer, more thoughtful editor. You're the best! Thanks also to Karen Walsh for her good work and creativity in publicity and Reem Abu-Libdeh for her meticulous copyediting.

We owe a quick word of appreciation to all those who read the book and gave us suggestions or simply offered crucial moral support, including Leon Gellert, Brian Zittel, Jenn Cohen, John Taylor, Sam Dolce, and Brian Groh.

Can you thank locations? Why not? To the wilds of the Sinai Peninsula, where the two unlikely coauthors met, and to the city of Paris for incubating our artistic collaboration, deepening our friendship, and providing expensive but first-rate cheese.

Finally, a wise Dormian once said, "Always thank your wife twice—once awake and again while sleeping." And so, as we nod off to sleep, let us say this:

To Nancy Celia Rose, my muse and love, you are the soundtrack of my life. —P.K.

To Kasia Lipska, my best friend, who first showed me the haunted and melancholy woods of Niedźwiedzi Róg, where the spirit of Dormia resides. —J.H.